SIN

SIN

SHARON PAGE

APHRODISIA

KENSINGTON BOOKS
http://www.kensingtonbooks.com

APHRODISIA BOOKS are published by

Kensington Publishing Corp.
850 Third Avenue
New York, NY 10022

All Kensington Titles, Imprints, and Distributed Lines are available at special quantity discounts for bulk purchases for sales promotions, premiums, fund-raising, and educational or institutional use.

Special book excerpts or customized printings can also be created to fit specific needs. For details, write or phone the office of the Kensington special sales manager: Kensington Publishing Corp., 850 Third Avenue, New York, NY 10022, attn: Special Sales Department, Phone: 1-800-221-2647.

Aphrodisia and the A logo Reg. U.S. Pat. & TM Off.

ISBN 0-7582-1470-7

First Kensington Trade Paperback Printing: September 2006

10 9 8 7 6 5 4 3 2 1

Printed in the United States of America

To A.J.

PROLOGUE

London, April 1818

There was nothing like money to pique a lady's desire . . .
Lydia Harcourt smiled in triumph at the two open letters
sitting beside her plate. Humming happily, she refreshed her
chocolate with a splash from the china pot.

Promises of generous payment. Enough to pay her bills, if
she were so inclined. But the tradesmen, so desperate about
their unpaid accounts, were also so easily distracted.

She lifted the letter closest to her and reread it as she sipped
her chocolate, savoring her victory. A thousand pounds.

Still, Norton really should be good for more. Perhaps if
she pressed . . .

Lydia settled her cup on its saucer and gave a luxurious
yawn and stretch. She was one of the few Incognitas who
knew what morning was. She picked up the third letter delivered in the morning's post. This one promised to be her coup
de grâce.

None of her lovers could ever keep their secrets from her.

A talent that now served her well.

A flick of the letter opener and she smoothed out the thin
sheet. For a duke, Montberry used the cheapest paper. He'd
not wasted much ink either. One stark line sprawled across
the page.

Publish and be damned.

And *Montberry* written beneath, with a flourishing 'M' and 'y'.

Blast the man! Did he really wish the polite world to know what a dreadful bore he was in bed? To know about his preferences? The *haute* ton thought him a hero. A great man, larger than life. What a grand joke it would be when all learned the truth.

She tossed the letters aside, shook out her loose hair. Rodesson preferred her hair down and tousled into shimmering waves. For some reason, the eccentric artist enjoyed his carnal pleasures before noon. Her cunny bubbled at the thought of their upcoming encounter and she allowed a vindictive smirk to curve her lips, despite the risk of aging lines. It would be a delight to destroy Rodesson after the mocking pictures he'd painted of her! She would not even give him the chance to bribe her.

In fact, today she would start on the letters 'R', 'S', and 'T'. She leafed through the small leather bound book that sat by her right hand. A good thing she'd kept meticulous records. Over twenty years, a woman did tend to forget the men she had entertained.

When so few had entertained her.

Two hours later, Lydia stretched out on her bed and skimmed her hands suggestively along her naked curves. She plucked at her nipples, then delved her fingers into her neatly trimmed nether curls.

She gazed with coquettish invitation at her visitor, but inside she glowed with victory at the pained look that burned in his green eyes. Handsome eyes that narrowed at the sight of her feminine juices soaking her curls, droplets sitting atop the bush of black hair like morning dew.

Even nearing sixty, with thick hair of pure white, Rodesson was a handsome man. Lean and well muscled. The lines on his face gave him a grizzled, sensual appeal. An artist, he appreciated that women enjoyed an aesthetic body on a lover.

How she longed to laugh. The great Rodesson, lolling at her feet like a lapdog.

"I would like to tie you up," he said, hoarsely.

He was the sort of man that allowed the submissive to hold the power in the game. He would not force her, but he was waiting, his emerald eyes afire, to see what she would allow. What she would suggest.

Excitement rushed through Lydia, dampening her cunny even more. Rodesson sought escape in games of bondage when he was haunted by worries—either money or guilt, or when he'd sunk into maudlin contemplation of the woman he'd loved and lost.

"I am your servant," she promised.

He was not yet fully aroused, though even in its semi-slumbering state his cock was long and beautifully formed. He would often be sexually excited without having an erection, eager to slide into her mouth and have her bring him to attention.

She merely flicked her glance to the bedside table, to the tangle of silken rope and ribbons jumbled on top.

Sunlight spilled through the paned windows, drawing crisscrossed shadows over her nude breasts, belly, and thighs. The thought of bondage at the time when most were rising to sip their coffee and chocolate did indeed titillate.

She closed her eyes as Rodesson left her bed to rifle through her playthings. She heard the sharp intake of breath as he discovered the true treat amidst the heap of restraints. A gift from the Marquess of Chartrand—jeweled bracelets designed to be locked to her headboard. They clinked as Rodesson lifted them.

"Roll onto your stomach, lass."

Lydia obeyed. How could she despise this man yet delight in the deep, gravelly sound of his voice? Sometimes she thought she seduced herself.

She buried her face between her two plump pillows and shivered at the softness of silken sheets brushing her hard nipples and her wet quim. Once more she closed her eyes, anticipating the touch of a velvet rope or silver shackles to her skin.

A deeper excitement set her heart pounding. A troubled man enjoying kinkier pleasures was more apt to spill his secrets.

Why had he not yet touched her?

She lifted her hips and wriggled her bare arse to tempt him. Now she was truly aroused.

"Bind me," Lydia whispered in a throaty, alluring voice.

A pressure, a roughness touched her calves. Finally. But this was not the softness of velvet or silk.

Startled, she lifted, shoved a pillow aside, as something rasped across her ankles. She twisted to watch Rodesson wrap a length of rope around her ankles. He had brought rope!

"I prefer velvet," she protested. The rough fibers scratched. And would leave angry red burns.

"Silence, captive." The rope wound tighter, cutting into her skin. She could not escape these bonds. Her ankles were well and truly trussed and she found the sensation exciting.

Perhaps she'd betrayed her apprehension, her shock at the way she was growing delightfully wet, for he gave her a gruff laugh and then bent to kiss her bare arse. No, not a kiss. He bit her cheek! Gently, but really.

"Mind. I don't wish permanent disfigurement."

He laughed, paying her no heed, and bestowed love nips all over her buttocks. Which, despite her protests, left her soaked and throbbing. The rasp of his jaw along her curves made her yearn for a deep and thrilling penetration in her derriere and she lifted her bottom up to him, hoping he took the hint.

But no, the man instead resumed his work of tying her up.

He labored with the knot at her feet for so long she was moaning in exasperation.

"Shackle my wrists! Please, oh yes, please, my master."

Lydia fell back to the bed, burying her face into the softness of her mattress. She heard the clatter as he lifted them from the table and let out a happy whimper. They were locked, but the gold key was in the lock, ready for him to open it.

She waited and waited, squirming against her sheets.

"Damnation."

Bother, had he lost the key? Her heart thudded for long moments, her frustration grew. What was he doing? Apprehension grew beneath her irritation. She arched up again to see what he was doing.

He knelt at the foot of her bed, his handsome features distorted in a grimace.

Wincing, Rodesson dropped the shackles to the bed and massaged his hands. "Bloody rheumy hands." He appeared to be in genuine pain. With her ankles bound, she rolled up onto one hip, watching him try to work his hands, to flex out the stiffness.

But his gaze met hers and a look passed through his eyes that intrigued. He ceased his manipulations of his fingers. Instead he picked up a second length of rope. "Back on your belly, minx."

Truly excited now, she lay down again. Her famously large breasts squashed against the mattress. He slid the rope under her legs, and circled it around her thighs.

"Your hands must pain you greatly when you paint." Lydia kept a tone of sympathy and sensuality.

His answer was a curt yes.

He did not wish to speak of this. Was it due to shame? Or something more?

He began to knot the rope that bound her thighs together, struggling, and she could barely breathe with excitement.

Her honey flowed like a river between her thighs, her heart pounding, her throat tight. She would never wish to be truly captured, bound, raped. God in heaven, she knew what it was to have a man force himself on her. She had spent a lifetime ensuring she would never have to endure that again, yet by some perversity of her nature, she enjoyed—no, *needed*—to have Rodesson make her his prisoner.

He lifted the jeweled cuffs. With muttered oaths, he struggled to control the key. She couldn't see how he could hold a brush with such ruined hands. How it must hurt him to paint. How that gave her a sense of smug satisfaction. He had just produced a beautiful volume and every moment of his work must have been excruciating agony.

Lydia turned to watch him once more.

"Ah lass, it's no use." His broad shoulders drooped. So did his cock.

"Give them to me."

He looked ashamed.

"It is exciting to do this," she prompted. "To shackle myself because you wish it. I know I dare not disobey . . ."

He handed them over but his shaft did not swell or straighten. She must work harder to assuage his ego.

He followed her gaze. "No need to worry about that, lass. That still works. It's the hands that don't. Can't even bloody well paint—"

Can't paint? Had that one volume been his last? Did that mean she had no need to destroy him? She unlocked one cuff and clasped it around her wrist. Lined with velvet it was comfortable—she might enjoy the game, but she didn't truly like discomfort.

"Lydia, love—"

She gazed up, looking as innocent as she could while locking the second cuff in place. The gold chain between them allowed her movement but she entwined it around her wrists to give the illusion she was completely trapped.

"Lydia, you can't let anyone know I can't paint."

A secret. How delicious. How useful.

"You are my master and I will obey."

"I am serious, gel. I can't have it known that I can no longer . . . perform in that arena."

She smiled, the submissive once again controlling the man who wished to play dominant. "Now, my master, do you wish to fuck me?"

"I do indeed." His eyes narrowed and he licked at his lips. "My *houri*."

His hands did not trouble him as he lifted her hips up into the air, presenting her derriere and her quim like a heated mare. She no longer knew where she wished him to penetrate. The blunt head of his cock slid from her puckered anus to her bubbling quim and back, soaking her along the way. Her heart thundered as she waited for him to choose, to push inside. Something large pressed against the entrance of her bottom and she lifted toward it, relaxing. She felt herself open to receive . . . one of her own gew-gaws, a wand of ivory carved like an enormous phallus. His ministrations were gentle and slow, coaxing her to spread for her gigantic toy. Within a few strokes, he had it halfway inside.

"God yes," he groaned, "Take it deep, my beauty."

Lydia moaned in answer. "Push it to the hilt, my master."

Realistic ballocks had been carved as part of the phallus and these pressed into her parted cheeks. Goodness, it meant she was completely filled, the entire length within her. Rodesson held it in place with one hand and she felt him part her nether lips. Her moisture released in a flood, drawing a hungry groan from her lover.

His cock began to do battle with the phallus in her bottom. As his thick, hot staff slid inside her quim, it pushed the other out of her arse. He pushed it back in, stretching her impossibly.

His secret. She must think of his secret . . . there was something significant in what he had told her . . . But she was stuffed so wonderfully full. And he began to paint her an image . . .

"What if you were caught like this by a man in your employ? A young footman of twenty. Randy, brawny, but still a virgin and eager to be taught by a voluptuous, experienced woman. His swollen cock would stand tall for you. You would be imprisoned yet you would control him. And then, his friend would come to see where he was. Another young man, another enormous cock. Both thrusting into you and determined to please. It would be torture for them to control their climaxes until they pleasure you. And you, my beauty, would enjoy their pain."

She must concentrate but his fantasy was so perfect she couldn't resist letting herself imagine . . .

His cock thrust deep and each plunge of his hips crammed her toy deep within her bottom. She rarely reached orgasm with her gentlemen. But with Rodesson it happened every time. It would happen now. The double penetration brought her to her peak without fail. Her anus was so delightfully sensitive and he knew it.

He pounded into her, brutally hard, just as she liked it. She was so wet and slick, she loved the pounding of his hips, the strike of his solid groin against her cheeks. The ripple of her flesh with each slap sent an answering ripple of ecstasy through her butt and quim.

"Yes, harder," Lydia cried. She wriggled her captured hands between her belly and the bed. With a moan of pure pleasure, she reached her nubbin, the trigger for her pleasure. She must work quickly. She loved to have many climaxes this way and he would reach his peak soon. He was almost sixty after all.

"Oh God, yes." Two strokes took her to her first. The orgasm slammed into her, roaring through every nerve. *Oh yes, yes. Such pleasure.* So long had it taken her to learn of pleasure like this. She saw stars, as she did each time with this man. Stars that sparkled like priceless jewels against black velvet.

Barely did she gain her senses from her first climax, before she brought herself to a second. And then a third. By the fifth, she no longer needed to stroke her throbbing, abraded clit. It took one deep thrust of Rodesson's magnificent cock to make her climax again. She was soaked and finished. But he was not.

"Withdraw," she instructed, panting, "You must withdraw."

With a groan of frustration, he did. Wet, exhausted, she rolled onto her back. Her bottom hit the bed, driving the phallus impossibly deep inside her. She came with it, but the orgasm was a mere ripple through her sated body. She didn't need to give more instruction. Rodesson moved to straddle her shoulders and he held his rigid cock down to her lips.

Once he forced himself to wait it became almost impossible to bring him to climax. Sometimes she had to leave him unsatisfied—on the days he took her by her arse. But today, she must give him special pleasure, for she knew he had secrets to reveal.

She tongued the head, drawing out a moan. His story had been true. Even shackled she possessed great power. She kissed the bubbling eye. "You can't paint at all?" she whispered.

He tried to thrust himself inside her mouth, but she kept her lips together, teasing the engorged head. "But that is not so tragic," she reassured. "Wouldn't your books become more valuable if it is known there is to be no more?"

"I wish there weren't," he muttered, speaking more by reflex than by conscious thought.

She took him inside then let him out to torment him once again.

"It doesn't work that way, love," he said louder. For a man experiencing skilled pleasure to his cock, he looked decidedly grim. "I done a few things considered shocking in the world of publishing. Keeping me copyright, for example. But if the volumes stop, me blunt will."

So if she wanted anything from him, she must get it now.

"And hell, since me money's gone, I'm to be in dun territory. Again."

"Don't think of such things, master. Let your slave suckle you and please you."

"You're a talented and cunning lass, aren't you, Lydia?"

No, she could not let him think her cunning and calculating. She must play the courtesan who loved to please, even if he could readily see through the ruse.

She took him deep into her mouth and he rewarded her skill by swelling large. She grabbed his buttocks and let him thrust into her as vigorously as he needed to. She curled her lips over her teeth and endured. His explosion rocked him, and for a moment she feared that his heart was not strong enough. He collapsed to the bed beside her, muttering endearments and words of appreciation.

She breathed hard and murmured words of pleasure. He still seemed to be semi-conscious as he struggled to free her of the ropes, as he gave her the key to free her own hands.

"Yes, you're a talented woman . . ." He flopped back.

Knowing Rodesson, she guessed he'd played cards all night and had not yet slept. Curling up beside him, she stroked the damp gray hair on his chest, and waited until he drifted into a post-coital slumber.

Lydia slipped from the bed and drew on her silky wrapper. As she tied the belt around her waist, she padded out of the room.

Once in her library, she scanned the leather-bound books on the crowded shelves. To extract the one she wanted, she had to tug hard to free it. With a warm sense of pride, she surveyed the books surrounding her. Her library was as well appointed as any gentleman's.

Stroking a finger across the gilt letters embossed in the rich leather, she lay the book on the large table. Opened it, flipped the pages until she found the first erotic picture. She then took a second book and laid it beside the first. Rodesson's last two books, *Tales of a London Gentleman* and *A Gentleman's Pleasures*.

Why should his inability to paint be a secret, unless . . .

She studied the pictures closely. The poses. The expressions. The style.

Her guess had been correct. These pictures were . . . different.

Who had painted Rodesson's work?

Chapter One

What would her jaded lord do with his hands while the lovely courtesan knelt between his legs and kissed him intimately?

Venetia Hamilton tapped the end of her brush against her lips as she studied her watercolor painting. Even though her earl—yes, she'd decided he was an earl—was a most experienced man, this time he'd met his match in the delightful auburn-haired woman pleasuring him.

She couldn't resist smiling at her imaginary earl's downfall in the arena he believed he reigned supreme. Since his lordship was so steeped in vice, so bored by customary sensual acts, he'd begin with definite ennui, merely an onlooker to his own seduction.

In his right hand, Venetia sketched a glass of fine champagne. In his left, since he was in the theatre box of the pretty woman, she gave him a peeled orange the size of an ample breast, large enough to fill his strong hand. No, he would not touch the woman, she decided. But in his expression . . . there she could show not only the desire, but the growing wonderment as his heart began to open, to unfurl, to delight in the pleasures bestowed upon him.

She turned her attention to the audience, for her earl was receiving these daring caresses to his intimate parts in full view of the Drury Lane theatre. Ah, the expressions told the tale—the matrons pretending to be scandalized, but really enraptured by his magnificent proportions, his exquisite form, his handsome face. Envy on their husbands' faces. And the leering looks of the mob in the orchestra.

Now she must tackle the earl's expression. Capture perfectly the growing astonishment on his face as this act that he must have experienced a thousand times—at least—became new and special and wonderful once more . . .

She took short, unsteady breaths as she stepped back from naughty fantasy to the reality of her tiny studio. When she drew, she became one with the scene—not a participant, but a figure in the shadows, holding a brush, telling a life's history in one erotic moment.

Her body hummed with desire, ached with it. She should be ashamed to admit it, but she wasn't at all as proper as her mother had raised her to be. She was, after all, her father's daughter.

With a sigh, Venetia plopped her brush in the jar and swirled it until the water blushed pink, lit by the fragile spring sunlight that spilled through the paned window. The only raven-haired scoundrels in her life lived on the canvases stacked on the narrow shelves of her studio, all safely hidden beneath muslin covers.

She knew perfectly well that love was a woman's folly. That rakes never truly reformed—

A sharp rap on the door had her almost knocking over the water glass. The rap came again. Followed by a breathless, "My heavens, Miss Hamilton!"

She had to take the time to turn the easel so her painting faced the wall and Mrs. Cobb burst through the door just as she hid the scandalous picture.

Mrs. Cobb puffed from the jaunt up the stairs. Her cheeks blazed red, her cap was askew. She held out a card. "There is a *gentleman* to see you, mum. A gentleman calling upon you alone!"

"Which gentleman?" Her father? Rodesson outwardly appeared to be a 'gentleman'. But he wouldn't dare visit.

Her housekeeper pushed her cap upright. "The Earl of Trent, mum! I put him in the drawing room. Tea? Should I put the kettle on?"

Venetia's heart tapped a frenzied dance in her chest. She pushed her chair back, snatched up the studio key, and crossed the floor in a heartbeat to take the card. Her thumb slid over thick, textured vellum embossed with a crest. Her gaze fell to the title, in bold text. It did indeed read—THE EARL OF TRENT.

She slumped against the doorframe in disbelief. How *could* the earl know who she was?

Mrs. Cobb lurked over her shoulder, demanding a decision on tea as Venetia locked the door to her studio with shaking hands.

"N—no tea," Venetia stuttered. Lifting her skirts, she hurried down the hallway in the most unladylike way. But if she was running into disaster, she wanted to get it done with.

Plodding footfalls told her Mrs. Cobb was following but couldn't keep up.

The most preposterous notion dawned as Venetia sped down the stairs. What if her father had gambled again, hoping to win his vowels back from the earl? What if this time Trent had won *her* at cards?

Reaching the open drawing room door, she stopped, smoothed her skirts, and gulped down steadying breaths. She must be careful. If she ruined her reputation, she ruined her sisters' reputations. Maryanne, Grace . . . they at least deserved a chance at the lives Mother hoped they would lead—marriage, children, happiness . . .

The earl, she noted, had found the only warm spot in her chilly drawing room. As soon as she stepped inside, the cold seeped through her dress and wrapped its icy fingers around her bare neck. Since she never received guests, she never heated the room. At least a fire now crackled in the hearth.

His lordship stood so close to the licking flames, she feared a spark might set his trousers alight. His left elbow was propped on the mantel, between the unfortunate bric-a-brac left by the previous tenant—two candlesticks shaped like nude women and a bronze of his favorite mount.

Venetia closed the door gently behind her, then stopped short, still clutching the doorknob.

The earl balanced an open book in his large gloved hand and he lazily flipped the pages. The faint sunlight cast a bluish gleam on his coal-black hair and slanted across his straight shoulders. Even in a casual stance, he easily topped six feet and she couldn't help but admire how his midnight-blue superfine emphasized the taper from wide back to narrow waist and lean hips. Skintight trousers displayed magnificent legs and disappeared into Hessians with a mirror finish.

She arched on tiptoe to spy around his broad frame. Pictures. The book did indeed contain pictures but she couldn't see the detail—he stood too far away. But *Tales of a London Gentleman* was bound in burgundy leather, in exactly the same shade as the book lying across that massive hand.

The earl paused at a plate, then turned the book in his hand to study some detail that had caught his fancy. A flush prickled along the back of Venetia's neck.

He moved to capture the light more fully on the page, and she saw his profile. Raven hair, darkly lashed eyes, patrician features, and wide, firm lips.

Her stomach pitched to her toes. *Trent* was the dark-haired gentleman who had appeared in her father's pictures. The man she'd copied for *her* book. She'd thought him an invention of her father's brush. But since he stood before her in the flesh, obviously her assumption had been wrong.

It made sense. Rodesson attended brothels and orgies and hells. Why wouldn't he base his pictures on actual patrons? On the actual scenes he had witnessed?

The titles flew through her whirling mind. *The Fair Lady Bound. The Jermyn Street Harem. The French Kiss.*

Even *The Trapeze* in which the nude lady had been seated on a suspended bar over the gentleman's upright—

Venetia pressed her hand to her churning stomach. Her father had changed Lord Trent's appearance, she saw that now. She, in utter innocence, had decided to make *her* gentleman more handsome. By horrific accident, she had succeeded in making him look more like the actual man.

A soft groan spilled from her lips.

The earl looked up sharply and she stared into vivid turquoise eyes, the color startling and beautiful in contrast to his long sooty lashes and straight black brows.

That extraordinary shade had not appeared in her father's pictures. Could *she* capture it? If she blended cobalt blue with a touch of—

"This is my personal favorite, Miss Hamilton. I think you have caught my likeness perfectly in this one." Dangerous amusement rippled through Lord Trent's seductive baritone and his deep masculine voice held her transfixed. "You have a remarkable talent."

A remarkable talent. She felt a warm flush of pride, even as her knees almost buckled.

"My—my lord." She managed a curtsy, a wobbly one, her plain gray skirts crumpling as she dipped. "I am afraid I don't understand to what you are referring."

He closed the book. His brows arched over those turquoise eyes—*cerulean* blue would do it, blended with a dab of yellow oxide—

"Your book of erotica in which I play the starring role."

Erotica. The word flowed off his tongue in a nonchalant manner, as though they had met in the park and he had just touched his hat and commented on the rain. But it struck her with the force of a lusty slap on her backside. She thought of the pictures he was looking at, pictures she'd created, and all the confidence she'd struggled to earn evaporated in a heartbeat.

His lordship rested his elbow on the mantel and smiled at her confusion.

No. She had finally succeeded in taking charge of her life and she wasn't about to surrender her control. Earl or no. She must bluff him. And, for the sakes of her mother and sisters, she must prove better at bluffing than her father.

She stiffened her spine. Prim disgust. That's what she sought. She imagined Lady Plim, the wife of Sir Plim, and the sharp-tongued tartar of Maidenswode. "My lord, it may be the fashion amongst the aristocracy to carry scandalous tomes about and view them before unsuspecting women, but I am afraid your behavior is—"

He waved an elegant hand. "Don't waste my time, Miss Hamilton. You've got paint on your sleeve."

"Watercolors. A lady's pastime."

He chuckled and a shiver raced down her spine. She'd never heard a laugh like that. A low, rumbling, purely masculine laugh. It held a naughty suggestive sensuality that she'd never been treated to before.

He inclined his handsome head. "Rodesson has told me all about you, my dear. He came to me to plead for the return of his vowels—for the sake of his illegitimate daughters."

Venetia flinched at the word *illegitimate*. It never failed to make her feel her parents' actions had been her fault.

"But—" Her last-ditch attempt to protest that Rodesson was not her father died on her lips. His lordship knew the truth and she was not going to convince him otherwise.

He crooked his gloved finger. "Come here, Miss Hamilton. I don't wish to shout our conversation across the room and I suspect you wouldn't want that either."

She glared, not willing to go at his command, but he was right, of course. She would bet pounds to pennies that Mrs. Cobb had her ear pressed to the keyhole. Reluctantly, Venetia marched toward the fireplace and the analogy of flinging herself from the pan to the flames leapt to mind.

She stopped at the worn and sagging wing chair, keeping it between them. But even separated from Lord Trent by a bulky piece of furniture, she felt small, dainty, and vulnerable confronted by his size and superb build. Her throat tightened. Her heart galloped. A quiver that she hoped was fear, but suspected wasn't, arced down her spine.

The earl left the mantel and strolled toward her, the spine of her book cupped in his large palm. "Your father insisted he had no means of supporting his family other than the royalties for his books. He explained that his innocent eldest daughter has been forced to embark on a dangerous career painting erotica."

What a fool her father had been! Trent was a rake, a scoundrel. He exuded so much sin and devilment, she suspected he didn't dare walk into a church. Everything about him screamed debaucher. He moved with a tantalizing predatory grace, his twinkling eyes threatened disaster to an innocent heart, and as for his seductive, insolent grin—

"My father is aging!" she cried. "He was despondent, confused. He forgot he had painted pictures that were not previously published. Really, how could I have possibly created that sort of risqué work?"

"I don't know, my dear. But you did, since it is obvious Rodesson didn't paint them."

Her heart hammered as Trent paced around the chair until he stood behind her. She refused to turn, but glanced back out of the corner of her eye. He towered over her. Trapped between his large body and the chair, she couldn't retreat. He bent until his warm breath whispered along the rim of her ear, exposed by her severe chignon. She lurched back in shock, rewarded by the rasp of his closely shaved jaw along her cheek.

Despite her skittering nerves, she forced herself not to move. If she turned, her lips might touch his.

The maddening temptation to tilt her head toward his

took her by surprise. She was hot, perspiring beneath her corset and tight-fitting bodice. Tense and wound up like a coiled spring.

This man had made love to a bound woman! This rogue had lain on a sumptuous bed, suckling the breast of one woman while another took him in her mouth—

Yes, the earl might look exactly like the sort of fantasy man she created with brush in hand—the gorgeous libertine felled by love—but it was an entirely different matter to have a real rake in possession of such devastating knowledge. And she didn't think for one moment Trent would be felled by anything.

He rested her book on the back of the chair. To her astonishment, he flipped it open, turning the pages until he found a plate. "Ah, *The Page Turner.*"

She knew the picture by heart, of course. A young man holding a candelabrum and turning the pages while his fetching lady played. The buck's pants were open, the lady's breasts freed from her dress, her skirts pooling over her bared thighs. The lady pursed her pink-lipped mouth delicately toward his member. In the shadows beneath the instrument, another man—Trent as the lady's secret lover—pleasured the lady with his fingers. A silly fantasy really—created because she had hated practicing her pianoforte.

Now devastating, because it involved him. Even over the crackle of the fire, her quick, shallow breathing seemed to fill the room.

"Exquisite." The earl's smooth rich voice wrapped around her like silk. "But while your style is very similar to your father's, there are marked differences."

"Impossible," she lied. "Since the drawings are my father's."

"The lady's hands are playing a chord that corresponds to the music sheet. I know the piece, my sister played it a thousand times—I used to be conscripted to hold her sheets. And in your father's work, the females are vacuous, simpering, all of a type. But in this book, every woman is different. Distinct."

"You look at the ladies' faces, my lord?"

"Yes I do, Miss Hamilton," he murmured by her ear. "Evidence of a lady's touch, I believe."

She kept her attention straight ahead but his scents teased her, enveloped her. A tinge of sandalwood soap. Starch in his shirt collar and cravat, cedar in his clothes, smoke and coffee on his breath. Horse and leather and the lightest hint of his sweat. The earl must be one of those gentlemen who enjoyed a good gallop on the Row at the crack of dawn.

Despite herself, she breathed deeply. Intrigued. Painted men did not have such alluring smells. She was cloistered in her studio all the time—she never met real gentlemen. To remember his scent would help her be more creative. More inspired.

His lordship's hard biceps bumped her shoulders. The sensual brush of his body against hers set her legs trembling. Venetia balled her hands into fists, stiffened her spine. "You must be a true connoisseur of my father's work, my lord Trent."

How else could he have spotted her slight deviations from her father's style? How likely was it that other gentlemen would?

"*My* father was," he said. "He owned every volume of Rodesson art. He introduced me to it at an early age. I believe I was eight when he gave me my first volume."

Eight? Eight was the age of a boy, not a man. Was a boy of that age even able to understand the drawings? To find them arousing?

If he'd started looking at such pictures at eight, when would he have first made love?

The instant the shocking thought raced through her head, Venetia found herself picturing the earl at his first sexual experience. With a voluptuous dairymaid or perhaps a bountiful courtesan. Eager. Sweaty. Naked.

Venetia, good heavens, stop! She took a shaky breath. "Are there other . . . differences?"

He turned the pages. "This one."

She gaped at the picture framed by his large gloved hands.

A simple alfresco luncheon scene. This one featured the earl with his back against an ancient oak tree while his mistress rode atop him.

"This, to me, is a distinct clue your father did not do the work."

For the life of her, Venetia could not see why. Her father had in fact done similar pictures.

"The position of the woman is the telling thing."

Mystified, she studied the mistress. The lady's skirts were up, revealing her plump bottom, and her head was thrown back, eyes closed, lips parted in ecstasy. Venetia had copied the expression from Belzique, the French artist of the last century who drew women in bizarre costumes, wielding whips. Pictures that disturbed her, which she would never wish to copy, but that she found inexplicably intriguing.

"In your father's works the women are always lifted," he explained. "In the upward portion of the stroke—" For the first time, his voice faltered.

"Yes?" Her query came out as a husky whisper.

"That position reveals the man's . . . equipment."

"His equipment," she repeated.

"His shaft. It appeals to the male to see the shaft disappearing inside the woman. For a start, they know actual penetration is taking place."

His tone was teasing but her chest felt squeezed, as though she'd been laced too tight. She stared at her picture, strangely hurt. "It doesn't appeal to the male to see the woman seated back, the way she is shown here?"

So it was more than just differences in style. She'd thought her work tempting, seductive, pleasing. But, as a woman, had she not understood what men desired? Was it more complex than she'd thought?

Did this mean her career—her key to independence—would fail? Perhaps her book had only sold well because of her father's name. Perhaps she would never sell another.

"You look so heartbroken, love," he murmured. "I can assure you that men enjoy your drawings. Your work is unlike anything I've ever seen. Far more arousing."

He settled his hands on the back of the chair. She was caught between his powerful arms as his breath skimmed the nape of her neck. Tiny loose tendrils of her hair stirred and tickled.

He bent forward at the exact instant she drew back. Her bottom bumped against a solid ridge. His lordship's . . . equipment, hard and jutting against her derriere through her skirts and his trousers.

He turned to the next page, revealing *Two Ladies Painting Watercolors*. Two young ladies of the ton sat in a garden with easels in front of them and the statue of a naked god to inspire. Both women had been attempting to sketch the nude man, but had become distracted in their arousal. Skirts and petticoats spilled over smooth thighs and they employed their paintbrushes on themselves in inventive ways.

And from the shrubbery, the Earl of Trent spied on the pretty girls.

"Now you see why I am here, Miss Hamilton." His tone hardened. His jaded amusement was gone. Anger burned beneath his words. "You've depicted me as the most promiscuous and perverted man in London. At a time when I put my patronage behind Lady Ravenwood's charity—a charity to save young women from brothels. Lady Ravenwood—my sister—was horrified when rumors reached her ears that I was doing the very thing she was trying to prevent."

Venetia fought panic. There was no point in denying the truth anymore. "It was not intentional, my lord! I did not even know you were a real man. I did not even know your name! You were in Rodesson's books. You did those things in public. You were naked—"

She broke off. She had just said 'naked' to an earl. Guiltily, she thought of *The Theatre Box*. Suddenly, she wanted to burn it. "I will never draw you again."

"No, you won't, my dear." He lifted his hands from the book and stepped back, as though giving her room to breathe. "Your career is about to come to an end."

She spun around. "But I must paint! How else will my family survive? My publisher expects a book in a month's time!"

A part of her quailed at the earl's sheer size, his intimidating pose with arms crossed over his wide chest, the hard line of his lips. But she tipped up her chin.

His lips softened. "I do not normally cancel gaming debts, Miss Hamilton. But I won't be responsible for your ruination. I will tear up your father's vowels."

She should be overjoyed. He would return the money. They were saved. She had saved them all. She would return to the country. She would have to give up all her hard-won independence.

Solemnly, she shook her head. "My father always enters into deep play, my lord. He will only lose his money again. I am the only hope my family has. And you need not worry, I am not innocent."

The lie rolled off her tongue before she could stop it.

His black brow lifted. He took a sharp breath. "Your father lied?"

"He doesn't know, of course."

She shivered again as his gaze swept her from curls to hem.

"You blush very prettily, my dear. But I have known of several courtesans who could summon a fetching flush on demand."

Her face flamed hotter. "I am not innocent and I . . . I can prove it."

"Can you?" Trent traced his gloved finger along the length of one of the paintbrushes in her picture. "So you have experienced the pleasures that you paint?"

Venetia was riveted by the sight. Her voice, where was her voice? "Y—yes," she lied.

"If you are not innocent then you must know how such a caress would feel." He circled his fingertip over the painted vulva. "You must know how a man delights in parting those soft lips and finding the heat and honey within."

He paused. Silence stretched for many fervent heartbeats. She heard her soft, quick breaths. The tick of the mantel clock. The greedy roar of the flames.

"Do you touch yourself like this, sweeting? Do you paint your quim with your brush until you are creamy and wet? Do you enjoy threesomes? Do you prefer two cocks at your command, or another woman's juicy cunny?"

Her knees felt as insubstantial as sea foam.

He lifted her hand from the back of the chair, gave a light brush across her knuckles with his lips. Gentlemanly. Safe. But he drew her index finger into his mouth and she was shocked and thrilled. His tongue toyed with the ridge of her fingernail, soaking the thin cotton.

How could the stroke of his tongue on her finger make her ache between her thighs?

But it did.

Why didn't she pull her hand back? Stop him? She couldn't. His words, his forbidden words, cast an irresistible spell.

She must relax. How would the auburn-haired courtesan she'd created behave? A woman bold enough to pleasure her lover in a theatre box wouldn't be gasping in shock at a kiss on her fingertips.

He released her finger and reached for the hem of her glove. Goodness, she was about to lose an article of clothing. He bared her hand and her glove fluttered to the carpet.

"In one kiss, sweetheart, I'll know if you are innocent or not."

No, he wouldn't. She would kiss him like a courtesan. She wasn't certain how a jade kissed, but it must be with great passion. Unfortunately, she was entirely on her own. None of her father's pictures depicted kisses.

With a gentle tug, he drew her to take a step closer. She lost balance, fell into his embrace. Her body pressed along his and his erection nudged her stomach. So close, so intimately close.

His lordship caught her other hand by the wrist, surprisingly quick despite the lazy grace of his movements. In a heartbeat, both her hands were captured in his.

Fighting the urge to gulp, she stared as bold as brass into his turquoise eyes. But she felt anything but bold as his lips—his perfectly sculpted, sensual lips—lowered toward hers.

She must behave like a wanton.

She *was* wanton. His mouth was a work of art, but all she could think of was pressing her mouth to that perfection and making it yield to her. Feigning sauciness, she slid her foot up his lordship's polished boot. Her soft slipper followed the shape of his bulging calf. The leather fit him like a second skin.

He caught her around the waist, his large hands splayed over her hips. Her nipples ached—she needed something . . . some pressure against them. She arched up against him, so sinfully close her breasts pushed into his hard and solid chest.

His lips slanted over hers and her moan vanished into his mouth. She tasted his morning coffee, a trace of smoke, and heat, delicious heat.

She had no chance to pretend passion—he lured her lips apart and slid his tongue inside. She'd never kissed like this. She'd only had one peck, one boring, meaningless peck in her whole life! This was scandalous, luscious. His tongue filled her mouth, touched hers, and coaxed it into sensual play.

Venetia slid her arms around his neck and dared to let her fingertips stroke his black hair, softer than the sable in her treasured brushes.

He moaned. Hoarsely.

She'd made him moan. A thrill of power rushed through her. She felt, wild, reckless, mad. Deep in her throat, she moaned again, too. She lifted her leg, seeking to wrap it around his hips. To hold him close. To never let him go.

Why had she never thought to draw something as spectacular as a kiss?

Her body burned with need. Dizzying desire swamped her. She slipped her hands up his back—the earl's broad, hard, beautiful back. She stroked the planes she'd drawn, imagining bare skin, sculpted muscle. His hands cupped her rear, squeezing, so she grabbed hold of his rump. Goodness, he had beautiful buttocks—hard and smooth and tightly indented at the sides. If he were on top of her, inside her, she would grab him there and clutch his muscular derriere as he plunged into her—

He set her back on her feet, pulled her hands from his rear. "That's enough, sweetheart. You *are* every inch a gently bred virgin. That unskilled kiss was definite proof."

She clung to his hands, unsteady. Unskilled kiss? Wonderful kiss. Dizzying kiss. She'd been passionate. How could he *know* she was innocent after that?

"I—" She wanted another kiss. Wanted more. She couldn't think.

"Eventually your secret will get out, Miss Hamilton. Do you want to ruin your sisters too?"

She shook her head. No, that she couldn't do. "But I want to be independent. I can't bear living each day knowing that disaster will come at any moment. Can you not understand that?"

"It's not safe, Miss Hamilton."

"So you will save me against my will? Why?"

His lips lifted in a lopsided grin and her heart somersaulted in her chest.

"Because my sister, Lady Ravenwood, insisted it was the right thing to do," he said. "My father made a career of ruining innocents. I do not intend to follow in his footsteps. Unfortunately for the males of England, Miss Hamilton, your career is most definitely finished."

CHAPTER TWO

"**A**nd here is your brand-new nephew!"

Marcus Wyndham, Earl of Trent, stood as Minerva, Lady Ravenwood, walked into the drawing room, a beaming smile on her face. She cradled the tiny baby against her chest. He could barely see the child amidst the frothy white bundle of blankets and blue ribbons, but Min . . . he'd never seen her look more radiant. Only two weeks from childbed and she glowed.

Sunlight spilled into Min and Stephen's drawing room, the fire roared with cheer, and being a part of the family gathering filled Marcus with a reassuring sense of warmth. He grinned as Min approached. Even his mother, who sat silently by the fire, had tolerated his presence without shrieking or throwing something at him.

This was the happiest he'd felt in a long time. Nothing seemed to please him these days. Nothing . . . except Venetia Hamilton's kiss.

He hadn't been able to sleep since kissing her. Hadn't even gone to a bloody brothel to ease his pain because he'd vowed he wouldn't and because it had been infinitely more pleasurable to lie in his bed with a cock as hard as a bloody iron bar and remember their kiss.

A phrase of his father's came to mind. *I was shaken to my gleaming boots by her kiss.* He'd been talking about a debutante—a virgin. A proper young lady, untouchable, off-limits, and oh, so ready to play, his father had claimed.

Damn his father—he understood exactly what the old debaucher had meant.

Hell, not the sort of thing to be thinking at a happy family gathering. He pushed the thoughts aside, and lightly kissed Min's cheek.

"David is smiling already," she announced, raven curls bouncing. "If you smile at him, Marcus, I'm certain he'll smile for you."

With shock, Marcus saw she was offering his nephew to him. He was at once honored and terrified. Min's large, luminous eyes implored. She was so proud, so delighted with her joyous gift, that she would be hurt if he refused.

He couldn't hurt her.

"Take care to support his head," Stephen warned from his chair, "He's a strong lad and when he throws his head back he can catch you by surprise."

Marcus flashed a grim look at his brother-in-law. "You've rapidly turned into an expert, have you? I seem to remember you were all fumbling hands that first night."

"True enough." Stephen chuckled, raking his fingers through his hair. "Several bottles of port will do that to you."

"Don't you want to hold him?" Min asked.

Marcus swallowed hard and nodded. "But he's such a tiny little thing."

"I can assure you he didn't feel tiny," Min admonished.

He blushed at the quip and awkwardly slid his hand around his nephew's head. For once his hand felt large, unwieldy, dangerous, but the baby's head fit perfectly within. He cradled the tiny bottom, his gloved fingers squishing into the thick cloth there. Large blue eyes ringed with dark lashes gazed up at him as though he was the most fascinating sight ever beheld. Dark blond hair dusted the strangely shaped head, thickest in a ring above the ears.

He shifted his hands, trying to ensure he had the best grip, and he felt as though he were trying to juggle china.

"There!" Min crowed, "A smile!"

His nephew's hands fisted, then waved. He'd always thought infants were swaddled tightly, but Min had explained that she did so for sleep. She wished to let David explore and play.

Some madness seemed to overtake him as he gazed down at the bubbling lips and the large eyes. Suddenly he was cooing and gooing.

Beside him, Min giggled. "I think you are smitten, aren't you, Marcus?"

He couldn't help but answer her smile. "I have to admit I am, Min." She was so at ease with the little one even after a mere fortnight. Would he be the same as a father? He suspected he'd be the talk of the nursery if he had his own son— watching his miracle every moment of the day. He'd have to take care to employ an indulgent nanny, not a strident one.

"Find a wife and you could be blessed as well."

He tried to tease. "You have a child dependent on you. I forbid you to launch into a matchmaking project." But he wasn't going to find a wife or, if he could help it, be a father.

Min laughed. "I wouldn't dream of attaching any female of my acquaintance to you." He knew she'd meant to tease but her face sobered instantly and the vivacious light faded in her green-blue eyes.

What was she thinking? Remembering how she'd caught him at twenty-one kissing Miss Wallace, who was her bosom-bow? He'd been cradling the lady's full breast. Never a wilting flower, Min had accused him of trying to *rape* her best friend. She'd brained him with a vase to save her friend's virtue.

In that one moment, his beloved sister had revealed what was deeply in her heart—she thought he was like their father. She'd thought that he was capable of forcing himself on a defenseless woman. Miss Wallace had thrown herself at him, but Min wouldn't believe it.

She'd thought he was a brute. A debaucher. A rapist.

How could she think he was like that? He used to cry himself to sleep listening to Min's tears at night. With a child's instinct, he'd known the way Father had touched Min had been tainted by lewdness and nastiness. He'd known it was wrong.

The baby's loud burp startled him. "Bravo, David."

Min dabbed at the baby's pursed lips with her cloth, cleaning chunks of white. Cooing sounds ensued between both mother and son. David gave Min a gummy smile that tore at Marcus' heart. "What about love?" she asked softly.

"I have friends who married for love," he said, "Who speak highly of it—call it the most perfect happiness. You know more about love than I."

Min looked up, her large blue-green eyes alive with perfect happiness. "I could never begin to explain love. Intimacy. Friendship. Something glorious that both hurts and enriches. And you know that if you lost it, your heart might never mend."

"But love is not for me. Nor is marriage."

Concern cast shadows in those eyes—concern for him—as she reached for David. "I thought you'd given up your sinful ways."

He relinquished the baby with relief—too small and precious for his big hands. "So did I. But some temptations are too great to resist." That kiss. Venetia Hamilton had tasted of sweet tea, sugared biscuits, and feminine heat, and he had wanted to devour her.

"Did you help Miss Hamilton? I know your honor balked at forgiving the debt—"

"Yes, I protected Miss Hamilton as promised. And now my heart shines with the joy of a good deed."

"What was she like? Was she truly a proper lady?"

"She blushed often. She wore a frightful gown and had red hair."

"Marcus!" She laughed. "Was she pretty?"

"Yes. A country beauty with peaches-and-cream skin and curls the color of fine sherry bouncing around her wide hazel eyes—eyes both amber-brown and green. She has her father's nose, unfortunately, and his sharp chin."

And a lush and lovely mouth. An enticing mouth. Miss Hamilton had wrapped her leg around his hips and pulled herself tight against his erection. Her kiss was eager, artless, and delightfully tentative—and the touch of her hands on him had sent shivers of pleasure down his spine and a surge of blood to his groin that had shut off his brain.

Min's eyes had widened at his flowery description. "And why are you so curious about a woman who draws naughty pictures?" he asked, to deflect her interest.

"I just wondered if she was a bold woman, the sort with henna-dyed hair. I can't imagine how a well-bred woman could do such a thing."

He shrugged. "Survival." Miss Hamilton had moaned into his mouth as he kissed her. Desperate little moans. He'd never known a woman make such lusty sounds at just a kiss. And he, blackguard that he was, had grabbed her derriere. A gentleman didn't fondle an innocent woman's derriere. But apparently a maiden did grab a gentleman's arse, for she had caught hold of both his cheeks and squeezed. His cock had reared against his belly. He'd been aroused, damn near out of his mind, with the enticement of introducing her to pleasure.

He wanted to speak of it. But he couldn't. Couldn't admit that he might be like their father.

Min was caught up in watching David's eyes flicker shut. The boy would fight, the lids would open wide, then slowly sink down again. Marcus couldn't help but smile.

"So what do you seek in your perfect countess?" Min asked, cuddling her child against her shoulder and rocking him.

"Beauty, brains, breeding. A fortune. A good heart and quick wit. But Min, sweetheart, I am not getting leg-shackled."

Min's enormous eyes twinkled. "But I'd love to play

matchmaker for you and force you look in all the places you hate to go—balls, routs, assemblies." A naughty gleam showed in Min's eyes. "This Season, my project is Stephen's brother Frederick."

He gave Min a severe brotherly look. "You're not to strain yourself at those events. I hope Stephen made that clear to you."

From his chair, Stephen laughed.

"You cannot dictate to me through Stephen! He is too much your friend—he tolerates your interference too much."

"I didn't look after you when I should have, Min," he murmured.

She blushed and looked down at her son, giving a loving pat. "It wasn't your fault."

She was so strong it humbled him. She'd endured and found happiness and comfort in Stephen's arms, found love in her marriage bed. The only worthwhile thing he'd done with his life was to find Stephen for Min.

His heart soared to see her happy, but it would never be enough. It didn't atone for the nights he buried his head into his pillow. For the years when he didn't protect her.

Cradling her baby with one hand, Min touched his arm. "You gave me a great gift. You forced me to see my future was to be a wife and a mother." She looked over to their mother, rigid and emotionless in her chair by the fireplace. "I would like Mama to hold him."

He shook his head. "It's not a good idea."

Their mother stared blankly toward the flames, as though unaware of her children, her first grandchild. As though she could not even hear the laughter. He never knew how to handle the countess. No matter what tactic he tried—to soothe, to coerce, or to inflict his will, his mother fought him. Punishment, he figured, for what he'd done.

"Please, Marcus," Min implored. "If we watch her and just let her touch him for a few moments. She wouldn't do him harm, I'm certain of it."

She looked so anxious, that it broke his heart. "She won't even remember holding him."

"Marcus, I would like to try."

Oh, the man was a disobedient scoundrel!

Venetia tossed her paintbrush into the water glass and slumped back in her chair. She fixed the canvas—and her recalcitrant hero—with a scowl.

"You are supposed to be a blond war hero! Dressed in scarlet with a lethal sword at your side and an even more magnificent weapon between your thighs. You are not supposed to be a raven-haired earl with a wicked smile!"

Goodness, she was raving at a two-dimensional man. And like the Earl of Trent, he was not listening to her.

Her lips still burned from his kiss. A kiss he'd used to prove her innocence, a kiss that had shaken every fantasy she'd had about a love affair. She couldn't forget it. Or him. Was this what lust did to a woman?

Venetia balanced her elbows on the desk, taking care not to dip them in wet paint, and dropped her forehead against her hands. Four pictures started and in each one the male looked exactly like Trent. She'd even attempted a drawing of two voluptuous, randy courtesans exploring each other's succulent breasts, her heart pounding as she drew, her throat tightening, but suddenly, in the background, a *portrait* of the sensual earl had appeared.

She'd tossed and turned in her bed all night. Imagining him in her bed—without a stitch—kissing her, moving over her, parting her thighs—

Her elbow hit her teacup. It tottered and before she could catch it, it tipped in the saucer. Tea sloshed over her picture. But what did that matter? Her career was over.

Out of habit, she had come to her studio, picked up her brush, and painted to ease her confusion, to give her time to control her whirling thoughts. She had no choice but to forfeit her independence, but she didn't want to give it up!

It was more than just the money. She would have to slink back to the country. And do what? Become an eccentric spinster doing good works for the church? If she was a guest of the country gentry she could always peruse their libraries to see if they had copies of her books.

She could marry. At twenty-four, she was on the shelf by London standards, but if she were very fortunate, a widower might consider taking her on. There was one in Maidenswode who had offered—he was fifty, fat, had eight children, and drank.

To return to the country would mean hiding her paints in the stables, sneaking out to the woods to draw . . .

She would have to paint in secret once more. After her mother had found that first portrait—of a nude male statue—painting had been forbidden. Her mother feared that it was the artistic temperament that made Rodesson so licentious. Olivia Hamilton had been horrified to discover her eldest daughter had been compelled to sketch naked men.

Venetia stroked the ivory handle of her brush. What was he doing now, the roguish Lord Trent? Was he asleep, curled up with a woman or two in his bed? She could envision the threesome, with him sandwiched between, his groin pressed again a bottom just as it had pressed into hers, and the other woman would press her breasts and privates against his backside. His beautiful, sculpted backside—

The ache wasn't only in her quim—for some reason her heart ached too.

If she were in his bed, in his arms, she could reach out and touch his bare back. Boldly trace the line of his spine down to his tight buttocks, to those iron-hard muscles she'd loved having beneath her palms.

What if she'd dared to explore more?

As though compelled, she bent and opened the lowest, deepest drawer of her desk. She should just shut it now. Instead, she lifted the first book from the stack. The rippled leather caressed her bare fingertips. Gently, she set it on the middle of the desk, so it wouldn't make a sound. Guilt made her heart pound.

In the middle of the book, she would find Rodesson's famed picture of a gentleman reviewing his 'harem' of willing wantons at a Jermyn Street brothel. That gentleman, the Earl of Trent, was shown in aroused glory . . .

All she had to do was look.

All she had to do was open the book and satisfy her . . . curiosity.

No, that was . . . improper. Invasive. Rude. Unforgivable. But she could just peek. After all, the earl had performed in public. It was his own fault he had ended up in a book—

Really, one peek could hardly hurt.

She flicked past two courtesans entwined like the numbers six and nine to find *The Jermyn Street Harem*.

Trent was shown reclining on silken pillows, dressed in a dark blue robe, covered but for his spectacular . . . cock which curved upward into the air. Dozens of women stood before him, displaying their breasts and quims. His lordship appeared as jaded as always as he selected one for his entertainment.

Throat dry, Venetia studied the picture. Trembling, she traced his length with her finger.

This was so very . . . wrong. To touch . . . him. This way. But she couldn't resist.

Was he exaggerated in the work? She doubted it. He'd felt enormous, impossibly so, when pushing against her backside.

His . . . cock looked so rampant. Thick at the base, it curved toward his lean stomach like a sickle and was crowned with a large, dusky head. It was clearly the centerpiece of the picture, rendered in great detail—even to the veins on its shaft.

She found her fingers stroking between her thighs. The way she did, without conscious thought, while she drew.

Women were not supposed to touch themselves there. Even bathing was to be done with a cloth and with haste. But if she didn't touch herself, she'd die from the pain.

Rubbing in a slow, sensual spiral, she remembered his words. *"Do you touch yourself like this, sweeting? Do you paint your quim with your brush until you are creamy and wet?"*

She lifted her brush from the water goblet, stroked it against the rim to smooth the bristles and squeeze the water out.

Do you prefer two cocks at your command, or another woman's juicy cunny?

She thought of him watching her, amused, intrigued, with his hand on his large cock . . .

She wanted him so, this man she couldn't have. He was an earl—one who frequented the wildest brothels, lavished fortunes on the most desirable mistresses—but in her fantasies, she could have him. He would be hers.

Yanking up her skirts, she listened. Her door was behind her, closed. From beyond it, nothing but quiet. Feeling illicit, she parted her thighs on her chair and touched the wet brush to her nether lips. She drew a line of water to the apex and dabbed there, teasing herself with the cool wet against her heat. The sable bristles, soft but slightly stiffened by use and washings, rasped her clitoris.

She could just imagine the look of approval on Trent's handsome face . . .

Sliding the brush down, she held it tight to her bud and rubbed herself against it. Wanton. Wild. Not longer caring about a delicate performance . . .

Yes, yes, he was right. She *was* wet and sticky. Heat and honey.

Oh, yes. Oh!

She had to hold the edge of the desk as the climax roared through her. She shook with it, rocking the chair on the plank floor. Her fingers dug into the blotter; she dropped the brush to the floor.

She gave a weak, giddy giggle as she imagined Trent applauding—

She gasped at the quick rap on the door.

Mrs. Cobb. The doorknob rattled. Twisting in her seat, she saw it begin to turn. She'd forgotten to lock it!

The book fell into the drawer with a bang just as her housekeeper pushed open the door and peeped through the opening. Facing forward, Venetia prayed Mrs. Cobb didn't notice her hiked up skirts, prayed that her racing heart didn't explode.

"This came in the post, mum."

Fluffing out her skirts as casually as she could, Venetia felt the hem swish over her ankles. She dropped a cloth over her painting in progress—it didn't matter if it smeared.

She knew her face must be beet-red but she had no choice but to walk over on shaky legs and take the letter. As she took it, she gagged.

"Pooh, scent! It stinks of the stuff." She sneezed. Her eyes watered. She stretched her arm out straight to keep the offensive thing away. Eyed it warily. Who would send a letter drenched in perfume? The return address was Compton Street, on the fringes of Mayfair. Instinct warned that this wasn't the sort of letter she could allow anyone else to see.

"Thank you, Mrs. Cobb." She began to swing the door shut.

"Is it trouble, mum?"

"No." She closed the door firmly. Guilt stabbed. Mrs. Cobb might like gossip, but she was truly concerned.

Venetia strode back to her desk and tore open the envelope with the end of her paintbrush.

Her gaze riveted to one word in fussy, lavish handwriting. *Rodesson.*

Scanning the words . . . *your father revealed . . . can no longer paint . . . his talented daughter . . .*

Her stomach tightened. Nausea roiled in her belly. She reached the last line. *One thousand pounds to preserve your secret.*

And the loopy, flowing signature, almost impossible to decipher. *Lydia Harcourt.*

"Lyd, what the bloody hell are you about?"

With three silk gowns draped over her arm, Lydia gasped in shock. A gown slid from her grasp to pool on the floor. The voice came from behind her, from the doorway of her bedchamber. A voice she hadn't heard for years . . .

She trod on the skirts as she turned, to see Tom lounging in the doorway, dressed like a dapper dandy. She gulped. The second to last time she had seen her half-brother he had been wearing his butcher's apron and it had been splattered with fresh, bright red blood. The last time he'd demanded money . . .

She was suddenly conscious she wore only a corset and a shift and her large brown nipples were obvious beneath the flimsy lawn.

"Haven't you a good word for yer own flesh and blood, Lyd? After so many long years?"

"I thought you were in Italy."

"Missed the home shores, lass. And missed me family."

Run out of blunt, no doubt. Though most men fled to Italy because they could live in decadence there without money.

"I've nothing." She laid the dresses on her bed, as smoothly as she could. Her traveling trunk was already half-filled. "I can't spot you a thing this time."

He laughed. "Sweetheart, I could pawn the contents of your drawing room and buy a villa fit for a king."

And where did that leave her? "The house was rented furnished, Tom." And she had a mere month to vacate it.

"I've been in London for a while. And the tables have been bloody fickle—"

"I won't give you money for gambling."

"I'm worried about you. Blackmail's a rum business, Lyd. A bloody dangerous one."

She jerked up. Her peach satin snagged on the trunk hinge and tore. How did he know?

"I was playing whist at The Sin Room and overheard the very foxed Duke of Montberry."

Montberry! Oh, how annoying that man was. She'd thought he would at least use some discretion. That was the problem with dealing with aging men. Montberry might have been a military genius but in the years since Waterloo he was quickly losing his wits. What a fool to get drunk at Mother Maggie's horrid brothel and spill secrets.

Tom grinned. He was a strikingly handsome man. Why hadn't he found himself a post pandering to an Italian countess and left her alone? But she owed him her very life and she couldn't deny him what he wanted.

"I've looked after myself my entire life, Tom. I've nothing to fear." Nothing to fear but age. She was almost forty. It had been so easy when she'd been young—eighteen. Lord Craven had believed she was fifteen. Of course she hadn't been a virgin, but she'd put on the act for Craven. A sponge, a bit of blood, some sobbing and tears.

And what other choice did she have? What future was there for an aging woman with no means?

"Ye could come with me back to Italy, Lyd. Venice is a beautiful, decadent city."

Italy. So far away from England. She needed to escape London. The carriage this afternoon as she'd walked to Hyde Park . . . it had been a near miss. And last night, the man in the shadows . . . the footpad. He'd grabbed her arm, a knife had glinted, he'd swiped, but then he'd ran. She'd been in the company of Lord Brude, thinking herself safe . . .

Since mailing her last letters, the ones to R, S, and T, she'd been beset by accidents . . .

Accidents. No reason to think they weren't. Other than the fact she'd now made enemies. Powerful enemies . . .

Blast men! All she'd wanted was her due for all her years of servitude. A little protection for her retirement. And instead of paying a few thousand pounds—a mere trifle to these men—they'd rather do her harm . . .

Italy. She could flee to Italy. Buy a villa. Buy a handsome Italian or two . . .

No, she couldn't escape to Italy with Tom. Not now. Not yet. She doubted she'd make it to the coast alive. She had to go to Chartrand's orgy first. He would be there. As would Brude, Wembly, and Montberry . . .

Tom stretched out on the side of her bed, watching her with his head-of-the-family arrogance, his booted feet dirtying her expensive ivory counterpane.

"How much do you want?" Lydia asked on a sigh.

"Madam is not in."

The breeze tugged at the hood of Venetia's cloak. She caught hold of it to keep it in place, shadowing her face. Not in? She must speak to Lydia Harcourt. She stuck her foot on the threshold so the door could not be shut. "When will she return?" she demanded.

"Not today." The housekeeper frowned at her foot.

"Then when?" Her father was now lying in sickbed. She needed to reassure him that Lydia Harcourt was taken care of. What if he had another attack of his heart from the worry?

Beneath her clean, starched cap, the servant's eyes narrowed. "I cannot say."

"Mrs. Harcourt sent me a letter requesting my prompt response." Venetia tried to infuse haughtiness in her words but, standing on the steps at an unfashionable hour with her cloak's hood pulled low to hide her face, she knew the servant wouldn't find her intimidating. The servant would know she had secrets to hide.

"Madam has left for a stay in the country. She will not return before a week hence."

An Incognita leaving London at the beginning of the Season? "Where has she gone?"

"A house party." Raw greed gleamed in the housekeeper's dark eyes. "Now, madam, if you have a package or a letter ye wish to leave for my mistress—"

And have her pluck a few notes from the stack that Lydia Harcourt expected to receive? Or perhaps take the lot and run off? She wasn't that naïve.

She bit her lip. The physician had assured her Rodesson would recover. But he had looked so frail last night . . . and anxiety over this wouldn't help. "I would prefer to deliver my . . . gift to Mrs. Harcourt directly," she said. "Where is she staying?"

"I've been instructed not to say. Ye'll have to come back when she's returned."

The housekeeper pushed hard on the door. Venetia admitted defeat and drew her foot back. The door snapped shut in her face.

She trudged down the steps. She worked so hard to ensure her servants didn't know about her secret life. But Mrs. Harcourt was careless. The housekeeper obviously knew what sort of business she was here to transact. The hood, the veil, the face paint had hidden her appearance at least. But why would Mrs. Harcourt race off without waiting to get her money?

She stomped down the last two steps. She hated this. Hated to be at the mercy of this woman.

She paused at the stairs that led down to the servants' entrance, cast in shadow. An idea dawned. Could she bribe another servant to tell her where Mrs. Harcourt was? She nipped down the steps and raised her fist to knock—

"I might be wearing drawers and I might not, milord!"

Startled, Venetia glanced up. A couple stood at the top of the steps. The girl, blessed with golden ringlets, coyly stroked the chest of a fine gentleman.

"I knew the instant I set on eyes on you whether you were or not, strumpet," the gentleman returned and he boldly cupped the swell of the woman's breast beneath her poppy-red pelisse in full view of Compton Street.

"Strumpet!" Giggling, the young woman slapped the man's broad chest with a dainty reticule. "Miss Harcourt to you, sir."

Was this giggling twit was her blackmailer? Some courtesans merely used the title 'Mrs.' to appear respectable to their neighbors. Just as her mother had pretended to be a widow.

"You've no idea what is beneath me dress, milord," the girl challenged.

Venetia chewed her lip. Should she walk back up and announce herself? The girl was silly and young, and hardly seemed capable of creating a clever scheme of blackmail.

"What if I were to toss your skirts right now to find out, sweet strumpet?"

His lordship was tall, alluringly dark, and radiating dangerous sensuality, just like Lord Trent. This silly flirtatiousness reminded her of her kiss with Trent. Of the thrill of bandying naughty words . . .

A strange wistfulness blossomed in her heart—jades could be bold and flirtatious and have fun. She'd spent a lifetime in Maidenswode being rigidly correct lest someone suspect the truth—that her mother wasn't a respectable widow.

The gentleman inched up the girl's skirts.

"Swansborough!" the girl cried. This time she slapped his hands.

Laughing he let her skirts drop. "And where is your sister, angel? Why has the lovely Lydia left London?"

Venetia stood absolutely still.

"She went to a dull house party. She was ever so . . . tedious, going on about how she would be spending a week at Lord . . . Oh, Lord Chartrand's estate. Why should anyone wish to rusticate in the country? At least I shall be able to use her theatre box."

Lord Swansborough gave a throaty laugh. "Angel, Lord Chartrand's house party is the most wicked orgy of the Season."

"My sister has gone to an orgy? How utterly scandalous."

"Indeed. I just might retrieve my invitation and go myself."

An orgy. Venetia's jaw dropped. How the devil could she

go to an orgy to speak to a courtesan? But she had to! Rodesson could not travel. Once again, it was up to her.

Venetia saw the girl's eyes widen to the size of sovereigns. Even from several feet away she could read the young lady-bird's sudden desperation. "But I want you to take me to the theatre, my lord. You promised it would be a most reward-ing—"

A squeak escaped Venetia's lips. Men really did indulge in sexual activities in the theatre! Then she stayed motionless, her heart thudding. Had that noise given her away?

But the girl and Lord Swansborough swept up the stairs, oblivious to her hiding place in the shadows. Venetia breathed out in happy relief. Lord Swansborough had given her a brilliant idea. She knew exactly how she could go to an orgy.

Lord Trent. No doubt he would be attending. It made perfect sense. He was the only rake she knew in London. She could ask him to take her.

CHAPTER THREE

Venetia darted along the path that wound through Hyde Park. In the afternoon, the ton would flock here. A stroll in the park was *de rigueur* in the Season for the *haute volée*. But in the morning, gentlemen rode the paths. Handsome, sleekly muscled gentlemen on sleekly muscled mounts.

Even on this gloomy day, the panting of lathered horses filled the air. Bold, deep-voiced shouts rose from the men racing on the track—calls of victory, curses of defeat.

A massive black horse thundered up the Row, black mane flying, hooves throwing up sand. Horse and rider charged as one, streaking up the track toward her. Exultant power showed in the rider's aristocratic face.

She tipped her hood back enough to view him.

It was the Earl of Trent and he rode like a god. Astride that giant coal-black gelding, he rose up, his powerful thighs clamping the horse's body. Beneath his hat, his raven hair streamed back. Pure ecstasy gleamed in his eyes. Sweat shone on his high cheekbones.

She was mesmerized.

At the end of the track, he reined in and turned the giant beast with a twitch of his thighs. He frowned as he saw her. She began to walk toward him, to make it clear he was her intent.

He urged the horse into a trot and reached her side. She

had to hold her hood in place as she looked up at him. On that enormous horse, he towered over her.

"How did you get here?"

His cool voice didn't hold promise. For the last day—even knowing she was being blackmailed—she'd thought of him. Of that kiss.

"A hackney. It's waiting for me. I came to find you—your butler admitted you were here."

"If this is about your career—" he broke off. Smiled. "Don't look so devastated, my dear. I would like to offer you a commission."

Confused, Venetia asked softly, "For a book of erotica?" Drawing naughty pictures specifically for him? Her every nerve ignited at the thought.

Heat flared in his eyes but he shook his head. "No, for a portrait. A miniature. Of my nephew. He is but two weeks old, and his mother insists he changes with every moment. I wish a keepsake of him as he is now."

There was no mistaking the tenderness in his voice, the wistful look in his eyes. "You wish me to paint you a portrait of your nephew?"

He was giving her a reason to stay in London. A reason to paint. A career. "But what of your sister's family? Do they know who I am? The ton do not accept female artists."

"I believe my sister, Lady Ravenwood, would be willing to give you the opportunity. She is very strident about rescuing women. As you said, if your father gambles again, what will you do?"

Strangely, she was almost happy her father would recover and be able to gamble again. But she was so astonished by the earl's offer. How could his sister's family accept her in their home and let her be in the presence of their child, knowing she painted scandalous art?

"Why would you—would they—do this for me knowing what I've done?"

"Lady Ravenwood believes you are an innocent woman forced to do what you must to survive."

In that mad moment, she loved him. It was the kindest thing anyone had done. Noble, wonderful. She couldn't imagine why he had even spared her another thought. Face aflame, she snapped herself to rights.

"Why would you do this for me?" What did she want him to say? That the kiss had entranced him as much as it had her? That she'd captured his fancy?

"Do you accept?" was all he said.

He was giving her everything she'd dreamed of—freedom, independence, her art, the excitement of London—but she couldn't accept. Not until she could stop Mrs. Harcourt's blackmail.

"Well?" he prompted. Her silence had offended.

She swallowed hard. She thought she'd known despair when Rodesson lost everything. But that had been nothing compared to having this presented to her when she must refuse it. "I came here, my lord, to ask you to take me to an orgy."

The horse shied. She leaped back, almost tripping over her cloak. The beast reared, hooves flailing. Would it throw him? The earl pulled hard on the reins, forcing the horse down. The earth shook beneath her as the huge hooves pounded into the ground. He'd brought the horse down away from her, saving her life. He stroked the horse's gleaming black neck, steadying the beast with soothing words and sheer dominant will.

With fluid elegance, he dismounted, swinging his long, powerful leg over the horse's rump. She watched the beautiful play of his muscles beneath his breeches, the bulge of his calves in his polished boots. In a heartbeat, he was at her side, reins in hand.

Other men watched them with avid curiosity but none approached. Who did they think she was? His lover? The thought made her tremble.

Filled with concern, his turquoise eyes assessed her. "Are you hurt?"

She shook her head.

A sensual smile touched his mouth. "I'd give you another kiss to make certain, my dear, but this is not the place."

Her heart thundered like the horses.

"Now the truth, my dear. Why have you searched me out to invite me to an orgy? I can assure you I have no intention of taking you, but you've piqued my curiosity."

"I must go because you were correct. Someone else knows about me. I'm being blackmailed."

"By whom?"

"A Mrs. Harcourt," she whispered, "I must speak to her. Stop her. She is going to a scandalous orgy at Lord Chartrand's. You are the only gentleman I know—"

"We cannot speak of this here," he interrupted. "You must come to my home—you know where I live, of course."

"So what does this Mrs. Harcourt want from you?" Lord Trent asked as he poured brandy into his glass.

Venetia cradled her enormous, delicate brandy balloon between her palms. Her mother had only taken spirits before noon when she mourned her broken heart—in the parlor, with the drapes closed. As Venetia nervously caressed the smooth glass, she realized, with shock, that the Earl of Trent was the only person she could confide her problems to.

At least she'd taken care to hide her face and hair as she'd walked back here. There had been only gentlemen about, no one had spared her a glance.

She took a sip of her drink. The spirit slid down her throat, igniting fire.

"Money," she said. "Lydia Harcourt is a courtesan. My father was so foolish! She discovered that his hands are crippled and that he can't paint. She learned about me. I don't know if he told her everything or if she guessed, but she wants one thousand pounds to keep silent. I haven't got one thousand pounds!"

She took another gulp of the brandy—it was easier now to take more than a sip. Courage blossomed in her heart.

"Does Rodesson know about this?

"Not until I told him yesterday afternoon."

"It seems to me it is his dilemma to solve."

With sarcasm, she said, "He creates the troubles that must be fixed. At first he assured me that her intention was to hurt him, not me. He insisted that she had no intention of revealing what she knew but that we should pay her. He decided to set off last night in her pursuit—or he would have done, but he had a mild attack of his heart."

The earl's brows shot up. "He survived, I gather?"

She nodded. "I was summoned by his footman and sent for a physician. The doctor looked dour and serious, and lectured, but he's confident my father will recover. Still my father is in no condition to go to Mrs. Harcourt and I fear about what will happen to his health if he is trapped in bed and worrying."

"And what does the orgy have to do with this, love?"

The earl smelled delicious from his ride—of leather from the saddle and his riding boots, heady sandalwood, his perspiration. Even his library was a delight for the senses. The room contained lavish color—rugs of crimson, indigo, ivory; a daybed heaped with silks and pillows of scarlet, sapphire-blue, deep green. Pillows were strewn on the floor, beside low tables, as though he sprawled there to read. Her book was there, on a table inlaid with jade.

"I went to Mrs. Harcourt's house this morning and learned she has gone to Lord Chartrand's orgy."

"You went to her house?" The earl's brows rose, then he strolled over to his desk. He picked up a card. Presented it to her. "Chartrand's bacchanalia. Held in the Cottswolds. Near Moreton-in-Marsh."

Venetia could barely breathe as she stared down at the printed card, tracing the gilt design with her thumb. It was not addressed to him in particular. With this in hand, she could easily attend.

"You aren't going to attend an orgy." He plucked the card from her fingers, tossed it back to his desk.

"But I must go. I can't wait for her to return! What if she talks before then?"

"Hell and damnation," he muttered. "You want to go to an orgy because you are afraid that anxiety will kill your father? I would say that he deserves some anxiety."

But that would only cause her more, so she could not agree. "I believe if I go, I can understand what kind of woman Mrs. Harcourt is. And plead with her not to ruin my family."

He sauntered over to a bookshelf, with his long predatory stride, and pulled out a slim volume. "*A Gentleman's Choice*," he read off the spine. "*Or a Guide to the Fashionable Impures of 1818*. Anything you wish to learn about this Season's courtesans can be found in here. Lydia Harcourt is featured."

"Someone publishes an annual guide to courtesans?"

"Illustrated as well."

Given her own pictures, why was she blushing? "Do you select your mistresses from descriptions in a book?"

"You disapprove?"

Well, she did, but she had no right to.

"But you know how enticing a book can be. Here, take a look."

She found Lydia Harcourt's picture near the back of the volume, a voluptuous woman shown wearing only a corset. Large breasts pointed boldly at the viewer, her legs were crossed to hide her quim but to reveal her full thighs and generous bottom. The sketch was ink, in black and white, depicting Mrs. Harcourt with a pretty face and masses of black curls.

"Lydia Harcourt was once the Queen of London's courtesans," he said. "But now she is nearing forty, her charms are fading, and the men she once entranced are seeking out new, younger lovers. Rumor has it that she raved at the publisher of that book for placing her at the back and blackened his eye before he had her thrown out. Under her veneer, she's a coarse scrapper who will do anything to survive."

"Not very sympathetic, then." She read the text that accompanied the picture. *Magnificent forty-inch breasts . . . most skilled mouth and clever hands . . . conquests include the Duke of Montberry, the Earl of Brude . . . Rodesson's mocking pictures . . .*

"My father painted her picture." She hadn't even thought to look.

Trent nodded. "Several unkind ones that revealed Lydia's origins as a coarse butcher's daughter and mocked her aspirations to bed dukes."

Venetia frowned. Yet Lydia had still let Rodesson come to her bed. Why? Had revenge been Lydia's goal all along and her father had stupidly played into her hands? Venetia closed the book. "Then I shall have my father write out an apology and take that to her. Surely that will help." Now she understood—Lydia wanted her father to suffer, she wanted to torment him by threatening to ruin his daughters.

"You can't go to an orgy, my dear."

"I want to see what an orgy is really like," she protested. "It would be . . . an adventure. I don't wish to be good and proper and pure anymore! I want adventure. Even if only for once, I want to be part of the world I draw."

"Have a love affair then, sweetheart. Do you ride horses?"

That surprised her. "Not well," she admitted.

"Would you want to climb on the back of Zeus, my horse, and race him down the Row?"

"Heavens, no."

"Then your first sexual adventure should not be an event

that exhausts even London's most experienced and randy men. At Chartrand's orgy, you would be seriously out of your depth."

"I know what happens at orgies. I've drawn them!" Venetia cried.

Marcus picked up Venetia's book, *Tales of a London Gentleman*, and flipped the pages until he found an orgy scene. Rodesson had drawn dozens of such scenes and his father had insisted he look at every one. For his sixteenth birthday, his father enacted his favorite at a brothel. A bloody wretched night it had been, he reflected. Six young ladybirds had sprained their ankles, three of his father's friends were laid up for a month, and he'd spent the entire occasion fucking one woman with his eyes shut, embarrassed by the wild, heaving display—

Venetia Hamilton's orgy scene was unique, set amongst gods and goddesses in a temple in the clouds. She had succeeded in turning a tangle of naked human bodies into something playful and undeniably romantic.

He looked away from her picture and sighed. "My dear, you have a very starry-eyed view of an orgy."

She crossed her arms beneath her breasts. "I am well aware that reality does not sell books, my lord. After all, when is the hero of a romantic story ever balding, pot-bellied, and riddled with gout?"

He laughed. God, she was enchanting. And mulishly stubborn.

"Besides." She stuck out her chin. "Some Rodesson paintings are more humorous than erotic. A set of plump buttocks sticking up, a gentleman's tilted sword, a lady tumbled on her back with legs waving in the air. All very silly."

His throat tightened. His cock began to rise. "At the orgy, would you announce to your host that he has a virgin in his midst, one who has delivered herself willingly to the wolves? Do you have any idea what Chartrand would do with you the moment he discovered a virgin had come to his party?"

Hazel eyes wide, she licked her full lips.

"He would introduce you to the darkest pleasures but first he would make you compliant by stripping you naked before his guests and spanking your nude derriere with a riding crop to teach you obedience. He would be the one to plunder your virginity, likely in public—"

He wanted to frighten her—to protect her—but she stood with a straight spine and a fiercely determined expression.

"I would pretend to be a jade," she said, "I would go masked. And if you will not escort me, I can hire a body-guard to do so."

"Chartrand's orgy is a weeklong event. A week of men fucking any woman they can get their hands on."

Her nostrils flared. "A week . . . they have . . . they rut for a week? How many encounters do they have?"

"Many."

"Don't they . . . tire?"

"The men, certainly. Women can enjoy, or endure, many partners. At the last one I went to, Chartrand wagered that a woman could not service one hundred men, and he paid a jade to do it."

"One hundred men are there?"

"He rounded up fifty—she had each man twice. One of his favorite games is to assign six men to pleasure a woman at once—especially if the woman is a novice."

Her startled look encouraged him to press. He lifted her hand to his lips. Kissed her middle finger. "One man's cock in your cunny."

He kept his tone casual, as though he was speaking of the latest Drury Lane play, not sex. If he lectured, she'd close her ears. Presenting sin so calmly would shock her all the more.

A light flared in her vivid eyes. Lust, desire, interest. A be-witching fire. Her breasts heaved in the most endearing and enticing way. He pressed his lips to her index finger. "One for you to pleasure with your mouth." Kissed her thumb and baby finger. "One prick each for your hands to explore and one to explode and shower your breasts with come. And the last, of course, to be buried deeply in your ass."

"I must be completely wicked . . . because I'm aroused." To Marcus' surprise, she turned the tables on him, sensually stroking his lips.

"The words excited you . . . the reality would be very different. Would you wish to lick the cock of a man you don't know? Would you be willing to kiss his rump? Would you like to be tied up by a woman like Lydia Harcourt and have her kiss your quim?"

Her moan rippled down his spine. "I . . . I don't know. You've enjoyed such adventures. You attend orgies." Her soft voice teased his cock into painful hardness.

He fought to stay distant. "I used to find it diverting to attend orgies where men and women are indiscriminate with their pleasure. I don't go anymore."

"Have you made love to six women at once?" she asked.

The innocence of the question seared him. "No love, only three at once." But even as the memory of it made his cock pulse, it was her curious face that made him hunger the most. He leaned back against his desk, shifting his hips.

She stepped toward him. "And you think it is perfectly acceptable for you to do it, while you condemn a woman for wanting to be adventurous? If a woman doesn't expect marriage, if she is completely independent, why shouldn't she enjoy erotic games?"

"And you think you would?" He'd never expected a woman to argue women should be as promiscuous as men. Usually women argued that men should learn to be faithful.

"Men will demand things of you. What would you do if a man did this to you?" He tipped up her chin and forced a kiss upon her. He quickly changed to the kiss to a sensuous melding of their lips, and slid his tongue within. Demanding. Filling her mouth.

She kissed him back until he broke it, breathing hard.

"I am not afraid of a kiss," she said.

He grabbed her left breast. "Then I shall have a squeeze of your lovely tits, my dear." God, he hated behaving like this—but at orgies, he'd seen it all the time amongst those drunk or fired by aphrodisiacs. Her breast was a lovely weight in his hand, ripe, soft, warm.

Her nipple hardened and poked into his palm. Her hand snaked out, grabbed his ballocks in his breeches and squeezed hard. "Christ Jesus!" he yelled, and he let her go.

"Try that at an orgy and you'll only enrage a man," he warned. "They think a woman is there to play."

"Then I would tell the man I was ready to play, arrange a meeting and then slip away."

"And what if he doesn't want to wait." His blood thundered in his head. "What if he tosses up your skirts where you stand?"

He felt her heat steaming through her dress. His head swam. Enough blood had surged down to his cock so he could barely think straight. "You are a beautiful woman. You tempt a man to madness."

"I want you to toss up my skirts." Desire—innocent, tentative, but fiery—burned in the hazel depths of her eyes.

"I won't deflower you, angel, but there are many ways to pleasure you."

"I know. Pleasures with mouths and hands." Her voice was soft, throaty. "I've drawn many pictures of that—of women swallowing a man's privy member, of men licking a woman's quim."

Her words played havoc with his soul. He didn't debauch virgins. He would not do it.

But her hands slid down, between their bodies. Marcus heard her gasp as they slid over her breasts. She began drawing up her skirts. "Pleasure me, please."

He glanced down. Her skirts were at her waist, lacy petticoats spilling over her arms. The erotic scent of her arousal flooded his senses. She possessed an abundant bush of sherry-red curls between her smooth creamy thighs. Demure white stockings and ivory garters graced her shapely legs. Her juices shone on her nether lips.

He cupped her naked bottom. Her skin was satin-smooth, her cheeks full, firm, enticing. Sweat beaded his brow, prickled along his collar.

He began to sink to his knees, then stopped. No, he wanted her on her back, legs spread, with her cunny displayed to him.

Scooping her up, Marcus carried her to the daybed.

Venetia tumbled gently back against the silky fabric. She felt as though she were floating, even though she was firmly anchored to earth by the earl's strong, powerful body. Her dress was a jumble at her waist, her legs spread wide.

The earl kissed her lips, nibbled her ears, brushed his mouth down her neck, and licked the sensitive spot in the hollow of her throat. She arched with each touch of his tongue. Sensation swamped her senses. Her sensitive skin, his wetness, warmth. She wanted to see, smell, taste his naked skin—

With shaking fingers, she tried to push off his coat.

He took over, sliding his tight-fitting riding coat from his broad shoulders. She watched, breathless, as he dropped it to the floor, leaving him in his shirtsleeves. She wrapped her hands around his biceps, rock hard bulges beneath exquisite lawn. With one hand he undid his waistcoat buttons, with the other he cupped her breast. Her bosom seemed so small beneath his large, masculine hand. Pleasure sizzled from his touch. Like a firefly seeking light, it raced through her and burst between her thighs. *Oh!*

She shut her eyes as he kissed her deeply. Their tongues twined. His hands slid between her back and the daybed, splayed wide over her. The buttons dropped from their loops. He pulled the neckline of her bodice down. Her breasts perched atop her crumpled bodice, lifted for his admiration and pleasure.

He licked the valley in between. "Lovely."

"But not large." In pictures, women possessed succulent breasts. "Don't men favor large—"

"I assure you that you have beautiful tits."

He nuzzled her nipples. He'd been shaved close, his cheeks and jaw wonderfully smooth, skimming over her sensitive skin. His mouth opened—her nipple disappeared inside. Her touches to herself had been nothing compared to the suction of his mouth, the swirling of his tongue. He laved, licked and suckled, and her dampened nipples gleamed in the faint daylight.

She fumbled with the buttons of his shirt. Freed the first. Then she sensibly let him do the rest. It was all she could do to breathe.

His shirt fell open, revealing ridges and planes of muscle, swirls of dark hair, dusky brown nipples. She stroked the soft curling hair, tracing it down over his flat, rippling stomach to the snug waistband of his breeches. Daringly, she coasted her fingers lower, and touched the hard ridge of his cock. She skimmed her hands back up. Her thumbs brushed his nipples, which tightened instantly. "Your nipples are so different than mine."

"But they are as sensitive and they enjoy the same attentions. Stroke them, pinch them—"

"Suckle them?" she suggested softly.

"Yes, sweeting, but for now you are to lie back." He moved off the end of the daybed and dropped to his knees. He was going to . . . to kiss her there. Yes, she'd drawn the act, had trembled with illicit desire each time she sketched a man's head between a woman's thighs, and now she was burning with anticipation.

Soft golden light traced his cheekbone, his firm lips. In the candlelight, his skin was the color of toasted meringue.

Her breath left in a whoosh as he kissed her nether curls. His tongue tangled within them. Luxuriant pleasure washed over her. She dug her fingers into the smooth fabric of the chaise, curled her toes.

He slid his tongue down to her quim. Warm and slick, it flicked her nether lips apart. He tasted her juices, groaning as he did.

He watched her over her nether curls—she stared helplessly into his turquoise eyes, a slave to the pleasure he was giving. Then, above her mound, he winked at her.

How could she be so shocked—and suddenly worry about Maidenswode propriety—while arching and moaning on his chaise?

He slid his tongue into her passage, filling her with wet heat. Plunged it in and out and she cried out with each spearing thrust.

He lifted his mouth from her throbbing quim. "Tell me what you like, love. Do you like my tongue to slide inside your cunny?"

She nodded, unable to speak.

"Have you seen your beautiful pussy, my dear?"

Again she nodded. She'd held a mirror there to look. She'd been so curious. In paintings it was a mysterious oval-shaped opening. She'd had to know for herself.

"Have you touched your clit?" he asked wickedly. And with that, his mouth closed over her sensitive bud.

Her moan turned to a scream. "My lord!"

He licked her nub with demanding strokes that sent explosions of ecstasy and agony, shock and delight, racing through her. She was pleading for mercy. Crying "my lord" over and over, clutching at his hair.

But he wouldn't stop. He stroked, stroked, stroked. The tide of sensation, of agony, was building in her. But it was too much.

He caught hold of her hands so she couldn't push him away or pull free. Relentlessly, he suckled and teased. This was so much more intense than her caresses. She arched her hips up to him. She had to close her eyes, grip his hands.

"Oh! Oh! Oh! My lord!" She wanted him to never stop, to take her over the brink—

She exploded. Her body clenched and pulsed and she thrashed with it. Saw fireworks—worthy of Vauxhall—then sparkling darkness. She was screaming!

He stopped her shouts with a kiss, covering her mouth with his. His lips tasted of her quim, rich and primal and musky, and his fingers stroked her. She was still coming, still pulsing, still caught up in ecstasy. Then, she opened her eyes to find him leaning over her, braced on his muscular arms. He smiled down at her. She touched his cheek, and he kissed her palm. A gesture that made her heart tremble.

Then she realized she was half-naked, drenched in sweat and her juices, and had screamed his house down in the middle of the morning.

She sat up abruptly, almost falling to the side as she did. Her head was dizzy—lovemaking was as intoxicating as liquor. She must put herself to rights but her bodice was crumpled beneath her bare breasts, her skirts a wrinkled mess.

"What is wrong, my dear? Why the haste?"

"I—oh, what have I done? I am—" Horrified, she thought of his offer. "You see I'm not good and proper at all, my lord. I am not the sort of woman who should paint Lady Ravenwood's baby."

As she slapped at her skirt to try to smooth it, he kissed her cheek. "Marcus. After that intimacy we are Marcus and Venetia, my dear. And you aren't wicked, love. However, you aren't going to Chartrand's."

"I do not require your permission!"

"I could stop you in a heartbeat," he warned, "Merely by telling your father."

"You wouldn't!"

"I could dispatch a footman with a note immediately."

He crossed his arms over his bared chest, forearms and biceps bulging—how could she notice such a thing when he threatened to betray her? How could he do such a thing after giving her an intimate French kiss?

To protect her. She almost laughed at the madness. He was the noblest man she'd ever known yet he had just licked her quim until she saw stars.

She stared down at her hopeless skirts. "Then you have won, my lord. I cannot go."

CHAPTER FOUR

"I take it I am here to play Devil's Advocate?" Viscount Ravenwood leaned back and sipped his brandy.

Sprawled on his leather chair, Marcus raked his hand over his jaw. "Miss Hamilton has every intention of going to Chartrand's bacchanalia and I suspect that nothing short of chaining the woman to the bed would stop her." The sudden scorching mental image of Miss Hamilton in playful bondage sent blood racing to his groin.

Firelight was the only light cutting the blackness of his library. Marcus wasn't certain why he'd summoned Stephen here, and before his brother-in-law could counter, he said, "And you bloody well know I can't snitch to her father. Miss Hamilton will hire an escort—some seedy ex-Runner who will likely rape her. Or Chartrand will find out who she is and make her the centerpiece of some perverse sexual display."

Stephen grinned. "You're looking for an excuse to go with her."

"Hell and damnation, Stephen, she's a virgin. If she wanted to drink an entire bottle of brandy, I'd stop her." But he was trying to justify taking her, not stopping her. "She's sensual . . . innately sensual, but innocent. And a day at Chartrand's event should shock her into realizing she must give up her career."

"And she needs a noble escort who won't ravish her?"

He'd already ravished her—with his mouth. Rock-hard at the memory, his cock strained against his trousers. He would love to do it again. The delectable Miss Hamilton deserved to discover her sexuality. He could teach her without hurting her, without spoiling her future.

"I began with a kiss. A kiss to prove a point." He lowered his head, unable to look Stephen in the eye. "I've never been kissed like that—it was more passionate, more heated, more explosive than any other kiss I've had. She was so . . . untutored, but so giving." And then, in his library, he'd begun again to 'prove a point' and been overwhelmed by desire.

He launched to his feet to pace. "Damnation, Stephen, is it her innocence that tempts me? *Am* I the same kind of blackguard as my father?"

"Christ, no!"

The vehemence of Stephen's cry gave him the answer he needed, even as Stephen assured him, "You are not the same kind of man as your father, Marcus."

Marcus tossed back his brandy as he strode across the carpet. "Lydia Harcourt is blackmailing me."

Stephen's liquor sloshed over his ice-blue waistcoat. "Hades, over what? Everyone in England knows your reputation for bedding women. I believe it even extends to the Continent and the Americas."

He frowned. That might be true if Venetia Hamilton's book found its way there. "Father's scandals."

His brother-in-law's face went stark white. "God, not—"

"Not Min," Marcus lied. "Lady Susannah Lawrence, the young woman who got with child and killed herself. And the details of my father's disgusting practice of having madams procure innocents for him. I'm terrified what having that in print would do to Min. To Mother."

Stephen rubbed his temple. "Why in Hades would your father confess to Lydia Harcourt?"

"Drink. He spent his days in a brandy bottle and was possessed by devils. The witch—I quote from her letter—'sought to ease his pain by encouraging him to confess his troubles'."

The rest of the letter haunted him. A *subject of great delicacy . . . Lady Ravenwood . . . secrets . . .* Damn that bitch, Lydia.

"How much does she want?"

"Ten thousand."

Stephen grimaced. His white hand gripped the glass. "Do you plan to pay her?"

"I'd like to wring her blasted neck. But I'm thinking of negotiating a trade. If I can get hold of her manuscript, I can trade it for her silence. I imagine she's taken her book to Chartrand's with her. I'll burn it page by page until she agrees."

"And Miss Hamilton?" Stephen prompted.

"Taking a pretty new mistress to Chartrand's orgy would be the perfect disguise."

"Take her because you want to," Stephen advised. "Don't take her as a way to punish yourself with temptation."

Marcus swung open the door as his carriage clattered to a stop on the street outside Venetia's narrow townhouse. A slim figure in a swirling black cloak darted out from the shadow and hastened down the steps.

Leaning out, Marcus reached for her hand. At this hour the street was deserted, save for his servants loading her trunks. Her delicate fingers slid across his palm. As he drew her up into his softly lit, private world, she pushed back her deep hood. He caught his breath as he gazed into effervescent hazel eyes.

Holding her cloak about her, she settled in the seat opposite him. He raised a brow—after the sensual session in his library, he'd expected her to cuddle up against him.

She smiled happily. "My father is much improved. His color has returned and he's had no more pains."

"I am pleased to hear that. So there is no need to take you to Chartrand's?" Why did he feel the pain of regret?

She shook her head, curls bouncing. "He's not well enough to risk travel. No, that wouldn't be wise."

"I suspected it wouldn't be." He couldn't help but smile. "You might want to open your cloak. I've kept the coach heated."

Slowly, teasingly, Venetia tugged at one end of the ribbon that tied the wool shut. His throat dried. He'd watch dozens of women undress, but the sight of Venetia playing seductress aroused him instantly.

She drew the sides of her cloak apart, revealing a stretch of pale satin skin.

It took him a full minute to realize he was looking directly at her bare legs. Not quite bare—she wore creamy white stockings and pale blue garters. Rigid with sudden tension, he gazed upward at the stretch of her bare stomach, the curves of her naked breasts, at her cheeky, hopeful smile.

Other than stockings, she wasn't wearing a damned stitch beneath the cloak.

"What in damnation are you thinking?" Marcus demanded.

Venetia sat demurely, despite her nudity, her legs crossed at the ankles. On the seat opposite, Marcus was glorious. The buff breeches he wore displayed the hard muscles of his legs. Blue superfine fit like a second skin across a broad chest and broader shoulders. A heavy greatcoat lay discarded at his side. He was a man who had seen everything—done everything— and she'd gambled on a bold, wild tactic to intrigue him.

She took a deep breath. "I want you to understand that I am not a frightened virginal miss, Marcus."

He gritted his teeth, growled between them, "You can't travel to Dorset naked." He rubbed his jaw and she watched the pass of his hand. Freshly shaven, his skin would be smooth, soft, and smell of his soap.

"Why not? This is our own private world in your carriage, is it not? Who will see me other than you?"

"What of meals?" he snapped. "Using the necessary?"

She hadn't expected him to be so enraged. "I can just hold the cloak closed."

"You plan to walk in public completely bare beneath your cloak?"

"No one would know but you," she protested.

Agony flashed across his handsome features, twisting his sensual mouth. "God, and that's the bloody magic of it, isn't it?"

Venetia summoned her courage and stood in the lightly swaying carriage. They were making haste out of London before the streets became congested. She lowered to her knees on the floor, the comfortable carpeting and the thickness of her cloak cushioning her. Heat rose from bricks in the floor, warming her skin.

"Venetia—"

She cut him off by cupping her hand over the bulge in his breeches. "I painted a picture," she told him in a breathy voice as she fumbled with the first button on his flap. He was so engorged the placket was pulled tight. "A picture of a man who looked like you being pleasured this way by a courtesan with auburn hair. In his theatre box in Drury Lane."

When he didn't immediately speak, she gazed up and saw turbulent thoughts behind his turquoise eyes.

"In front of the audience," she whispered.

The solid ridge jumped in his breeches, straining against the buttons, making her task of undressing him more difficult. She couldn't tell him more about her picture—that the earl fell in love with his ravishing courtesan.

"Are you certain you want to do this?" His voice was raspy, hoarse.

"Yes," she whispered, freeing the second button from the loop. "I want to take you into my mouth."

Her hands shook with expected nerves, but also with weakening desire. When she'd seen this act in pictures, she'd marveled. A man's penis was so long, how could it fit in a woman's mouth? It couldn't go down a woman's throat, could it?

With trembling fingers, she opened the last button. Parted the falls of his trousers, peeled down his soft linen underclothes. And gasped.

She was eye to eye with his cock.

She marveled at it, running her fingertip along the shaft. It bobbed at her touch like a top-heavy rose swaying in the wind. In pictures, rendered in purples and angry reds, it had looked enormous. Close up it was gigantic. Carefully, she closed her hand around the shaft, surprised to feel it swell and firm against her palm. A droplet of moisture gathered at the tip. The head was surprisingly adorable and begged for a kiss. It even possessed a small beauty spot—a dusky brown spot beside the glistening eye.

"Is it so fascinating?"

She met his gaze and noticed he was waiting, quite tense, for her response. Despite his power, his privilege, his experience, he was concerned about her opinion. Were both men and women always nervous in this arena?

"What do you call it?" she whispered.

"My cock, my prick . . . staff, rod, maypole . . . John Thomas . . . sometimes my Commanding Officer, for that's what it often seems to be. So tell me, does it please you?"

She nodded. "It is very aesthetic, my lord." She used his title, excited to play make-believe. To step into the erotic scene she had created where she was courtesan to his earl.

"Really?" He leaned back, obviously proud and pleased, and she had to giggle. "What makes it so? In an artist's opinion?"

That was easy to answer. "The proportions of the head to the shaft." She toyed with the surprisingly soft, velvety head. "Perfectly made to ease the beast into a woman's cleft, allowing the passage of the thick steely shaft behind it."

"Not too big?"

"The whole is very big, my lord. You have a fine cock of considerably generous proportions."

He laughed.

She couldn't believe she was having a discussion about his intimate parts. But it gave her courage, this teasing exchange. "And the color—"

"The color?" His black brows went up. "I'd never considered the color to be at issue."

Some erotic pictures featured unattractive pasty white members. "It's a lovely dusky tan."

"I must remember to let it get more sun. Keep it from losing its appealing tanned look."

Venetia giggled. Marcus was panting, and he no longer looked jaded like the earl in the theatre box. His fluid was flowing now, the heat taut and shining.

Closing her eyes, she bent down and pressed her lips to the head. She stuck out her tongue and licked him. Dabbed at him. Then she flattened her tongue, swirling it over his satiny skin. His juices wetted her tongue, tantalizing her with a taste both rich and slightly sour.

He gave a soft groan that sent a surge of triumph through her. Though she held power, she still wanted to please him. Flattening her tongue, she caressed the head, then licked the shaft. Oh, it was delicious, warm, beautifully velvet.

She traced a vein with the tip of her tongue.

His head arched back. "Temptress."

She bobbed her head on him with no idea what he truly wanted. She sucked hard, then slow and teasingly, with lavish, slobbering strokes. She touched his ballocks, terribly afraid to hurt him. They squished when she lightly squeezed and seemed to scurry up, away from her hand.

His hand settled in her hair. To stop her? No, he moaned lustily and she fondled his balls with one hand while gripping the hilt of his cock with the other.

Gathering courage, she drew his cock into her mouth as deep as she could. She gagged in shock and pulled back.

She tried again. Tears drizzled from the corners of her eyes.

"Sweetheart, no, you needn't do that." He cupped her cheek and drew her back.

"In *A Gentleman's Choice*, courtesans who could take the entire shaft into their mouths were highly prized."

"Hades, you read that thing?" He caressed her cheek. "I don't want you to think you must do that. It pleases me to be in your warm mouth as much as you desire."

He stroked his thumb along her lip and a bolt of pleasure streaked from there to explode between her legs in a flood of wetness.

"Come here, my beautiful naked temptress. I want you to sit on my face."

"Sit where?"

Within a moment, she understood. He lay on his back along the carriage seat as she slowly dropped her cloak to the other seat. She clasped her hands in his, swung her leg over his chest, and climbed aboard.

"Now move back, my sweet. Smother my face with your wet quim."

"But—but how will you breathe?"

He laughed and she felt terribly naïve as she wriggled back. She glanced around, saw the heat in his eyes as he drank in the sight of her nether lips dangling above his face. Clamping his hands on her hips, he pulled her down so her sex sank down over his mouth. Pleasure swamped her as her aching cunny made contact with his wet, hot tongue. His tongue caressed her everywhere, and he rocked her so her fragrant quim rubbed over his face. His nose was buried against her derriere.

He held her hips as the carriage swayed on the road. She felt completely safe on top—as long as he held her tight.

She moaned at the forbidden eroticism of this—of sitting on an earl's face. Fired by wanton naughtiness, she closed her eyes and danced her hips on him, twisting and grinding her wet, aroused, ripe sex into his mouth. His tongue slicked over her clit.

Ooh! Eyes shut, she arched back, pushing her privates even more aggressively on him. She felt a rhythmic pounding and opened her eyes wide to see his hips and bottom bouncing on the seat. His cock jutted toward her, his fluid dripping from the head.

"Would you like me to bend forward and take your Commanding Officer into my mouth?" Venetia asked.

God, yes, temptress.

Marcus answered her question by suckling Venetia's hard clit until she melted over him. She must have seen pictures of *soixante-neuf* and she knew exactly what to do. He fought for control as she gobbled his cock into her mouth. Her soft, moist lips skimmed the sensitive places on the shaft. She sucked him hard, gripping him tight in her hot mouth. Beautiful, beautiful sucking in a perfect rhythm, driving him wild.

He was forgetting his part of the bargain—he'd stopped licking her. He quickly rectified his lapse, tonguing the snug entrance of her wet pussy. She tasted rich and feminine and delicious.

She licked the length of his shaft with her tongue. Up and down, driving him mad.

Erotic art had provided a remarkable education.

She licked his balls. He instinctively tensed even as he moaned at the pleasure. But she was gentle and cradled his sac with infinite care. He enjoyed scrotum play, even though he balanced on a knife's edge of tension throughout. When her tongue traced the seam of his ballocks, he cried her name into her quim. She treated his balls to glorious delights, tugging the fine hairs in her mouth, even holding one delicately in her hot mouth to suck it.

Oral sex never brought him to orgasm anymore—hell, he was eight and twenty, he'd experienced it too many times, had taught himself too much control, but Venetia's enthusiastic exploration was bringing him close.

He didn't want to come in her mouth. She wouldn't want that. With her weight resting on his face, he couldn't even warn her. He must practice intense control, make her come, then attend to his rigid, throbbing prick himself.

A complete assault was needed. Two hands and a mouth to take her to ecstasy. He tipped his head back to penetrate her snug anus with his tongue. She was bent over, her plush bottom jutting in his face, her puckered rosebud ripe for his tongue. He ran his tongue around the rim, gently pushed in. Her muscles slackened to let him gain entry. Then closed tight.

She was scorching. Unbelievably tight. Delectable.

He thrust his tongue deep, filling her rear, his fingers were in her pussy as deep as he dared, and he stroked her clit.

She dropped his cock from her mouth. "I can't . . . can't . . ."

He grasped her hand and led it between her thighs. She soon knew he wanted her to rub herself. Shyness had vanished and she masturbated with lusty abandon.

He gripped his cock, jerking it hard, ravaging the length of it. Pumped like a wild man.

"Oh! Oh! Yes! Yes!"

The scream was hers, triggering his explosion. She bounced wildly on him in her orgasm, her greedy cunny clutched at his fingers, her bum slapped his face.

His whole body went tense, and arched up. His hips launched off the seat as he came in a fierce stream. His face lifted, burrowing right into her sopping, melting, eager sex. White fire exploded in his head as his spine melted, his limbs turned to water, his very soul raced out of his cock.

Wet heat surrounded the swollen head. She'd taken him in her mouth. Each pulse of her suckling pulled on his cock, lashed him with agonizing pleasure. She was drinking his come. To please him.

Spent, exhausted, he lifted her quim off his face so he could breathe. "I'll understand if you wish to spit."

"I swallowed." Her eyes showed ingenuous confusion. "Was I not supposed to? You taste quite remarkable. I liked it."

"I'm honored that you did, my sweet." He arched up and kissed her derriere, rewarded by her pretty giggle. Returning Venetia to London with her virginity intact might very well kill him.

Cradling Venetia against his chest as she slept, Marcus kissed the top of her tousled red curls. He buried his face in her sweetly scented hair, inhaling roses, lavender, a hint of freshness like spring rain. The scent of her sweat and earthy female juices clung to her skin. She smelled like a woman just tumbled in a meadow. He could taste her delicious juices on his lips, the flavor of his come on hers.

She'd slumbered blissfully against him for miles. He felt every breath she took, felt it in the rise and fall of her breasts against him, in the gentle movement of her back against his arm. He steadied her, so she could sleep despite the rocking of the carriage.

When had he ever let a woman sleep in his arms?

He normally sent courtesans home. Never let his mistresses stay in his bed. Over the years, his father had drummed a warning into his head. *Nothing but trouble ever results from waking up with a woman.*

CHAPTER FIVE

"Welcome to your first orgy, Venetia."

Marcus' devilish grin stole Venetia's breath as he casually relaxed back from the carriage window. He stretched his muscular arms along the back of the blue velvet seat. Fighting to hide the churning of her nervous tummy, she peeped out. Ahead loomed the symmetrical façade of Abbersley Park at the end of a long, straight gravel drive. For a house of sinful debauchery, it stood dark and solemn in the downpour. Black thunderheads massed behind it in the gray sky. Trees whipped in the fierce wind.

Instinctively, she tightened her cloak around her. She was thankful to be fully dressed. He'd been absolutely correct—it would have been foolhardy to arrive naked.

"This cannot be the place. It looks . . . so normal. So quiet and sedate. What will happen?"

"Sex. In every position, every grouping you could imagine."

And he wanted her to return to London a virgin? She knew exactly what she wished to do at this orgy—have a decadent love affair with Marcus. Pleasure without penetration was quite delicious but she wanted more. She craved more—

"Rules first, before you set foot inside."

"Rules?" she echoed.

"You are to stay with me at all times. If you stray, I can't guarantee your safety. Remember, men at these events do not take no for an answer—not from an unprotected woman."

"Do you mean you will never stray from my side?"

"Yes, sweeting, that is exactly what I mean. Second rule—mask at all times."

Mask?

He turned his attention to a pocket of his greatcoat and drew out a black velvet bag. Loosening the gold strings, he reached in. Puzzled, she watched as he drew out a mask, which he dangled before her eyes by its two long green velvet ties.

This was no mere mask. Venetian style, it was an exquisite sculpture of silk-lined paper maché, feathers, paint and sparkling glass. A work of art. Silver and gold paint and glittering diamondlike 'jewels' decorated the face. Dark paint outlined the eyes and mimicked eyebrows. Emerald-green feathers swooped from one side.

"But why?" she asked. "No one will recognize me. I am not of their class. And they are all attending an orgy too!" But she knew, from village life, of the hypocrisy of the upper classes.

"Turn around, temptress."

That teasing name, on his lips, made her heart pound as Marcus swung over to her seat.

How ridiculous it would be to wear a mask every day. But she was responsible for her sisters' futures. Their good reputations depended on her discretion.

She turned to present the back of her head. With his long, elegant fingers, he fitted the mask to her face. Lined with silk, it was beautiful and a perfect fit. The almond-shaped slits allowed her to see, though not well at the sides. But the shape of the holes cleverly disguised her eyes. The curves at the bottom of the mask clung to the upper line of her lip. Silk tickled there.

"I can guarantee that this mask will intrigue every gentleman here," he murmured beside her ear. "They'll know immediately you aren't a professional. Your identity will be a mystery that they will long to solve. You will have to be very careful. And I will watch you every moment."

That promise made her tremble with desire.

Behind the mask, she felt as though she'd become an entirely new person. Sensual excitement burned in her. She felt exotic. Also free. Unfettered. She could now be anyone she wished to be. A woman of her own creation.

She must remember her goal. To stop Lydia Harcourt from destroying her.

"You look extremely seductive, Venetia."

To her surprise, Marcus kissed her. A light kiss but even just the brush of his lips made her burn. But she knew there would be no more. No more caresses. No more touches.

She'd been restless and edgy since they had stopped at an inn in Lower Dentby and he had engaged a room. She'd hungered for more pleasures but he had refused to play. He'd led her upstairs simply to dress her.

When he'd laced her into her corset in that bedroom, she thought she'd go mad. She'd wanted—no, needed—his touch on her bare skin. She'd thought he would stroke her breasts, play with her cunny, fondle her derriere while she dressed. But he hadn't. He'd watched her with his arms crossed over his chest until she'd needed his help with corset stays and the buttons of her gown. He'd even dressed her hair and all the while she'd stared at the large bed. He hadn't even appeared to be aware of it.

She touched the mask, aware of how flamboyant it appeared. "Are you certain my dress will be acceptable?" A simple gown of white muslin with a square neckline and long sleeves, it was pretty but demure.

His lips twisted in a wry smile. "Chartrand will think you are pretending to be a country miss as part of a sensual game." His voice hardened. "I have no choice but to let him think that. That it pleases me to dress you like an innocent."

With that, he settled back on the seat at her side and looked out the window.

They were almost at the house. In the gloom of the rainy afternoon, she could make out spots of crimson and circles of black streaming down the stone steps. Liveried servants carrying umbrellas. Golden light gleamed in the hundreds of paned windows—the glow from candles and cozy fires, now giving the stone house the look of a comfortable haven.

"There is one more rule."

She turned and met his turquoise eyes.

"At all times, you must obey me."

Before she could protest, the carriage stopped in front of the sweep of stone steps. Marcus drew up the hood of her cloak, covering her hair. "Ready, temptress?"

He swung open the door and climbed down before the servants could rush to his aid. Reaching up, he caught her around the waist and set her beside him. The hem of her cloak snapped in the breeze. At their side, a footman struggled to tame a broad umbrella.

Under its shelter, they hastily mounted the steps to the house. Venetia felt a tug of disappointment as a perfectly proper, utterly correct butler met them at the door. Was this truly an orgy? It seemed a normal house party.

Tall and thin, the butler obviously recognized Marcus. He bowed. "My lord Trent." He bowed again to her. "Madam."

The servant hadn't mistaken her for a wife. Surely there were no wives at an event like this.

Marcus offered his arm. She felt reassured by his hard, solid forearm. He gave her fingers a gentle squeeze as they followed the footman across the foyer in search of their rooms. It seemed an endless stretch of black and white marble tiles to glassed double doors at the end of the intriguing octagonal room. The ceiling rounded over like a dome, decorated in a delicate rococo style.

She'd only ever been in one country home as lovely as this— that of her maternal grandparents, the Earl and Countess of

Warren. And that had only been because the home was open to the public that day. She, her sisters, and her mother, had been one of many families led through the ballroom, the music room, the indoor gardens, the famed gallery.

At the sight of her grandparents' portraits—the first time she'd seen them—she'd almost fled from the room in hysterical laughter. It had felt like a strange dream.

Had her mother Olivia's scandalous relationship with Rodesson been worth losing everything? Not just Olivia's home but her parents, their love?

"Penny for your thoughts, temptress," Marcus whispered.

"I was thinking about your last rule," she murmured. A lie, but he didn't seem to notice. "Complete obedience."

He grinned.

They were passing through a carpeted center hall. On each wall were several doors, all painted delicate pale blue, each with a gleaming gold knob. Massive rust-red marble pillars framed the doorways, and a giant stone fireplace stood at the very end of the hall. A fire blazed cheerily behind the grate.

Once again, it all seemed so ordinary. So proper.

As they turned a corner, Venetia realized the hall was 'L' shaped. Before them stood the curved staircase, rendered in cream, salmon-pink, and ivory, festooned with delicate scroll-work.

"I cannot believe that behind these closed doors people are doing naughty, forbidden things," she murmured. She could barely breathe, expecting a door to fly open. To see an orgy scene for real, to watch many men grunting and thrusting and striving for pleasure, the women screaming with ecstasy . . .

"They are, I can assure you."

"Why does it matter so much to you to protect me? To help us?" she whispered. Could he even hear her over the roar of the flames in the fireplace?

His voice was equally low and devastatingly sensuous. "Because there were women I didn't protect. That I didn't help."

What women? Protect from what? She remembered their very first conversation—just days ago!—in her drawing room. He protected innocents from brothels. But who had he not protected?

With the footman so close, she didn't dare ask—

"My lord Trent!"

Perfume swirled around her, rich, spicy, intoxicating. A woman stood behind her.

Soft, purring tones confirmed it. "Does this intrigue, my lord?"

Long slender hands pressed against her sides, at the ruching that framed her breasts. Venetia froze at the reality of a woman's hands on her breasts. Shock spiraled through her. She was too stunned to do anything but gaze helplessly at Marcus' face.

The beautiful fingers slid up to cup and lift her bosom. The hands were warm, soft. Rings sparkled, stones of red, blue, green, and some as clear as ice. Every finger bore a ring, each set with an enormous stone.

Distracted for a moment, Venetia wondered if the stones were real—and worth a fortune.

For several seconds, Marcus merely looked at her breasts and the mysterious hands cradling them. Then he spoke, with the full brunt of noble hauteur. "Enough, Lydia, my dear. My *partner* is weary from travel. We have no interest in your games."

Lydia? This was Lydia Harcourt? Venetia wished she could twist around to see.

But Lydia did not move her hands. Too tongue-tied to speak, Venetia realized her nipples had hardened, just as they did with Marcus' touch. Her breasts did not care whose hands caressed them, they just enjoyed the attention.

Indeed, she was growing wet between her legs at the caress, just as she dampened when she drew such erotic scenes.

"How delightful to find you in attendance, my lord," Mrs.

Harcourt continued in a voice dripping with sensuous pro-mise. "I thought you now eschewed these events."

"Normally, I do," Marcus drawled. He was playing the jaded rake to the hilt, leaving her stranded as Lydia Harcourt's thumbs spiraled over her hard nipples. Of course, she was supposed to be a courtesan and no ladybird willing to attend an orgy would be mortified by the touch of another woman's hands.

It did feel shockingly good. And the look on Marcus' face, the expression of pure rough male hunger, stole her breath. He liked this. And she . . . she liked exciting him.

In the carriage, he'd resisted her further attempts at seduc-tion—the touch of her fingers on his inner thigh, the brush of her lips to his biceps, flirtatious exposure of her breasts, but this scandalous display was obviously arousing him.

"I must think of something to spark your interest once more, mustn't I, my lord?" Lydia mused in her throaty purr. "Your partner has delightful breasts, my lord." The woman pinched—pinched!—her nipples.

"Oh!" Each squeeze set her quim throbbing. Lydia pressed against her from behind and sinuously rubbed her hips back and forth. Between her tight corset, her shock, and her for-bidden sexual excitement, Venetia feared she'd swoon.

"Play along, my dear," Lydia whispered. "You do want to pleasure your protector, don't you? You don't want to bore him and lose him, do you?"

She didn't answer. She couldn't. She understood her mistake.

Her obvious horror had piqued the woman's curiosity. She took an unsteady breath, drinking in more heady perfume.

"I suspect her nipples taste delicious, my lord. Would you like to watch me sample one?"

Marcus! She glared into his turquoise eyes. He wouldn't let this continue. Would he?

"That's enough, Lydia. Release her." He spoke with dan-gerous calm.

Venetia felt her chest expand on a desperate breath as Lydia dropped her hands and stepped out from behind her. Her heart tumbled in her chest as she moved to Marcus' side.

Lydia Harcourt was a beautiful creature. Blue-black hair arranged in a complex, elegant coiffure of curls and braids. Smooth, glowing skin. As for her figure—it was full, voluptuous. An ivory satin gown displayed the famed enormous breasts, swathed a nipped waist, and shivered over broad, rounded hips. Lydia gave a mocking smile and Venetia fought a tremble as Lydia's appraising gaze swept over her.

Then Lydia chuckled as though at a private joke and turned to Marcus. "Very lovely, my lord. And untutored— how novel for you."

"Cork it, Lydia." His gentlemanly veneer vanished. "We have business to discuss."

Suddenly, Lydia's beauty dropped away, and she appeared hard and mercenary. Lydia dropped into a curtsy, giving him an eyeful of her deep cleavage. "Of course, my lord. At your pleasure."

Marcus managed to appear completely bored—how did noble men perfect that expression? Venetia knew she wore her every emotion for all to see. Thank heaven for the mask.

To her surprise, Marcus bowed—a courtesy she hadn't expected him to give a courtesan. But his voice was brittle ice. "We will see when the whimsy strikes. I dislike having my pleasures interrupted."

Lydia Harcourt's confident smirk wavered at Marcus' noble disdain.

Venetia's nerves felt strung taut, and she almost stumbled as Marcus caught hold of her waist and led her to the stairs.

Curious, Venetia watched as Marcus walked the length of the wall in her assigned bedchamber, a femininely decorated room connected to his. He moved deliberately and slowly, like a stalking predatory cat, and brushed his hand over the ivy-patterned wallpaper. Mouth dry, she let her gaze linger on his long, lean legs, the muscles bulging with each easy step. His polished knee-high boots gleamed in the firelight. Unfortunately, the tails of his coat hid his sculpted derriere.

"What . . . what are you doing, my lord?"

He turned and flashed a grin, a lock of raven hair drifting over his eyes. Her heart gave a little jump as her gaze met his vivid turquoise eyes. Then he winked. "Checking for peepholes."

"Peepholes?" In that one word she realized that while she drew sinful pictures, she knew nothing of his world. "Goodness, people can watch us?"

"Possibly. There are some in the wall between our rooms, so I can watch what you do when you believe you are all alone." He infused such naughtiness that her nipples tightened beneath gown and shift.

"Now that I know you are watching," she protested, "I won't do . . . things."

"What things won't you do?" Spoken in his deep, sinfully suggestive baritone, the simple question sounded vastly wicked.

She flushed, thinking of . . . not of scandalous things, but of using the chamber pot, and of other personal moments.

Venetia sank down on the edge of her enormous bed, balanced on her slipper-clad toes.

Before she could stop herself, she blurted, "Why do you enjoy public sex?"

He crossed the room and leaned against the bedpost nearest her, elegant and casual all at once. "It is the nature of men to posture before other men."

He tipped up her chin and bent down so his lips were just an inch from hers. "Imagine an audience of gentlemen watching you, all enraptured by the sight of your hands caressing your naked breasts, and all entranced by the sway of your hips as you ride your lover. You could make them all come just by the way you move your hips."

"Why do you do this?" she cried. "You tell me that I don't

belong at an orgy. You make me promise to dally with no one else, and then you . . . you tempt me, you arouse me until I can't stop thinking of wild, scandalous things!"

"Now that we know no one can see, you no longer need to be masked." He pulled the strings, undoing the bow. Some hairs snagged and tugged at her scalp, and he whispered, "Sorry love."

Strangely, the quick apology made her heart flip. Why did the smallest gestures he made send her heart into palpitations?

Thankful to be free of the mask, soft as it was, she watched as he laid it on the bed. It seemed a precious, beautiful gift, but it likely meant nothing to him. A mask was necessary and he would purchase the best because he expected nothing less.

"I have something for you," he said.

She knew he would not answer her question, but she was trembling in anticipation. *Something* for her? He gave a wink, then left through the connecting door to his room. Leaving her alone on her enormous bed in her exquisite room. The bed was thoroughly decadent, a delightful confection of gleaming gilt and ivory silk, the mattress thick and soft. Above her, an elaborate canopy dripped tassels and bows. Fine ivory curtains were tied with forest green ropes. A mass of green velvet bolsters and pillows were strewn across the head.

"I hope you like it." He leaned in the doorway, a long blue box in his hands. A box of the sort her mother received from Rodesson. Her heart leapt into her throat.

Marcus crossed the room in long, elegant strides. Struck dumb, she looked from his handsome face to the box and back. He looked pleased with himself. He yanked off the lid as he reached her.

Green glittered at her. Emeralds. Dear heaven, *emeralds*. A necklace of a million winking stones and one magnificent pear-shaped one at the center. Within the loop of the necklace sat a matching bracelet and earbobs.

"You may touch them. They are yours."

"M—mine?"

"No one will believe you are my lover unless you wear a flamboyant token of my desire." A grin widened his sensual lips. "Allow me."

He draped the cool necklace around her neck. At the brush of his fingers on her nape, she felt her legs quiver. "Emeralds to match the green in your eyes. And they look spectacular with your auburn hair. They are yours to keep."

And she thought his apology had sent her heart careening in her chest? "No . . . no, that would not be right." She turned to gaze solemnly at him. "I haven't earned them."

"Perhaps you have." He stroked her cheek. He began to open the buttons of his dress coat. "So what did you think of Lydia?" he asked casually. "Do you still believe she can be convinced to spare you?"

Startled, Venetia watched him undress. She was sitting on a bed. He had fastened the most gorgeous, heavy, *expensive* necklace around her neck. What did he plan to do?

Lydia. He had spoken of Lydia. "I—I don't know what to think," she admitted. "Why did we not speak to her? We could have had the business finished in the foyer."

"If you want to keep your identity a secret, you must leave Lydia to me." He stroked a fingertip along the length of her throat, caught it in the necklace, brushing both the beautiful stones and her skin. Her legs dissolved like sugar in tea.

He shrugged off his coat. Laid it on her bed.

"What are you doing?"

"We must dress for dinner, love." He opened his waistcoat while she stared, her mouth gaping. "I would pay her off for you . . ."

He would pay Lydia for her? But she didn't want that. She didn't want him to rescue her. She wanted to be independent! To be in control.

"I visited my father last night. To ask him to write an apology about that picture—" She was embarrassed to admit this.

"Good God, he knows you came here with me?"

She shook her head. "Of course not! I wouldn't reveal that. But I couldn't find the courage to ask him to write the note. He, at least, was in much better health."

He stripped off his waistcoat and was working on his shirt. "I doubt your apology would work, sweeting. I know Lydia Harcourt. She has expensive tastes. She wants blunt."

Venetia couldn't help the surge of jealousy that sent her stomach plummeting to her toes. "You've had an affair with Lydia Harcourt, haven't you?" The instant the sour-sounding words spilled out, she regretted them.

"No." He undid the buttons of his shirt, then reached for the first one on his trousers.

"I don't believe you!" She looked up, into his eyes, but her gaze strayed back to his crotch "Downstairs, she was offering herself to you."

He paused, with trousers half open. "Actually she was offering to have sex with you for my amusement. And no, on my honor, I've never bedded Lydia Harcourt. She's ten years older than I am. By the time I was a randy young man visiting orgies, she was a favorite and she refused to fuck anything less than a marquess. It's only now, when her charms are waning, that a mere earl looks much more appealing."

That sounded . . . cruel. Hard. Something flashed in his blue-green eyes. Anger? "You sound like a rejected suitor."

"No, hardly that. But Lydia likes to cause trouble. And I'm not bloody impressed that she's blackmailing you. You've worked hard, taken great risks for the welfare of your family. Lydia has no bloody right to threaten you."

No one had ever championed her before. *Don't let it go to your head.* It meant nothing. Merely kindness. After all, a man could forsake the woman who bore his children.

"Now, have you taken a look at your other gifts?"

Startled, she glanced where he pointed, but at first she could only see his hand. His beautiful hand—tanned, patterned with veins, with large, graceful fingers. He pointed at the gilt escritoire that stood by the window, framed by open drapes of deep green velvet. Beyond, rain slashed down in the gardens. "Other gifts?" she asked.

"Specially selected by our thoughtful host, Lord Chartrand. You will have to look and see."

"I do wish you wouldn't keep teasing me!"

"I am delighted to see that even emeralds do not quell your spirit. Why don't you go and have a look?"

Chastised, she stomped over—she especially disliked being teased—and lifted the card from the top of the box. It bore two words, in a woman's beautiful handwriting. *A Gift.*

Cautiously, she flipped open the lid. The most curious items lay within. Two gold balls attached to a fine gold chain. She reached in and touched a long ivory wand, tapered and rounded at the end, but attached to leather straps. There were two other such wands, carved to look like cocks—perfect replicas, right down to the veins. They were attached at the hilts, hinged. Small rubies encircled their bases.

"What is it?" he asked, behind her.

He must think her embarrassed. She knew that people used devices for pleasure—the art of Rodesson and Belzique included many pictures of women sliding such things inside them.

"Sex toys, I assume?"

"Yes." A giggle bubbled up. She held one member around its thick shaft, let the other dangle. "What is this supposed to do?" With her other hand she held up the two balls. "And these? Tell me, oh rakish guide."

He prowled to her with his shirt open. "The balls are for your pleasure. Shall I show you?"

Yes. Yes, she wanted this. Wanted to learn. He was the master and she was the student and he had an illicit game he wanted to teach her.

She held the balls in her hand, heating them. Soft and fine, her shift teased her thighs as he drew her skirts up.

"Now I make you moist, vixen." His thick fingers parted

the lips of her quim. She moaned as her wetness flowed onto his fingers. She couldn't help but squeal as he eased the first ball between her nether lips. Oh, how she wanted it but she tensed at the pressure.

"The balls move inside you, pleasuring you. You leave the chain out, to withdraw them. If you move with them inside—walk, dance—you bring yourself to orgasm. And if you are quiet, it can be your own naughty secret."

"Will the other women have these . . . inside?"

"Yes. But you cannot use them, sweetheart. Not without breaking your barrier."

"I don't mind doing that."

"You might regret that choice later. You might want to marry." He slipped the first ball just inside her cunny.

"I don't want to marry—" She gasped at being filled. What did she care about marriage? All she wanted was to breath in his male scent, gaze at his lust-heated eyes, hear his deep, seductive baritone, and rub her clit against the toy he held in his powerful hand.

"Do you pleasure yourself?"

Mute with passion, she nodded, grabbed his hand, and held it tight to her cunny.

"How?" he whispered.

"I touch my bud. Stroke it. It brings my release swiftly—" Venetia understood what he was making her reveal—even though she'd decided never to marry, she had preserved her barrier. Why? "The first time," she admitted, "The first time I touched my fingers to it, the release came almost immediately and I thought I might die. I was young . . ." Why did she feel she could tell him such things. Because he had shared such things with her? *I was eight when he gave me my first volume.* "Fourteen. I'd been painting a picture of the village smithy's muscular son."

Marcus groaned, dropped the ball, and thrust his fingers between her curls. The rough tips stroked, teased, and then he caught her abraded clit between two fingers. "It arouses me to think of you bringing yourself to climax. It doesn't surprise me that you took control of your own pleasure."

Yes, but she couldn't take control of her own life. But stroking her pearl was more fun when shared, she realized, and then he rubbed with his big fingers, and she couldn't think at all.

"Yes, yes, yes!" She rocked violently against his hand as the orgasm streaked through her. Still climaxing, she grabbed naughtily for his cock—she wanted him coming too!—but to her surprise, he drew her hand away. "But you're hard," she managed between pants, "Huge! Don't you want release?"

"God yes, sweeting, I do. But I will have to wait."

Chapter Six

Standing at the top of the gallery, Venetia surveyed the elegantly dressed peers and courtesans who strolled below. Chandeliers dazzled. Jewels sparkled on powdered bosoms. She let her fingers stray to her own magnificent necklace. Every woman was beautiful, every man breathtaking.

"This early in the evening it looks like a tedious ton ball," Marcus advised, bending to let his voice tease her ear. "When I was young, the contrast used to amuse me. Knowing that the party would degrade into unfettered, wild sex."

Her hand tightened on her necklace and the cool edges of the stones tickled her palm, damp inside her glove.

"But tonight," Marcus admitted, "it sets my teeth on edge. Tonight, leave Lydia to me and tomorrow we will return to London."

One look at his intense turquoise eyes told her he would brook no argument. One night only. One night for adventure.

"Now paste a pretty smile on your face," he said, "It is time to meet your host and hostess."

That startled. "*Lady* Chartrand is here?"

"In the flesh." He nodded toward the foot of the stairs, to where a voluptuous blonde stood, flashing a coquettish smile at the Duke of Montberry. Even Venetia recognized His

Grace, the famed hero of war. A man with gray in his thick ash-blond hair, he exuded a potent sensuality that made her instinctively lick her lips. As for Lady Chartrand, she was tall and curvaceous, with elegantly dressed curls of gold. Paint gave color to her beautiful face but beneath the artificial bloom, she was deathly pale—as though gripped by despair, or shock.

Venetia followed Marcus' lead to the top of the steps.

"Lady Chartrand is a submissive. Her back, beneath that gown, bears the scars of many whippings and beatings."

Beatings. He must mean like those in the Belzique paintings. "Have you ever—"

"Only a few spankings." He stared down at her hands. "She loved it, but eventually begged for it harder, and that I couldn't do for her. She loved pain—I hated giving it out. I've never wanted to whip a woman."

"I can't . . . I can't imagine what woman would want to be whipped and hurt by a man!"

"Many do, my sweet."

She lifted her satin skirts as they descended the stairs—it was like casually walking into a demon's lair. She felt the curious gazes the way she would feel the heat of a fire. Voices rose in a furious buzz of speculation.

No one could know her. She wore the mask and a low cut ivory satin gown, the most beautiful one she possessed. Her fingers lifted to her mask and she touched the sides, the strings, felt for the snug bow at the back of her head.

He squeezed her hand. "Confidence, my dear. We're in this together."

They were at the bottom of the stairs, close to Lady Chartrand and Montberry. Her ladyship watched them, head cocked, curiosity blatant in her enormous blue eyes. Venetia felt her cheeks prickle with heat behind the mask. She pasted a confident smile on her painted lips.

"Trent!" A booming voice carried through the elegant hall.

"Our host."

Venetia saw a huge gentleman charging up, with a voluptuous henna-haired jade clinging to his arm. Who else but a jade would be poured into a tight gown of black lace—with holes cut out to expose her scarlet nipples? As for the gentleman, he possessed the brawn and bulk of a Corinthian. He gave a broad grin, flashing missing teeth, yet his hawklike brow, large nose, and wide lips were compellingly sensual.

Lord Chartrand clapped Marcus' shoulder. "Pleased to see you here, Trent. Heard some rubbish that you've been practicing abstinence."

Abstinence? But before Venetia could think more on that—and the fact he had most definitely not done so with her—Lord Chartrand's gaze raked over her. He leered at her breasts, then studied her masked face. "Who is your lovely companion, who has her secrets to keep?" He shrugged off the courtesan's hand. Venetia had no choice but to let him lift her fingers to his lips.

Her body was as stiff as a board and heat flared behind her eyes, as though she might faint. All her bold courage fled at the lascivious hunger in Lord Chartrand's eyes.

"It amuses me to call her 'Vixen'," Marcus drawled.

"Vixen, indeed. I do hope you plan to share, Trent."

Share! But that was exactly what happened at an orgy.

"Not this time, Char," Marcus said, "She's new to this."

"All the more reason to introduce her to all the carnal delights on offer."

"I plan a slow seduction, Char."

Chartrand licked his lips—as though contemplating feasting on her. "You don't mean to say that she's a virgin?"

"Not a maiden, just a lass who hasn't been exposed to more inventive sexual practices."

She remembered his words—*do you have any idea what Chartand would do with you the moment he discovered a virgin had come to his party?*

Chatrand smirked. "She might resist at first, Trent, but I guess she'd heat up quickly. You might discover she has a taste for rough sex."

Her head buzzed like a beehive. She'd enjoyed the pleasures she'd shared with Marcus, but she didn't want Chartrand to touch her.

Marcus rested his hand on the small of her back. He stroked, and she remembered, at his side, she had nothing to fear. She could relax and pretend to be an intrepid explorer.

Chartrand gripped the redheaded woman's wrist, and dragged her forward. She dropped into a graceful curtsy. Chartrand's voice was a rough growl. "Miss Vixen, may I present to you Miss Rosalyn Rose."

Vixen? Venetia bobbed down in return but her nerves showed in a slight wobble. She wasn't certain she liked the name Marcus had bestowed to protect her identity. She raised her head to see Lord Chartrand squeeze Rosalyn Rose's large breast, then bend and sink his teeth into the upper swell. Miss Rose squeaked but endured without defending herself. The red indent of Chartrand's teeth showed plainly on the jade's smooth flesh as he straightened.

"Take your pretty Vixen to the drawing room," Chartrand advised with a wink, and with that he and Rosalyn Rose moved on.

"Enjoying yourself?" Marcus asked.

They were alone. It was safe to speak.

She tipped up her chin. "I'm not afraid."

"You should be."

She refused to quake at his low, dangerous tone, but she certainly would never leave his side.

Seminude girls wandered among the guests—lovely girls wrapped in transparent robes with loose, shimmering hair that reached to their bums. Men grabbed at their breasts and cunnies, kissed lips and scarlet nipples, slapped their bottoms. She was supposed to be like one of those girls.

"Men won't paw at you like that." Marcus slipped an arm around her waist and drew her close. "They are aware that you are my property. Even in this game, a man doesn't poach on another's preserve. Definitely not on the preserve of a crack shot."

"You mean duels?" Horror echoed in her whisper. "But they're illegal."

Splaying his gloved hand over her bottom, he nudged her to move her along.

"You can't kill a man over me!"

"Don't show your claws in public. Wise harlots keep them sheathed."

"But I'm supposed to be untutored," she returned. "Please, you *must* promise you won't call anyone out."

But before he could answer, a dark-haired man bowed before her. Dressed head to toe in black—even his cravat was dyed the color of coal—this gentleman quirked his full, sensual lips in a sardonic smile. Long lashes brushed his black brows and he possessed beautifully sculpted cheekbones. He was the gentleman who had been with Miss Harcourt.

The man dropped into a careless, theatrical bow. "Viscount Swansborough at your service, my lady." Instead of pressing a kiss to her fingertips, the viscount tipped her fingers back to present the flat of her palm, which he kissed with his mouth open. He even dabbed his tongue into the sensitive center and she bit back a squeal. Of surprise, of forbidden enjoyment.

"Back off, Swansborough," Marcus warned. His chest seemed larger, his spine ramrod straight, his eyes glittered like a predator's. She recognized male posturing and gulped.

Lord Swansborough released her hand, but not before caressing her fingers. "A private treasure. Does your jewel have a name, Trent?"

"Vixen," Venetia breathed. Both men drew in sharp breaths at the husky melody her nervous voice played.

But as they moved to pass, Swansborough caught Marcus' shoulder. His expression twisted. "Who is she, Trent?" He spoke in a jaded drawl but with lethal sharpness beneath. "What in hell have you brought a woman like that here for?"

With a self-mocking grin, Marcus said, "She's a jade entertaining me by playing the novice. Fancies a future on the stage."

"The apple doesn't fall far from the tree."

Venetia felt as helpless as a witness to a carriage accident as Marcus seethed at the remark, his hands fisted, his teeth gritted. All she could do was clap her hands to her mouth and pray.

Swansborough turned to a pair of almost-nude courtesans, both blondes. He grabbed both round derrieres and nuzzled each set of pert breasts in turn. Venetia began to fear that if she became any more shocked, she would turn to stone. But at least the viscount's insult to Marcus was lost to lusty passion.

Marcus clamped his hand over hers and dragged her away. Venetia scurried to keep up with his pace. "What is wrong?"

They'd reached a set of open gilded doors before he stopped. He stroked her cheek. "You're going to have to act a more convincing whore, sweeting," he murmured. "One look at you and a man knows you're innocent."

Venetia felt a stare on her back and glanced around to meet Lady Chartrand's thoughtful gaze. She managed a smile. Her ladyship stood between two men she recognized from the gossip sheets and her father's books. Lord Brude, the dreamy poet, and Mr. Wembly, the arbitrator of men's fashion, the king of the Bow Window Set.

"How do you wish me to act like a whore?" she asked.

"Grope me, flirt with me, and make lewd suggestions."

She snuggled close and laid her hands on his steely thighs. She slid her hands up and up the insides of his thighs, until she reached his delicate balls—a large bulge within his trousers.

She cupped them with both hands. Warm. Soft. Large. They overflowed her palm.

His breath hitched. "Sweeting," he groaned, "Your act doesn't need to be quite so convincing. Your touch there is sweet torture. Heaven help me for encouraging you."

Someone passed—Swansborough and the two ladybirds. "Do you wish to . . . fuck, my lord?" She asked like a bold strumpet, trying to be as opposite to her true self as she could be.

Marcus' brow jerked up. The instant they were alone again, he warned, "You cannot use words like fuck."

"Why not? You do!"

"Because hearing an angel like you say such a crude word makes me hunger to fuck you until neither of us can walk. And that I can't let myself do."

Why not? she screamed within.

"You are tempting me to sin, dear angel." He drew her hand away from his crotch, shook his head as though fighting the haziness of lust. "You make me forget why I'm here. To rescue you from Lydia and not to watch you learn a harlot's skills."

"She's not out here." She glanced behind, around the quieter foyer. Lydia's dark curls—or enormous breasts—were nowhere to be seen.

"She'll be in the blasted drawing room."

Why did he sound so reluctant to go in? She could see only fashionable guests strolling inside, drinking champagne and sharing heated glances. "What is in there?"

"Fucking." His wry laugh rippled down her spine.

Just the naughty word sent heat coursing through her. "I've drawn such things. I want to see everything."

Venetia feared her eyes might pop out of her head. She clutched her champagne flute.

By the pianoforte in the drawing room, a young man held

a candelabrum and turned the pages while a pretty young woman with golden ringlets played. The strapping young buck's pants were open and he pushed down on his rigid cock, forcing it down toward the girl's pink-lipped mouth. In the shadows beneath the instrument, a dark-haired man had his head between the young lady's legs.

"It's *The Page Turner*! He's copied my picture." She gulped in shock. The dark-haired man was supposed to be the Earl of Trent, indulging in some illicit fun with an eager virginal daughter at a house party. Marcus would be furious.

"Apparently Chartrand admires your work." Marcus' hard, ironic tone made her shiver.

"Oh dear God," she groaned.

"But—" His deep murmur surprised even as it set her on fire. "He hasn't quite captured the remarkable flavor of your exquisite work, my love."

My love. So much more intimate than 'love', or was it a mocking address, one that hid great fury?

"Now that you have met me, now that I've made you come, do I live up to your fantasy of the Earl of Trent?" His erection brushed her bottom and robbed her of words.

What did he mean? She could tell nothing from his seductive tone—was he truly feeling playful or was he hiding dark anger? She stared at her picture come to life, at the elegance of the erotic action. But there was no secret story here. Only artifice.

Marcus slid his warm, powerful hand up her spine. He was real. His scent. His warmth. Strangely, even though she was certain he was angry, his touch gave her courage in this foreign world. Nor was that the cold caress of an angry man.

"You are more seductive than I could have ever imagined," she whispered. It was true.

Unlike her picture, this scene was not a moment trapped in time. The fake earl's tongue lapped hungrily at the woman, who made pretty moans. Venetia's quim ached in response to each cry. The man with his member exposed moved closer to the woman's mouth and she stuck out her tongue. They drew together, inexorably, until the tongue and cock touched and the woman's tongue slid over the swollen head in a wet caress.

The man moaned but it was Marcus' groan that electrified her every nerve.

His teeth grazed the top of her ear, sending honey flowing in her cunny. "Do you think I would be a better fuck than your fantasy man? Am I better at eating cunny?"

Her tongue flapped uselessly in her mouth—she took a fortifying sip of champagne.

"Magnificent artist, Rodesson. *Tales of a London Gentleman* is a masterpiece. Hope you don't object, Trent."

A purely lecherous laugh washed over her from the left—too close—along with the strong scent of brandy. Venetia coughed and sputtered in shock. Marcus drew her into his embrace, and she turned to the speaker—Lord Chartrand.

"Your mistress appears to be choking." Chartrand grinned. "So, Trent, is your lady accomplished on the pianoforte?"

"I've never given her time to play," Marcus returned. Venetia shivered. He was presenting her as a whore, while making it clear she wasn't available to anyone else.

"But does the young lady possess talented hands?"

"She is very talented with her hands," Marcus replied in a dangerous growl.

If he'd been a wolf, his hackles would be raised, his fangs bared. She felt as though her chest were being squeezed. She wanted to be in control. Yet she didn't dare even speak in case she made a mistake.

Chartrand—even though he was bigger than Marcus—gave a cold smile and took a step back. "I only hope that my tableaux provide inspiration."

Venetia let out her caught breath on a whoosh. Chartrand had blinked first. Then he muttered a virulent 'bitch', and glowered over their heads. Venetia twisted to look.

The Duke of Montberry was approaching—with Lydia Harcourt on his arm.

Venetia swallowed hard. Lydia knew that she, not Rodesson, had drawn *The Page Turner*. What would Lydia say when she saw it?

Furtively, Venetia touched her mask to reassure herself it was still there. Lydia couldn't know who she was. Thank heaven she hadn't revealed herself yet. Lydia could not point a finger at her and scream 'She's the one who painted it.'

Marcus murmured, "Don't speak to her, Vixen. Be careful."

Lydia's large blue eyes shifted from Montberry's patrician features to Marcus' face, and a catlike smile curved her scarlet painted lips. Lydia's coloring was magnificent—pink cheeks, rosy lips, endless dark lashes. Any portrait artist would love to capture such beauty. She wore scarlet silk, with plunging neckline and a slit up the side that showed her legs.

"Publish and be damned, Your Grace?" Lydia asked the duke in a low voice. "Indeed I shall, but I will not be the object of ridicule."

The elegant war hero lifted his quizzing glass. "Pah, you already are, minx. Do you not know the polite world is laughing at your ridiculous aspirations to become an author? Lud, gel, can you even compose a sentence?"

"Well enough to mock you, Your Grace," Lydia snapped. With that the courtesan spun, nose in the air, and stormed off.

Montberry drew a cheroot from his breast pocket. "Stupid, stupid tart," he muttered.

"Oooh!"

Legs trembling, heart racing, Venetia snapped her attention back to the piano. The young lady writhed as the man beneath the piano clutched her to his face. The 'earl' had made her come.

The erotic moment captured her, held her spellbound. She

became aware of Marcus' heavy breaths, of his touch on her hip—so wonderfully sensitive there, even through clothes. Of the insistent push of his erection against her bottom.

She wanted him, ached for him, and reached for his hand, twined fingers, led his hand up to rest beneath her breast . . .

Marcus groaned as Venetia watched Trixie Jones suck a cock down her throat and grind her quim into another man's face.

This had to be a punishment for his sins, Marcus thought.

Emeralds flashed around Venetia's wrist as she brought his hand up to rest against her tight bodice, beneath her full breasts. His gift. The pretence that she belonged to him, his to seduce tonight.

He'd seen the condemnations in the eyes of Brude, Swansborough, Wembly, even Helen, Lady Chartrand. Each and every one thought he was playing the sort of game his father had done. Debauching a naïve girl. They wouldn't intervene, but he hated to be considered to be that kind of blackguard. Yet to protect Venetia, he had no choice.

"He . . . he hasn't got it quite right," she mused.

"Who?" he bit out. "The one underneath or the one standing?"

The scene set his blood thrumming, as it would any breathing male, but knowing Venetia had created this fantasy made him ache with need. Even though he should be furious that it was depicting *him*, he was aroused by it. He hadn't felt so rigid, so swollen, so close to losing control since his youth. He hurt as though he'd denied himself for months. Of course he had, but it wasn't that. It was a few hours in Venetia's tempting presence.

"Chartrand." Venetia pursed plump lips. The scarlet cream made her mouth look large, wet, and tempting. But he preferred it bare. Soft, natural, and tasting of her.

"The woman is a bit too brash for the part, I think," she continued. "I envisioned a woman caught up in deception and sin and passion against her better nature. A more tentative woman."

"A woman like you?"

A flush bloomed in her cheeks, visible below the mask. He pressed close. Her bottom was a lush cushion for his erection. Her exotic-tinged scent swirled up and he took a deep breath. Not her usual perfume—the clever woman had realized how identifying scent could be.

Other couples strolled by and stopped to watch *The Page Turner*. Helen on Wembly's arm. Rosalyn with Brude, who nodded in approval. "Ah, Rodesson's latest work. Excellent choice."

Marcus gritted his teeth as the ladies winked and sent carnal invitations with the motions of their fans. Wembly and Brude shared a bawdy laugh at his expense. But the truth was that Venetia was a remarkable artist. And she was correct—Chartrand's copy of her work didn't possess the arresting sensuality of the original.

Brude and Wembly bestowed kisses on Venetia's hand, but as he turned for one moment to kiss Helen's fingertips, both men squeezed Venetia's bottom. She jumped. Her champagne glass tipped and spilled.

Marcus pulled her possessively to his side. "I don't intend to share," he growled.

Wembly quirked a brow. "Then you shouldn't have brought her, Trent."

Venetia' eyes widened in shock as the couples strolled on and Marcus warned, "You see, fantasy and reality are two different things."

She shoved her empty glass at a passing footman. "I was surprised, not offended. I do recognize the risks here."

No, you don't entirely. Even after a night here, your soul will never be the same.

"I'll protect you from all risks, sweeting." And he would, but he knew now he was on a fool's errand. Preserving Venetia's virginity wouldn't save his soul.

He lured her from the growing crowd, arm tight around her waist, but he led her from *The Page Turner*, only to encounter a true Rodesson work, *The First Night*. On a large daybed, a starry-eyed debutante—a pretty auburn-haired whore who looked a convincing virgin—surrendered her innocence to a dashing rogue.

A rasping breath caught in his throat. The woman looked too much like Venetia.

The scene was in progress. Both lovers were nude. The rake parted pretty thighs, positioned his lance, then took his first thrust, sinking deep. Venetia gasped. While the woman in the tableau was doubtless not a virgin, she gave a convincing sobbing cry. It echoed though Marcus' veins and with every pulse of blood to his groin.

He urged Venetia to move toward the doors at the end that led to a gallery. A place for sanity.

"Wait, m—my lord." Venetia stood her ground as he tried to hurry her past the next scene. He glanced back at it. A tangle of nubile bodies, mouths at every orifice and large, erect cocks wobbling everywhere. She murmured something.

He only caught one word. Sketchpad. *Sketchpad?*

Venetia twisted him in circles. When he expected shock, she acted the bohemian artist. And sometimes she was sweetly startled, his heart ached . . .

"What is the haste, my lord? Aren't you intrigued by this?"

"I've seen it before, Vixen. Done it. What I want is to get you out of here."

In truth, he hungered to whisk Venetia back to the bedroom. To spend the night with his head between her silky thighs, breathing her rich fragrance, reveling in her taste, making her scream . . . wishing he could do it with his cock . . .

One night. All he had to survive was one night. He'd have Lydia taken care of and he'd return Venetia to London with her virginity intact. And he would have protected the damsel in distress.

Church was a place he rarely went, except for the obligatory christenings and weddings—he had a rake's unease about stepping onto hallowed ground—but he sent up a prayer as he steered Venetia away. *Give me the strength to resist temptation.* His father was rotting in hell for his crimes and no amount of prayer over a brandy bottle had saved him.

"Oh my goodness," she gasped. "Look at that!"

CHAPTER SEVEN

"I never—" Venetia stopped, lowered her voice. "I've never drawn anything like this. Certainly none with you—"

"I know. I know all your pictures." Marcus stroked her bare shoulders and shivers tumbled down her spine. "You've drawn women together. But this scene does remind me of your *Reunion of School Chums* and he's changed it to suit his catamites."

Two brawny young men shared the Grecian-style daybed. One lay on his back with a muscular arm resting on the bolster. The other had his arm flung across the first man's hips, his hand squeezing the plump sac that nestled between lean thighs.

Mouth dry, Venetia watched how an experienced hand played with a man's balls. The ministrations were so aggressive. Surely the one being fondled must be in pain.

But they kissed passionately, with mouths wide open, tongues jabbing and tangling. Both sported erections—the swollen cocks as unique as their owners. The one lying on his back had golden curls on his head, sherry-colored ones at his crotch and a thick, straight member that jutted upward. His partner was dark, his back and chest were tanned to the color of dark clover honey, and his cock curved toward his navel. A small head peeked out of his tight foreskin.

She was shocked at herself for studying them so intently.

Merely the interest of an artist in the human form. It was a lie and she sucked in deep, hurried breaths. "In *Chums*, the women were . . . daintily exploring each other. It was rather . . . innocent."

The dark-haired youth trailed kisses down the ridged abdomen of the blond man . . .

"And these two look playfully appealing too, don't they?"

Yes, she had to admit they did. Or she would, if she could find the breath to speak. Why she should be so aroused by two men kissing and caressing, she couldn't imagine. But she was. As the men began grappling each other's erections, her cunny throbbed in response.

With a shock, she realized the blond man was casting covetous looks at Marcus. He was all but fluttering his long, fair lashes. Even though his mate was kissing the nest of golden curls at the hilt of his erection, he only had eyes for Marcus.

She gave an icy glare and put her hand over Marcus', squeezing possessively. Not only did the women want him, so did the men!

There had been one Rodesson picture involving a coupling between men. A picture of sodomy, though the man being penetrated had worn a look of shock. He'd been buried deep inside a woman and another man was taking him from the rear, obviously without consent.

What had happened after that moment? Had the man in the center forced the other to stop? Had they fought a duel? How did a gentleman name his seconds for that?

Her dress slid up at the back, up to midcalf. Startled, she tried to twist in Marcus' arm. He let her hem drop and the ruffles skimmed over her gauzy fine stockings.

Marcus lifted her skirts again, caressing her legs with the brush of muslin and silk. She could hardly think.

"I can smell your delectable honey flowing, Vixen. The sight of two men excites you?"

She nodded.

"Intriguing."

What did he mean by that? And why, if he wished to keep her pure, did he have to tease her by lifting her skirts? Was it just part of the game? She burned—in the most wanton way!

"My lord Trent."

The breathy, husky voice of a woman. Lydia? Venetia managed to turn in his arms. No, this woman wore white. And a mask—a beautiful concoction of white leather and feathers. Her entire face was hidden, the holes at the mouth painted with a scarlet outline, the eyes rimmed with painted-on lashes. Floating feathers trimmed her white gown. They were all that covered her breasts, and as she moved feathers fluttered, revealing distended dark brown nipples.

"My dear Lady Yardley."

Venetia gasped as her skirts swooshed down to her ankles once more. Marcus bowed over the woman's fingers. His lips briefly brushed, but Lady Yardley's breasts rose and fell, parting the feathers.

Even she, far outside London's high society, knew Lady Yardley. The widow who did many charitable works and who actually ventured into the rough and grimy streets around Covent Garden to save prostitutes. Lady Yardley attended debauched orgies? And why do so masked, if all knew who she was?

Lady Yardley boldly stroked Marcus's hip. "Lord Trent, I didn't know you enjoyed the sight of a man's cock in another man's ass?"

Venetia coughed. Lady *Yardley* had just said that?

"My little Vixen wished to watch."

Still shocked, Venetia turned back to the daybed. The blond youth sprawled on his belly now, legs parted and he lifted his rump until the cheeks brushed his friend's dangling bollocks. The other licked his hand and spread his spittle over the swollen, purplish head of his cock.

A proper young lady should not see such a thing. But she wanted to watch, heaven help her. And not only to merely study for her art—

Both young men looked so agonized, so needy. A large male hand curved on one tightly clenched cheek, parting, opening. His cock dipped, forced down into the furry valley. Moans from both. A plea to hurry.

She knew the moment of penetration—the dark-haired youth gave an abrupt thrust of his hips, the blond man cried out. His friend immediately yanked back. Again and again they tried, until the thick, rigid cock slowly sank from view, until a groin dusted with dark curls slapped hard against firm buttocks.

"Yes, yes, John," cried the blond youth. Ravaging thrusts forced him into the daybed. His fingers curled like claws, gripping plump silk cushions. The pounding rocked the chaise, yet he arched his rear up, seeking more.

"God, I love fucking your tight, tight arse, Cole." Eyes shut tight, John plunged deep, his thrusts almost vicious. "I want to rip you apart, boy. I want to thrust me cock right through you."

Venetia flinched at the brutality. But Cole moaned and bucked in encouragement.

Lady Yardley flicked open a white and silver fan. She wafted it before her masked face with savage strokes. Warding off a faint?

No, not that at all. Venetia gaped as her ladyship stepped up onto the dais. While the two men engaged in their savage shocking sex, Lady Yardley stroked a white glove along the bunched thigh muscles of John, the dark-haired man on top. She snapped her fan closed.

Startled, Venetia saw the ivory fan had a rounded end. Lady Yardley stroked that end between John's clenched cheeks. He groaned, deep and harsh. "Are you going to ram that up me arse, milady?"

"Not now, dear boy. Perhaps later, and only if you please me."

"Yes, m'am," he answered, and even bobbed his head, suddenly becoming a proper servant in the midst of his violent thrusting.

Venetia's head swam. Heat raged over her skin. Her legs felt weightless beneath her. Marcus' grip on her waist tightened. "Too extreme?" he whispered.

It wasn't shock. Or was it? Venetia watched, dumbfounded, as Lady Yardley struck John's rear with the fan, turned, and daintily left the stage. Her ladyship smirked like a cat in the larder as she watched John pound hard enough to almost shove Cole off the bed. He was truly performing now and Cole howled with every thrust.

"I shouldn't worry, my lady. Chartrand's bucks are also willing to service ladies."

Venetia jumped at the mocking female voice. It was Lydia Harcourt, of course.

"*You*. What are you doing here?" Anger burned in Lady Yardley's eyes.

Lydia gave a careless wave of her hand. "I am here to offer you a second chance."

"You blackmailing tart." Lady Yardley pointed the fan at Lydia as though it were a pistol barrel. "You greedy, stupid little fool. You'll end up throttled to death, I promise you."

Venetia shivered at the venom behind the threat. But Lydia merely laughed. Perhaps she'd heard worse. With a curtsy, she moved on. Lady Yardley turned back to the dias, radiating fury. Venetia knew her face was flaming beneath the mask.

"Oh God, I'm coming!"

She couldn't help but look. Cole thrust his head back and his rear upward. "Coming!"

"God, yer squeezing me so bloody tight!" John yelled back. He climaxed with his head bowed, his mouth open and gasping, his muscles tense. Yet, as she watched, a voyeur to this intimate vulnerable moment, it was Marcus she was envisioning . . . the way he had come in the carriage for her . . .

Marcus' finger was tracing the valley between her cheeks through her skirts. Like Cole, she arched her rear back to encourage. Would he put his finger between, pushing silk inside?

He cupped her rear with both hands. Oh yes. He kept her positioned so she could watch the daybed. John collapsed on top of Cole. With surprising gentleness, he kissed his lover's neck, just beneath the damp blond hair. The gesture was so gentle and loving, such a contrast to the raw fervor of their joining.

Marcus' hands slid around her waist. One settled low, sliding down from her hip toward the place that throbbed and burned.

Relief. His hand would give her relief and his fingers were so very close now . . .

He idly stroked her bosom. Was he only acting? Other gentleman fondled their partners. Pinched nipples and bottoms. Lifted skirts or plunged their hands down low bodices.

She became aware of them all at once. Of the scent of rich perfumes and other earthy smells. Of the sighs of encouragement, the coarse words. Of the lust burning in the men's eyes. Of Cole rolling over onto his backside and offering his soft cock to his lover's mouth . . .

Marcus' thumb spiraled over her hard nipple. Yes . . . yes . . . She reached behind. Found him and stroked her hand along his hard length.

"We should stop," he groaned in her ear. But his breath there, hot and teasing, drove her wild. She could feel the shape of the head though his trousers. Softly she traced the rounded ridge, the cleft. She wanted him . . . to do what she wasn't sure and didn't care . . . but she needed to climax before she died from the pain—

"I'm not going to do this in public."

Do what? Anticipation tingled through her, setting her skin on fire.

"I need to take you out to the gallery. Now."

Marcus pushed his way through the crowd and it parted for him, though he didn't hold the highest rank.

Her mask had slipped, obscuring her vision and she had no choice but to blindly follow Marcus. Male voices called out from all sides.

"Did pretty Vixen enjoy the catamites' display?"

The deep drawl of fashionable Mr. Wembly. "Thinking of three in the bed, Trent?"

Three! Her wits whirled as Marcus escorted her forward. Her feet moved by instinct.

The clipped accents of Montberry. "Didn't know that was your pleasure, Trent. Allow me to entertain your little Vixen, while you indulge in a strapping young male—"

The husky, jaded voice of Lord Swansborough. "You'll end up in hell, Trent, but I can see how your little treasure would tempt you there. If you're seeking a third, I'm willing to damn myself in some sporting debauchery—"

Venetia struggled with her mask. She didn't tug too hard in case it came off. Mad thoughts—lurid images—spun through her mind. "Are all the men going to offer to join us?"

"To have a taste of you? I don't doubt it."

The cool night air spilled over him and Marcus felt as though he'd been delivered from the flames of hell. Panes rattled along the long row of windows as gusts struck them. Rain pelted against glass, and some windows were open, letting in the steady drum of the storm. Thunder boomed. Dark and quiet settled around them, and he took a deep, relieved breath.

"Do you often share women with other men?"

The blunt, matter-of-fact question wasn't what he'd expected from Venetia. He'd expected relief at escaping that den of sin. Shock over the bold offers. Not curiosity about his sexual practices.

Bracing his arm against the cold glass of a window, Marcus lifted her hand to his lips for a chaste kiss after the excess.

She drew pictures that astonished him. She had an imagination that stunned him.

"Do you?" She tugged at her mask. It had slipped down, half-covering her mouth.

"I have no intention of sharing you." He eased her hands away, set her mask to rights. Heard the sharp intake of her breath. He'd meant he had no intention of letting her give up her innocence.

Lightning forked, setting the room ablaze for an instant. Thunder cracked and Venetia squealed. He jumped too, but caught her hand in his. Not just a gesture of protection.

There were no candles in the gallery. No moonlight either. The brief flash had left him blinded. Only the light creeping around the double doors to the drawing room illuminated the room. "We're alone. Stand at the window, Vixen."

He saw her reflection in the glass. Wide eyes, parted lips.

She moaned as he whisked up her skirts from behind.

"I want you, my lord. I've tried not to think about how much I want you. Tried to think of Lyd—of my quest. Of art. Of the scandalous people I've seen here. Of anything other than you."

The clever wench lifted her slipper-clad foot and ran it along the side of his leg. She leaned back to tuck her head against his neck, to let silky curls tease his jaw.

Her skirts poured over his arm in a waterfall of silk and lace. The faint light caressed the rounded curves of her plump bare bottom. In the cool of the night, she promised fire and forbidden delight.

"Did it work, Vixen?" he rasped. "I couldn't stop thinking of you."

"Why?"

Such a simple question. So direct. One that deserved an answer.

"I don't know. Perhaps because I am your protector?" He stepped between her spread legs. "But mostly I think because you are a beautiful woman who captures my—"

Sinfully soft, her bottom brushed across his groin.

"You capture my imagination. And I very much fear you could capture my soul." He braced his hands on the window-sill, capturing her.

"After all the women you've made love to?"

"You are unique." He nibbled her lobe, the metal chain of her earbob cold against his lips, her skin hot. "You must know that."

Her wry laugh tugged at his heart.

"I've never met a woman like you, Vixen. An artist. A creator. So very talented." With his tongue, he traced the rim of her ear, enjoying the way she trembled. God, he loved her scent—the natural delicate perfume of her skin underneath a splash of jasmine and rose.

"Most men don't believe a woman is capable of true artistic skill. Even my . . . my father balked at the thought of me painting in oils."

She'd hesitated at the word 'father'. They had that in common, she and him. A father who kept their lives in turmoil, who created disasters for them to clean up.

"Tonight you've seen how many people you have enthralled with your imagination and talent."

"Truly—?" Her voice caught. "But you must be angry."

"Not at you," he reassured.

On a soft sigh, she thrust her rear back against him, engulfing his member with her luscious cheeks. "I want you so, Marcus. So much. I don't care about my virginity."

He shaped his hands to the globes, filled his palms, squeezed. God, he wanted to be inside her. And there were other ways, now that her knowledge of sensuality had grown—

Her bottom was lush and tempting. He splayed his right hand over both cheeks, slid his left to open her pussy lips. Heat and honey awaited him. Stickiness coated his fingers. He rubbed his wet fingertip over her clit.

Her back arched. "Please," she moaned.

The one word ripped through him. He pressed hard against her, trapping her against the window sill. "I can pleasure you without tearing your maidenhead, without risking pregnancy."

She shoved her derriere back against him, grinding hard

against his cock. "Oh, yes . . . how—?" Then insight dawned. "You mean in the way of the two men. Sodomy."

"Pleasuring you through your bottom." He used the gentle words for her. In his head he thought—*I want to fuck your delectable ass.*

Quiet stretched except for pounding rain, an angry wind. Then she half-turned her head. "Yes. Yes, Marcus, I want this."

He groaned. "I can't now, Vixen." Not with an innocent. He needed warmed oil. Needed to make her comfortable. To make her slick and prepared. He could lick his fingers, use his tongue on her, but it wouldn't be enough.

She moaned, a desperate, begging sound. "You can't resist now, my lord."

He gave a low chuckle. "No, sweeting, I promise I can no longer resist." He drew a finger down between her cheeks, dallying at her puckered anus. Sensual agony lanced through his groin. "But I need to prepare you. If I don't, I risk causing you pain. I'd never hurt you, Vixen."

"Pain?"

"Let me make you come with my tongue, Venetia."

"Yes," she whispered. "But I want more."

"And soon you will have more."

"Open your trousers. Take out your cock. Please, my lord Trent. I want to make you come."

He'd never ached like this. Had never been so sexually hungry. His hand went to the buttons of his placket, already straining. After easing them free, he reached into his small clothes. His cock twanged free and planted itself in the cleft of her ass cheeks. Snug and satiny, they clamped him, squeezing him. His cock dripped its readying fluid on her curves.

Even that wouldn't be enough to ease this for her. But he would tease her a bit, then stop and devour her with his mouth and tongue, lick her cunny, clit, rosebud anus . . .

Taking cock in hand, he stroked the tip against her tight, puckered anus. She pushed back on a sweet moan and he felt her blossom open around his cock. The wet tip slid in a touch. Enough to swamp his brain with lust. So tight. So fiery hot.

God, yes.

Hell, no.

He stroked her clit with his fingers, her rear with his cock. Her juices ran down his fingers, her ass was slick with his fluid. The promise of sex surrounded him. Speech left him. All he could do was grunt and groan.

Instinct sent his hips thrusting forward. His slick cock slid down, skimmed over the bridge between pussy and ass, wedged itself in her satiny slit.

He had to draw back. His fluid was flowing. He could make her pregnant—

A deep boom sounded, an echo playing though the long, dark gallery. Thunder? No. The dinner gong.

Marcus dropped to his knees and turned Venetia, so her quim was at his mouth, his to pleasure. His first suckle had her hips arching hard against him, his name in a cry on her lips.

She clutched his shoulders and skillfully he teased her clit until it plumped into his mouth. Until she was sobbing and incoherent. With his finger, he teased the tight rim of her anus . . .

It could be his cock. Clamped tight, stroked by strong muscles . . .

Not now.

Her fingernails drove into his scalp, holding his face tight to her cunny. In answer, he slid his finger in and out of her ass.

Strands of her hair flew free as she thrust back against him, a wink in the low light, the way fairy dust should be. She thrust against his face, pumped on his finger, taking him deeper into her derriere. Deeper than he intended to go. To the hilt and the length of his finger was gripped by scorching, silky walls.

"Oh. Oh. Oh."

Yes, sweetheart, come for me.

He furled his tongue around her clit, licked, circled, used every skill he'd learned. Then he just let his tongue rest flat against her, let her grind against him as she wished. Her fingers drove into his shoulders.

God, she was beautiful. Like a sensual *houri*, adept at using voluptuous hips to tempt, Venetia danced over his mouth. Curls flew, hands clutched, her head arched back, exposing the white, lovely arch of her neck.

As she came, her cry rattled the windows. He plunged his tongue into her passage, to revel in the pulsing of her cunny, and watched her surrender.

Making a woman climax was always a victory. But with Venetia, it was sweeter, more intimate. Despite the driving pain of his hard cock, he felt he was sharing her ecstasy.

Slowly, her cries descended into sobs and sighs. She dropped forward, eyes shut tight. Drawing back from her heat, his face slick and sticky with it, he planted a kiss above her nether curls, on the curve of dewy skin.

"Now that you are satisfied, Vixen, we must go to dinner." His voice was strained, his cock aching, standing proud of his trousers. Like a pointer on a hunt, pointing up toward her cunny.

"No." The poor sweet could barely stand. He held her hips to support her. Drawing back the curtain of her hair, she whispered, "I want to do it to *you*."

Her lips were plump and swollen. She began to sink down—

The double doors swung wide. Light and coarse laughter spilled in. Chartrand's jocular baritone rang through the gallery. "It appears we missed the performance!"

In a second, Marcus was on his feet and Venetia's skirts covered her once more.

The second bong of the gong swelled through the gallery, echoing off the row of windows.

Shit. He was destined to spend dinner in pain.

* * *

At dinner, Venetia had to survive by her wits.

Even here, in the midst of a bacchanalia, order of seating was preserved. Placed between Mr. Wembly and Viscount Swansborough, she sat across the table from Lydia Harcourt. As an earl, Marcus sat much closer to the head of the table, between Lady Chartrand and Lady Yardley, who had one hand permanently beneath the table. On Marcus' leg. Or worse.

Twice Marcus had lifted the countess' elegant hand and placed it back on the table, but Venetia's heart hammered like a trapped bird. Madness, of course, because she knew he was promiscuous and no doubt he'd made love to all these women before.

She tried not to think of it.

Without title—or even a full name—Venetia was surprised to be allowed at the table at all, but she was Marcus' partner, and that kept her from languishing at the very end, where the lesser jades and handsome, anonymous bucks downed their wine.

Lydia Harcourt's curious gaze kept falling on her. She would stare at her wineglass or her dinner but she had to plan how to best deflect curiosity. Appearing witless was the only tack she could think to take.

What other choice did she have?

She wished she could have an honest discussion with Lydia instead of hiding behind a giggle and clumsy speech but she couldn't take the risk that Lydia would identify her. She breathed a sigh of relief as Lydia turned her attention to Wembly. The famed dandy wore an elegant tailcoat and trousers, an ivory waistcoat, a simple cravat with crisp knot. His taste was subdued—rather like Marcus'. His hair was a tumble of waves of dark blond streaked with soft gold. His lips were soft and full.

Lydia swirled the red wine in her large glass. Rubies gleamed at her throat, ears, and wrists, the same deep scarlet as her lips and gown. The one in the center of her necklace was the size of a robin's egg.

Anger rose. This woman could live forever if she merely pawned her jewels.

Perhaps she already had. These could be fine fakes.

Wembly leaned suddenly close. He smelled of sandalwood and starch, just as Marcus did, but unlike Marcus', his scent didn't enthrall, didn't steal her wits.

"My dear Miss Vixen," he murmured, "I heard your climatic screams, even over the crashing storm. They electrified me, sweet nymph. I should very much like the chance to make you scream like that myself."

She stared, dumbfounded. This man was considered London's sharpest wit?

"You are a sensual woman," he continued. "Untutored, that much is obvious, but naturally wanton. I want you, my dear."

Fear uncoiled in her belly. "I belong to Lord Trent."

Wembly's fingertips, elegant in white gloves, stole to her hand, and stroked. "I'll obtain his permission, of course, sweet Vixen. Meet me at midnight in my rooms. How delightful to end this day with my head up your skirts."

Venetia felt her mouth gape open. Marcus would never allow it. She wouldn't go!

Lydia's rich tones spilled over the table, clear and distinct. "I gather you wintered in Italy, Mr. Wembly. Escaping debts or seeking the sun?"

Oh, thank you, Lydia, for the interruption.

"Both, dear lady, both," he returned. Laughter rewarded the quip and he raised his wine glass in a salute before draining it to the quick.

One of Chartrand's footmen—a muscular one with vibrant blue eyes and a cocky grin—began the parade of carrying in the main course. Each and every footman was striking. And as for the gentlemen . . . Chartrand had filled his event with the most handsome noblemen of the ton.

But not one made her knees weak, the way just a glimpse of Marcus did.

And that promised disaster. If the most handsome, delicious men of the ton couldn't set her heart pounding, it meant she had a partiality for Marcus.

Oh, hell and damnation, it meant she was falling in love with him!

"Did you encounter Princess Caroline on your travels, Mr. Wembly?" Lydia speared a piece of roast lamb.

"Alas, no. She had packed off her entourage to Pesaro, where she lives in seclusion with *il Barone*."

From mocking caricatures, Venetia knew he meant Mr. Pergami, the princess' 'servant'.

"Poor Caroline deserves to have a lover. And I think our dear princess is remarkably clever. Surely you must agree."

Wembly gave a jaded shrug. "She's remarkably tasteless. She's run to fat and seems to thinks she's a dozen years younger than she is. A clever woman . . ." He paused, stared pointedly at Lydia, "Recognizes her age."

"Indeed," Lydia agreed. "A *clever* woman does."

Venetia felt a stab of pity. Poor Princess Caroline was mourning her daughter's tragic death in childbirth. Wembly's cutting remarks were cruel. But then he was a favorite of the Prince of Wales. Prinny must reward him for his caustic comments about the Prince's despised wife.

"The Princess has found a clever way to flaunt English law," Lydia continued. "For Mr. Pergami is safe, being an Italian citizen. It would be treason, would it not, for a Englishman to have an affair with Caroline? Punishable by death?" The long dark eyelashes fluttered as Lydia spoke. Her hands made lovely, expressive motions.

"An affair with Caroline would be a punishment." Wembly drained his wineglass. A footman stepped forward to refill it but Wembly's hand knocked the stem, sending the stream to the table. An exclamation, effuse apologies and the mess was cleaned, the glass refilled.

Looking smug, Lydia turned to smile toward Lord Brude.

Venetia gave a furtive glance at him, thankful she had the mask to hide behind. Any educated country girl would be swooning to be in the presence of the brooding, darkly handsome poet. Glossy dark curls dangled before the famed, enigmatic black eyes. His hair was not raven black, like Marcus', more of the color of dark, bitter chocolate.

A country lass drawn into this world of high society debauchery would be fawning over Brude. To play her part, she sighed and gave him dreamy looks. Cow-eyed looks.

Having caught Brude's attention, Lydia embarked on a spirited discussion of literary work with the poet. *Tom Jones*, Cleland's *Fanny Hill*, Austen's *Emma*, Brude's latest collection.

A different gleam showed in Lydia's eyes as she mentioned her own memoirs. Venetia recognized the look. Tentative, a little fearful, but oh, so very proud, so very hopeful one's artistic effort would be a true success.

"Have you hired someone to write them then?" Brude asked with false innocence.

"Writing is rigorous work and often trying, I agree," Lydia said, "But my work is my own. I shouldn't think of having *someone else* writing my book."

Mussels arrived. Brude shoveled several on his plate, skewered a plump one and popped it in his mouth.

"Eat hearty," called out one buck, "To fortify one's strength for later sport."

Venetia flushed as the handsome man winked at her. "Mussels are a famed aphrodisiac."

She slid a glance down the table. Lady Yardley was trying to feed Marcus mussels.

"His lordship has no need of those," Lydia remarked, with a sly smile.

"I know," Venetia replied, trying for airy feminine spite. "He's inexhaustible."

Lydia's lovely eyes narrowed. "Who are you behind that

mask, my dear? Has Lord Trent really brought an innocent maiden here? What a delicious scandal. I plan to find out exactly who you—"

"Most memoirs are bloody dull stuff, Lydia," Chartrand boomed from the head of the table, interrupting. Venetia sent up a prayer of thanks.

"Tired of reading boring tomes about military men or Whigs or the trials of blasted reformers," he shouted. "I sincerely hope you plan to include the spicy stuff."

"Oh, I do, my lord. Unless, by special request, I choose to retract some of the more scandalous incidents."

Sipping her wine, Venetia sputtered. How could Lydia be so open about blackmail? But there had been no mention of memoirs in Lydia's letter to her. Only a request for payment for silence.

"You should have Rodesson illustrate it for you!" Chartrand exclaimed. He gave a nasty laugh. Guffaws followed this and Lydia's eyes narrowed, shooting sparks.

"But alas, my dear," Chartrand continued, "He's never been kind to you, has he?"

"I could hardly have him illustrate as he—"

Venetia stopped breathing. Lydia was going to reveal that Rodesson couldn't paint—

"Would hardly do justice to the eloquence of my tale," Lydia finished.

Thank heaven. But a red flush heightened Lydia's artfully rouged cheeks. Oh, no. Her father enjoyed making political comment when he drew, and he enjoyed having mean-spirited fun. He must have insulted Lydia viciously. If Lydia hated her father she must want revenge . . .

She should hate Lydia—but she couldn't bring herself to. No one took Lydia's literary aspirations seriously. As a fellow artist, Venetia could sympathize. Lydia's vulnerability had been exposed. No doubt she deserved the cutting treatment, but it must have hurt. No doubt Rodesson's pictures had hurt Lydia, too. Her father never worried about others' feelings.

"Still masked, I see."

The sensuous voice at her right startled her. She dropped her fork. Turned to Lord Swansborough. Dressed entirely in black, the viscount lounged in his chair like Lucifer. He studied her face as though he could see through the mask. "Who are you, that you are so careful of your identity?"

To hide her nerves, Venetia lifted her fork and did battle with a mussel. "If I were to reveal that, my lord, I'd have no need of the mask."

"I wonder if you could be coaxed to remove it."

She quaked. The mussel flew from her fork, landing with a humiliating plop on his plate.

Just as she was about to slither beneath the table to hide, Lord Chartrand stood and clapped for attention. Venetia had to jerk her hands up as her plate was taken away. Four mussels still remained, nestled in sauce within their shells, but her appetite had vanished.

Footmen returned, bearing silver trays loaded with delicate stemmed dishes. Frothy white syllabub trembled in crystal as the trays were whisked down the length of the table. The first to be served lifted gold spoons.

"Wait!" Chartrand called. "In one of the dishes is a gold ring. A ring to be worn on an erect cock."

Venetia stared at her dessert as it landed on her place. No sign of a ring from the outside, but the dish was large. But what on earth would she do with such a thing?

Slip it on Marcus, whispered her inner, naughty voice.

"If the finder is a gentleman," Chartrand continued, "He will be the winner of a delightful treat. If a lady finds the prize, she may award it to the gentleman of her choice."

And what would happen after that?

With trepidation, Venetia lifted her spoon. *Please, let there be no ring in my dish.* The spoon slid through the whipped confection with ease. Down, down, down . . .

But if another woman found the ring, that woman could select Marcus.

Her spoon hit the glass bottom with a ting. Instead of a flood of relief, Venetia felt her hand tighten with tension. She turned the spoon's handle in a circle, scraping metal against glass.

"Come now," urged Chartrand, "Surely someone has found it?"

"Hell and damnation."

The deep, rugged, utterly irritated male voice was unmistakable. Heart in her throat, Venetia looked up at Marcus. As she expected, the gold ring dangled from his spoon.

Chapter Eight

Marcus glared at the gleaming gold ring designed to slide over the wearer's cock and balls prior to erection. Once the cock stood proud, the ring tightened, enhancing size by restricting blood flow. To squeeze the base was to enlarge the head.

He dropped his 'prize' from the spoon to the gold rimmed plate beside the dish.

What should he do? Claim it but turn down whatever it brought? Would that raise suspicion?

He could hand it back to Chartrand and award his host the 'treat' in his stead but, for all he knew, whatever Chartrand had arranged might involve his partner—Venetia. If so, Chartrand, the devil, would try to claim her.

So, he would refuse to participate and refuse to let her do it.

Simple enough.

If he ended up over pistols at dawn, so be it.

Picking up the ring, he held it up to catch the light of the chandelier, then tossed it down the table toward Chartrand. "I've already planned my night, Chartrand. Why don't you give a demonstration instead?"

"The prize is yours, Trent." Chartrand clapped his hands and his footmen brought in a sedan chair, on which sat Rosalyn Rose, completely nude. Her nipples were rouged.

Her hand dangled demurely across her henna-red bush. She ran her tongue around her glistening lips.

Chartrand's grin widened. "Rosalyn shall give a demonstration to your country lovely on the best techniques for fellatio."

Marcus groaned. "My country lovely is inventive and adept in her own right. She needs no lessons. In fact, I'm aroused enough to take her up to my rooms right now."

"Upstairs?" Chartrand blinked. "Why such modesty?"

Laughter rose all around. Marcus ground his teeth. Given the number of public displays he'd given, he could never be called modest. Besides, the term was damned feminine.

Face covered by her mask, Venetia was staring at him, syllabub spoon still hanging from her fingers. He noticed Lydia's appraising expression.

"Are you suggesting I sweep aside your dessert and rut on your table?"

All laughed once more at the joke—Swansborough had done it at the event two years before—but Chartrand's face grew red. "I insist you claim your prize, Trent. You won in all fairness."

"But for a game I didn't know I was about to play." He quirked a brow. "I've decided to try a novel entertainment this year. I've promised my fidelity. And I'm sure any other gentleman here would be delighted to aid in the demonstration. Perhaps you should let Rosalyn choose the cock that most intrigues her."

All the women—except Venetia—tittered at that. It meant a competition. A display of male attributes, with invitations to bring the cocks to attention.

Lydia took up the cry. "Mr. Wembly posses an astonishing piece of equipment—one that would startle a horse. Perhaps Miss Rose should test her skill with that challenge. Not—" Marcus groaned as Lydia turned her radiant smile on him. "Not that you are not generously endowed, my lord Trent, but since you refuse . . ."

"Unless you're too foxed, Wembly," Brude called out.

Downing yet another glass of French red wine, Wembly stood with a slight stagger. "Never. The tipstaff has never failed me yet." He stalked toward Rosalyn, unbuttoning as he went.

Wagers began to make their way down the table. Brude began. "A hundred guineas he doesn't last for more than five minutes. The dear girl possesses remarkable suction."

"The liquor will make him slower, more insensate," mused Swansborough. "I say he'll outlast her."

Lydia gave a wicked smile. "Two hundred that our host claims privilege of rank and thrusts himself between Rosalyn's lips before the deed is done on Mr. Wembly."

Brude grunted. "Someone should record these."

Lady Chartrand summoned a quill and paper.

"Are you certain you don't wish to play, Lord Trent?" Lydia goaded. "I do love the sight of your magnificent cock."

Marcus heard Venetia's spoon clatter to her plate. Now would be the time to search Lydia's room for the manuscript but he couldn't leave Venetia alone in here. He would whisk her up to their rooms and lock her in, safe, for the night.

He scrubbed a hand over his jaw. *Ten bloody thousand.* His father would have hired someone to slit Lydia's throat. Likely why she'd never pushed before. Smug Lydia Harcourt believed she had him by the ballocks. He would show her just how wrong she was.

He glanced down the table to Venetia. Her mask shielded much, but her scarlet-painted lips were so expressive. Firm, tense, slightly turned down. Unhappy. Did she want to flee? All he wanted to do was take her up to his room.

Venetia caught herself staring at Marcus' face, at his beautiful profile gilded by candlelight. He caught her staring, too. As her face flamed behind the protective mask, he smiled gently.

He had refused his prize.

Had he refused because he had truly reformed, as he'd

claimed? Folly to think it was a sense of loyalty—or fidelity—to her. After all, he planned to send her home after tonight. Then, without the rigors of their masquerade weighing on him, he'd probably indulge in all the carnal delights on offer.

Cheers from the table warned that Rosalyn Rose and Wembly had begun their display. Yes, she was terribly curious about how a woman was supposed to delight a man with her mouth but she wasn't certain she wished to watch. Still, if she turned tail and ran, she would regret it. She wanted to find out just who she was—a prim country maiden or a wickedly sensual woman. She was determined to experience adventure.

Chartrand rose from his seat again. "Before Rosalyn begins to explain the mysteries of her technique, I must remind you of the delights on offer tonight. A Turkish theme in the ballroom. Cards and hazard in the east drawing room. Tomorrow night, if this blasted rain eases, the scavenger hunt will begin. But also tonight, for the more intrepid, there are scenes to take one to the darkest depths of lust. True torment beyond the usual bland birch work and ropes and whippings."

It would be like a night spent caught in a Belzique picture. Was she ready for that?

Lord Swansborough gave a lazy laugh. "Nothing like the depths of degradation amidst the height of luxury."

Venetia shivered. A cruel self-mocking note lay beneath the calm, casual tone. Not only did Swansborough look like the devil, he apparently liked to live in a hell of his own making.

Unease slithered through her, raising goose bumps on her skin. In her pictures, dark rogues were saved, but this was reality.

Chartrand clapped again and silence descended. Against her better judgement but consumed by curiosity, Venetia glanced up. Wembly was now sprawled on the sumptuous chair of red velvet, his trousers opened. Rosalyn straddled his thighs. She held her hair back with one hand and his monstrous cock upright with her other.

Heat raced through Venetia. Her breathing quickened.

"For many men, perhaps even all, this is their favorite sex act," Rosalyn began, in clear strident tones as though she was lecturing at a Royal Society gathering. "Your tongue can control the caresses in ways your passages cannot. Some men will be passive. Others will hold your head still and thrust deeply into you. To take such penetration is an acquired skill—"

She stopped there and abruptly took Wembly into her mouth. To the very hilt. Wearing a smug smile, Wembly held a glass of port in one hand and fondled Rosalyn's head with the other.

Rosalyn released him. "Many men like to hear a woman gag over their prick and like to see watering eyes. Makes them believe they are very large."

This brought laughter once more, wild drunken laughter. Wine with dinner, now port and sherry. No wonder.

"Bloody well get on with it," Mr. Wembly demanded.

"Of course, sir." Rosalyn replied and her head began to bob upon him. Her cheeks hollowed. Venetia heard soft slurping sounds, sounds she remembered from doing this very thing to Marcus—

Even though the displays aroused her, her every thought centered on Marcus. She glanced over at him. He kicked back his chair and stood, his gaze locked on hers.

She wanted him. But did she dare here amidst the wildness of Chartrand's games? She thought of the bold auburn courtesan in her theatre picture and desire sizzled through her.

She stood too, aware of all eyes turning to them, but she only looked at him.

Chartrand's robust voice resonated. "I think it is time to retire to the ballroom."

* * *

"I wish to at least see this—we will be here for only one night. I want one naughty night."

As Marcus frowned, Venetia worried he would never allow it. "Are you certain, sweeting?" he asked. He lifted her hand for a kiss. "You did not look happy at dinner."

"I was afraid you might choose Rosalyn."

"Were you? She doesn't tempt me, love." He tucked her hand in the crook of his arm and led her to the open ballroom doors. Light and heat spilled out. Most other guests were inside but a dozen pretty young courtesans in various states of undress were still making their giggling way through the doors.

His brows drew together, his mouth firmed. "I do not intend to let you take part."

She stroked his forearm, tense beneath his sleeve. "I just want to see what happens, just for a little while."

Venetia had never attended a ton ball but had heard they were crushes. Chartrand's bacchanalia was the same. Around the perimeter of the ballroom, handsome gentlemen flirted gallantly with beautiful women. But then they passed through the crowd and stepped into sin.

Pillows, chaises, sofas were everywhere. Lady Yardley reclined on a gold chaise. Lord Brude kneeled at her side, nude. England's most romantic poet wore not a stitch. Dark hair dusted his lean legs, his strong arms. She could see his firm, slightly furry derriere. He and another nude man were suckling Lady Yardley's breasts.

Venetia moaned softly as Marcus' hand slid lower on her back, to caress her bottom. He propelled her to a divan piled with silk pillows—one nestled between two soaring columns. "A safe place to observe the fun."

She was trembling. Aroused? Curious? A little embarrassed? All of those things. She sank into the embroidered chaise, unable to tear her gaze from the men at her ladyship's breasts. The second man lifted from his task, cried, "Such magnificent tits. I wish to be smothered by them!"

Lady Yardley spanked his tight buttocks with her fan and he dropped to his work once more.

Venetia gasped as both men's hands slid up her ladyship's legs, pushing up her skirts. Those two hands began stroking the countess' nether regions together while their cheeks hollowed with the force of their suckling. Lady Yardley moaned and slapped indiscriminately with her fan.

Marcus dropped to his knees before her, lowering his head to her clothed breasts. "To make it clear you belong to me. And because I hunger to do this." He ran his tongue over taut silk, circling her puckered nipples.

"People can see." She spoke out of instinct, out of an upbringing of propriety.

"That is the point of an orgy, my dear. To be aroused by other's excitement."

"I know. I am aroused, but I feel strange to be a spectacle. But it is exciting. Don't stop." People were watching. Men looked at them. A group of tittering ladybirds cast interested glances at Marcus, rubbing their cunnies. Some were already naked, others had their skirts pulled up.

Marcus lifted his mouth from her breasts. He brushed back rakishly tousled hair, blue-black as the night sky. Her dress was soaked over her nipples from his mouth.

Heady scents filled the room—burning wax, lush perfumes, and the intoxicating scent of sensual excitement. The room stank of it and it made her wet and fragrant too.

Marcus kissed the swell of her breasts, bare above her neckline. Wantonly, she grasped his hand, pulled it to caress her cunny through her skirts.

Over Marcus' dark, thick hair bent at her breasts, she saw Mr. Wembly drop his drawers. He laughingly bent over a hard-surfaced platform as Trixie Jones, the courtesan who had played the pianoforte, spanked him with a paddle. His white buttocks turned pink with the jade's determined smacks. Trixie was nude, but wrapped in bizarre leather straps—like a Belzique heroine. Her pert breasts jiggled as she punished Mr. Wembly.

Lord Chartrand came up behind her, brandishing a riding crop and an enormous, glistening wand. Trixie stopped flogging to hold her bum cheeks apart, crying out as Chartrand slid the dildo into her bottom. The marquess thrust and pushed until the entire impossible length disappeared, striking Trixie's rear with the riding crop as he worked. His face was flushed, his breathing fierce.

Venetia ground her quim against Marcus' palm, spreading her legs, needing pleasure . . .

She spied a tangle of bodies sprawled over pillows. Diaphanous skirts fluttered, women screamed, hard-muscled male bottoms heaved.

Venetia tried to look everywhere at once. The noble war hero, the Duke of Montberry, still dressed, sprawled on a sofa to avidly watch Lady Chartrand and Rosalyn Rose as they kissed each other's cunnies. Lady and courtesan lay side by side, mouth to cunny, moaning and nuzzling. Lady Yardley summoned a footman to her side from the group of spectators—handsome, muscular, he wore his livery, but no wig atop his dark curls. Now he alone feasted on her magnificent breasts as he released his large cock. Her ladyship moaned in pure rapture as she ran both hands up and down his thick shaft.

Sex surrounded her. Enticed her. Her quim clenched with each moan, each cry, each shriek. She was panting. Venetia glanced down as Marcus coaxed one of her breasts out of her bodice. His body shielded her, no one could see, but suddenly she didn't care if they could. She was melting with pleasure, grasping at Marcus' shoulders. She wanted him to pump on her the way she saw men doing to women. She wanted to be crying out in ecstasy. She wanted Marcus' thick, beautiful cock inside—

Arms linked, three women raced over to their chaise.

Marcus quickly eased her bodice up, covering her tingling breast, her hard nipple, before he turned.

"My lord!" the girls squealed. They giggled and batted their lashes at him.

"We wish to introduce your Vixen to naughty girls' games," they chorused. "To the pretty pleasures of women's breasts and quims and licking tongues."

They all wore nightgowns of transparent silks that clung to round breasts and crested over erect rouged nipples. One was willowy and tall, her chocolate brown hair loose and brushed straight. It swayed over her generous bottom. Her bush of abundant dark nether hair was visible through her thin gown. The smallest was the fairest blonde, with neatly pinned curls and enormous blue eyes, a nipped-in waist and full, large breasts—almost the size of soup tureens. Honey-gold hair spilled over the shoulders of the third, and she flashed almond-shaped eyes at Marcus.

Each carried different wands but Venetia couldn't help lifting her gaze from the assortment of toys to their sumptuous bodies. She remembered how her breasts had enjoyed Lydia Harcourt's attentions even as she'd been shocked at first . . .

"But please, my lord," cried the tallest, the brunette. "First you must stuff our cunnies and arses. We've been told you are dedicated to your Vixen, so we can only pretend these dildoes are your enormous cock!"

CHAPTER NINE

Venetia was enraptured with this game. If it were a painting, she could call it . . . *The Lord Stuffs the Giggling Jades*, for the women tittered like schoolgirls as they held up the wands and dildoes they wished him to use.

Venetia's face burned—as did her quim, her breasts, her very soul. Embarrassment warred with excitement.

Did she dare let him play? Could she stop him?

"It would amuse Vixen and me to watch you fill yourselves, my dears." His drawl sent shivers through her, delicious shivers.

Venetia caught her breath as Marcus elegantly lowered his firm rear onto her chaise, stretched his arm alongside her legs. Three bosomy, seductive women had offered themselves to him, yet for her, he'd refused. Raw desire glowed in his eyes as he shared a look with her. "Is this what you wish?" he asked softly. "A little adventure?"

Heart in her throat, she nodded. Her hand rested on her hip, he slid his fingers over hers.

In the soft light of the ballroom—the chandeliers were not all lit—the three women had the softness of a painting. As one they whisked off their nightdresses, exposing smooth, creamy naked skin. All three were unique—hips, breasts, legs, faces entirely different—yet each was beautiful. No wonder men sought to explore many lovers, for each woman's body was a novel adventure.

And then they began to kiss. With painted mouths open and pouting, the women kissed each other's lips, necks, breasts, leaving streaks of scarlet cream on fragile skin. Pretty sighs rose up. The girl with the china shepherdess coloring clutched her friends' heads to her enormous breasts. Dainty hands cupped the large mounds, lifting the nipples to hungry mouths.

The blonde's nipples were brown beneath the paint, and grew to an astonishing length. The girls used their teeth, stroking small white teeth along the thick jutting nipples.

For a fleeting moment, Venetia stiffened as Marcus bent to her breasts, but she was on fire as well, and desire consumed modesty. She held him there, hand on his warm, strong neck. Moaning. Lost to all but sensation. His mouth on her clothed breasts stoked and soothed the burning need. He lifted his head as the blonde squatted with her legs parted. The dark-haired girl winked at Marcus. "I am going to cram this toy into Sukey's cunt, my lord." She gave a curtsy. "I am Lizzie." She pointed at the honey blonde, who put a wand to her lips and licked it. "That is Kate."

And with the introductions made, Lizzie began to push the dildo she held between Sukey's thighs. She did so from the side, so Marcus could watch, and Sukey prettily played between the curls with each slow thrust. The thing was monstrous—it appeared to be a foot in length.

Venetia felt her quim pulse as each inch disappeared. Each throb was agonizing, demanding, and she thought of Marcus' beautiful cock . . .

"And now for her arse," Lizzie announced. She took the wand that Kate's mouth had wetted. Sukey bent over to display her nude rear, Kate licked her nipples and held the other thing in place as Lizzie invaded Sukey's tight rump.

"Oh, yes, yes," Sukey moaned as she was stuffed completely full. Both toys were enormous, she must be painfully stretched, but she appeared to be in utter delight. She immediately attended to Lizzie, and then Kate, slid the wands inside both girls' rears and pussies. Kate took the shortest but fattest wand inside her rump. Shaped like the bulbous decoration on a newel post, the entire thing popped inside her, with only the base exposed. Lizzie waggled her derriere in front of Marcus—which meant it was in front of her face as well. The toy inside Lizzie was the longest and half of it stuck out of her rump, swaying back and forth.

Eyes glued on the sight, Venetia felt Marcus move her hand. Wool brushed her palm, heat and hardness filled it. He'd pressed her hand to his rigid cock.

"Oh, I do love to have a big cock in me arse," Lizzie exclaimed.

Sukey had hold of each of her dildoes and was thrusting them into herself. Her face was red, her eyes glazed.

"Ye're not to come yet!" Lizzie cried, but it was too late. On her feet, hands clutching the rods buried in her, Sukey climaxed. She rocked with it, screamed with it, and when it was done, she fought to catch her breath. She sashayed over toward the divan, her breasts jiggling, her hips swaying as she sought to keep her toys inside as she walked. Sweat gleamed on her skin, and the ripe, exotic fragrance of her pleasure teased the air.

She held out her hands. "Join us, Vixen."

Venetia's heart pounded. To join a scandalous sex scene? Did she dare?

Her gaze met Marcus'. What she saw made the juice flow lushly from her pussy. Lust and desire, but there was a deeper fire in his eyes as he looked at her.

"What is your desire, my sweet? I would love to watch you have a sexual adventure. And this one would be . . . safe."

Safe because it did not involve men? The lure was there, the three women with dildoes within, squirming and sighing, the lure to have an adventure. With his permission. The choice.

And she wanted to be, if only for one night, a truly sensual artist.

"Yes," she whispered.

"But I forbid the use of toys on Vixen," Marcus instructed.

Kate clapped her hands. In an instant she was on her knees. Venetia watched as Kate parted her legs wide, Marcus moved to give room. To feel a woman's soft hands on her thighs . . . it was titillating. Shocking. Thrilling. So different from his strong, rougher hands.

She felt embarrassed as Kate's long fingers touched her nether lips and felt the dew there. "Oh, she's ever so slick!" Kate's shout made her blush more.

The golden curls spilled over her belly as Kate drew her lips apart to expose her clit. Kate gave it a good looking over, and Venetia let her head lay back, too shocked to look now. She closed her eyes. As Kate parted her lips more, the tug pleasured her hard, tingling clit. Cooler air washed over it. She opened her legs wider, wantonly displaying herself.

"Such a lovely cunny."

Was it? Venetia opened her eyes, to find Lizzie standing close, her cunny mere inches from her face. She saw the thick black rod sticking out from between Lizzie's glistening nether lips. Lips a darker red than hers—a purplish red. She inhaled the scent of Lizzie's juices. She became aware of Marcus' hand on her thigh—she knew it to be his without even looking. Two hands stroked her legs—his large, rough masculine one and Kate's delicate one.

Wet pressure slid around it. Kate's tongue! Luxuriant, loving, caressing. Then suckling. In such a wonderful rhythm that her every inhibition spiraled away. She stroked Lizzie's thigh. Daring herself to touch the curls, the fake cock. But Lizzie spun, presenting her derriere and the large dildo.

"Would ye hold that between your lips, Vixen? And let me thrust upon it?"

So close she could smell Lizzie's bottom—a ripe scent that excited. She realized that this toy also was carved to look like a cock on this end. She could hold it in her mouth, pretend she was sucking Marcus—

Oh! She had to moan at Kate's wonderful sucking. Fingers touched her. Large fingers. Marcus playing between her thighs while Kate licked. Naughty! But she could be the young lady in *The Page Turner*. A cock in her mouth while mouths and fingers played in her quim.

Sukey, on hands and knees, wriggled between Lizzie's spread legs. She got up on her haunches to pull down Venetia's bodice. With a good tug, Sukey tore the seams. Venetia gasped as her breasts popped out, then Sukey bent, ice-blond hair tumbling, sucked her left nipple, and robustly pinched the right. But Lizzie thrust her bum back, offering the long white cock, and Venetia opened her mouth. She caught the end of the dildo inside and held it with her teeth.

"Christ Jesus," Marcus muttered.

It became a mad, delirious, lovely tangle of bodies, of pretty moans, husky groans.

Lizzie's derriere pushed back and she had to hold the cock tight, to let Lizzie pleasure herself. The jade had a lovely bottom, full and smooth and round. It quivered as she rocked. To have her mouth so close to it—

Venetia reached up, to control Lizzie, and the girl grasped her fingers, dragged her hand to Lizzie's wet cunny. There she pushed the other rod in and out, gasping and sighing around the one in her mouth.

Her gaze shot about the room. To the tangle of bodies on the floor and their moans. To Chartrand, who led a blond woman by chains attached to her nipples and quim. To Lady Yardley, who sucked young Cole while John fucked her wildly from behind.

Pleasure rose, swelled, and she knew she was about to—

A finger teased her bottom. Kate's? Or Marcus'? All she knew was she wanted it inside. She bounced on it to take it in. Slowly her anus opened, the length filled her. Spiraling within to tease tight walls, her stretched rim.

Mouths on her nipples and quim. Two fingers in her anus—
moving with different rhythms at different times! Kate's tongue
lapping, while she bounced on the two dildoes inside her.
And Lizzie screaming, coming, drenching the black cock and
her hand. Lizzie's climax ignited Kate, who sucked her clit
throughout her release, and Sukey came too, squeezing her
nipples.

Venetia felt her senses overload. Felt glorious tension arc
through her, burst, and her orgasm exploded. Her teeth
clenched around the cock in her mouth, she sucked at it as
she came, salivating around it, loving having it in her mouth.
Her dutiful lovers licked at cunny and nipples and the pleasure racked her endlessly.

The little death! How she understood! Her cunny and clit
pulsed, her nipples stood as tall as they could. And she
moaned and whimpered around the cock between her lips.

Finally, she slumped back, and the other girls tumbled
against the divan. They sighed and panted like she did, and
she floated in communal ecstasy.

Then, all four of them together looked to Marcus. He still
wore his evening dress—though sweat trickled into his cravat. Venetia realized that she'd been so captivated with her
pleasure, she'd forgotten him and his rigid cock. Four women
had climaxed in front of him—he must be in the most intense
sexual agony.

Kate and Lizzie reached for the buttons on his trousers.
Four slender hands, and two enthusiastic mouths. But he
shook his head. "No, angels. I wish to share private pleasures
with my Vixen."

How could he turn down such a delight?

The girls pouted, but got to their feet, gathered their discarded dresses, their used toys. They quickly surrounded another dark-haired man. Lord Swansborough. "Let us wash
our toys," Lizzie said, "And then let us whip you with three
sets of tits!"

But what private pleasures did Marcus want? He got to his

feet, adjusted the placket of his trousers with a groan. "Come upstairs with me, Venetia."

She smoothed down her bunched skirts. "To protect me from more?"

"No, because I want to spend the rest of this night with you. Only you."

As Marcus locked the door of her room and Venetia undid the strings of her mask, guilt rose. And propriety. "You must think me . . . w—wanton for what I did. It's improper. I'm improper."

"Sweetheart, I don't think there is anything improper about a healthy enjoyment of sex." Rumbling, low, suggestive, Marcus' voice rippled over her. His scent wrapped around her. Her senses sang as he stood in front of her, cradled her cheek. His signet ring gleamed, cool against her heated skin. His gloves were already discarded on her bed.

"But you wouldn't marry a woman who wasn't a virgin." Why had she said that? It had been his concern all along. Losing her virginity. Now, he would think she pictured him in a marriage. To her. She didn't. Preposterous.

"Let us not talk about marriage," he murmured. "Or propriety. Tonight is your night of pleasure. Tell me what you want."

"You with me . . . inside me. I saw couples rutting in the ballroom, saw the men plunging deeply into the women. I know that is what I want. Kissing and licking is lovely, but I ache to be filled." She reached out and let her fingertips trail over his swollen cock. His eyes shut at her touch, his mouth tightened. "You need your release, don't you?"

"I won't be a slave to my cock, love." He turned her, kissed the back of her neck, his mouth hot and silken on her skin, the touch of his hands so familiar now on her back. He dispensed with the row of buttons in agonizing moments, nibbling her nape all the while. Truly, her limbs felt as frothy as the syllabub. "I can't go inside your cunny, sweeting. I won't tear your maidenhead. But there is a way for us to make love but preserve your virginity."

A shiver of anticipation coiled along her spine as he brushed one fallen curl aside. "If you trust me, I would like to pleasure you through your bottom."

The warmth of the room caressed her back as he slid the gown off her shoulders. Silk slithered over the curve of her hips, to pool at her feet.

"But are you certain you trust me enough?"

"I do trust you, Marcus." And she did. Yet this man had thwarted all her plans. Her plan to paint. Her plan to deal with Lydia. He'd stolen her independence away. Yet she trusted him.

His hand cupped over her hip, warm and large, bunching her thin shift. "That means very much to me, Venetia."

He knew what to say, her rake. But she knew not to believe in romantic sentiment.

He tugged the ties of her corset loose. "Take off your shift but leave your garters and stockings on for now."

No. In this she would be independent and she wanted to be completely naked. Lifting her foot to the edge of his bed, she rolled down garter and silk stocking in slow, seductive motions. She hoped she looked truly tempting.

At his raised brow, she murmured, "I want to be nude for you. To be completely unclothed is . . . exciting. Naughty." Even in her art, her participants were never entirely naked. Stockings remained on the women and often the men were fully dressed, only revealing their staffs.

He dropped to one knee, hooked his finger in her other garter. It would be so easy to be enthralled by the intimacy, to forget he was a lofty earl and she a scandalous artist.

No, that couldn't be forgotten. Not ever.

In a heartbeat, she was a nude artist. She stepped out of her last stocking, her best gossamer-fine stockings. He drew the filmy fabric across his lips. It looked like a mask, made him look even more dangerous.

"Undress me," he invited as he let the stocking flutter to the carpet.

How could she deny such a request? But he didn't let her do it alone. He opened the buttons at the top of his ivory waistcoat as she worked at the bottom. On tiptoe, she could reach the knot at his cravat but she fell against his chest as she attempted to undo it. Laughing, he righted her, then loosened it.

Like a dutiful mistress, she took the folded length of fabric and smoothed it over her bare arm. It smelled of his starch and sandalwood and his skin, the delicious skin of his neck. Venetia couldn't resist stroking it against her cheek, a silly thing to do.

His breath sucked in sharply. Quick motions freed the buttons of his cuffs. Then, one by one, the buttons of his shirt slipped open. He hadn't worn boots over his trousers, just shoes, and these he kicked off easily.

She reached out to the buttons fastening his trousers. The back of her hand skimmed along the ridge of his erection and they groaned softly together.

Fire warmth filled the room, kept her from getting chilled, even as she stood naked and watched him slide his trousers down, revealing strong, muscular magnificent thighs dusted with dark hairs. His gaze never left her . . . nipples? Or her face? She wasn't quite certain. Her nipples stood erect, flushed a deep red. She had to admit they were fascinating to watch as her breasts bobbed and swayed.

Her proportions couldn't begin to compare to Lydia's ample endowment, and though fashion favored small breasts and willowy shapes, she knew most men did not.

He hooked his thumb into his linens and drew them down. Kicked them away. He took hold of his prick, cocked his hips forward, and stroked the thick length. No doubt he admired it. As did she. She was a virgin who'd seen more male members than she could count—in pictures—and now, tonight, she'd seen dozens in rampant, naked glory.

But none were as beautiful as his. The erotic sight of his hand on his cock made her whimper.

Marcus licked his lips. The soft, intimate smile vanished. He looked predatory. Large, male, and dangerous.

For twenty-four years, she'd lived in strict propriety, not raising a ripple of scandal, but, as bold as a jade, she strutted in front of her lovely bed. Then she blushed, and hid her face.

Marcus levered up onto her bed, landing in the middle with a bounce. Beneath the green canopy, his eyes became a richer turquoise. Amusement glowed in them as he held out his hand. "Climb aboard, temptress."

The mattress dipped as she crawled to his side. With one arm beneath his head as a pillow, he reached out in invitation. She tumbled on top, and he pulled her into his commanding kiss. She met his open mouth with her lips parted, dueled her tongue with his. Her hands roamed—over solid chest, hard nipples, tracing the beautiful planes of ribs and muscle.

She let her fingers play over his stiff cock, touching stickiness and finding a damp trail on the curls below his navel. Wrapping her hand around him, she gently squeezed. Her hand barely closed around him, her fingernails grazed the soft heel of her hand.

She bent, enticed by his scent, by the fascinating beauty of his cock, and explored with her tongue. So velvety, but hard. A luscious taste—his fluid sour, the light hint of his urine, and such a heady scent. She flicked her tongue over veins, along its intriguing spine. Then stopped.

He groaned as though in pain. "Don't stop now, my sweet." His lids half-covered his eyes, his mouth tense. Sharp lines framed his lips, deep sexy lines. Dark stubble shadowed his jaw.

Her heart lurched in her chest as she gazed at his handsome face. "But am I doing it as I should? As good as Rosalyn?"

"Rosalyn is a professional. You, my dear, are a goddess."

Venetia kissed the tip, licking up the salty, rich fluid there. "You aren't in pain, are you?"

"Repeated erections without relief cause a lot of pain. Nature's way of encouraging a man to get on with it and make love to a woman."

"I want you to make love to me—the way you said."

He slid off the bed and she watched him walk across the room, to the box of toys on the secretary. The sheets were heavenly soft against her bare skin. He rifled through the box as her breathing sped up.

"What are you looking for?" she asked.

"This." What he held between his fingers was too small for her to see.

He lifted the candle that stood there. The flame licked toward him as he carried it.

"Are you going to put it out?"

"No, light another. I want to see you, temptress." He lifted the white taper from the brass holder and put the wick to the candle on the bedside table. It sputtered and caught. Two flames from one fire.

Even the way he dripped the wax to the saucer on the table was elegant. Hot, white, molten droplets splattered. He set the base of the candle into the puddle. Then he sat on the edge of the bed. "Do you know I was so jaded I once visited a woman who bound me up and dripped hot wax on my chest."

She shouldn't be shocked—she'd seen Belzique's pictures—but she was. Marcus seemed to be waiting for her reaction. He stroked the sheets beside her shoulder, plucking at the cream silk, not touching her. As though he would not dare touch her until she spoke.

Even with the candlelight, she couldn't see his shadowed eyes.

Keeping her voice even, she asked, "And that was arousing?"

"Not in the least. Highly recommended by Swansborough

but I didn't see the fun myself. But I was willing to try anything."

She glanced at the candles. "You don't want me to drip
wax on your person do you?"

He smiled ruefully. "Never, Venetia. And I'd never hurt
you." He turned his hand palm side up. A glass vial rested
there. "Oil. To ready you for me. Are still willing to trust me?"

CHAPTER TEN

"Of course, I trust you, Marcus. You've protected me, denied yourself pleasure to be with me." From beneath a tumble of sherry-red curls, Venetia's hazel eyes glowed with innocence.

"Denied myself pleasure?" Mystified, Marcus repeated what she'd said, trying to understand it. "I've denied myself nothing." He hadn't meant it to sound curt. Abrupt. Surprise showed in her eyes, confusion in the tremble of her lip.

Silk whispered as he drew the sheets down from her body, displaying her like an exquisite work of art. Dropping them in a puddle just below her feet, he bent and kissed her expressive mouth. Her fingers slid up into his hair.

But she broke the kiss. Her bare breasts rose and fell with frantic breaths. "What do I do?"

"Turn over and display your lovely bottom to me."

She rolled over onto her tummy, onto folded arms. Golden light bathed her plump cheeks, her smooth, full thighs. Shadows enhanced the curve of her spine.

He held the vial of oil under the candle's flame until the glass was warm to his touch. He drew it back, flicked open the stopper. A spicy scent filled the room.

"Mmmm." Venetia breathed in and squirmed seductively on the bed. He watched her lush derriere sway over the shimmering sheets and his throat parched.

She knew how to tempt. She knew it instinctively.

Marcus tested the oil with his baby finger, which actually shook. His heart had never pounded so hard before sex. Tipping the vial, he watched a droplet gather, then fall. It splattered on the shadowy cleft beneath Venetia's cheeks, rolled into the warm, dewy valley

He parted her cheeks, revealing her puckered entrance, tightly closed. He poured a stream of oil there. It flashed like molten gold and she arched her hips off the bed with a happy squeal.

"Oh, that tickles!"

He massaged the oil, circling and stroking until her muscles relaxed enough to let his fingertip within. A considerate lover would start slowly with the first finger, working with great patience to ready her . . .

She twisted to look at him. Lust and need and a plea for more burned in those entrancing eyes. He winked as he straddled her smooth thighs.

"Now?" she whispered. So much tension in her voice.

"Relax, temptress." A caress of his hand down her spine and she purred once more. "There will be pain, because of your innocence, but it will vanish, and you will know the most exquisite pleasure. My experience," he added wryly, "has to be good for something."

That left her bewildered, he saw. Braced on his arm, he stretched out, balancing his weight. His cock bumped her slippery cheeks. Blood drained from his brain, filling his prick to bursting.

He rasped, "Touch yourself."

Her hips lifted, her slender hand slid along silk sheets, dove down between her thighs. "I'm soaked," she confided.

God, yes. "Stroke your clit as I enter you. The pleasure there will ease any pain. I'll start with fingers—"

"I want your cock."

Her bold words set him on fire. He fought for control.

Her leg slid up the sheets, knee bent, as his finger went

deep. In and out into her tight heat until it was swallowed up to the last knuckle. Over the spiciness of oil, the smoky scent of the crackling fire, Marcus breathed in the musk of her pussy, the earthy scent of her ass.

Venetia rubbed her fingers over her quim. "Oh! When I stroke myself as you do that—it's wonderful!" She was grinding her finger over her clit—no shyness about touching herself. He dared to try two fingers.

She arched her head back and moaned. Her tumbling curls shivered over her back, glinting red and gold like flickering flame. On a whimper, she took both his fingers in.

He shouldn't do this—he could pleasure her with his mouth. His cock throbbed but—

"Oh, it's good now."

All the air squeezed from his chest. He pumped his fingers in and out with slow, steady strokes, her muscles clutching him tight. His throat was raw from panting as he fucked her derriere with his fingers. She was slick and open now.

Ready for more.

Three fingers. Almost the thickness of his cock.

He'd expected her to lay still, to be cautious and demure. Instead she thrust her bottom up to him, sawed her fingers against her pussy, turned and clawed tangled hair from her face. God, he'd no idea she would be so driven by lust. So wild.

Heavy-lidded, her eyes burned with lust. "Give me your cock," she moaned. "I want you inside. Oh, please."

Bone-hard, his cock hurt as he pushed it down, forcing it to touch her slick, hot entrance. He had to pause, his hand on her bottom, to steady himself. But she drove back into him, almost bending his cock for one excruciating instant before the head surged by the tight rim with a pop. Pleasure roared over him like a flame. He heard her cry, his deep groan of heartfelt pleasure.

He drew back, pulling his throbbing tip back to her rim. Not enough to withdraw, enough to let her grow used to him. His biceps bulged, his forearm was rigid with the strain of supporting his weight.

"Move with me, temptress," he urged, "Rock with me."

There was no shake of her head. No plea that he stop. He eased in, one more delightful inch. Then another. Her moans encouraged. She began to chant, "Yes, yes, oh yes."

Yes. Muscles quivering, he gave slow fluid strokes.

Her curvaceous bottom was in the air, her legs splayed, her pose receptive. Welcoming. Three long thrusts and his cock was buried deep, engulfed in fire and velvet. His groin struck her cushioning cheeks with each plunge. She cried loud with every thrust.

She wrapped her hand delicately around his forearm, slid down and found his hand. Her fingers, sticky with the rich honey from her quim, twined with his.

It was his undoing.

His controlled veneer fell away like his dripping sweat. He thrust like his goddamned life depended on it. His mouth twisted with grunts, growls, and fierce moans. His sweat rolled down his brow, coated his back, ran down to his lips.

Beneath him, Venetia was a wanton, fiercely pounding her bottom along his prick, ravaging her quim with one hand, holding his fingers with the other. Even half-mad as he was, crazed with the fight not to come, even as he hovered on the brink of orgasm, he reached down, joined his hand with hers at her pussy and rubbed her clit.

She screamed his name. Shattered beneath him. Inside her scotching derriere, her muscles clutched at him. *Control, control, control.* He clung to the mantra as he watched her come. Exquisite. Beautiful.

Between her thighs, her hand stilled and he knew she was feeling the climax pulse around her fingers.

The thought had him almost over the edge.

He drew his hands away from hers, splayed them on the bed as he slowly withdrew. His cock twanged upwards once free, glistening in the candlelight, drenched in oil.

She turned her face to the side. Tears spilled on her cheeks but a smile touched her lips. His heart lurched. Damp with sweat, her red hair spilled over her shoulders, a wash of dark fire over perfect, flushed curves. Her eyes were dreamy. As though he'd given her a glimpse of heaven.

"It was so . . . so intimate, so perfect having you inside."

"I want to make it even more intimate, Venetia." He stroked the sensual curve of her naked back, unwilling to stop. He didn't want this to end. "I want to do more. I understand if you don't want to. If you need to rest."

"More intimate? Of course I want to try!"

Venetia reached out for Marcus' hand again. Could anything be more intimate? She caressed his long, elegant fingers. Traced the large knuckles, felt the pattern of raised veins, the dusting of soft hairs. How she loved his hands, and it had been scandalous magic to hold his hand to her quim.

Yes, she was tired, floating on a cloud of sweet sensual pleasure, but how could she resist being more intimate with him?

"What will we do?"

"First, angel, you must roll onto your back."

She did as he asked, sighing as her damp back and bottom sank into the soft mattress. "Are you going to . . ." She shrank from the word. "Are you going to fuck my quim?"

His eyes, that mysterious blend of blue and green, burned brighter at her words. "No, sweet, but I want to look into your eyes when we make love. Trust again, if you can give it."

Why did he fear she wouldn't? What had he done with women—or what had they done with him—to make him so cautious?

Then he was on top, his big body pushing her lightly into the bed. This was glorious, having the chance to touch and explore, to follow the long curve of his spine. She squeezed his buttocks, giggling as he made them rock hard, then soft enough to pinch.

"Will you let me lift your legs?"

Baffled, she nodded. Then gasped as he gripped her ankles and bent her legs back until her feet were at her head. He opened her legs wide until her muscles tugged and complained. Could she do this? "Now, hold the backs of your thighs."

She held tight, feeling her muscles stretch. She'd never imagined such an exposed position, her quim and bottom on display, her belly bulging where it curved. Did she truly look sensual like this?

She must. His cock was still a rigid pole standing before the black curls on his stomach.

Hand on his cock he approached. He stroked the thick head against her anus. She shivered, tried to let muscles go slack, tried to open her body for him.

She touched her clit, stroked with her finger and saw stars. Caught it between two fingers, gasping at the jolt of pleasure as he pushed, gently, slowly. With lashes lowered, he watched himself go inside. She could see the thick veined shaft disappear. She felt the pressure, the delicious fullness.

Then he was inside her, his cock deeply inside, his ballocks bumping against her bottom. This truly was more intimate. His expressions were exposed to her. She saw his eyes hot with lust as he drew back and sank in again. His jaw went slack, his lips parted, lines framed his mouth. His face became a portrait of sensual agony.

She stopped rasping her clit, leaving it throbbing and aching. Ran her fingertips along his shadowed jaw, her thumb over his lower lip. On his upper lip, she found sweat, and stroked it away. He stopped his thrusts to kiss her fingers. "Rub my kiss over your clit."

She obeyed and he pumped into her, his hands bracing her legs. She was stretched to the limit. But she begged for him to thrust harder, even as she saw that the gentlemanly veneer had vanished. This was a man, a man driven by lust. With a man's raw strength and his primitive need to be buried deep. She should be frightened.

But it drove her too. The need to fuck. Venetia wanted him wild. Rough. Uncontrolled.

Goodness, her bottom was slick, her cheeks slapping him.

His teeth grazed his lower lip making him look so vulnerable. As new to this world as she.

The need to touch consumed. To massage bunched shoulders, taut biceps, steely forearms. To explore matted curls on his chest. To caress harsh cheekbones.

His thrusts lifted her from the bed. Their wild dance banged the headboard against the wall. Above them, the canopy rocked, the tassels shook and swung wildly. Could it fall?

She didn't care. She felt bent in two, but didn't care. She grabbed for his hip to hold him to her. To pull him deep, impossibly deep. Each pound of his groin against her bottom sent sparks through her. With two fingers, she ravaged her poor clit, astonished she could be so rough, and it could be so good.

Another stroke. Another—

"I'm going to come," she cried. Why the urgent need to tell him? But she had to. Over and over, she moaned, "Yes, yes, yes."

The excitement in his eyes urged her on.

In amazement, in delight, she plunged her fingers between her nether lips, pressed her clit hard. The orgasm took her, stinging and fierce. It flooded her heart, her head, her soul, swamped her with delight. Her breath left her. Her thoughts fled.

His name. Hazily she heard his name shouted up to the canopy.

All she clung to was Marcus and pleasure, holding him tight as her body came apart, as she soared in ecstasy.

So lost in her delicious whirling climax, she barely heard his strangled cry. She snapped her lids open wide. He drove his hips tight against her, as though trying to climb within her. Shudders racked him. His mouth went slack. He didn't scream like she did—he panted. How could he not cry out? How could he be so reserved? His come shot into her in a hot flood and he bucked with it, launching his hips ahead over and over.

His head dropped forward. "Dear sweet temptress," he murmured.

She'd called his name in her pleasure but he'd held himself back.

"We must get you under the sheets, Vixen, before you catch cold."

Sweat was cooling on her, a chill flowing over her skin, raising prickles. Marcus kissed her nose, her cheek, her lips, her chin. Such sweet concern after wild sex. He brushed his palm against her softening nipples, stroked back her hair.

"Do all men enjoy such things? Do all men like to pleasure a woman's bottom?"

He gave a wicked smile. "Some men are too proper to try."

She reached up to touch but he was off the bed. Confused, she asked, "Won't you join me?"

"I wish I could."

He intended to leave? Despite the warm sheets, she went cold. "Is it . . . me?"

"Not you," he assured as he headed toward his trousers, but did he speak too quickly? "I need to attend to Lydia Harcourt tonight."

Fighting a yawn, she sat up and the sheets fell away. "Of course." Guilt quickly banished sleepiness. She'd thought of drifting off in his arms, he was thinking of protecting her and her family. The sight of her gown, on the floor, filled her with dread. It would be horribly wrinkled, even now, and she hated to be buttoned into it.

"You will stay here with the door locked."

"Here? But I want to go."

He brushed a kiss on her forehead. "You must go to sleep. And don't worry."

She wanted to ask if he would come back to her, to sleep with her, but she couldn't bring herself to. What if he laughed? He was going out alone into an orgy. He would probably end up in another woman's bed.

But she couldn't bring herself to protest. She'd look a fool.

He blew her a kiss from the connecting door and Venetia felt her heart fracture.

Lydia Harcourt yawned and gazed sleepily in her mirror as Juliette arranged her hair. She dared not take too deep a breath. Juliette had drawn the black silk corset to excruciating tightness. But the effect was dramatic. A man's one hand could almost span her waist, but her breasts overflowed the cups. Her hips swelled voluptuously below, her legs clad in black-dyed stockings with scarlet garters. She tugged the cuffs of her long black silk gloves.

Ironic that at these events she never shared anyone's bed for the night. She much preferred her own. She looked at it longingly in the mirror. But that would not be for a few hours yet. Perhaps not until dawn.

The silver brush winked in the soft firelight as Juliette drew the bristles through her hair, smoothing the pass with her hand. She'd snared Juliette away from the Countess of Yardley, since she was far more generous, and far more fashionable.

Her hair tumbled down her back and she purred. Stroke, stroke, stroke. The tug on her scalp soothed. "Leave it down, Juliette."

It had been a very tedious night. She'd successfully reminded her more affluent and stubborn victims of the dangers they faced, but there'd been no promises to pay. Good God, Wembly would be shot for what he'd done. Treason. She'd thrown a few shots at dinner, enough to shake his sangfroid. Surely he'd cough up the blunt. And it had amused to taunt Brude about plagiarism, when London's ladies swooned over his words.

Lydia waved a dismissive hand. "There is a man waiting

for you tonight, Juliette. You will not see his face, nor know his name. He will degrade you. He will be brutal, but you must not defy him. Do you understand?"

Juliette licked her thin lips. She bobbed a curtsy. "*Oui*, madame."

Juliette was not pretty or young. Gray threaded the fine black hair, which was drawn, as always, in a tight bun. Hatchet-faced, sharp eyed, with a thin, prim mouth, Juliette was not the sort to attract men. Yet she wanted men. Her predilection was sex with an unseen brute.

Lydia smiled at the reflection of her maid. How amusing to think that beneath the severe black dress beat the heart of a perverse woman. From the coarse men she'd paid, she'd learned of Juliette's peculiar, unsavory tastes. It didn't cost much to buy such men. But it required a discerning eye to avoid those who would take the game too far.

All in the name of control.

Juliette drew back her chair and Lydia strolled to the secretary. Her nightdress lay on her bed, waiting for her. Peach silk, her favorite. She was not like other courtesans, who favored flannel nightgowns when not entertaining men. She surrounded herself with beauty at all times.

Behind her, Juliette's black wool rustled as she left. The door clicked. She would lock it before she retired.

Lydia brought out a sheet of paper from the drawer, then sank down on the plush stool. Thoughtfully, she wrote a list of gentlemen's names. Brude. Chartrand. Montberry. Trent. Wembly. She dipped her pen in the inkwell. Scratching it across the page, she wrote in one more name.

Swansborough. He'd wished her to bind his arms, to drip hot wax on his chest. He'd wanted to howl in pain . . . then he had made her howl, too. He had drawn her to do acts she would never submit to for any other man. Not even Rodesson.

But Swansborough had been too dark. Too disturbing. She loved Rodesson's games much more than his. But Lord Swansborough proved a great enigma.

She could not learn what drove him to enjoy such torture. He was careful with his secrets. Rather like Trent. But unlike Trent, Swansborough did not have a father with a loose tongue. Though the late Lord Trent would have throttled her rather than paid her . . .

She tapped the pen to her lip, thinking of the women in attendance. Those of interest to her. Lady Yardley. Rosalyn Rose. Lady Chartrand.

Approaching Lady Chartrand as well as her husband had proved a lucrative strategy. Her ladyship had dipped into her pin money and had paid. As for Rosalyn . . . she would not be merciful to Rosalyn in her book, but, for a price, she wouldn't reveal that the Duke of Thorndale had not been the father of Rosalyn's child. Thorndale had been generous to all his bastards—two lived in his London house, others were reputedly named in his will. Alas, she'd never quickened during her affair with the great duke.

And Lady Yardley would crack. Soon. Her rage was a sign she was on the brink. All Lydia had to do was continue to play a cool hand.

The sharp rap at her door startled her and she blotted ink on the page

"Mrs. 'arcourt, ma'am?" The lazy vowels, the deep timbre identified Tom's voice.

Relief surged. He was an ally in a house of foes. Clever of him to finagle his way into Chartrand's employ.

Not that she would have ever pegged Tom for a guardian angel.

The silver and scarlet of his livery set off his dark hair, his swarthy skin, his deep blue eyes. Two years her junior, Tom was no doubt a handsome man. He'd likely fuck every young maid in the house by the time the party ended. No wonder he wore such a cocky grin.

"A message from your host, ma'am." He gave a bow, a wink, and retreated.

"Thank you, Polk." Even in private, she used his false name. He was careful around Chartrand and the guests. No one could possibly guess he was her half-brother.

She unfolded Chartrand's note. *I'll pay, you bloody witch. Gallery. Ten.*

Finally. But she sighed. Did he mean ten in the morning or at night? Bother the man. Chartrand would rise that early, she knew. Regardless of how he punished himself the night before, he always rose for breakfast.

Before noon, Chartrand's chapter might be closed. And she would have enough blunt to flee to Venice.

With victory in sight, she turned her thoughts to another puzzle. Trent's fancy piece. Who was she? Was the disguise amusement or necessity?

The late Earl of Trent had pursued wellborn virgins. The last had been a fool of girl who became pregnant easily. A foolish fall, a hope to lose the babe, and the girl was in the ground.

A sad story of a dupe and a wicked man. Lydia crumpled her paper and threw it into the fire.

So who was the girl in Trent's company? And what would such information be worth?

"Join us for a game, Trent?"

Lounging in the doorway of Chartrand's study, Marcus made a pretense of considering Chartrand's invitation. He scanned the card tables filling the room. Most were in use. A nude woman sat on the lap of each man. Rosalyn's prostitutes earning their keep and some looked young. The one on Chartrand's lap possessed tiny breast buds and petite pink nipples, which Chartrand pinched with one hand as he held cards in the other. Most men did likewise, while the girls giggled. Some couples had progressed to fucking—the men's falls open, the girls bouncing eagerly, chairs thumping on the ground.

Marcus rolled his eyes. Despite being buried in snug sheaths, the men were still gambling. "No, thanks. I think I'll tour the other entertainments."

The more experienced courtesans such as Lydia, Trixie, and Rosalyn were not in the room.

"Bored with pretty Vixen?" Chartrand leered. "I'd be happy to purchase her for the night."

"She's awaiting my return."

"So who is she, Trent?"

Without answering Marcus turned to leave, but a slim waif clutched at his arm, making an admirable job of looking shy and sweet. The jade brushed back her curtain of auburn hair, then lifted her tiny breasts for his admiration.

"Now, that's a lovely redhead, Trent," Chartrand called. "Swap her for your treasure?"

Marcus gave a curt, dismissive shake of his head. Wembly, who already bounced a blonde on his knee, snapped his fingers. The girl crawled onto his other knee. With a laugh Wembly laid down his cards and nuzzled first the auburn-haired girl's nipples, and then the blonde's.

Wembly grinned. "Never thought I'd see you tamed, Trent. Makes me intrigued to discover exactly who is the woman behind the mask—"

"And you won't." Marcus turned to leave, ignoring Wembly's parting words. "Care to wager, Trent?"

Talk at the table nearest the door caught his attention.

A man in regimentals was complaining. "Chartrand had ordered up a dozen more whores. But the river's flooded its banks and taken the bridges with it. All that delectable female flesh is trapped on the other side."

"Blasted luck," agreed another officer. "And it looks like the erotic scavenger hunt might be postponed—or cancelled— the only bloody reason I came this year. That and the chance to do some pretty birch work."

Marcus rubbed his temple. If the wenches were trapped in the village, it meant he—and Venetia—were trapped at Chartrand's. He knew the geography well enough—the river separated Chartrand's estate from the village. A tributary fed into it, so two bridges joined Chartrand's to the King's highway, and likely both had been lost.

There would be places where the river might be crossed on horseback, but given the flooding, he wasn't sure. To try to travel in other directions required travel through dense wood, and up unforgiving hilly terrain.

There would be no way he could whisk Venetia away from this place tomorrow. And her blunt question raced again through his mind. *Do all men enjoy such things?*

He grimaced as a healthy dose of guilt hit him. After tonight, how could a sensual woman like Venetia Hamilton find happiness in a typical staid, proper English marriage? She would lie on her back for her husband, too afraid to express desire for the pleasures she truly wanted and endure frustration. He should never have allowed her to come here. He'd never expected she would tempt him so much. He'd made a mistake.

The thoughts haunted him as he headed toward Lydia's room. He tried to concentrate on his mission—find Harcourt's book, then find her, and teach her a lesson for threatening to hurt Min.

As Marcus strode up the back stairs, he had to skirt around maids entertaining drunken men. Bleary-eyed women grabbed at him, pinching his buttocks, and clutching at his cock. They offered him their tits and arses, shrieked his name. Gentleman offered him higher and higher sums to purchase Vixen, all of which he rudely refused.

A drunken lieutenant grabbed at his lapels. "Fifty pounds for the tart."

Insulted, he shoved the officer aside and the young buck swung wildly at his head. A neat step to the side and he watched the officer land face first on the floor.

Various aphrodisiacs were in use and lust-driven couples rutted in the hallways. Two gentlemen sprawled with a pretty chambermaid around one corner, both thrusting eagerly into her. One sucked her breasts, the other clamped his hands on them to gain leverage. "Coo, this is heaven!" she cried.

He couldn't resist a grin. He loved to hear a woman enjoying herself. He'd loved to hear Venetia enjoying herself. Damn, why shouldn't she enjoy herself? Why was it forbidden for a good woman to know carnal pleasure? Because men were proprietary beasts, he knew. The girls had been a pretty diversion, but he knew, here, he would not let another man touch Venetia.

Lydia's corridor was deserted. He rapped on the door, waited, then sprang the lock.

CHAPTER ELEVEN

Venetia threw her stack of linen sheets and her box of brushes on her bed. The mahogany lid flew open and her brushes bounced out, scattering over the wrinkled counterpane. She knelt to find the pots of paint hidden beneath the shifts and corset in her trunk.

Marcus had no idea what she'd smuggled inside. No doubt he'd be furious if he found out. But she kept the key on her person, so curious servants couldn't search for her secrets.

She hesitated over the pots wrapped in linen.

Paint would be too much bother. She would use charcoal. She could sketch figures and poses in the dim light, capture the more spectacular scenes from last night. But she would not draw Marcus. She feared what she might see if she did.

My heart laid bare.

Was it so impossible to have love affairs without feeling the pain and tug at one's heart? No, it wasn't impossible, for Chartrand's guests did it with ease. She had shared orgasms with Kate, Lizzie, and Sukey, but she wasn't the sort to lose her heart to another woman. Though she felt warm, sensuous, and deliciously sinful as she remembered what they'd done.

It should be easy to resist falling in love. Her mother had shed a lifetime of tears over Rodesson. She knew the consequences. Even though Rodesson hadn't lived daily in their lives, they'd lived at his pleasure. Every time her mother began to be free of him in her heart, he'd come back into her life, seduce her all over again, then vanish the way red paint did from a brush dropped in turpentine. The brush came out clean, but the stain of red tinged the fluid forever.

Venetia flopped down on her bed and hiked her robe so she could sit, lotus positioned. Plunking her sketchpad over her crossed legs, she feathered the stick of charcoal onto the page.

Why had Marcus not come back to her room? Why sleep alone in his?

Had he even spoken to Lydia? How could he leave her in suspense? But the truth was that, if he had returned to her bed and slept with her, she wouldn't be angry that he hadn't let her know about Lydia. No, she would have curled up to him, been happy and content, and stayed at his side until he awoke.

Oh, she was a fool. How could she be so easily dazzled, how could she so easily let him touch her heart, when she had her mother's example? She couldn't let herself fall in love with a man who hadn't thought enough of her to even slip a note under her door.

At least she knew there was no other woman in his bed. Heaven help her, she'd opened the door a crack and peeked.

Embers glowed in the fire, adding light to the faint dawn gloom. With long strokes Venetia blocked in the lines of the daybed, then the shape of Cole's head, the planes of his broad shoulders. Quick sketchy lines gave him his sleek, youthful limbs. She wanted to capture . . . the intimacy . . . that surprisingly potent aftermath of sex. Which meant drawing slumbering cocks instead of erect ones. The moment had delighted her. Would it delight men? Did they only wish to see erect, rampant cocks?

What did it matter? These pictures couldn't be sold. They were only for her.

Flowing strokes brought Cole's tumbled curls to life but she couldn't lose herself in the erotic moment. She could only think of Marcus and draw by instinct.

Had Marcus offered to pay Lydia? She could not allow it. But what could she do?

What a tangled mess.

She flipped the page and tried to capture another scene. Lady Chartrand and Rosalyn, each lapping her tongue between the other's thighs—just as she and Marcus had done . . .

She tried another. Lady Yardley and the raven-haired footman . . . Her ladyship's expression wasn't merely lust—there was vulnerability . . . She looked so enraptured. The highborn lady captured by the sensual skills of a handsome, low born man as he sucked her breasts and slid his entire hand in her cunny—

Her heart raced. Her hands shook. And her fingers were black with charcoal.

Venetia closed the book, inexplicably clutched it to her chest. What if Lydia demanded more? Even if Marcus allowed her to paint his nephew—and she doubted he would since he knew how wanton she was—she would have to give all her money to Lydia.

His offer had been a wonderful gesture of trust, of kindness. He had invited her into his family. She still could not understand why he had sought to help her rather than just stop her. Did his sister's good opinion mean so much to him?

Suddenly, she felt guilty to be betraying him by painting. She hid away her supplies and sketchbook, then padded to the window as she wiped her hands on a cloth.

Thick black clouds covered the sky. Rain beat down, a gray sheet of it, striking the paned windows and the stone walls. She couldn't even see the terrace or the garden fountain for the rain. Lightning forked the sky, slashed through the thick clouds. Thunder rumbled, exploded and she jumped on the spot.

She didn't fear storms, but she stood, with bare feet on the thick carpet, within reach of the connecting door. It tempted her again.

If she crept into Marcus' room quietly, she could see him sleeping. She'd never seen a man sleep—other than some country husbands, dozing off their drink. She ached to steal a look. To catch Marcus with eyes shut, mouth relaxed, lost in his dreams. Did he look innocent and sweet? Or ruthlessly sensual?

Folly to do it. He might wake. How would she explain herself?

Fool that she was, she wanted to climb into his bed and wrap her arms around his lean, firm waist. She wanted to press herself along the length of his beautiful back, her cunny to his ass, and hold him.

Footsteps. She heard someone walking in Marcus' room. A servant? As she watched, the doorknob of the connecting door turned.

She couldn't help but watch it, as the latch clicked free, and the door swung into her room.

He stood there, wearing only an inviting smile, with tousled hair and boyish charm in his eyes. Oh yes, this man could break her heart.

Thank heaven she'd hidden away her artist's tools.

Brimming with confidence even without a stitch of clothing, he smiled. "Join me, Vixen. Come into my room."

He issued his invitation with every confidence she'd race to accept. It was peevish to ask, but she truly wanted to know. "Why, my lord, didn't you come back to mine?"

Marcus sat back on his rumpled bed with his legs spread. In the silver-gray light of morning and the warm glow of his candles, Venetia's thin cotton skirts were translucent, revealing shapely legs, the alluring gap between. His cock rose to half-mast, curving toward his hip. With his legs open in invitation, he had a warm spot between for her to sit. "Join me."

She stood in the doorway, her right hand clutching the sleeve of her opposite arm. Last night, she'd been wild with him. This morning she looked vulnerable.

"I assume your fire hasn't been made up for the day? Mine hasn't." He glanced at the window, the drapes drawn back. Rain pelted at the windows as though the storm wanted to break the glass and get inside. Blasted rain. He'd brought her into a storm in many ways.

But now, he wanted her in his arms. He patted the bed again. "Come here."

She'd slipped her nightgown on—a simple long-sleeved gown of muslin and modest lace. She padded across his room, bare feet visible beneath her hem. In her country village world, a glimpse of ankles was a scandal.

She drew up her skirts and crawled onto his bed. Without concern for grace or seductive display. Her thoughts were elsewhere, not on being appealing to him, and he liked that about her.

"You asked me why I didn't return to your bed."

"I didn't intend it to sound possessive. We are at an orgy, after all."

He drew her back, enfolded her in his arms. "So no proprietary feelings, love? Not even after the intimacy we shared?"

"I wouldn't dream of spoiling your fun, my lord."

He knew that tone of voice. The primness of a woman teased. "Ah, sweeting. I didn't sleep with you because of a piece of advice my father gave me."

"Which was?"

Her breasts were full, tempting swells against the soft gown. He filled his palms with them, strummed her nipples with his thumbs. The most tempting feminine moan drifted up, like smoke from their solitary candle. "You may touch me, if you want. You may fondle my cock at any time you wish, Venetia. It now belongs to you."

She giggled. "But what *did* your father say that kept you out of my bed?"

"He warned that nothing but trouble came from waking up with a woman."

She pushed his hands from her breasts. "Well, my lord, I may have been nothing but trouble to you, but you've been nothing but trouble to me!"

Who else but Venetia would answer him like that? He was a powerful earl, and people toadied to him all the time. She was indignant, he was laughing. "Indeed. And how have I troubled you? Was last night a great trouble?"

From above, he saw cheeks blush. "Last night was wonderful." She turned in his arms. "What about Lydia? Did she agree? And what did you offer?"

Marcus skimmed his hands over her belly. "I have to admit failure there, love—"

"She refused?" Venetia squeaked.

"No, I couldn't find her," he admitted.

"You got *distracted*, you mean!"

Her accusation stung. "Not in the way you're thinking, sweet. The only distraction for me here is you."

She waved away the sentiment, but it was the truth. The tapes on her gown were loose, he slipped his hands in to stroke her breasts. Even in her disappointment, her nipples greeted him by growing hard. "How could you not find her?"

But despite her abrupt and accusatory question, she squirmed between his thighs, obviously enjoying his touch.

"I can't saunter through gentlemen's bedrooms and search for her beneath the covers."

"Here?" she snapped. "I would have thought that part of the fun."

"Not entirely, sweet. And she wasn't a participant in the public displays."

She half-turned, resting her hand on his thigh. The gesture spoke of forgiveness and he cherished it. "What type of public displays?"

"A lot of fucking, love. In the ballroom, the drawing

rooms, the hallways. Couples, groups. And all I could think of was you upstairs in your bed."

Hell, he hadn't been able to stop thinking about her. Of being in her bed, spooned snugly against her lush body, instead of downstairs, pawed by squealing women, watching his step on a floor strewn with drink and spilled seed.

The truth was he'd spent most of the night searching fruitlessly for Lydia's blasted manuscript. He'd finally picked the lock on one trunk, to discover it filled with books. But then he'd heard footsteps. He threw the books back and hid in the wardrobe while a woman with a dubious French accent had sex with a coarse speaking Englishman on Lydia's floor. Her maid, he'd assumed. After finding nothing in Lydia's room, he'd braved the storm to search her carriage—another wasted effort.

Was it possible he'd been wrong? That she hadn't brought the book with her? No. He'd get another look at that trunk of books today.

But now . . . he had Venetia in his arms. In the quiet cocoon of his room, with the storm raging outside, the magic of the moment captured his senses. She was beautiful as she leaned back against his chest, all slender limbs, long hair, and rounded curves. The cleft between her cheeks teased his hard cock, which stretched up against her spine. Her breasts were velvety soft and delightfully heavy against his palms.

"We won't leaving today—not until we find Lydia?"

"We won't be leaving for days, Venetia. All this bloody rain has swelled the river over its banks. The torrent washed out the bridge and has turned surrounding roads into mires of mud. Travel would be next to impossible."

She was silent, thoughtfully stroking his thigh. His cock twitched with each long, lazy brush of her fingers. "So we're trapped here," she said finally.

"Last night most gentlemen I encountered wanted you. Wanted to buy you from me. I want to get you the hell out of here, but I can't."

She looked startled.

"You've intrigued them and they want you. Eventually one might decide to take you."

Marcus tightened his embrace, buried his face into the crook of her neck. "I won't let that happen—but I want you to understand the risk."

"And you don't want me to leave your side."

She still smelled of sex, ripe and arousing. The truth of her words hit him. He was a bloody fool. He should have slept with her last night.

Clarity struck—he'd lost something he could never regain. He could never have that night again.

She was alone with a man who had strangled his wife.

Wiping her gloved hands nervously on her skirts, Lydia rose from the bench to greet Chartrand who arrived in the gallery surrounded by sniffing hounds. Dressed in breeches, tweeds, and boots, he looked more country squire than dissolute marquess and he held the whining dogs on tight leads.

"Good morning, my lord." She dropped into a curtsy, an abbreviated one, not the low one that gave a view of her cleavage, aware of rage in his narrowed gray eyes.

She trembled as she rose.

"You're a lying bitch, Lydia. I had nothing to do with my wife's death. The gypsy swung for it."

Had he remembered what he'd told her? Perhaps not. That night he'd been so foxed with drink, so riddled with opiates that he had passed out on her floor and almost choked in his own vomit. That frantic night, the thought of a dead marquess in her drawing room had spurred her to action. She'd dragged him upstairs, had dunked him in a frigid bath to rouse him, had listened to his confession.

Had it been a sexual game or rage? That much she'd never known.

"I brought you back from the dead that night, my lord."

The hounds whined. A curt command had them lying at his feet. "To bleed me dry."

"No. I've named my price and I will be satisfied with it. That I promise."

"Your story would be a pack of lies. No one would believe it."

"It was grief then, that drove you into neck or nothing carriage races, foolish duels, brutal sport? That drove you to have your head knocked sideways at Gentleman Jackson's? Grief and not guilt."

His hand jerked and she flinched, expecting a slap. But it lowered, clenched in a fist. "You witch. I loved her."

"But you beat her."

"As a husband should. And she submitted the way a proper wife should. *She* knew her place."

His indignation rang out into the still, silent room.

"The man, the one tried for the crime, he was young, wasn't he? Twenty-two?"

"Blasted gypsies. Should've run them off." He dropped the leads of the dogs. The beasts stirred, growled, but another command had them lowering hackles and muzzles. "There's another group of them camped outside the estate now."

His threat was obvious. *Her* body could be found in the woods, *her* brutal death attributed to the gypsies.

A clumsy threat. But then Chartrand was a big brute of a man, lacking finesse. Still, his large hands filled her with apprehension. He massaged his fisted hand with the other and she heard the crack of his knuckles. Then the beefy hand swung up and she reeled back.

Wearing a triumphant smirk at her cowed position, he slowly put his hands to his coat, drew a slip of white paper from his inside pocket. "A bank draft."

She reached for it but he lifted it high. She would not demean herself by stretching. She arched a brow. "Then give it to me."

"Down on your knees first, Lydia, love. I want more than your promises for my money."

How many men had she performed fellatio on? Dozens. With eyes shut, thoughts elsewhere, the bobbing and sucking a mechanical act. With some—those men she desired—she'd enjoyed the act and enjoyed dazzling them. Desire made the slurping sounds erotic rather than coarse, desire made the taste sublime, desire turned the ripe scents of a man's cock, sweaty ballocks and arse into a tempting fragrance.

She didn't desire Chartrand. When he had been her lover, he'd been generous, exceedingly so, but only because his demands were high. She knew what he was. She would not sink to her knees before him now and place herself in such a vulnerable position. Chatrand might kick her in the head. She'd been kicked before, almost been kicked to death.

"You'll do it, witch, or you'll watch this burn."

"Give me that paper, my lord, and I will consider your request."

His mouth worked. Spittle flecked his thick lips in his frustration. Then he tossed her bank draft—a veritable fortune—into the air and grabbed her by the throat.

His beefy hands closed on her neck with enough pressure to frighten. Meeting his round, gray eyes, she tried to stare him down, tried not to show her fear. But he took a step and she had no choice but to stumble backward in response, and to keep doing so, until her back hit the wall. The corner of a frame gouged her shoulder blade. She winced. The picture rattled.

"Blunt won't shut you up, will it, Lydia? There's only one way. One way." Relentlessly, his hands tightened. There was no rage in his eyes. They were empty. Terrifying.

She clawed at his hands. Damn the gloves, they covered her fingernails. She was helpless. Trapped. She was going to die.

God. Oh God.

She couldn't die like this. This was a fool's death.

He'd take her, just as he'd done to his young wife, and carry her out to the woods. He'd arrange her prettily, tear her clothes, her skirts . . . point his villainous finger at the gypsies . . .

His ballocks.

She couldn't force her legs to move. Her fingers clung to his hands, digging, gouging, but she had no strength.

Please move!

Her knee jerked up.

His howl echoed, his body jumped back, but his hands tightened—

CHAPTER TWELVE

She no longer had the strength to claw at him.

Lydia fought the fall into blackness, clinging to Chartrand's hands. Die like this? No! She wouldn't . . . couldn't. But any moment, she'd tumble into the dark and then—

Fear and strength flooded and she kicked out, kicked wild. Her knee jerked up, hitting softness, then the solidity of his pelvis.

"Bitch!" His hands instinctively clenched tighter.

Her last chance . . . she must fight. His eyes! She struck his eyes with her hands, half-blind, that spurt of strength fading. Fingers curled like talons and she gouged. He screamed, high-pitched, but his hands never left her throat. Her arms became both heavy and weightless, and a red-tinged blackness beckoned.

She felt herself falling.

"Milord—milord!" A man's shocked cry pierced the enveloping dark.

Abruptly the hands yanked from her throat. Fierce pain shot from her neck as it expanded. She slumped against the wall. Sliding down it—

"Get out!" Chartrand roared to the servant, her savior.

No, no, please . . . but what would the footman do but obey . . .

"Her ladyship sent me, milord. Urgent matter, she instructed."

Lydia caught hold of the paneled molding as she slid lower on the wall. She pushed up with aching, dead legs, trying not to fall. That cocky voice—

Tom! She forced her eyes to open.

Chartrand barked a command—but not to her or to Tom, to his dogs. They bounded up on splayed, rigid legs, then loped off in pursuit of their master. He stooped, snatched up the bank draft. The bastard. Then left . . . without a word, a backward glance, as though she didn't exist . . .

Lydia stared after Chartrand, slowly taking in air, her throat so sore it hurt to breathe. How could even he be so bold as to almost a strangle a woman in front of a servant and then leave without even an attempt at a lie?

"What sort o' sick games are ye playing, Lyd?"

She rubbed her throat. The skin burned and she winced at the tenderness where his fingers had dug in. She imagined bright redness and bruising . . .

There were those who enjoyed sex while having their breathing cut off, who claimed that being near death enhanced the pleasure.

They must be mad.

Still stroking her neck, Lydia met Tom's dark, inquisitive gaze. She couldn't let him know the truth. "The man is a brute and bully who enjoys disgusting pleasures."

Suspicion burned in his narrowed eyes. "What the 'ell is it you want 'ere?"

"His lordship pays well." She gave a jaded shrug, but worry gripped. Tom might be a village butcher and he'd been sharped at cards in London's hells, but he wasn't a complete fool.

She needed that bank draft! She'd promised to pay Tom's debts, and the amount he needed had staggered her. Even if she could free him now, what of the future? And the past . . .

she couldn't forget the past. The fireplace shovel. One deter-mined swing.

There'd been so much blood from the gash in the head. She, of all people, should have known that. They were al-ways coated in it, her father and Tom, their leather aprons slick with it, stinking of it.

When did you ever stop repaying the man who'd blud-geoned his own da to save your life?

"Ye don't fool me for a minute, lass. This is over yer black-mailing. Did he pay ye?"

"No. He wouldn't pay me and then strangle me, would he? But don't worry. His lordship will give me what I want. And then I can leave here. *Venezia.*" Softly, she reminded him of Venice, of escape. But if she gave him Chartrand's money, what would be left for her? She needed more. If Montberry would pay . . . or Trent . . .

Tom's hand snaked out and gripped her arm. He shook her, wrenching her arm in the socket, bringing tears to her stinging eyes. "I'm a dead man if me debts aren't paid, sis-ter."

She needed his protection, needed him on her side. "You have saved my life twice. Trust me."

Blast men and their stupid wagering, Venetia fumed. Her entire life had been continually twisted about in knots by ridiculous bets and male boredom. "Well," she decided, "They can wager away but they will not discover my iden-tity!"

Marcus' big, naked arms were wrapped around her waist. In the safety of his embrace, on his rumpled bed, it was easy to make vows.

Was that why he laughed? "Bravo, Vixen. You have my word that they won't."

He sounded impressed. But she had the strength of her own vow and that was what she would put her faith in. She held no doubt Marcus would move heaven and earth to protect her—a certainty that melted her heart, but she refused to surrender responsibility for her own fate.

"So you aren't too horrified by all this? You can endure a few more days?"

What other choice did she have? She heard worry in his words. But she wasn't a simpering twit who swooned at scandal. "It isn't so . . . horrifying."

He chuckled. "You enjoyed Kate, Sukey, and Lizzie?"

"Yes." Venetia thought of her orgy picture set in a temple amongst the clouds, *Zeus Summons*, in which Marcus played Zeus, and couldn't help but giggle. Silly to laugh amidst disaster, but it helped. "But it most certainly isn't . . . it isn't what I expected. Though you did warn me."

His hands slid up her back, leaving a trail of tingling nerves. Big hands cupped her shoulders, deeply massaged. She sighed, ecstatic, and let her head loll.

"And not that way—the way you're thinking. It isn't the sex." She tried to explain, even as pleasure engulfed. "There's a tension to all this, an undercurrent of . . . of anger."

"No surprise, there. Almost every gentleman here is expected to pay to keep himself out of Lydia's bloody book."

Icy disdain coated his words. A flame of fury ignited in her soul. "Well, they shouldn't be angry with her," she protested. "They should have watched their tongues. What else did they think she would do?" She half-turned her head. He looked puzzled.

His lips parted but a rap at the door interrupted and his words never came out. Marcus shared her look of surprise. A feminine voice with coarse accents announced the arrival of breakfast—the food he'd summoned.

"Hide your face, love."

She flopped down, flung the sheets over her head. Her body would be an obvious lump in the bed, but here, no one would care. It was expected! Scents made her tummy rumble.

The rich chicory smell of coffee. Warm, sweet fresh bread. Heavy, spicy aromas—the meats—ham, sausage, kidneys . . . At the click of the door, she drew down the sheets.

"All clear." He grinned and lifted a plate. Two trays groaned with their magnificent breakfast. "Care for chocolate, Vixen? Or coffee?"

The sheets spilled over her belly as she sat up. "Chocolate."

He poured a brimming cup. "Aren't you angry with Lydia?"

He was blaming the woman for the follies of the men. "No. I'm most angry with my father for not watching his tongue. Confiding in tarts while my mother is in anguish! Why couldn't he have visited her and not Lydia?" Tears stung her eyes. She tasted one on her lip.

He sat on the edge of the bed, by her side, and handed her the cup without spilling a drop. "Who is your mother, sweet? You've never told me and Rodesson wouldn't. Why didn't they marry?"

A fine actor—he sounded as though he cared. He must only want her to stop blubbering like a silly child. She took a deep breath. In her anxiety, her cup tipped, hot chocolate splashed to the saucer. "My mother is—was—a lady. An earl's daughter. The Earl of Warren, though he'd never admit it. As for why they didn't marry—I don't truly know. How they ever came to be lovers, I can't imagine. She loves country life and he—well, you know what he is."

Marcus bent, slid his hands down to her hips, down to tickle her nether curls. The fire crackled, rain drummed in the stretch of silence. Finally, he kissed her, at the top of her spine. Heat flowed over her, luxuriant heat over her skin, wet heat between her thighs.

"Tell me, sweeting."

Oh, she didn't want to talk . . . she wanted to kiss . . . to do more carnal things . . .

"Tell me what you think your father is."

She didn't completely understand. "He's an artist." Surely that explained it all.

"Couldn't he be satisfied painting the countryside?"

His fingers brushed her nether lips, stealing her breath. She struggled to speak. "No. He's a bohemian who loves his brothels and tarts, his drink and cards. He revels in male excess."

"I see. Of course, you are an artist and you aren't satisfied with country life either."

That startled. No, she hadn't been. She hadn't been unhappy, though, just restless.

To her dismay, he stopped touching her. Instead he stood and sauntered back to the breakfast trays. He lifted lids. "So how did two such unlikely people meet?"

Because you came to end my career. But he was speaking of her parents, not of her and him. "Rodesson came to paint the portraits of my mother and her sisters."

"And passion ensued." Selecting a plate, he piled it with sausages. From a steaming dish, he ladled kidneys beside those. Added eggs from the platter.

"I suppose. I expect she fell in love with him."

He paused, cutting a slice of ham. "I expect he fell in love with her."

Venetia hadn't expected romantic sentiment from a jaded rake. She shook her head. "He was never faithful."

"Which doesn't mean he didn't love her."

"He certainly didn't respect her, then," she snapped. Though she knew in Marcus' elevated world where titles and bloodlines and wealth dictated marriage, women ignored their husbands' infidelities. Most ignored their husbands.

"My mother became pregnant, of course, and they fled to Gretna Green in a flurry of passion to marry, but they never quite got there. I suppose he thought he'd make her a bad husband, and there was still chance she could marry well. I believe they stopped along the way, took a room as husband

and wife, and the next morning she was sick, so she guessed she was pregnant. But she discovered Rodesson hadn't been faithful and she made a decision. She set herself up in a house, with the help of friends, and created a new identity. A friend posed as her husband, so the village believed there was one. The story was that he was a sea captain who had decided to travel to India to make his fortune. There were doubts and gossip, of course, so she, and then all of us, had to live above suspicion."

Cathartic to spill the entire story. But her face burned. Surely he didn't really care.

He returned to the bed, handed her the plate, a knife and fork lying across the impossible mound of food. She'd thought that mountain was to be his.

"Eat what you can," he advised, eyes twinkling.

She took it, mumbling thanks as he returned once more to the trays. He glanced up from his plate. "So despite the child—you—your father didn't marry your mother or live with her?"

"She chose not to force him and she decided to make her own life."

"A brave choice for a lady with little experience of the world," he mused.

"A romantic notion for a woman who thought the way to impress a bohemian artist was to be as wild as he." Her mother had been hopelessly, foolishly in love.

"But she wasn't wild."

"She was willing to be anything—for love." The tremble in her voice angered. This was a logical discussion—she refused to cry. "Her friends dissuaded her from being truly scandalous for the sake of her babe—me. There was still hope that her future could be salvaged, and her true nature won out. She lived quietly and devoted herself to noble work in the village."

Marcus selected a bun, sliced it, then buttered it completely, right up to the edges. He looked up—caught her staring. "Is this how you like it?"

"Yes. Thank you." Venetia sighed. "Only you, my lord Trent, could seduce a woman by the way you butter her bread."

"I've never seduced a woman that way before—in fact, I don't believe I've ever buttered a woman's bun."

She giggled helplessly at that, her cup rattling perilously on the saucer. He brought his plate and her lavishly spread bun to the bed. "Your mother had noble friends, to stay by her. Yet Rodesson visited her obviously—you have younger sisters."

She set down her chocolate. "My mother traveled to him. She pretended to be meeting my father on his arrival at Plymouth, but she would visit him in London."

"Did she? A forgiving woman, your mother."

"A besotted woman. Every time she seemed free of him, she fell under his spell once more."

"And this way your sisters were explained? What of the friend posing as her husband?"

"He truly did leave to seek his fortune in India. He sent letters and gifts, which made the tale look true. Then he died, and she claimed she was a widow."

"Interesting. Then there could be no more children."

By that, of course, he meant that her mother and father could no longer be lovers. Was that true? Her mother had visited Rodesson after that, yet her mother never quickened again.

"Well, there would be no more letters or packages sent and she had to explain that. I expect if anyone's curiosity was truly piqued, they could have found the truth, but my mother flung herself into village life with all her heart, ever proper in her speech, her dress, her behavior. And all the while she lived a secret life."

"Like her daughter." Sprawled on the bed, with his plate laid precariously on the covers, he smiled between devouring his slices of ham.

She had her plate safely on the bedside table and she nibbled off it. "You see, I don't even really exist. Hamilton was a name my mother invented for herself. My certificate of birth is a lie. She didn't want to return home in disgrace—there was a marriage waiting for her. A man willing to overlook lost virginity. But she wanted to be free."

"A romantic tale. Didn't her parents search?"

"Yes. But then they found her and were shocked. They were happy to wash their hands of her. I'm sure that if you asked any matrons of the ton about the scandalous youngest daughter of the Earl of Warren, you'd hear the tale of her supposed elopement with a sea captain as fresh as though it happened this Season. She gave up everything for love. And all she received was heartbreak. In the night, if I crept down, I would see her alone, drinking the sherry we saved for company, and staring into the darkness. Love is a very frightening thing."

"I'll agree with you there, sweeting, though I've been told that it can be the most enriching experience there is."

"By whom?" Venetia asked.

"My sister. And my father—though he wouldn't have known love if it bit him on the arse," Marcus said. He got up from the bed, tossed back the rest of his coffee, and carried his empty cup back to the coffee urn, thinking about love. Other than Min, he'd never had a discussion about love with a woman before. It was a dangerous path to tread. How had Min described love? *Intimacy. Friendship. Something glorious that both hurts and enriches. And you know that if you lost it, your heart might never mend.*

Intimacy. He'd never shared intimacy like this with anyone. Was this what his sister found with her husband?

He'd never shared breakfast in bed, spilling crumbs and smearing butter, learning about a woman's soul. No wonder his blasted father advised him against waking up with a woman—

"Did you truly have hot wax dropped on you?"

He wasn't expecting that question. He set the urn back before filling his cup. "Yes," he answered with a wry grin. "Though afterward I wondered if Swansborough had lied about his interest to entice me to do it. It's the sort of bizarre joke he'd enjoy playing."

Her green-flecked eyes were serious, contemplative. "He's very like you, but he's not."

That surprised him. "A woman's riddle."

A whim had him lifting the carafe of chocolate. Filling his cup with the cooling treat. Carrying the cup, he paced back to the bed, aware of his erection swaying.

Venetia was kneeling on the bed in her sweet nightdress, legs curled beneath her. The picture of innocence. "No, I mean he is like you in that he is—"

"Handsome and charming?" He stirred the chocolate with his index finger.

"Bother you, yes, but I meant that he's . . . rakish and jaded about the most shocking exploits. But with you I feel safe and comfortable. He makes me uneasy."

"Has he propositioned you? Touched you?"

"No," she said quickly. "No, he hasn't."

"Why the interest in Swansborough?" Even he heard the jealousy behind his light tone. He saw her tense as his finger approached her lips, a light coating of chocolate running down.

"I was thinking that if I were Lydia, I wouldn't blackmail him. Or you. Or any of these men. You are all too dangerous. But he seems the darkest. He wants to be punished."

He painted her mouth with the rich drink, and her tongue flicked out, licking his finger clean. A tremor raced down his body, thundered through his cock. "I understand now why your paintings are so exquisite."

He undid the tapes of her nightdress, gently opened the neckline to expose her breasts. Dipping his finger again, he traced her nipples, circling them until they were dark with chocolate. He bent and sucked them, tasting the bitter tang, the sweetness of her skin.

"W—why?" Her eyes were wide.

"Because an artist's eye can see into a man's hidden soul," Marcus said.

The thought startled Venetia. But in her pictures, she feared he could see her hidden soul. What if Marcus looked and realized that, at the end of the book, the roguish earl fell in love with the mysterious lady who had made love to him on his journey but who had never offered her heart? For that was the forbidden story behind *Tales of a London Gentleman*. The rake falling hopelessly in love.

"I didn't know you when I painted those," she protested.

"Now I must look," he teased. "And I know Chartrand has a copy. Or perhaps I should have you paint my portrait."

He painted her nipples again, making them large and dark. With a heavy-lidded gaze, he admired his handiwork, then surged forward to suckle.

How could she paint his portrait? Shock filled her, tumbling with desire, as he held her tight, as he nuzzled, nibbled, licked her breasts. She wished she could—but she couldn't.

Every brush stroke would reveal how much she desired this man. How could she hide how awe-inspiring she found his wide shoulders? Shoulders that made her hands seem small and inconsequential. And his chest—she couldn't help but lovingly depict the chest that made her feel warm and protected.

It would destroy her to draw his face—to put her skills to the test to capture the color, the life, the naughtiness, the kindness, the sensuality and the honor in his eyes. Anyone viewing his lips would know that they'd been drawn by someone addicted to the wide shape, the playful dip of his upper lip, the firmness, the seductive color—not quite pink, not bronze, but so tempting . . .

Those lips tempting her now. His eyes waiting for an answer.

"I don't wish to talk anymore," she whispered.

He laughed. "I've never had a woman accuse me of being too chatty." But he fell back on the bed, pulling her with him. She sprawled over him, breasts still at his mouth. Her nightdress flew up. The ridge of his erection pressed against her mound. She mustn't . . . she shouldn't . . . she couldn't resist.

She brushed her quim along his prick, the lips wet over the shaft. She kissed his shoulder, inhaling the musk of his underarms, and dabbed her tongue there, in the soft hair, to taste sweat.

He groaned. "No, sweeting. My juice is flowing. Even a touch risks pregnancy."

She lifted her hips in a hurry. "Oh no! Not a bastard child."

"There are all the other ways we've explored . . ." Eyes wild and wicked, he asked, "Do you want me? Or do you want more breakfast?"

He skimmed his hands down her spine and licked her neck, taking her to madness with a flick of his tongue. Her belly rumbled but she didn't care. "You! Dear heaven, yes."

"Then, onto your tummy, Vixen."

As she rolled, presenting lush curves, a loud knock rattled the door once more. The footman called, "A message of importance, milord."

Venetia collapsed into the mound of pillows as he shrugged on his robe, padded to the door. She wasn't going to ask about his private business, but to her surprise he gave her the note to read.

My lord Trent,

Gentlemen are wagering on the identity of Vixen. I must meet you and your partner in the south drawing room before her identity is revealed.

Lydia

*   *   *

Lydia sat back with an exasperated sigh. Trent's clever companion had locked her trunk. She rose and stole to the bedside table of Vixen's room. The surface was bare, the drawer empty except for the obligatory ropes and a short riding crop. No key was to be found.

She stroked her sore neck—she could barely speak, it seemed her throat had swollen, and the pain had grown worse, not better. She had half a mind to publish Chartrand's secret anyway.

Half a mind indeed—he'd kill her.

At least her ploy to lure Trent and his jade away had worked.

She should be recovering in bed and her door firmly locked. This was madness—but she wanted this business finished with haste, and if she wanted her money from Trent, she required leverage.

Stroking her poor bruised neck, Lydia sat down on the edge of the rumpled bed. Would this prove to be worth the money she'd paid to bribe the maid?

There was the escritoire. The screen around the chamber pot. The mantel. The wardrobe.

Her only hope might be the wardrobe but she doubted the key was to be found in the room. She pulled the doors open quickly, releasing the scent of lavender. She fingered the dresses, testing the quality of material.

There were few dresses—silks and muslins—but not the latest fashions or the best quality. The seamstress who had constructed them was adequate but not talented. Trent had not purchased these dresses, she would wager on that. There were too few of them. And he would insist on purchasing from the most fashionable modiste.

The girl's underclothes were in the drawers and some were positively ghastly. Functional cloth not expensive silk. Plain and dull.

But it made no sense. Even if Trent had acquired a country girl as his paramour, he would buy her decent clothes.

Who was Trent's lover?

Did she dare take the time to search Trent's room? Really, what would she hope to find there? But she had this opportunity, one she would not have again . . .

Lydia moved swiftly across the floor. Smug delight soared when the doorknob of the connecting door turned beneath her hand—

Footsteps. Outside, in the hallway.

Numbing panic rose. What if Trent had seen through her ruse? What if he'd only left long enough to lure her to walk into a trap. He could accuse her of stealing. Have her arrested or transported—

Her legs felt mired in mud. She must stay calm. Her neck throbbed. She must remember she was not a desperate, friendless, penniless girl anymore . . .

Get out. Get out. The words beat at her, like a desperate bird trapped against glass.

She ran for the door.

CHAPTER THIRTEEN

Shadows filled the south drawing room, but exotic lamps illuminated the sensual entertainment on offer. Venetia blinked in astonishment.

It was only late morning, yet Chartrand's events had already begun.

In the middle of the room, a woman was upside down! Suspended from the ceiling by a golden chain that winked in the candlelight, she twirled in the center of the large room. The chain bound her ankles together. She was nude and her large breasts hung toward her lips. Blond hair spilled down, a golden waterfall spiraling over the floor.

The blonde didn't appear upset by her predicament. Her hands were free—she lifted one pendulous breast to her mouth, until she could lick her own nipple

Venetia's legs trembled at the sight. Her breasts weren't large enough for that . . . and as the tongue flattened over the swollen nipple, her legs swayed. As though she, too, were spinning.

A burst of applause broke in. Two men were reclining, watching the woman's performance. Fully dressed, they lay amongst a jumble of silky pillows. It looked like a decadent scene from the East. A curious scent clung to the air—smoky, sweet, hazy. The men appeared half-asleep, in heavy-lidded languor, but their breeches were open, their cocks out, and they ran their hands lazily up and down the rigid lengths.

The iron lamps sent patterned light dancing over the men. One had dark brown hair. The other's was raven black. Lords Brude and Swansborough.

"The scent is from an opium pipe," Marcus murmured, "And I don't see Lydia."

The woman's hand was at her quim, sliding something in and out of her. A long ivory toy. Her face was growing flushed and the position must be painful, but she only smiled enticingly.

Venetia couldn't tear her gaze from the woman, hypnotized by the way her breasts pointed and swung, by her long, seductive strokes. She must think about Lydia. About danger. "Could she be late?"

She felt him watching her and glanced up, blushing.

He winked. "Do you wish to go in? To relax on the cushions and watch?"

"No." But the men stood up from the cushions and strolled toward the woman. Their erect cocks protruded and she couldn't look away. Swansborough approached the hanging woman from the back. He buried his face against her bottom.

Brude set to work on the woman's cunny with his mouth. At first, the blonde thrust into herself with the wand, moaning as the men pleasured her. But then Brude withdrew the wand—impossibly long—and he held it down to the woman's mouth. Obediently she flicked her tongue over it, then took it in deep and held it there. The jade couldn't moan any longer, it acted as a gag.

Marcus brushed a kiss against her ear. "Shall we wait?"

This was naughty. Scandalous. To watch.

Marcus cradled her breast and she allowed it, loved it. His hot breath on her neck tangled her senses. "Do you wish to stay for the climax?"

Brude was tying the woman's hands now. What would the ton's ladies say if they saw their romantic poet doing that?

"The woman," she whispered. "Who is the woman?"

"Sarah. A protégé of Rosalyn Rose."

She'd guessed he would know but still her heart gave a twinge. He'd given her the name without a moment's hesitation—as though it had been on the tip of his tongue.

"Is she . . . enjoying that? Or . . . is it just to please the men?"

"Sweetheart, in truth I can never tell when a woman is acting a part to please me. Does watching it excite you?"

"Yes." She was ashamed that she'd admitted it.

He fondled her breast, her derriere, whispered, "There's no shame in that, sweeting. Many women fantasize about bondage, and enjoy it."

Venetia wanted to believe that he would understand. "I've looked at Belzique's work. It . . . it fascinated me even as it horrified. But those pictures were impossibly tame compared to this. To what people truly do."

Marcus was stunned. Innocent Venetia enjoyed Belizique's depictions of dominance and submission? Already hardened by the display before him, by watching other men taste and enjoy an aroused woman, he felt his cock pulse in response to her words.

"Bondage can be playful and safe between partners who trust." Even as he spoke, his brain screamed—*what in hell are you thinking?*

"Are you . . . offering to try it with me?" she asked softly.

He conjured an image. Her naked legs spread wide, waiting to be bound and her quim exposed to him, soaked with her juices. He would tie her. Velvet ropes would bind her hands, truss her breasts, saw into her wet pussy. He would make her come just by the way he tied and tightened the ropes.

In the bottom of Chartrand's box of toys had been clamps for her erect nipples. His great weakness was a woman with her nipples clamped, with chains or jewels dangling there. He loved to watch heavy gold weights suspended from a woman's breasts, and he loved a woman stuffed with sexual toys, pleasuring herself with her every movement—

Swansborough was sliding a slim unlit candle into Sarah's bottom. He added another and Sarah moaned around the carved dildo she held between her lips.

Marcus' cock throbbed in time with her moans. With gentle strokes, Swansborough added another candle.

"Hold those in place," Brude directed to Swansborough as he picked up a rod of pale ivory with a rounded end.

Marcus heard Venetia's excited breathing as Brude filled Sarah's cunny with the smooth rod. Swansborough picked up a third candle, holding it before Sarah's eyes. She hesitated, then nodded.

God, he was going to explode in his trousers at the display. No, it wasn't the display. It was watching the scene while thinking about slowly introducing Venetia to wilder and wilder games . . . exploring her innate sensuality . . . .

Venetia whimpered as she watched Sarah reach her first climax. Sarah couldn't scream for the dildo in her mouth, but she writhed and bucked in midair, swinging around on the rope while the men relentlessly fucked her.

Venetia panted heavily. The room was filled with hazy, drugging smoke and the wondrous scent of a woman's pleasure.

Marcus groaned and pulled her tight against his lean, hard body. His solid thigh pushed between her legs, parting them. Pins scattered as his fingers slid through her hair. Heat flared as his mouth devoured hers. Wet. Firm. Masterful. Wonderful.

He pulled away, gazed into her eyes. "Which Belzique pictures fascinate you most, Vixen? The ones where the women torment the men or those where the women are bound to serve their masters?"

Shock, excitement, desire thundered in Venetia's soul. What had her admission done? What did Marcus think of her? His fingers were harsh against her scalp, his thigh rubbed hard, but she loved the roughness of it. His sudden madness.

"Which do you wish to be?" he demanded, voice husky. "Dominant or submissive?"

"Marcus!" Her face burned—her skin was flushed, heated, dewy with sweat—but was it embarrassment or desire? What would it be like to be bound . . . to be at his mercy? To be under his control?

But she was already.

"We could try both," Marcus continued, as alluring as Lucifer. "Expand your education."

Breathless moments followed. She need only say 'yes' and then she would be plunged into a world of untold pleasure, untold adventure, untold sensuality.

Suddenly he groaned. A sound of frustration, not desire. "Blast. Lydia intended this to distract us," he ground out, his voice tight. "We have to go back upstairs. Now."

Panic raced through Venetia as they approached the door to her bedchamber. Her trunks were locked—Lydia couldn't have discovered her paints and sketches, could she?

She heard her own frantic breathing . . . and another sound, a soft, steady thrum. His breaths? Not her heart—it pounded like a drum.

The sound grew louder—it was in her room—and something beyond the door rattled. Marcus had heard it too. Venetia's hand clutched his arm; she felt him become alert as he eased away from her.

"There's something wrong . . . the sound, that's it. The wind is loud—can't you hear it? And it's cold." She felt it now on her ankles. Frosty air eking out from around the door. "There must be a window open."

"A forgetful maid? Do maids air rooms in the middle of storms?" Marcus frowned, approaching the door with lethal quiet. "Lydia wouldn't open a window—she wouldn't climb up a two story stone wall. There's a terrace outside my room, but it still means a climb." He twisted the doorknob. It turned freely and the door opened.

Icy air breezed out.

"Please, Vee, stay behind me."

Vee. He'd never called her that. Always temptress or vixen or sweet. Endearments that he could bestow on anyone. 'Vee' was special. It was hers.

Strange that it would matter so much when her heart was beating wildly.

She stayed so close her fingers brushed his back. Nonsensical detail struck—the deep green of his jacket, the whisper of trousers, the soft thud of his boots as he stepped in the room. Her slippers made no sound as she crept behind him—

"Christ Jesus." Quick, harsh, the words raced out on his sharp exhale.

Her heart jumped and she reached out to Marcus but he was gone, by her bed. There was no one in her room. But something dark was on her bed. She could barely see around his broad back and she moved to his side to peek.

It was a shape. A body. The skirts of a violet gown spread wide over her sheets. The woman's legs and hands were splayed, one hand dangled off the bed. A silent woman lay on her bed.

Waiting? Sleeping?

No. Venetia began to shake. Her knees. Her hands. Shaking.

Marcus shifted, moving forward and through the space between his back and the bedpost she saw the face—or the place where the face should be. It looked like a palette— blotches of blue and red and purple. Shapeless. Not human. The face and the dark hair were one borderless mess of color. As though paint had spilled on the bed. Blue and red, running together to make a lake of purple, streaked by tendrils of the pure color . . .

The eyes. Suddenly she saw those. The whites of the eyes were stark, the irises deep blue. Lifeless. The glass eyes of a waxwork. And that . . . that was the tongue, discolored to black, like a charred stump of log, sticking out from blue lips, the teeth bared.

Lydia. Lydia's face.

A whimper slid out. Her own tongue felt thick and immobile. She tried to speak. "M—"

He turned at once.

The room lurched. The house seemed to slide beneath her feet.

His hands closed on her shoulders. She feared he might crush them together and snap her ribcage. He was only trying to hold her up. Protect her. One moment Lydia's face was in front of her gaze, the next she was staring into his waistcoat. Dragons. Embroidered dragons frolicked there, across his large chest.

"Out," he commanded, pushing her backward. Her feet obeyed, even as her hands dangled as useless as Lydia's and her eyes stared as fixedly. "Come, Venetia, back to my room. You must come out of here."

His voice. Firm. Autocratic. Yes, of course she must do as he said.

But there was something she must do. That she suddenly could do.

Her lips parted, her lungs filled.

She screamed.

Venetia heard other screams. And voices. So many voices, pounding inside her head—shrill, deep, excited, frightened—screaming, shouting, arguing all at once.

She sat up on Marcus' bed and put her hand to her head. The connecting door was slightly ajar—the catch hadn't clicked and it had swung back after Marcus closed it. But no one had come in. She shivered beneath his counterpane—Marcus had bundled her in it, had rubbed her through it until her arms and legs began to feel warm, instead of heavy and . . . and dead.

But he'd had to leave her to deal with the guests barging into her room, making that awful discovery . . .

She should get up. Help him. Face this.

What sort of independent woman was she, cowering beneath the bedsheets? She kicked the bedclothes back with shaky legs. She couldn't just hide here while he dealt with . . . with Lydia's body.

She had to keep forcing herself to think of that. To think of the image she'd seen. She had to deaden herself to the shock.

Helping her mother aid village women had brought about enough shocks, enough to think she was a tougher woman, forged of sterner stuff. She'd seen women beaten to a pulp, punched until they didn't look human, and she'd helped to tend wounds.

Those were times for true courage because there had been no other choice. But now she had choice. She could hide. Or she could be at Marcus' side. She could be of some use instead of being a burden—

She had courage. The shock had robbed her of it, but she could find it again.

Venetia slid off Marcus' bed and landed unsteadily on her feet. She pawed her skirts down as she took a step. Her legs shook. She clutched at the bedpost.

There was a knock now at Marcus' door.

"Brandy, ma'am," called a masculine voice. "For yer shock."

Walking to the door gave her a chance to test her trembling limbs. She had to hold the bed, then the wall to ensure she didn't fall, but once she reached the door, she felt improved. Still, her fingers fumbled with the doorknob. Of course, she couldn't open the door. Marcus had the key.

Her voice shook as she tried to shout that through the door—the footman obviously had no master set because he left with a promise to return.

Perhaps brandy would be a good idea before she went back into her room.

Within a few moments, she heard the rap again, heard the soft scrape of the key going into the lock. The lock turned, the door swung open, and the footman swept in with a silver tray and a large balloon glass of brandy. It was the dark-haired servant—the one with black curly hair. The one who'd kissed Lady Yardley's breasts. Earlier he'd worn a smirk on his handsome face, had looked cocky, now his face was ashen beneath his powdered wig, his mouth a grim line.

"I expect yer room'll be set to rights, soon, ma'am," he promised, his tray hugged to his hip and her brandy placed on the bedside table. "His lordship's directed others to get a sheet. They'll like as not move the poor lady to 'er own room."

A sheet. A winding sheet. To cover her. To carry her.

"Ye'd better 'ave that brandy now, madam."

Venetia found herself reaching for it, before she remembered he was a servant. What had become of her that a masculine voice had her automatically obeying? "Thank you . . ."

"Polk, madam."

She said, as austerely as she could, "That will be all, Polk."

She knew this man was shocked by the death too—he banged his tray against the half-open door in his haste to leave and muttered a ripe curse. There was a strange, nervous quickness in his step and he pulled the door shut behind him with a too-loud bang.

Someone had throttled Lydia Harcourt, deliberately, cold-bloodedly, and boldly. Someone whom she had threatened had turned on her. Someone in the house had killed.

She downed a glass of neat brandy, and found herself caught up in the heated dizziness left by the drink, her throat burning, but her entire body shivering. The most horrible thought settled on her. Evil. Selfish. Terrible. But it stuck there and she couldn't dislodge it.

She was safe. Her sisters, Maryanne and Grace, were safe. Her entire family was safe.

Someone had saved her family.

And, heaven help her, she felt relief.

*   *   *

"It's the gypsies. Bloody thieving gypsies."

Marcus let the sheet drape over Lydia's destroyed face, surprised to feel a twinge of sympathy for both the victim and the gypsies Chartrand claimed had killed her.

He leveled a cool glance at his host. "Gypsies? Bold to break in here in the middle of the morning. You believe they scaled the wall in the pouring rain to steal?"

Chartrand paced alongside the bed, arms crossed over his large chest. "They came through that window." He jabbed a thick finger toward it. The wind snatched the paned glass panel and threw it back in place.

"Could that window be closed before it shatters?" Marcus snapped and a footman leapt forward to do his bidding.

Chartrand's gaze locked into his, hollow, unblinking, shocked.

Of course. He remembered now—incredible to think he'd forgotten. The gypsies. Chartrand's blank, stunned look. Chartrand's first wife had been attacked in the woods by a gypsy boy and killed. The senseless murder had stunned the *haute volée*. He'd been a typical bloodthirsty adolescent, fascinated by the details. The lurid newsheet descriptions of the body, the blood, the wound—

God help him, but so had most schoolboys his age. And the gypsy boy had dangled on a rope.

He motioned for the footmen to help him move Lydia. "It was locked on the inside, Chartrand. I know, I locked it myself."

"Might be appropriate if you don't mention that, Trent."

Sliding his hand beneath Lydia's shoulder, Marcus stared at Chartrand, who wore a mulish, petulant look. "Appropriate if I don't mention the truth?"

Chartrand wheeled around and stalked to the fireplace. Marcus turned his back on him. At this moment he had to move Lydia, lay her out on the bed in an unused room.

A clanging sound came from behind him. Chartrand idly

striking the poker against the grate. "It's obvious the gypsies got in some other way and had to use the window to get out," Chartrand said. "It's easy enough for the likes of them to get into a house. They all but destroyed Lydia's room and took her jewels. Must have stole in another way—by the kitchens, or a first floor window. Don't muddy the waters by making things look complicated."

"Put that bloody poker down, Chartrand." He didn't want to direct Chartrand to take charge—Chartrand would be burning out the gypsy camp if he did that. "Have you sent for the magistrate? I want to have Lydia Harcourt's room locked—and this one left untouched until I say otherwise."

"Until *you* say otherwise?" This roused Chartrand from his corner by the fire. Heavy footsteps crossed the floor. "Lydia's room will stay locked and the key with me."

"I'll need new rooms for Vixen and I."

At this Chartrand's bullish stance eased. "Of course, Trent. The girl's suffered a bad shock. Rutledge will see to this."

Chartrand rang the bell pull, but the butler appeared in the room almost instantaneously. "The green room is in readiness, my lord, for the body. I regret to inform, my lord, that it will be impossible for Lord Aspers, the magistrate, to journey here at this time. Reportedly the entire lower road is under water, the bridges destroyed. No carriages can enter or leave. Even travel of horseback would be impossible."

"Bloody hell," Chartrand groaned. Marcus agreed. They had a murdered woman on their hands, and no hope of seeing the law for several days.

"Do you require more men to assist in removing the body?"

"Under control, Rutledge. But my companion will require a new room." Marcus scrubbed his jaw as he spoke. He didn't trust Chartrand to act as the law. Hell, he had no idea exactly who Lydia was blackmailing but from the tension, the anger boiling amongst the men here, he'd guess every man in attendance.

Rutledge bowed and withdrew.

"Now that we know the magistrate isn't coming—" Pointing, Marcus directed one brawny footman to Lydia's shoulders, the second to her legs. "I'll help lift, but you two are to carry Mrs. Harcourt upstairs."

But before they moved her, he lifted the edge of the sheet and studied the wound in the throat once more. Neat and deeply gouged—a slice into her throat. A wire had been used, he guessed. He let the white cloth drop. "Take her up."

He turned immediately to his host. "Chartrand—send Rutledge or someone upstairs to deal with the body."

Now he wondered as he watched Chartrand shuffle out, looking a confused, beaten man instead of the bully he usually was. Was he racked with grief, remembering his first wife's death? Or had Chartrand murdered his wife and Lydia had blackmailed him over it?

Marcus gave a grim smile as he was left alone. He'd loved the serial book, *Gentleman of Justice—Tales of a Bow Street Runner*, a romanticized work but with some sound thoughts about logical detection, including the lesson to not leap to conclusions.

A soft sound caught his attention and he glanced up. His heart lurched in his chest at the sight of Venetia trembling in the doorway, her hand checking to ensure her mask was still in place. He was in front of her in one quick step, and took her hands in his. Like ice. He stroked his hands gently all over hers.

"Sweeting, what are you doing here?" Marcus asked. "You need to be in bed."

Venetia tried to look around Marcus' large, solid body to see into her room. The brandy had left her a bit woozy, but revived. She hadn't come in earlier while Marcus spoke with Chartrand and Rutledge. Shameful though it was, she'd listened at the connecting door.

"It's horrible," she said softly.

Marcus wrapped his arm around her shoulders, turning her back toward his bedroom. Gently, but the command was unmistakable. So easy to surrender . . . to rely on his strength to see her through . . .

"Marcus, I want to go in there."

"What in Hades for, Vee? You've had a shock. You need to rest."

She tried to resist—she wanted to go in *her* room. She would find the courage! "I want to see if there are clues to who did this. It wasn't a gypsy who did this—it was someone Lydia blackmailed. Why—why do you think she was killed in *my* room?"

"I think it happened in your room simply due to opportunity," he said gently.

"You mean they followed her here and caught her by surprise? But why not in her room?"

"She wouldn't have screamed at first, when caught in here. She would have been afraid to give herself away."

Venetia blinked away the sudden thought of Lydia Harcourt's horror when she knew she would die. Poor Lydia. No one deserved that. No one deserved to be brutally killed.

Marcus propelled her through the connecting doorway. "This is not your concern. She did bring this upon herself, pet. No one deserves to die that way, true, but Lydia was a tough, surviving bitch, and would destroy anyone to get what she wanted. She teased tigers and they attacked."

Pulling her hands free of Marcus', Venetia stepped back and faced him. She'd thought him a protector, noble despite his licentious ways. Yet he seemed to be blaming Lydia for being the victim. Frowning, she pointed out, "Lydia was worried about her future, just like I am."

She stood on the threshold between their rooms. She faced two choices—retreat into obedient safety in his room or confrontation in hers.

"Lydia is not at all like you, sweeting. You aren't hurting anyone else with what you're doing." He met her gaze, his eyes questioning, confused. "How can you champion the woman? She set out to destroy you."

"She had to survive," Venetia protested. "What was Lydia going to do when men wouldn't pay her any more? Yes, she had to be scandalous. Yes, she had to break rules. But I can understand the desperation. I, of all people, have no right to judge her. And neither do you."

He snapped back at that, those stunning, almost unearthly greenish-blue eyes narrowing. "And just what do you mean by that?"

"You don't know what it's like to be desperate."

"Nor do you." A dark anger rumbled in his voice. "You had other options, sweeting. The truth is that you didn't like them. I do know what it is like to be desperate. Hell, I know what it is like to be willing to kill."

Chapter Fourteen

"Who were you willing to kill?" Venetia asked.

What in hell had possessed him to say that? Marcus reached out to Venetia, to turn her abruptly by her shoulders and direct her to his bed, but she darted free of his grasp. She rushed back into her room and ran right for her bed—where Lydia had lain.

She might have been raised as a proper young lady, but she most definitely hadn't been molded into one, and in more ways than just her unrestrained sensuality. She was too blunt, too direct, too questioning, and most definitely the daughter of the parents she'd described—a rebellious lady and a flamboyant artist. She began lifting the pillows, searching through the sheets.

"Stop it," he snapped. "You are not to involve yourself in this."

"There must be some clue . . ." She bent and slid her hands under the mattress. "Do you mean you killed a man in a duel? That isn't the same thing as being truly desperate and afraid."

"It wasn't a duel."

She glanced up, frowning. "Then why did you do it?" She frowned. Pushing—like a fencing opponent driven to draw first blood.

Should he just answer her and be done with it? Say simply 'I killed my father' and ignore the rest of the inevitable questions? Instead, he snapped, "Blast it! It makes no difference why, but it was over a point of honor. A matter of decency."

But it hadn't been. It had been blind rage driving him.

"You took charge in there," she said. "You took control away from Chartrand. Are you going to search for Lydia's killer?"

"I'd leave that to the magistrate. Let the law deal as it should." His only concern was protecting his sister, his family's name. His only plan was to search again for that blasted manuscript.

Venetia stood. "But will the law also dismiss Lydia for what she was? A courtesan. Will they care?"

"Stop this." Marcus grasped her hands and drew her away from the bed. She still wore her mask, and he untied it and pulled it away. Her face was stark white. Her eyes enormous.

She clapped her hand to her mouth. "She spoke of a manuscript at dinner!" she cried. "What if she brought it with her? What if everyone's secrets are there? What if mine are? I must look—"

"You will stay here. In my room. I will search for Lydia's manuscript."

"But we must go now! What if someone else finds it?" She bit her lip. "The room is probably locked—"

"I have a lock pick."

She frowned. "A lock pick?"

"A tool designed to spring locks," he explained, as though it was normal to bring one along to an orgy. "I searched Lydia's room last night. I didn't find a manuscript, a diary, or any sort of journal. Admittedly, I had to abandon the search before I was caught by her maid." He fought to keep his voice cool. To appear detached. He couldn't let emotion show—couldn't let her guess that Lydia Harcourt knew his family's secrets too.

"You searched her room last night?" Ingenuous innocence shone in her green-flecked hazel eyes. "For me? You weren't having sex with other women?"

He read the uncertainty in her voice—knowing he'd been faithful had been a relief. Did it mean she wanted more from this experience than he could offer? "No, I was not having sex with other women. And if the book is in Lydia's room, it's cleverly hidden. Or she didn't bring it. I want you to stay in bed—my bed—and do not go into—"

"Oh no, her book is precious to her," she broke in. "Lydia wouldn't trust it at home. What of fire? Or some other disaster? Her housekeeper certainly knew she was blackmailing, so would guess she had valuable secrets. I know how one worries over creative work—I'm certain she brought it with her. I am coming with you to search."

"You are definitely not. You've had a bad shock—"

"And I want to get out of this room! If there is one thing I've learned it is not to cower and wring my hands, but to take action. And I'm a woman. Did you ever search for your sister's diary?"

An arrow lanced his heart. He had, but not to tease Min over it. "All right. I admit it. I did and I never found it."

"The killer must have found it!" Venetia forgot to whisper as her heart sank to her slippers. Lydia's room was utterly devastated. Her gowns and corsets tumbled out of the standing wardrobe. The sheets had been ripped from the bed.

Marcus slid the slim metal tool—the lock pick—into his coat pocket. He shook his head and explained in a low voice, "This looks like a hurried search. There's a chance the searcher didn't find it. Ensure you leave things as they are—we can't move things before the magistrate arrives."

The magistrate! Venetia froze in shock, one of Lydia's gowns drawn tight by her clenched hands. The horror of the morning had kept her from seeing the danger. To prove their innocence she would have to reveal to the magistrate that they had been witnesses to that bondage display.

And the magistrate would insist she take off her mask. All her secrets would be revealed.

"Jewelry box." Marcus lifted a large cream and gilt box inlaid with winking stones.

Legs trembling, Venetia looked over and let the gown fall. Lined with velvet, the box was empty but for one glinting bit of gold. An earbob stuck in the bottom corner.

Venetia's thoughts whirled as she sifted through the gowns, searching for pockets, for a book. She couldn't face the magistrate. She was going to be ruined. Her family would be ruined.

She searched the wardrobe, the chest of drawers, the escritoire, the back of the cheval mirror. Nothing. She explored each gown—feeling the bodice, kneading skirts between shaking fingers. After that she rummaged through the undergarments in the drawers.

Marcus flipped up the lid of one of Lydia's trunks. "I didn't have time to thoroughly search this one." It was filled to the top with books. Frowning, Marcus lifted one.

"*Tom Jones*." He picked up another. "*Pride and Prejudice*."

"She read." Her voice wavered on even just the two words.

After flipping through the pages, he stacked each volume on the floor. The trunk was empty. "Novels. Biographies. Nothing else." He felt around the interior of the trunk and she stared in surprise.

"Checking for hidden panels." Grimly, he shook his head and stood.

Venetia searched the mattress, feeling beneath it, as Marcus stretched to search the bed canopy. He splayed a hand on the mantle and leaned into the unlit fireplace. Venetia crouched at his side, peered in too. A cloud of soot rained down. She shut her eyes, felt it dust her face. She spit out the taste of the ashes. Opening her eyes, she saw Marcus' black-streaked face. "Goddamn," he muttered. "Oh, Vee—" He brushed at her cheek.

She slumped back, sprawling onto her bottom. "It's gone. And my secrets along with it. My sisters' futures will be ruined. And Mother . . . after defying my mother to come to London and paint, I'll bring disaster to them all. You were absolutely right."

"We don't know that anyone else has the book yet, sweetheart. And if someone took it, I promise I will get it back."

She could not do it. Venetia realized she could not just simply rely on Marcus' promise and not worry about her own future. She stood by her new bed, in her new bedchamber, spine stiff, hands fisted.

Marcus massaged her shoulders, firm, sensuous, until the tension in her back melted away. Until she sagged back against him. "Perhaps she didn't bring her manuscript," he said.

If only she could believe that. "I fear she did. But I keep praying that the murderer didn't find it. Lydia must have expected her victims to try to steal the book. Perhaps she hid her work with extraordinary care."

He slid his arm around her chest, just below her breasts, and cradled her. His arm pressed sensually against her curves, but his touch was meant to be tender, she knew.

She'd survived the threat of poverty. She could survive scandal. She need only think!

"We must search Lydia's b—" She broke off, unable to say the word.

"I searched her body, love. I would have noticed something large in her dress or underclothes. There was no book, no papers, no mysterious key. I also searched her carriage."

"We need to know who she was blackmailing. We need to discover who killed her." She bit her lip. *Think. Think.* "We must question her maid! Servants know everything."

"Later, sweeting. You need to rest, relax, to recover from shock."

Venetia moved his arms away and stepped toward her es-critoire. She wanted to hide in his arms. She couldn't. "I heard Lady Yardley warn Lydia she would end up throttled to death."

"*Lady Yardley?*" Marcus followed Venetia. He couldn't imagine sultry Sophia, Countess of Yardley, as a murderess. On the other hand, how much would Sophia pay to keep her licentious lifestyle out of print? "I doubt a woman strangled Lydia—"

He broke off. Inclined his head. "You are absolutely correct, sweeting. An enraged woman could have killed her, with the advantage of surprise. Or Lady Yardley could have hired a man to do it. I don't know all the men here."

Venetia sat on the small chair. "But you know many of them." She drew out the inkwell, a pen, sheets of paper. "I think we should make a list."

He frowned. Perhaps this was healing for her—to keep her mind busy. He realized she wouldn't rest. Many women would have taken to their beds, but not Venetia.

He moved to her side, leaned over the chair, so his chest brushed her shoulders. He wanted to be close to her. "Montberry was Lydia's most prestigious protector, but it was rumored he didn't satisfy her. Chartrand was her lover once—he bought off her contract after only two months. Gave a generous settlement. To the best of my knowledge, Brude and Swansborough were never protectors but they bought time with her at events like this. For the right price, Lydia would play any game."

"What about Mr. Wembly?" she asked.

"He was her protector for a year, I believe. He became famous. Lydia adored that, and overlooked his lack of title. He threw her out when he became a favorite of Prinny's."

"At dinner, Lydia spoke to him a lot of Princess Caroline," she mused, tapping pen to lip.

"Which would irritate any friend of the Prince Regent."

"But what secrets does he have?" she asked. "Who has secrets that are worth killing over?"

I do. But Marcus pushed that thought away. He dropped to one knee, resting his hand on her delicate forearm. "Chartrand's first wife was strangled—supposedly by a gypsy boy who raped her. Fifteen years ago."

"S—strangled?" She went tense in her chair. Her beautiful hazel eyes met his.

"There were rumors—quickly stopped—that he killed her himself. Either deliberately, or by accident. He enjoyed rough sex and he forced her to play."

"But how could he escape prosecution?" she cried angrily. Her pen threw splatters of ink on the page. "Could he really have had an innocent man hanged in his place?"

"Easily enough, I'm afraid. But as for the others, I don't know their dark secrets."

She wrote with quick, sloping strokes. "The characters reveal themselves like a painting. They can be pigeonholed, yet the simple words to describe them hint at their conflicts and secrets."

She intrigued him—this woman who was logical and artistic, pure and wanton. He breathed in her spicy perfume as he watched her write.

Montberry—duke and war hero.

Chartrand—the sporting Corinthian who might have strangled his wife.

Lady Chartrand—the submissive wife.

Lady Yardley—the wicked widow.

Lord Brude—the brooding romantic poet.

Mr. Wembly—the jaded dandy.

Lord Swansborough—the dark, dangerous lord.

He was about to give his approval when she tapped the pen against her lip. "I could include myself," she said and she set about doing so. *Desperate virgin.* So that was how she saw herself? "But, of course, I didn't kill Lydia."

Perversely, he said. "You should add me."

"But I know you are innocent." Still she wrote his name. *Lord Trent.* He waited to see what would follow.

Protective, seductive earl.

That surprised him. Of course, she thought his only motive to strangle Lydia would be to protect her. She knew nothing of Min, his father, the secrets of his family.

Tipping her head, she looked at him. He bent to nuzzle her neck, so he could avoid her inquisitive gaze. "There may not be any special secrets, Vee. Lydia might just have threatened to expose the affairs she had. Chartrand and Montberry are married."

"But would someone kill over that? It must be a very valuable secret, to warrant murder." She stared down at her list. "Lords Brude and Swansborough could not have killed her. We saw them pleasuring that girl with dildoes."

"They couldn't have strangled her by their own hands but they could have paid someone—if the motive was to silence Lydia. Someone who followed Lydia to your room."

She frowned. "Did you find any clues in my room? Anything to help point the way?"

He shook his head—the truth—but she fixed him with a suspicious glare. "I suspect you wouldn't tell me if you did. I understand the danger, Marcus, but I must protect my family."

Her words resonated through his soul. "This is what I saw, Vee." He gave her as much as he'd taken in. The window open. No dirt or water on the floor. No signs of a search, except that Venetia's trunk had been out of place, dragged out but not opened.

"Thank heaven," she breathed.

He hesitated as he described Lydia. "Her bodice was ripped but the bed wasn't torn up enough to indicate she fought on it. I think she was strangled standing and then laid out on it."

"She wasn't . . . raped?" Venetia asked.

"No. I wondered why the killer had gone to the trouble of arranging her on the bed. Quicker to let her drop to the floor, and then run. She was strangled with a garrote or a thin cord—but given that every room here is filled with cords for use in bondage games, the weapon used doesn't point to the killer."

"There are the women, too." Venetia poised her pen over the paper once more. "What about the other prostitutes here? There are a dozen or more! You will have to help me," she added pointedly, "I only know three by name. There's Rosalyn Rose. 'The aging madam.' Surely Rosalyn wouldn't strangle Lydia because they were rivals. Trixie—the saucy young jade, who seems willing to do anything to entice men. Did she have secrets?"

"I have no idea."

"And there's Sarah," she continued, "Well, Sarah did not strangle Lydia. She was hanging upside down with candles in her derriere and—"

A discrete knock sounded on the connecting door. "It's ready, milord," called a feminine voice, and then another door—the one from his room to the hallway—clicked shut.

Marcus's heart pounded, blood roaring in his head, rushing to his cock. "Enough for now. Come with me, Vee."

"But we must—" She broke off as he lifted her into his arms.

Venetia gasped in surprise as Marcus carried her into the opulent dressing room attached to his bedroom.

An enormous claw-footed bathtub stood in the center, thick towels piled around it. Steam rose from the water and hung in the now humid and hot room. The fire roared, so one wouldn't be chilled while bathing. Lit wall sconces added a golden glow to the reddish, sensual light of the fire. Drapes were drawn shut, closing out the dull and dreary outside world. Closing out the loud, driving storm—the shrieking wind, the explosions of thunder, the pounding rain.

Closing out past tragedy and looming disaster.

Her heart raced as he set her on her feet. "But we must assess our suspects and—"

"You've had too many shocks today, love. I wish I could get you out of here. Send you somewhere safe."

"I wouldn't go. Protecting my family is my responsibility, not yours."

For a moment, there were shadows in Marcus' eyes, but then he smiled wryly. "We are both covered in soot. We can't appear in front of the others like this. I insist we bathe."

"Together?"

"A warm bath, a loving embrace is the best medicine for shock. Searching for murderers is not." He was laying his jacket over the back of a wing chair. His white shirtsleeves and pale waistcoat set off his lightly tanned skin, his blue-black hair. He was unspeakably beautiful. Worthy of a thousand portraits.

His eyes twinkled wickedly. "I am looking forward to ensuring you are deliciously clean. Everywhere."

She watched his long-fingered hands undo the simple knot of cravat, then toss the starched cloth, and quickly open his waistcoat. He smiled and motioned toward her buttons, which ran down the front of her day dress. "We should get in before the water cools."

Her breath caught at the thought. "Am I to wash you?" She wanted to. Wanted to touch him everywhere with soapy hands.

He began to peel down his small clothes. A smile tugged at her lips as he carefully worked them over his erect cock. It wobbled, bucked up toward the sky. He gave it a stroke as he stepped out of his underclothes.

She wanted to lose herself in this exotic moment. She whisked off her gown, light demi-corset, her shift.

He straightened, nude, sleekly muscled. As perfect as a statue of a male god. "Turn around as you roll down your stockings. I love the sight of your naked derriere."

His eyes were brilliantly blue-green, his hot gaze scorching her. It wasn't his title that made her obey. Or his lordly dominance. It was the knowledge that she excited him.

Suddenly, she realized she could think of them as just Marcus and Venetia—not rake and innocent, earl and commoner, peer and artist. A man and a woman . . . a woman who needed comforting arms and a man well capable of providing them.

She presented her bare rear and slowly rolled down her silk stockings. Nude, she turned to face him. His eyes blazed with desire as he swept his gaze along her body. He held out his hand and led her to the tub. Even the sight of his bare feet was strangely erotic. Her breath caught as she watched his snug rump flex and relax with each step, the cheeks hollowing to hard, tight globes.

His strong hands slipped around her waist. In one easy motion he lifted her over the side of the tub and lowered her in. Luxuriant heat teased her toes, then they dipped into the steamy water.

He held her there, his biceps bulging into large mounds. "Is the water right?"

"Blissfully perfect," she breathed and at her approval, he lowered her in. She held tight to his muscled forearms as she sank down onto her bottom. Her fingers touched the raised lines of veins, tangled in his dark, silky hairs.

It was sheer heaven to be engulfed by the hot, spice-scented water. The tub was so deep that water lapped at her shoulders and her breasts floated. Her nipples tightened and the dangling tendrils of her hair dampened. Her hair swirled in the water, tickling her neck and shoulders.

Marcus reached down and cupped her cheek. His thumb traced her lips, and she wrapped her fingers around his wrist and took his thumb into her mouth. Sucked it, licked it, watching his eyes all the while. In the rich golden glow, his eyes were like flawless aquamarines—the color she still had yet to capture exactly.

He slung his leg over the edge of the tub. She released his thumb, moved to give him room.

And then he was in with her, lowering his beautiful body

beneath the silvery, rippling surface. A sigh of pure pleasure escaped his lips as he sank down. He tipped his head back, letting the water soak into his raven-black hair. The steaming water covered his chest to his hard, brown nipples. His black curls plastered to his broad chest. Groaning, he ran his wet hands over his hair, slicking it back. Droplets sprayed on her and landed on his high cheekbones, his sculpted lips.

He dropped his hands back to the water, and swept his arms through it, to rest them on the sides of the massive tub. Waves lapped over, her breasts bobbed in the water. She glanced down to see that his cock waved in the water too as Marcus shifted and reached for a cake of soap. He grinned. "You are a truly delicious sight when wet, Vee."

Men saw the same sight with different eyes than a woman. When she had bathed in a few inches of tepid water in a tin tub back home, she had felt more like a drowned rat than a vision. But Marcus, nude and wet, would be beautiful in any setting.

He lathered soap on his hands until a white froth covered them. An exotic jasmine scent filled the air.

"Flowery soap for a gentleman's bath?"

"It was known I wouldn't be alone." Water sloshed over the tub's rim as he slid over to her. She held her breath as he washed her shoulders and her neck. As he dabbed froth on her nose and chin. As his smile wrapped around her heart like a warm embrace.

He covered her breasts with his soapy hands. She sighed with unspeakable delight. With great attention, he washed them. He cupped and stroked them, until they must be squeaky clean, but he didn't stop. Foam covered her nipples—he blew it away. She felt the brush of his breath through every nerve, in the throbbing of her cunny.

"May I wash your chest now? Is there any soap appropriate for you?"

With a laugh, he took another cake of soap off a towel and handed it to her. A fresh bar that smelled of sandalwood. As she turned in the tub, lathering her hands, she realized they would carry this scent, the scent he would wear.

Shyly, she pressed her hands to his chest. She roamed over his pectoral muscles and felt his nipples harden beneath her fingertips. Daringly, she even washed the long, soft hairs in his underarms, and sighed at the earthy, intoxicating scent there.

He groaned at that, and then she swept her hands up, to his magnificently straight shoulders, perfectly proportioned, perfectly symmetrical. She had to move closer to him, and he spread his legs to allow her knees to slide closer. There it was. A small scar that her fingers had found.

"A beating," he said.

"With what?"

"Riding crop. Broke the skin."

"A sexual game?"

"No. My father's rage." He turned his head to kiss her hand as she made soapy circles on his shoulders.

She could see he was trying to distract her. It must hurt him to speak of it. She washed his right arm, amazed as she always was by the hardness of his biceps. All the black hairs on his forearm streamed down his lightly tanned skin. She stroked his wrist—was it as sensitive as hers?

He moaned as she washed him there, then massaged his palm.

"I love your touch, Vee. You are truly an artist in sensual matters."

He so easily touched her heart. He soaped his hands again. Slick with suds, his hands gently washed her belly.

He winked. "Now, sweeting, you will have to stand so I can wash between your thighs."

To support herself, she had to brace her hands on his shoulders. He rubbed soap through her curls until they were frothy with it, then splashed warm water on her to rinse. The water teased her clit, dripped off her lips, rolled in tickling rivulets down her thighs.

He gazed up, locks of blue-black hair plastered to his forehead. Droplets of water clung to his long, curving lashes. Venetia arched her hips forward. In answer he grabbed her bottom and pulled her cunny tight to his face. His lashes closed completely, his tongue danced over her clit, lapped, then circled with long, strong strokes.

She loved this . . . the hard pressure, pushing, abrading . . .

He coaxed her foot up. Unsteady, she balanced it on the rim, then his strong hands held her derriere, giving her the confidence to open herself to his questing tongue.

He licked her everywhere—her clit, her lips, her passage. He dropped his head back, lifted her onto his face and licked the rim of her anus, around the soapy outside. Shivers of pleasure consumed her. If he stopped holding her, she would fall.

She was drowning in this. She bent forward, wrapped her arms tightly around his neck.

He found her clit once more, suckling, mercilessly teasing.

She closed her eyes. Water splashed. Rivulets ran from her lips, nipples, fingertips, down her thighs, teasing her skin. She rocked over his mouth, knowing now what she wanted. No longer content to linger and explore.

This was heaven—to hold beautiful shoulders, to feel like a queen while taking pleasure with the most gorgeous earl in existence . . .

But it was so much more.

His fingers drove into the soft skin of her buttocks as his tongue played. He pulled her against him in the rhythm she wanted. Needed. She danced with him. Driving. Pushing.

Pleasure grew, built, burst—!

The orgasm rippled over her, lush, vibrant, perfect. She sobbed with it. Grasped wet, raven hair. Held him tight, through the mad swaying of her body. Through the wild pleasure. Bone-melting pleasure.

She feared she might fall, but he lowered her carefully.

"Now you must stand while I wash you," she urged.

With a surprisingly shy grin, Marcus obeyed. Water sluiced off his lean hips and long legs as he stood. A steady stream ran off down his cock and dripped from his tightened ballocks.

Venetia tried to commit the sight to memory. To paint—for her own pleasure.

The soap made her hands slippery and she slid her palms along the length of his cock, tracing bulging veins, the fascinating shape. He moaned and shut his eyes at her touch.

Splashing water along him, she rinsed him clean.

The cheval mirror reflected them. His gaze went from her to the mirror and back, hot, admiring, lustful. She grasped his hips, toyed with his cock with only her tongue. He tasted of soap. The lush, ripe taste of his cock had been washed away and she ached for it. Even his balls, usually earthy and rich, tasted of clean water and fragrant sandalwood.

Clutching his hips, she took one of his ballocks into her mouth and held him there, swirling her warm tongue around its delicate shape. She stroked his anus, toyed with his cock, then teasingly released his sac and gobbled up his cock once more. Wantonly determined to please.

His fingers clawed through her hair. His hips thrust.

She sucked him deep, as deep as she could, sliding his length in and out. She wanted to pleasure him. It excited her to please.

He moaned hoarsely. Threaded his fingers in her hair and gently acted as guide. "I love your tongue wrapped around me like velvet. God—"

He began drawing himself in and out, urged her to bob on him. He murmured, so low she barely heard, "I love fucking your face, sweet angel."

So deliciously coarse. She groaned around him. She found his tight anus, his ballocks, and teased both. Suddenly, his cock swelled in her mouth. The head grew taut, bursting taut. With a rush, his come spurted onto her tongue, into her mouth.

She drank it, sucking it all out, and he collapsed forward. "Vee, you know how to make me your slave."

He was so tender with her afterward. He lifted her from the tub, wrapped her in the embrace of a thick white, warm towel. She stood before the blazing fire while he fashioned a smaller towel into a turban around her hair. "There." He let the towel drape on her shoulders and nibbled her ear lobe.

She turned in his arms, still holding the towel tight. He wore a matching one draped around his hips, the lean bones of his hips jutting above it.

He began to massage her towel against her skin, drying the dampness. He rubbed it against her quim in a way that made her legs shudder. He dried with extra care between the cheeks of her bottom.

"You make me forget," he said softly, "I'm supposed to be a reformed rake, Vee. There is something about you that tempts me as no woman has ever done."

"I don't believe that," she whispered. She didn't want him to think he had to make those romantic statements a rake always did.

"You condemn me for being a rake, don't you? You are judging me on what I was."

Yes, she was. But that was how a clever woman protected herself. He had been a rake, he would continue to be a rake. He would *always* be a rake.

"I have never known greater intimacy with anyone, Vee, than I've known in just a few days with you."

I've never known greater intimacy with anyone than I've known with you.

Venetia stared at the blank page facing her. Her hand, holding the charcoal to the pristine white surface, trembled. Marcus thought she was napping in her room, but she could not sleep. She flipped back to her sketches of the orgy. She began to work on those, to add more detail to the quick, loose pictures she'd created. It soothed her to draw. Gave her comfort. Let her gain control of her shock, her whirling thoughts and emotions.

She glanced up at the door. If Marcus caught her sketching, there would be hell to pay.

CHAPTER FIFTEEN

Marcus braced his hands on the back of Venetia's gilt chair and watched her brush her hair. Each pass of the bristles through her long red-gold hair made his fingers ache to touch, to stroke, to play. The smooth oval glass reflected her face, ivory satin dusted with freckles.

"You deliberately disobeyed me at dinner."

The brush landed on the marble vanity with a sharp rap. Her hazel eyes widened in her reflection. "I did what, my lord?"

"I expressly told you not to speak to the gentlemen. Not to question them."

"They sought me out. To offer sympathy on my horrible experience. And I was very careful. They did not suspect a thing." She stood abruptly, stalked over to her escritoire. "I am perfectly capable of looking after myself."

He followed, irritated. "This is not a game, Vee."

Blazing, her eyes met his. "I saw what one of these people did to Lydia." She unlocked one of the drawers, withdrew a folded paper. As she laid it flat, Marcus saw it was the list she'd made. "Should we write down what we learned of their alibis? What of the Duke of Montberry?"

She plunked down on the chair and picked up the pen.

Of course, recording what they'd learned made perfect sense. And it involved no risk. He conceded defeat and paced to her side. "Montberry claims he was with Trixie and two other courtesans in the morning."

"Goodness, he made love with them all? Very sprightly of him."

Her dry tone made him laugh. "The women cavorted for his pleasure while he watched from within the wardrobe. The other two whores substantiated the story—though they could have been paid to do so."

She wrote swiftly beneath Montberry's name. *Morning of Lydia's death he claims to have been making love with three women.*

"Chartrand still blames gypsies," she said. "Do you think that indicates guilt?"

He shook his head. "He might be innocent but not want to believe he has a murderer in his home. But he gave no alibi for the time of the murder. As for the women, Lady Chartrand was receiving a whipping from Captain Clarke—one of the bucks parading around in his regimentals. Helen craves a man in a uniform."

"Helen?"

"I'd attended orgies with her for years—yes, we are on a first name basis." He shrugged. "And Sophia—Lady Yardley— claims she was enjoying two lovers at the time. So was Rosalyn Rose. But, again, the men could have been bribed to lie."

Venetia made quick notes. He leaned over her chair, unable to draw his gaze from the thick fall of red hair, the soft curve of her cheek, the solemn intelligence in her eyes.

"Lydia made hints at plagiarism to Brude, but we know he and Swansborough have alibis," she said, and a flush touched her cheeks. "Mr. Wembly claims he was playing cards until dawn. He says he retired to his room and slept—with cucumber slices on his eyelids and a restorative mask of porridge oats on his face—until just before luncheon."

"Porridge oats?" Marcus shook his head in disbelief. "An alibi that can't be proven."

"Brude, Montberry, and Lady Yardley tried to leave, but

their carriages became stuck," she said, "Do you think one of them found Lydia's manuscript?"

A sharp rap at his door interrupted. Venetia followed him into his room as a sharp female voice called out. "I am Mrs. Harcourt's maid. You wished to speak with me, my lord?"

At Venetia's surprised look, he smiled. "As you said, servants know everything." And with that, he urged her back into her room and closed the connecting door. But Venetia opened it and peeped in.

She felt a surge of pity for Juliette La Fleur, Lydia's lady's maid, as the woman stepped into Marcus' room. Plain-faced and broom-thin, Juliette bore red-rimmed eyes and a defeated manner as she faced Marcus. He glowered with lordly command, but his first questions came in a low, engaging voice that seemed to make even Juliette sparkle.

"My lady entertained no men in her room, my lord," the maid explained, plucking at her severe black skirt. "She left last night to attend to a special gentleman and told me she would not return until late. I did not see her again—" Juliette broke off with a choked gasp. "But why do you wish to know, milord?"

"What of her book? Her memoirs?" asked Marcus, arms folding across his chest.

"*Non*, I never saw my mistress' manuscript. But it must be of great value—her memoirs. I believe there were many who did not wish to be named. There had been *accidents* in London."

Hands on the door, Venetia trembled with excitement.

"What accidents?" Marcus demanded.

Juliette took a step closer to Marcus. "I am left without a position and suspicion attaches itself to me. What if I cannot get another post? But I could tell you more of these incidents in London. This knowledge I offer to you for a price."

But Marcus, Venetia saw, was not willing to negotiate. He questioned Juliette until two tears rolled down the maid's cheeks. Venetia's heart lurched—she almost pushed open the door to beg him to stop. Juliette cried, "I do not know! I hoped for money. I don't know who tried to hurt my mistress!" She spun abruptly and raced from the room. The door slammed behind her.

Venetia flung open her door. "Should we go after her?"

Marcus shook his head. "You look exhausted, sweeting. It is time for bed."

To her surprise, he led her by the shoulders to his bed. His sensual hands reached around her waist to untie her robe. "What—what are you doing?"

"Tucking you into bed."

He had shrugged when talking of Lady Chartrand, implying the intimacy had not mattered to him. Was that true? Was that worse? *I have never known greater intimacy with anyone than I've known in just a few days with you.*

Rakes knew how to tug a woman's heartstrings. She tried to remember that as he drew back the white sheets for her and she slid into warmed silken bliss. He paced around the bed to the other side. Lifted the sheets. Startled, she watched him climb in.

"But you don't sleep with . . . share your bed with—"

His fingertip touched her lips, silencing her questions. "I want to hold you in my arms and keep you safe and protected." He snuggled up to her side, pressing his wonderfully masculine, utterly naked chest, hips, groin against her. His muscular arm reached across her. She touched his hand, held his fingers.

He settled into the pillow with a sigh that whispered to her foolhardy heart.

Marcus stirred, stretched, yawned. Warm, naked feminine curves pressed against him. His sleeping cock rested against the pillow of Venetia's hot derriere, his leg lay between hers, his arm casually fell across the lush curve of her hip. Her curls tickled his lip and he brushed a kiss against them as his senses returned. They were nestled in his bed like spoons in a drawer, beneath tousled sheets. The intimacy of it speared him. He had never felt such warmth, such bone-deep contentment.

With each deep breath he inhaled a magical blend of fresh washed hair, roses, lavender. He levered up on his elbow to watch Venetia sleep. Dark gold lashes lay against her cheeks, her lips curved in a smile.

She looked delectable.

He wished he could wake her by sliding his cock into her and slowly making love to her, rousing her on a wave of pleasure. His cock swelled as he entertained the thought, increasing the torture by wedging into her curvaceous bottom. He had to roll away.

She murmured as she began to wake. Her lashes rose slowly. Her smile widened as she saw him. "You did stay."

"Of course." His chest felt tight. Desire raged in him like a fire.

"Is it morning?" she asked, "It is terribly dark."

"Still storming." He was more abrupt than he intended.

Venetia nodded. "I can hear it now—the rain against the windows."

She sat up, curls tumbling, sheets sliding down her lovely nude curves. "I want to search Lydia's room once more. I thought of something last night. She had many books with her—why bring those to an orgy? She must have meant not to return to London for a long time. And her maid spoke of accidents. She must have brought her book with her." She wrapped her arms around her knees. "I want to believe that it is still there—that no one else found it."

Marcus clamped down on his desire for her. Was there any point in searching again? But Venetia wanted it and in that moment of intimacy and desire, he couldn't have denied her a thing.

"How could we have missed this the first time?" Venetia stared in amazement as Marcus pressed on the metal banding that crossed the lid of Lydia's trunk. It depressed with a small click. She waited, hopeful, expecting a panel to spring open. But nothing happened.

"Damnation," Marcus muttered. "This activates something . . . but it's not engaging." His dark brows drew together. "Something's stopping the mechanism . . ."

"Is it broken?"

He tipped open the trunk lid, ran his long fingers over the silk lining, his eyes thoughtful, intense. A smile came to his lips. He slid the lock pick from his coat pocket, held it out to her. Mystified, Venetia took it. "Turn it in the lock, as I press in on the band."

Dutifully, she did. She watched his thumb push the metal strip down, heard the click, then the metal piece dropped down flush with the trunk lid and a second, louder click came. The lining of the lid seemed to magically drop open a half-inch.

Venetia pried the panel open another two inches, as far as it would go. "It's here!" She pulled out a sheath of papers bound with a red satin ribbon. Heart pounding, she undid the ribbon, aware of Marcus at her side, aware of the warm feather of his breath over her neck. It made her tremble as much as the victory of finding Lydia's book.

Venetia flipped through the first pages. "Goodness! She begins with meeting her first protector—she was only fifteen! And then she seduces the man's son when she is eighteen."

"Lord Craven and the next Lord Craven."

"Yes. Aptly named." Shock spiraled through her but she couldn't resist reading about Lydia's adventures at eighteen.

As soon as Lord Craven finished tying my ankles, he snapped his fingers. At once the door opened and three large men entered. Grooms from his stables—I knew them at once. All were nude—except the youngest still clutched his cap. And all had been selected for their gargantuan male equipment.

*The new Lord Craven looked smugly down upon me. I
was tied to his bizarre rack and quite unable to move. I was
at his mercy. Me, an untutored girl of eighteen!*

*I could see at once how swollen and bloated his was—his
modest member pushing at his breeches. He rubbed himself
there as he explained his desire. He demanded that I rut with
all three men at once. One in my cunny, one in my arse, and
one for me to suck!*

*I'd never done such a thing, and was terrified. I even began
to sob but my tears were to no avail. I had never allowed arse
play with his lordship, even though he offered me a king's
ransom to do it. I suspected it would be painful. Lord Craven
had me penetrate him once with an appendage I attached to
my hips. There was blood! And how he did scream! And it
was dreadfully hard work to thrust it, for his lordship was as
tight as a virgin lass.*

*I vowed never to allow my own rosebud to be entered—
but that night I was to be forced to delight in those craven
pleasures, and taught to yearn for more—*

Venetia skipped the next pages, face aflame, breathing unsteadily. She dared attempt to read again at the next chapter.
"Oh my goodness, this passage is about my father." Embarrassed, she shoved the papers toward Marcus. "You must
read that. I cannot."

Though it was worse to wait as he read through them all,
for she kept envisioning a young woman tied to an evil-look-
ing rack while three beautiful men surrounded her. Lydia's
'memoirs' were erotic scenes prefaced by jaded observations
about the men who had wooed her.

She watched Marcus read. From the brightness in his eyes,
his slightly faster breathing, she knew when he'd found the
racy parts. He spoke as he skimmed the pages. "There are a
dozen chapters—detailing her affairs with Craven, Montberry,
your father, and Brude. And since he paid, she makes no allu-
sions to his plagiarism. Her passages on Montberry are

mocking but include nothing dangerous. None of the other suspects were mentioned."

Lydia's affair with her father. Tears stung as she thought of her mother—hopelessly loving a man who sought Lydia Harcourt's bed.

But there must be more. Where did Lydia keep her blackmailing secrets? Venetia worked at the panel of the trunk lid, but it definitely would not open wider. She slipped her hand in and felt around. She touched only smoothness. Did Lydia keep everything in her head?

"I know why Lydia blackmailed you—why she was so determined to hurt Rodesson." Marcus spoke quietly, as quietly as the soft sound of the pages falling as he turned them. "She fell in love with him and, I gather, never recovered from it. He rejected her."

More hopeless love. Two women with broken hearts—one who threw herself into good works, the other who became bitter and hard and wanted only revenge.

"Lydia speaks of a rival in the most bitter terms. I believe she meant your mother—" He broke off. "Have you found something?"

Straining to reach deep into the lid, she shook her head. "But why would he go to Lydia's bed if he loved my mother? Why do men do that?"

"I don't know," he said softly.

Her fingers collided with a hard edge. Wiggling her hand in, Venetia felt the leather face of a book. Luckily her arm was slim, her fingers small. She caught the very corner of the book, drew it out. The moment the red leather cover came into view, she forgot herself. "This must be it! It must be a journal!"

Marcus' warm hand covered her mouth in a heartbeat. She heard it—the slightest creak outside. The gentle rattle of the doorknob. Then footsteps, going away. Marcus moved his hand, put his finger to his lips. His eyes glittered, hard as gemstones. "Don't look at the book. Put it down, don't touch it," he ordered in a harsh whisper.

She didn't understand. Why shouldn't she look at it? But she did as he asked, laying it on the floor in front of her. As though satisfied, he turned and stalked to the door without a sound.

He was looking to see who had been standing outside the door. She wanted to know, but the red book sat in front of her. Tempting. Why shouldn't she look? Shaking, she picked it up. The front cover fell open, a folded paper drifted out to the floor. She picked it up and smoothed it flat on top of the journal, revealing a list scrawled on the page in Lydia's flamboyant handwriting. Her heart hammered.

Brude—plagarism £2000 pd.
Wembly—affair Caroline £10000
Chartrand & Lady C—first Lady C £10000
Montberry—male lovers £2000. Won't pay!!!
Yardley—heir £5000 pd. More?
R Rose—bastard £10000

Her hands shook. She pressed her thumbnail into the page beneath the last name.

Trent—incest, death £10000

Chapter Sixteen

Marcus waited with impatience as the footman bowed and closed the balcony doors behind him. Though the man's expression had been impassive, he'd obviously assumed he had been leading guests outside for a tryst.

This balcony was mostly sheltered by the one above and overlooked the extensive grounds behind Abbersley. He frowned as rain blew at him and wet his face and hair, as the wind caught Venetia's skirts and tossed her curls. "You'll catch your death out here."

Lydia's manuscript was rolled beneath his arm but Venetia clutched Lydia's book.

"I needed to ask you something. In private." She opened the book and drew out a folded piece of paper. She turned her back to protect it from the rain and wind.

"What is that?" he demanded.

"Lydia was blackmailing you." She pushed wild curls back from her face. "You told me you wanted to stop Lydia because of me. It was nothing to do with me. You could have trusted me, Marcus."

"You looked at the book?" he snapped. "After I asked you not to?"

She frowned, her eyes pained. "I only looked at this list, Marcus."

Damnation, why was he yelling at her? Suddenly, he

needed her to understand. It mattered that Vee understood. "I couldn't tell you because those secrets aren't mine to reveal."

"What does it mean—incest?" She spoke quietly, but even above the wind and the rain, he heard.

"You don't know?"

"I do . . . I mean . . . was it you . . . you didn't—?"

Her words stunned him as though a lightning bolt had seared him on the spot. "Jesus bloody Christ, you think I did it? You think I'm capable of that?" He remembered the pain that lanced his skull when Min had hit him with the vase, but the agony of her condemning expression had been worse. But he couldn't betray Min by revealing the truth to Venetia. He would have to give her a lie—but what lie could he give that wasn't wretched, revolting?

He strode away from her, out to icy rain and buffeting winds. She followed. Confusion showed on her face. She caught his arm. "It wouldn't have been your fault. You would have been young . . . a child."

He knew she was becoming soaked, even knowing she was being drenched, he couldn't move. "I wasn't the victim, love."

"Your sister?"

He tipped his head back. Here they weren't beneath the overhanging balcony and he could look up at the black thunderheads. He couldn't tell her. These were Min's secrets and he had no right to share them with anyone. The sudden memory speared him. Of the day he'd confronted his father, praying he could act like a man, yet giving in to one wretched tear. "No, not Min."

He turned abruptly. "Give me the book, Vee."

She hugged it to her chest. "But my secrets are in it, too. I found it."

Was he going to have to rip it from her hands—?

Movement. A flicker of movement in the corner of his eyes. Someone on the balcony above?

He craned his neck to see. The wind dropped for a moment, and he heard it. The light clang of metal. For one crucial moment, he froze. Overhead was an urn and the base jutted over the edge of the balcony. Too far—

He grabbed Venetia's arm and hauled her against him as he jerked back. His momentum flung him down with her on top. A dark shape fell in that instant, struck with an explosion against the terrace flags. Stone shattered. Dirt sprayed. Shards flew and he clutched Venetia's head against his chest, praying nothing hit her. Something hard struck his leg—a dull pain through his thick leather boots.

Silence reigned except for the swishing sound of rain and wind. Then Venetia turned her face away from his chest, sucked in a deep breath.

"Are you hurt?" He asked it softly, to reveal nothing to their assailant.

"No," she breathed. "What in hell was that?" She tried to twist on top of him to see.

Despite the need for quiet, he found himself laughing beneath his breath—the way he'd heard some men did when facing death. But his humor came from relief. "Sweeting, only you could ask that."

He could have lost her. If he hadn't looked up—

His chest ached. He rolled her off him as gently as he could. His right calf ached, only bruised. Levering up to a sitting position, he caught her wrist. "Wait. He might still be there."

"You saw someone? Someone pushed this?"

He put his arm around her, protecting her. Using his body as a shield, he helped her to a crouch, then bent over, he led her to the shut doors. "I think so. Someone who knows we have Lydia's book."

"But why try to crush us?" Venetia crossed her arms beneath her breasts. She still trembled, even here, in Marcus' warm and secure bedchamber, comfortable in dry clothes.

Marcus sat on the edge of his bed. He reached out to her. "That I can't answer. Possibly to keep us from reading his or her secrets. Or to injure both of us and steal the book. Probably the killer saw the opportunity and took it. Or he might have felt if he killed me—"

She walked into his embrace, between his spread thighs. He pulled her close and she locked her arms around his neck. Her quim and skirts cradled the ridge of his cock. A thick bulge, but not hard. His powerful arms slid around her back, pulling her to him. Silk and buttons pressed into her cheek.

She felt a soft pressure against the top of her head—his lips.

She shivered. What chance would she have had, alone, against someone capable of strangling a woman to death?

"The urn was full of dirt and flowers," Marcus said, as he stroked her hair. "Very heavy."

She remembered how impressed he'd been when she insisted on racing right up to the balcony. They'd done it cautiously, but there had been no sign of the culprit. Gouges on the balustrade post showed that the urn had been pushed. It was definitely no accident.

Shock had given her bravery. And so much had happened after the attack. A footman running to their aid. Then that dash upstairs. The reactions of their hosts. Fury from Lord Chartrand who blamed the gypsies. Lady Chartrand had sternly insisted it must have been an accident. They'd seen no other guests.

Reality set in now. In a shaky voice, Venetia apologized, "I'm so sorry—now your secrets are not safe. The killer must have heard . . . ." How would she feel in his place? Furious. He must despise her! She'd dragged him to a dangerous place. Forced a confrontation.

She hadn't thought. She'd been so hurt that he hadn't trusted her. So she'd let her passionate side take over—her *artistic* side—and exposed his secrets.

Guiltily, she broke out of his hug. She bit her lip as she

faced Marcus, as she took in the breathtaking beauty of his austere face. With his mouth set, his eyes narrowed, he withdrew Lydia's book from his pocket. He weighed it in his hand. "Does this really contain secrets worth killing for?"

She watched as he flipped through. "Meticulous woman," he remarked, "Lydia kept her blackmailing notes in alphabetical order."

With one swift pass of his hand, he ripped a group of pages from the book. These he fed into the fire. They curled, blackened, flared into flame.

She realized he had just destroyed the secrets Lydia had blackmailed him over.

"I will have to tell the magistrate that she blackmailed me," he said, "but I don't need to hurt anyone else. Nor will I tell him about you, Vee. Do you want me to destroy Rodesson's—or do you want to read them first?"

Did she want to read her father's secrets? She shook her head, hesitantly. Then again, with firm confidence. "No, I don't want to know!"

Tears blurred her view of those dangerous secrets turning to ash. "We're safe."

Marcus gave a rueful smile. "Someone did push an urn at us." He paced in front of the fire. "Whoever did it might try again—someone believes we know his secrets. We have to leave here, Vee."

"But will Lydia's killer be brought to justice if we leave?" Did that matter so much? As much as being safe and alive? But could they allow a murderer to go free?

"Your life is far more important to me, Vee."

Her heart tumbled in her chest and she tried to quell the sudden surge of girlish delight. He was a protective man—worrying about her life was not a declaration of love. She must be sensible. She opened Lydia's book, but could not focus on the words on the page. She was safe. They would return to London. She would probably never see him again.

Marcus pulled on the bell cord. Within moments, Rutledge

answered Marcus' summons, but even earls could not command the impossible to happen.

Solemnly, Rutledge shook his head. "You cannot travel on the roads, my lord. They are completely impassible and the storm is too fierce. No doubt it was the strong winds that dislodged that urn and caused that regrettable accident."

"No doubt," Marcus snapped.

Rutledge handed Marcus a card, bowed, and left.

Holding Lydia's book to her chest, Venetia scampered to Marcus' side. He handed her the card. Lady Chartrand's writing slanted across the back. *I do hope Vixen attends. This event will make her forget her shock.* And on the front . . .

An Invitation to a Night of Sin.

Dinner passed quickly for Venetia, though she was too nervous to eat more than a mouthful from each dish. Could she guess the murderer from his or her behavior?

Lady Chartrand looked stunned, wooden. In her journal, Lydia had detailed Chartrand's drug induced confession about the murder of Catherine de Lisle, the first Lady Chartrand. But was it true?

Rosalyn Rose wore a crimson dress, the skirt slit to her waist so it gave glimpses of her resplendent nether curls. Venetia thought of Lydia's notes in her journal—*The child she claims is the Duke of Thorndale's illegitimate son is merely the by-blow of a common footman, but she convinced the doddering duke of his paternity and convinced him to include the boy in his will. One hundred thousand pounds has been promised* . . .

Lady Yardley was masked from hairline to chin in a silver mask decorated with white plumes. She appeared most agitated. Her ladyship's hand shook as she reached for her wine. *The new Lord Yardley is not the heir to the title* . . . *poor Henry could not get his bride with child* . . . *he actually paid an impoverished gentleman to impregnate his wife* . . .

What would happen if it became known that Lady Yardley's

son was a bastard? A mother would be willing to kill to protect her son . . .

The Duke of Montberry fondled Trixie Jones' breasts between dinner courses, his expression haughty, as though murder was of no concern to him. But Lydia had detailed his love affairs with two young men under his command . . .

Venetia took a sip of her wine. Did fear prove guilt? Or was a murderer the one who was most calm? All the guests had secrets to hide. All looked shocked when Lord Swansborough pointed out that they were all suspects, as dessert—a plum tart—was cleared away.

"Ridiculous!" cried Lady Chartrand. "It was the gypsies."

Chartrand's voice cut in, bluff and booming. "We will deal with the gypsies. They won't decamp tonight—there's no where for them to go." He stood, waving his arms to demand silence. "We will not spoil tonight's pleasures, for we are all London's most notorious seekers of sensual delight."

"Debauched," corrected Lord Swansborough with a wicked grin. "We are all shamelessly debauched."

As the party began to leave, Venetia realized she must try at once to discover alibis—at least from the men closest to her.

With the utmost daring, she laid her hand on Lord Swansborough's sleeve.

"I was shocked to hear of your brush with death, Vixen." He lifted her hand to his warm, firm lips. "I was attempting to direct the removal of my carriage from the mud. Tonight, my sweet, you need only crook your finger and I am at your command."

She snatched her hand away. He smirked. This man had not been in Lydia's book at all. It seemed impossible to believe this dark, seductive man had no secrets.

She turned to Mr. Wembly, who cupped her derriere. "My twelve majestic inches could take away your cares, my dear," he whispered.

Her lips parted. But no clever question came to mind. She remembered Lydia's words. *His disparaging comments about Princess Caroline hide the truth—they shared a wild and passionate affair . . . I found letters while he slept. Stupid man— his lovemaking is a ticket to a hangman's noose for it was an act of treason.*

Arrest for treason and the possibility of execution was a powerful motive . . . .

As Mr. Wembly bowed and left her, Lord Brude leaned close. "Would you wish to twirl like a winking star while I pleasure you with enormous dildoes? Or do you enjoy rope work? I learned some delightful techniques this morning with Miss Rose—an artistic way to arrange knots for erotic pleasure—"

He broke off as Marcus slipped his arm around her waist. Brude hastened to apologize. The instant Venetia saw Marcus' face she knew why. With narrowed eyes, snarling mouth, he looked ferociously possessive. Marcus drew her aside. "You are not to speak to them alone, Vee."

"They approached me—to proposition me." She wanted to rebel against his demand but, in truth, she wanted to sink against him. "I learned that Brude and Rosalyn Rose have alibis—because he was tying her up."

Marcus stroked her hip possessively. "No one has an alibi, sweetheart. If Brude told you that, he was lying. He had finished his games with Rosalyn by then."

They were alone in the dining room except for the footman clearing the last of the dishes, snuffing the candles. "It could be any of them. What do we do now?"

"I take you to our room and keep you safe in my bed for the night." He pressed his hand to her cheek and she let her eyes shut and savored the caress.

"Would you wish to fulfill one of my deepest, most forbidden fantasies tonight?" he asked, his voice a sensuous growl by her ear. "One I've never revealed to anyone?"

She snapped her lids open, met his gaze. His turquoise eyes were hot with desire. But she saw the slight flicker of vulnerability in their depths.

"How could I resist that?" she whispered, "Most definitely, yes."

Marcus watched Venetia roll onto her stomach, her cheek pressed against his rumpled bed. She was naked, her skin a blend of peach-pink and ivory, like summer peaches topped with cream. Shadows enhanced the delectable curve of her spine, the rounded cheeks of her bottom, the hot fold where her derriere met her smooth legs.

And they were alone—in his room.

"You could—you could go inside me again." Seductively, she lifted her hips from the expanse of wrinkled silk, and she swung her lush ass in a tempting circle. Her ass—that had so recently clamped tight around his prick. She kept her face buried in his bed, obviously too shy to ask bluntly for his cock in her arse.

He knelt on the edge of the bed, beside her lovely, naked spread legs. Now he was exploring in a realm where he wasn't an expert.

He heard the seductive music of her quick, shallow breaths, and it called to him. Lured him. He could have lost her today. A second later—

Bracing his arms on either side of her rounded hips, Marcus ran his tongue over the bountiful expanse of her warm, soft ass cheeks. He licked them thoroughly, from the swell at the base of her spine to the sweet crease between her bottom and the backs of her shapely legs. She squealed and moaned and gripped the sheets. A glance down the length of lovely legs showed her toes curled into the mattress.

She wanted him, as much as he needed her. It was more than her innocence that spoke to his soul. He knew that now.

Heavy as lead, rigid as iron, his cock bobbed as though

nodding its approval. He was naked, his prick launching out from his groin, longer and thicker than he'd ever seen it.

He eyed it critically. *Don't begin to think you make the decisions.*

His groin tightened of its own will and his cock lifted again, as though mocking him with another saucy nod.

"Marcus?" Venetia's voice was soft and hesitant.

The servants had brought both the vial of oil and their chests of toys here. All stood on the bedside table, the glass winking and the brass gleaming like gold in the muted candlelight.

He left the bed. Lifting the lid of the box, he let it clunk against the wall.

God, he wanted to do this. Suddenly, he understood. He would lay himself completely vulnerable to Venetia. Reveal his most forbidden fantasy, because he knew she would give him acceptance.

Delving into the box, he closed his fist around the double-ended dildo. The cool ivory filled his grip and he shuddered in both lust and agony at the thought of what he intended to do with it.

Venetia watched Marcus return to the bed, taut with anticipation. Without a word, he sat beside her hips. She moaned as he spread oil over her tight anus. Each soothing stroke relaxed her, sending a wave of weakening desire through her. Something cool touched her back—the wand shaped like two cocks, carved ivory inlaid at the base with facetted glass. He skimmed her spine from neck to bottom, making her squeal.

She half-rolled to find him spreading oil on the curved tip of the wand. "Are you going to put that in my bottom?" Her voice was a breathy whisper as she watched his palm roll over the smooth, carved head.

A spicy idea blossomed. "If you wished, you could make love to me with that in my bottom. You could slide your cock inside me and fill me completely . . ."

Now she understood exactly what men thought of when looking at *The Page Turner*. The suggestion both shocked and excited.

The wand pushed between her cheeks. "Can you imagine two men in this bed with you?"

She closed her eyes, speared by the forbidden image of herself captured between Marcus and another man—another dark, powerful man, one who's face was hidden in shadow. Dark brows, sensuous lips, sculpted cheeks—like Marcus. Marcus would be kissing her everywhere, eyes heavy-lidded with arousal . . .

The wand pushed between her cheeks. "Tell me your fantasy. Tell me what you would wish two men to do to you. In fantasy, nothing is forbidden. Imagine you are painting a picture . . ."

"In a picture I would do something shocking, risky."

"I know that risk excites you."

Did it? It must—she was soaked, fiery hot, in pain with needing him inside. The orgy, the disguise, the risk of losing her heart, the scandalous encounter with three women, the luscious pleasures with Marcus—all those things only seemed to stoke her lust.

"What would be a risky scene for your picture?" he asked.

"A stolen moment. A mad moment of passion. Perhaps a betrothed woman dances at her engagement ball with a man she once loved but knew she could never have. Now that he is about to lose her forever, he craves her. As they waltz, he whirls her out to the terrace. They find shadows, seclusion. He presses his advances with dazzling kisses, forbidden caresses. She should stop him, but she is immobile with desire and fear and love. Her skirts are lifting—she's worn no drawers—"

"Don't stop, Venetia," he begged, rocking the wand against her entrance.

She remembered the three jades, stuffing their passages full. She grasped her cheeks and opened herself for him.

His breaths came in urgent pants. "God, looking at you like that—tell me more. The other man comes out to the terrace to find his fiancée. What does he discover?"

He eased the dildo inside her, just a little, enough to stretch. To entice. From behind, he slid his hand over her slick quim. She squirmed against the pressure of his cupped hand. His tongue skated over the swell of her buttocks, the touch both tickling and exciting, making her giggle and sigh.

"More story, angel. Please."

"He finds his rival on his knees before his fiancée, the rogue's wicked tongue turning her into a boneless puddle of desire. She is leaning back against the balustrade, weak and melting. And then she spies her betrothed and her heart pounds in fear. For once she lays eyes on him, as fair as her former love is dark, and she sees the pain, the shock in his large blue eyes, she knows she loves him. And has lost him."

"But she hasn't, has she, sweet? Now roll over for me."

He bent to her breasts the instant she did, suckling one and then the other. All the while he eased the wand in and out of her bum, until she was clutching the sheets by her hips, arching, digging her heels in.

"Are you all right? It doesn't hurt?"

He gave long easy strokes, until his knuckles grazed her bottom. "No. No, it's good." She shut her eyes and let her head loll back on his pillow, in the rumpled dent he'd left. The satin pillowcase smelled of his unique scent. Inhaling left her heady with desire. Her body smelled of him, too, his skin, sweat, all blended with spicy fragrant oil.

"What happens on the terrace?" he urged huskily. "Tell me more."

She couldn't believe her words had him enthralled, the way he claimed her pictures did. The scene was real to her now. She was just a voyeur to her characters. It didn't matter what she thought he wanted her to say. She could only report the lush vision she saw.

"Her fiancé sees the love shining in her eyes." Venetia

closed her eyes, imagining tears welling, blond curls dipping over a bare shoulder, lips parted on a sob of pleasure. "Anger and pain are tearing at his heart. Now he must decide what to do. Call out the knave who is suckling her cunny? Take a pistol and blow the man to kingdom come? The bold rogue is still devouring her, forcing her to moan in pleasure, yet her fiancé has never been harder. Never has his need been more urgent."

"Understandable," Marcus teased. Then he caught his breath. "It's up to the hilt, sweet angel, and it is huge." His throat groan sent ripples of excitement through her. He spoke as though awe-struck. "Every fat inch is inside your delightful bottom."

She was slick, so wonderfully slick from *his* words. Slowly she pumped up and down, pleasuring herself with the wand while he held the other. Her quim ached to be filled by it, but what she truly wanted was his cock inside her. It was rigid, standing tall, weeping in readiness.

He bent and kissed her clit, his dark hair feathered over her mound. Tantalized by her erotic tale, she arched beneath him, driving the toy deeper.

"Wait, temptress. I want to join you."

Join her? Mystified, she watched. He drizzled golden oil into his palm, then stroked the length of the other wand, turning it slick and glistening. He poured another dollop onto his finger and reached behind his back. To his buttocks.

Heavens, it was more erotic than anything she'd drawn. Than anything she'd seen downstairs. She couldn't breathe. His face contorted with agony as he rubbed the oil in his own entrance. He looked breathtakingly beautiful, with his raven hair drifting over his half-closed eyes, his mouth firm and tense. His head bowed forward as he massaged his opening and she knew he found the same pleasure she did.

Holding the other wand erect, he gently coaxed it to his bottom and lowered on it. The motion pushed the wand in her in a way that made her whimper. Intense, but oh so good.

He stopped, his hair dusting across his intense eyes, concerned. "Am I hurting you?"

She shook her head, and he groaned, pushing further. With a cry of "Oh God," he straightened fast. Slowly, he slid it in again. Eyes wide, she watched his fist wrapped around it as he sank and rose, up and down until they were joined together, the double-ended cock buried in both of them.

Joined in the most scandalous, intimate way. Balanced on his knees, he guided her hand to her clit. "So, temptress, get to the moment where the two men take her together."

She understood he wanted her to touch and play. But she was curious. "What does it feel like for you?"

"Like you perhaps. Intense. Full. I've never done this."

That startled. "Never?"

He took hold of his shaft and jerked his hand along the unyielding length. She'd painted women pleasuring themselves, never men. What a spectacular image she'd missed.

"Never, love. I've had fingers and tongues used on me in anal play. But I've never been penetrated. You tempt me to live out a pleasure I've never tried."

She did? "But why me?"

"Because you are delightfully curious and because I trust you. Now, tell me your story and make me explode."

How could she resist that? He began riding the cock, moaning with each bounce, and his motion rocked the cock in her bum, thrilling her until she couldn't speak.

So he did. "Her fiancé would take her virginity, would he not? Her special gift. And the other rogue would pleasure her up her ass. Her betrothed would enter her first, slowly, easing her to his size, before breaking her barrier."

"And the rogue would enter her arse, first with his fingers, and then, lovingly with his cock. He would feel her betrothed's cock pressing against him though the thin wall of her flesh. Feel the heads slide by each other, feel each thrust and pulse. She would be in ecstasy, the hands of two men on her breasts, their mouths—".

"Marcus! I'm coming! I'm coming!"

She arched back, letting the orgasm take her, command her, propel her to heaven. "Oh, I love you! I love you so much—"

"Venetia, Venetia—angel. I'm coming with you." He let his head drop back, his throat a column of straining muscle and he clutched his cock tight. The bed shook as he pounded himself on the wand and drove it deep into her. She exploded once more, half-blind with it. The last thing she saw was a white stream shooting from his cock to splatter on his flat stomach, his tensed forearm, his big masculine hand.

"I—" But his words dissolved in fierce moans. "God, God, God."

Slowly, her senses returned. She felt as though she was suspended on a summer's breeze, floating back to earth and—

What had she done?

She'd said she loved him.

Chapter Seventeen

"Let me guess, love. You regret what you shouted in the heat of passion last night." Marcus dipped a soft washcloth in the basin of steaming water brought in by the maid.

Clutching the bedpost, Venetia bent over and presented her bottom for him to bathe. He saw her reflection in the cheval mirror. Pert breasts tipped with taut nipples. Parted lips. Half-closed eyes. Wildly mussed hair hanging down her back.

"Ooh," she gasped as he brushed her snug anus with the hot cloth.

He made soothing, gentle circles with the warm, soapy water. "Professing love happens often at the moment of climax, sweet. Many men do it—and then panic."

She giggled, ducked her head, so her thick auburn hair shielded her face.

Rinsing the cloth, he cleansed the slick oil from her anus. She looked so tempting in this position. He'd love to enter her slick cunny from behind, and thrust long and slow and hard until her quim climaxed around him. He'd love to see her up on her toes, the sleek muscles of her legs flexed as she pounded back against him, taking his cock to the mouth of her womb. God, he wanted it—the one desire he couldn't indulge.

Restraint. Hell, if he could avoid brothels and orgies he

could resist this temptation. He gave her bottom a light, teasing pat. "Ah, sweetheart, you don't really think you are falling in love with me?"

She turned, still bent over, beautifully framed by her hair. "It frightens me that I might be."

He laughed and gave her one last careful wipe. "Not afraid of blunt words are you, even at my expense?"

"It's a very foolish thing to do, to love hopelessly. I promised I would be much too careful and too wise to ever let my heart be broken."

He kissed her rounded back. "All finished, love."

But she waited, watched as he washed himself with another cloth. As her bold, appreciative gaze raked over his naked chest, his groin, his legs, his nipples tightened and his cock swelled, as though determined to make a good showing. She reached out and slid her fingers along the shaft. He liked the way she treated it as though it belonged to her.

He didn't want to break Venetia's heart. His own heart felt strange—it hurt when he thought about this time being over, when he thought about saying good-bye to Venetia.

After the urn fell, terror had rushed through him. So close. It had been so bloody close.

He could have lost her.

"You aren't in love with me, Vee." Limned by candlelight, glowing after sex and sleep, she shone like a gem. "I was always told I was unworthy of the love of a good woman."

"Who ever told you that?"

On the bedside table, a plate of ripe strawberries beckoned. Beside, fresh cream sat in swirls in a gold bowl. Delivered by a footman when the maid brought wash water. Now it promised distraction. "Lie down on the bed, Vee."

She swung around the column and fell onto the downy mattress. She struck a beautiful pose, arms outstretched, breasts pointing high, legs half-tangled in the silk sheets. "Marcus, how could you be unworthy of a woman's love? What a preposterous idea."

Settling down on the edge of the bed, he reached for the bowl of cream and gave a shrug. He dipped in one perfect, large strawberry. "My mother warned me I was. My father had broken her heart and I had, in all ways but one, an even wilder reputation than he."

She sat up, outraged. "Your father gave you Rodesson's books when you were eight! You can hardly be blamed for growing up to be a rake, too."

With the berry, he dabbed dollops of cream on her nipples, sculpting them into foamy peaks. He sucked them clean and held the berry for her to take a bite.

"Mmm!" Her eyes closed in pleasure. A drizzle of juice ran down to her chin, and he scooped it up with his fingertip.

"Lie beside me," she whispered, after swallowing.

He cuddled by her side, and fed her the rest of the berry. She was small, her toes reaching his shin, her head tucked against his shoulder.

"I can assure you that you are most worthy of love."

He reached for another berry, swirled it in the cream. "My mother warned me not to marry a woman who loved me—not to break her heart. I think that's what drove her mad—she turned all her passion for him into hatred and it consumed her."

Venetia snuggled close and stretched her arm across his chest. A simple embrace, infinitely comforting.

"There's something I've never told anyone . . ." He'd never even told Min this. But he wanted Venetia to understand. Against his stroking palm, her hair was soft as down, touching it an indescribable pleasure. Her heart thumped gently against his skin. She would feel his heart beating, too.

"There was a girl. A girl of a good family. My father liked to seduce country virgins and most went to his bed willingly. He paid them generously, money that became dowries to tempt husbands. But this girl was of the ton. Ravishing. Naïve. She got pregnant and panicked. She tried to be rid of the babe and it didn't work, so she thought of causing a miscarriage in a fall. Broke her neck."

"That's a terrible tragedy! Your father . . . didn't he care?"

The fire crackled, flame licking at dry logs. Closing his eyes, Marcus remembered finding his father passed out by the hearth in the library. "He got bloody drunk, is what he did."

He caressed the waves of her hair. "I remembered my first thought—was the sod dead? I found his pulse, then flipped him over in disgust. Having his skull hit the floor roused him and, for once, he felt the need to explain himself to me."

His father's eyes had been glazed. Then they'd locked on his, pleading. He remembered his father's words. *The hell of it is, lad, is that I loved her. Always did. But the other . . . can't control it . . . it is hell.*

Only after several minutes, did he realize 'her' was his mother.

For some men, lad, the demon is drink, or the roll of the dice . . . for me it is innocence. The earl had struggled up, leaning on his hands. Sweat, or worse, had plastered down his gray hair. *Couldn't resist. Couldn't. I knew the cost. Knew she hated me, more and more. You can't imagine what hell it is to be possessed by the devil.*

"What did you do?" Venetia whispered, her breath a warm whisper across his skin.

"Rage drove me," he admitted. "All that maudlin rubbish was about his guilt. He wasn't really remorseful over that girl's death. I wanted to smash my fists into him. Instead, I shoved him forward, in case he was sick. I wasn't going to let him escape his conscience by choking."

He'd snapped in fury, yelled at his father, "Bloody hell, you're not possessed by the devil."

His father had wiped at uncharacteristic tears. Then his mother's cold voice had arced through the room. She stood in the shadow of the doorway. *It's indulgence,* she'd stated. *That's all it is. He ruins those poor girls for a fleeting moment of pleasure.*

Marcus, you are just like him, she had spat. *I despise you,*

just as I despise him. You will marry, of course, and I pity the
woman you do, for you will only destroy her. You are not
worthy of a woman's love. I don't even think of you as my
son.

His mother had not spoken to him after that for two
years—long after his father's death.

Strawberries and cream awaited but he needed to do this.
"When I met you, Vee, I desired you—hell, I hungered for
you. That morning you came to me to ask me to come here,
it was all I could do not to ravish you in every way I could
imagine. And believe me, sweeting, I can imagine many forbidden ways. I worried that it was the novelty of your innocence that enticed me so much. That I had the same weakness
as my father. But here, with you, I realized I'd met many delicious young virgins in the ton and never once had one made
my control snap. You were the only one."

She lifted to gaze down into his eyes. "Perhaps it's the
orgy."

"It's not." Gently, he rolled her onto her back. "But right
now, I wish to see you covered in cream."

He coated her quim with cream and feasted. The combination of sweetness and ripe, earthy woman proved delicious.
Reaching up, he handed her a berry, and delved his tongue
into her to taste her hot juices along with the cool cream.

Giggling, she urged him up. Supporting his weight on his
arms, he obeyed and let her feed him the berry, with her taste
still on his tongue. He swallowed tart juice and feminine
honey.

"I do like sex when it also involves sugary treats," she
whispered.

Charmed, he laughed. He bent to kiss her. His iron rod of
a cock bucked as their lips met. His juice damped her belly
and his. So easy to lower himself, to slide into her, bury his
cock in her heat, join them. So tempting to make love to
her—

Pounding on the door rattled it in its frame.

Hell, what was this? Marcus gave Vee a last quick kiss, before jumping down from the bed. He should tell whoever it was to go to the blazes—but the interruption had saved him from breaking Vee's maidenhead.

He grabbed his robe from the floor and held it against his crotch as he opened the door.

Swansborough stood on the other side, wearing hat and greatcoat. "Chartrand has gathered an armed mob—he's gone to flush out the murderer amongst the gypsies."

"Christ Jesus, the man is insane." Marcus flicked a glance at the pistols Swansborough held at his side.

"One is for you. Would you help me stop this madness?"

Drums beat a wild tattoo in her breast as Venetia ran with Marcus across the damp lawns. A nightmare had come to life and she was plunging into its vortex. The rain had stopped but a thick fog enveloped the grounds. Men charged across the grass, through the swirling mist, carrying rifles, pistols. Grooms, footmen, noblemen—all driven by revenge, maddened by drink and bloodlust. Racing to the woods—to the poor band of gypsies camped there.

Venetia's half-boots slid and slipped but Marcus' hand gripped hers tight and he held her up, kept her from falling when she stumbled. She tried to speak but the wind tossed her words uselessly behind her.

What was she to do? Resolute, determined, honorable to the point of heroic madness, Marcus planned to stop Chartrand and his armed men.

How? How could two men, Marcus and Lord Swansborough, stop a mob?

The gusts tore at her bonnet, pulling at the ribbon at her throat until she was choking. She clamped her hand on her hat to hold it on. She wore her mask still, amidst this insanity. It was as soaked from the fog as her cloak and bonnet and hair were. Through the curtain of gray, she couldn't see more than dark shapes. Shadows running across the gardens.

She clung to Marcus' hand. They reached the dirt lane that ran at the base of the lawns—now a mire of thick mud pocked with the deep plunges of footprints.

"They're armed! What can we do? There's nothing we can do!" Her incoherent, desperate words tumbled out between burning gasps, unheeded by Marcus as he followed the grassy edge of the lane.

Perhaps he couldn't hear. And she could barely speak. Her chest was on fire, her throat a torch. She sucked more mist than air into her lungs and sputtered. Trees shrieked in the wind, the men's shouts were a maddening pounding in her brain. The sounds of violence and hell. Marcus never let go of her hand—she'd insisted on coming, he'd been too afraid to let her stay—even when they reached the black void of the woods, where the close trees forced him to divert to the water-logged path.

Mud sucked at her boots, clung to the soles. In two steps, her feet were as heavy as full coal buckets. Impossible to lift. She pitched forward, Marcus pulled her up and his momentum hauled her free. He caught her with both hands as she took those sudden stumbling steps. Then he raced off again, gripping her hand tight, as though he didn't doubt she could follow, as though they were one in this—equal of courage and determination.

What was he going to do? He'd be shot. Killed. Chartrand was insane—he couldn't be stopped. What of the gypsies? There must be many of them but unarmed, with nothing to save them against rifles. Women and children as well.

Boots crunched between the trees. Shadows slipped between ancient trunks, barrels of weapons pointing their way.

A woman's scream sliced the curtain of rain. Guttural male shouts. Crashing of branches. Marcus' hand clasped tighter and she surged forward with him, rounding a bend in the road. She'd never known such terror—not even at the crash of the urn at her feet. In the middle of a group of tents, men battled. Great coats swirled around some—the gentlemen—and the others wore ragged bright colors. Those were the gypsies, fighting for their lives. They fought with branches, with knifes, swinging at the Englishmen. Color flashed though the mist as mothers grabbed their children's arms and dragged them back. She saw the desperate way the mothers held tight to their babes.

A shot exploded, a boom like the sound of Hades rising in the midst of rural England. Venetia screamed and Marcus hauled her back, to the shelter of an oak.

No—he was trapped with her. Forced to protect her. But what good could he do? She couldn't even see Chartrand! Men grappled and fought. Boots and fists collided. Bodies tumbled in the mud. Horses shied, dancing about the melee, hooves raised, heads thrashing.

"Stay there." Marcus pushed her back against the tree.

He pulled away.

Another shot. She saw Marcus' instinctive duck of his head, saw him turn. Bark exploded above her head—the tree jolted as though it would rip its roots from the ground. Her knees jellied. She sank to the ground, where it was wet and covered with rotten leaves.

Marcus' face was stark white. He stumbled to her, crouching as he came, hands outstretched. Shot! She'd been shot at. There was no pain. Only shaking. Horrible shaking. Her teeth chattering.

His hands were warm on her cheeks. His face blurry and indistinct. His voice—she tried to answer—*I'm alive. Alive. No pain. No pain at all.*

Blackness closed in.

Pain sliced into Marcus' heart as he cradled Vee, warmed her, stroked her face and spoke to her—trying to rouse her. He stared at the hole ripped through her bonnet. Mere inches lower—

Jesus, he couldn't even think of it.

Afraid that another shot could come, he used his body to

shield Venetia. She was slumped at the base of the tree, eyes shut.

"Wake up, sweetheart. Wake up," he begged. Her lashes flickered and hope rushed through him. He turned, scanning the woods around him, but even the dark trees disappeared in the thick fog. The men around him—who had seen Venetia faint after the shot—crashed through the woods, seeking the shooter, but the bullet could have come from anywhere. Shouts carried through the trees. Had it been an accident? Or the killer taking advantage of another deadly opportunity? Why? Over that blasted book?

Face pale, Venetia sat up, brushing at grass and dirt. Large and luminous, her eyes met his. "B—bother, I am getting a little tired of this." A weak smile flickered over her fragile lips. Heavy droplets of moisture dropped from the shifting leaves and ran down her face.

He scooped her into his arms, she was so slim and light. "Are you hurt?" His brain couldn't function beyond harsh terror.

"The bark scratched my back—other than that I'm fine. Alive." Large and luminous against her white mask, her eyes met his. "You're rescuing me once more. You seem to be making a habit of this."

He started back down the lane, men surrounded—shouted, laying blame for the shot, asking questions. Rage gripped him as he took the road in long strides. The need to rip a man to pieces surged, left him shaking. His back teeth ground together. "Go find the bloody bastard," he shouted.

They rounded the bend. In his arms, Venetia was shaking. Her lips were pale, trembling. She tightened her grip on his arm, her eyes poignant with worry. "What of the gypsies?"

"The shot that—" He stumbled, regained his balance. "That almost hit you, broke the tension—made the good men see the insanity of what they were doing. But Chartrand will take their leader hostage—"

"How can he do that?"

"To hold until the magistrate arrives. Swansborough will ensure there'll be no rough justice. No one was killed—" His gut wrenched at how close it had been. He didn't feel Vee's weight as he ran, as he dodged mud. He needed to get her back to their rooms. He would assign his grooms sentry duty, to ensure they were safe.

Returning to their house seemed an endless journey. At least it gave time for Venetia to calm. Once he had her in his room, on his bed, he took off her damp and muddy cloak, threw off his greatcoat. He handed them to the waiting footman. A maid stoked the fire, set it roaring, left a pile of thick warmed towels and went out.

He reached for Vee's bonnet but she'd pulled it off first. Shaky fingers traced the ragged edges of the hole. "It's huge." He grabbed it from her, tossed it to the flames. It hissed, sizzled. As though that could make the nearness of tragedy go away.

"Marcus—help me undress." Her hushed voice made his heart ache.

He opened her wet dress at the back. Heart pounding, he kissed her damp skin—her graceful neck, her slim shoulders, the top of her spine. Beneath his lips, the pulse at her throat grew steadier.

She let her gown fall to the floor.

"Your corset's knotted," he growled, but a quick zip of his razor along the crisscrossed lacing cut her free. He closed the razor, tossed it back to the bowl.

He wrapped her mist-dampened hair in a heated towel. Wrapped another—enormous and cozy—around her shoulders.

She was safe. Alive. He kissed her wrists until she closed her eyes at the pleasure of it. He kissed the crook of her elbows, her fragrant underarms. On his knees before her, he kissed and sucked her toes. He licked the sensitive place behind her knees, making her sigh in rapture as he drew stockings and garters down her legs. She stepped out of each, and stood before him, wearing only her dry shift and towels, never more beautiful or more tempting.

He rose up on his knees—the hem of her shift caught on his neck and lifted, exposing her glistening cunny to his mouth.

"I want you. I . . . I want nothing to be barred to us," she whispered. She gazed down at him, holding back her curtain of auburn hair.

He wanted to glory in the heavenly gift of having her with him. Gently sliding his hand around her delicate foot, he lifted her right leg, opening her sex to him. He balanced her foot on his shoulder. Her smell surrounded him, lured him, tempted him. He slid his tongue into the snug passage of her quim. Her rich taste exploded on his tongue—salty, sweet musk.

Venetia gasped and gripped Marcus' bedpost. She hung on tight as waves of pleasure rocked her. Oh, it felt so wonderful to have his tongue plunge in, filling her with wet heat, rippling against her walls.

So wonderful, but she wanted it all.

Heavens, she could have been killed. Why on earth was she preserving her virginity? She didn't want marriage, she wanted to make love with Marcus. He must understand she would make no demands of him. Earls didn't marry naughty artists who had no money or connections.

She wanted to seduce him but how could she overwhelm his defenses? How could she make him lust and desire with such intensity that he couldn't stop? He'd made love to so many women—women here had tried to tempt him yet he'd honored his promise to protect her. How to shatter his control?

She had no idea—

His tongue laved around her clit and she arched up on her one foot. *Oh . . . heavens!*

He played magical games with her hard clit, encircled it over and over with his tongue until she was dizzy and clinging to him. Expertly he slicked each side, and she rocked into his mouth. If he just did that . . . kept doing that . . . oh Lord, she would come for him. Come all over him. Like an on-slaught of tide, her orgasm built. She rubbed herself against his tongue fervently, so very close . . . so wonderfully close . . .

He stopped. She cried out, "No! No!"

"Touch your nipples," he said. "I want to watch you touch yourself."

From beneath his tousled hair, he watched. This was her chance to entice him. Gathering courage, she gave a flirta-tious smile as she cupped her breasts. The sensation of her palm on their undersides made her moan. Before his hungry eyes, she strummed her nipples with her own thumbs.

It worked. With languorous, sable-soft strokes, he tongued her clit more.

Closing her eyes, she saw stars. Bright, shooting stars against velvet black.

He flicked his tongue, right on the very tip of her clit. Torture, wonderful torture. He teased her anus with his finger-tip. Her leg became shaky, but she fought to stay balanced. Her breasts tingled with pleasure. Agony raced through her, flooding her cunny with hot liquid.

His gaze was approving as she fondled her breasts. She loved pleasing him. She grew more excited. More wild and daring. She pulled at her nipples and the spark of pain thrilled her. She wanted to be rough. Aggressive. Naughty and bad.

"Lick my cunny!" she cried, flushing, "Suck my quim."

He broke the rhythm to groan, "Yes," and devoured her like a madman.

She ground her clit against his tongue . . . lost control. All she could do was thrust her hips and rub and rub—

She came, crying out his name. Her hair flew wildly, slap-ping her breasts, her face, her lips. Moans and cries strained her throat. She pinched her nipples tight as the pleasure washed over her.

As the spasms died away, she thought she'd fall. He lowered her to the carpet. She was on her knees, he on his. She felt sensuous and wild.

"Lie down," she urged huskily. "I wish to suckle you."

He lay back on the carpet, legs spread so she could kneel in between. His cock stood in a rigid curve, the veins prominent, the head swollen and shiny. She planted a kiss on his ballocks, then traced her tongue up the shaft.

"Heavenly," he moaned. He arched his head back and closed his eyes.

Exactly the moment she needed. In a heartbeat she straddled his hips and settled her cunny down on his shaft.

"What are you doing?" His eyes snapped open. She splayed one hand on his chest, hoping to keep him down.

She rocked on him, drawing her wet nether lips along his cock, soaking him in her creaminess. "I want this. I want to make love."

"Venetia—" He caught hold of her hips, as though to lift her off but if he'd truly wanted to unseat her he could have. This gave her hope.

She settled her weight on his cock, so it was pinned between his flesh and her wet quim. "I could have died today. I want to have this one wonderful experience with you. Only with you . . ."

It wasn't just lust that made her want him so much. It was more . . .

No. She wouldn't think of love. Not now. Only sex and pleasure and filling the ache inside her.

She held up his cock so the magnificent length stood straight in the air, and poised her cunny over him. "I want you, Marcus. I need you. *Please.*"

"God, God, God," he moaned. "Sweeting, I want this. Hell, I do, but—"

His shaft was slippery and the head was slick with his juice. She sank her teeth into her lip and lowered. His cock slid in, gliding on their blended juices, until it pushed at her barrier. Her cunny clenched the hot thickness filling it and fireworks seemed to be exploding in her head.

"Please . . ." her voice died away.

He cupped her breasts, squeezing above her thundering heart. "God yes, let me make love to you." In a lower voice filled with masculine heat, he groaned, "Let me fuck you."

Chapter Eighteen

Venetia plunged down on his cock with one strong thrust and her lusty cry became a shocked squeal.

Marcus cursed himself. He should have stopped her. Should have realized she'd race to do the deed. She sobbed with shock and pain and he lifted her up from his prick, settled her down so she straddled his stomach. "Sweeting, the pain will stop."

She nodded, lids dipped over her eyes. "It's easing now."

Her maidenhead was torn. It was done. At least she had climaxed already, had been wet and relaxed. He'd never made love to a virgin and he hated to think Vee had felt pain.

"Now, temptress, we'll do this on my terms," he said, "And it will be good, I promise."

Not romantic, but the best he could do. He could barely think. He rolled them both over.

She made a delectable picture. Her fiery-red hair spilled around her. Lust and need and trust shone in her eyes. Arousal had tightened her nipples, and the dusky red points tempted his mouth. He bent to suckle and his cock, huge and heavy with his desire, pushed between her spread thighs. The swollen head nudged inside her sopping quim, determined to invade. She was so slick, his prick slid in a few inches.

He moaned. It was like dipping his prick into a river of fire. Before he could stop himself, his hips arched in the first long stroke. Her velvety walls gripped him with such exquisite snugness he had to marshal his control and thrust slowly to ease his cock inside.

She gripped his biceps, her eyes wide with wonder and surprise. "It feels so perfect."

"No more pain?"

"No, it's . . . simply perfect. Nothing is barred to us now."

Her innocent desire touched his heart and set his blood boiling. He wanted this to be unbelievable for her. Easing himself back out, he slid in once more. Deeper. He had to bow his head at the heat, the grip, the pleasure. Venetia stayed still, her brows drawn together as though concentrating on every sensation as he slowly, agonizingly, filled to the hilt. His black curls brushed her red ones, his cock entirely buried.

"You are enormous!"

He was only a man, and pride swelled at her guileless exclamation. Laughing, he nibbled the irresistible curve of her neck. "Relax, sweeting. We must let you get used to me."

He licked her erect nipples, so delightful to play with. He thrust slowly, worshipping her breasts with his mouth, her cunny with his cock. At the end of each stroke, he pushed his hips forward, penetrating deep. As deep as he could go. He wanted every inch inside her.

Her hands slid up to his shoulders, her nails gouged his flesh. Just her touch set his skin on fire. The softest stroke of her fingers sent pulses of pleasure to burst in the fire consuming his cock.

Venetia began to move with his thrusts, to lift her hips to meet his. Her eyes glowed at him—alive, beautiful, filled with delight. Awe and agony played across her face. He watched, mesmerized, forgot himself. He lost his rhythm and, like a callow boy, he backed off too far and his cock fell out.

She reached for his prick as fast and desperately as he did. Their hands collided. Fingers twined, they struggled to force his unbending cock back inside. She moaned in delight, he groaned as though his life had been saved.

"Your clit should be sweetly sensitive after your orgasm." Marcus lowered, resting close to her, so her hardened nipples stroked his chest as she arched up and he pushed down, deep into her blazing sheath. He had to arch his head back at the intensity. "I can ride high . . ." he had to stop, to suck in a deep breath. "And tease your lovely, stinging clit, but I want you to prime it. Rub yourself until you are close, my sweet, and then . . ."

His thrusts sped up—sooner than he'd wanted, but his cock, his body, no longer obeyed his command. "To make a woman come with just the thrusts of a man's cock is a miraculous business—"

She just looked up at him, enraptured, mystified.

"Move your hand now," he instructed. He wanted nothing in the way.

She did and her arms locked around his waist. Then she clutched hold of his ass, her fingers gripping into his cheeks. Sweat beaded on his forehead as he rode her faster, driving his cock in her cunny to the hilt, kissing her clit with his groin. Her moans came louder and louder.

"Yes, yes, yes. But do it harder," she demanded, "It's so good when you do it hard."

His sweat dripped now, his muscles bunched with each forceful thrust. What was he doing? She was precious, he was pounding her. But she cried out in pleasure at each slap of his body.

She clung to him. Her legs hooked around his. She thrust up to him, her hands separating his arse cheeks. He howled. Howled with the pleasure! God, it was incredible to have his anus tugged like that. Sensation roared from his hole to his balls—they were impossibly tight and ready to fire.

"Is it good? Tell me." He panted. "I want to make you come."

Her hips circled in an exotic dance. She was trying to milk him with her hips, trying to pleasure him. "Oh it's good. I love having you fuck me."

He almost fired. He clung to control. His brains evaporated, but he fought for that goal—Venetia's beautiful pleasure.

Her legs embraced his waist, exposing her tender anus. He reached down teased with his index finger, balanced his weight on his wrist.

"Oh!" she squealed as his finger slid up her ass, irresistibly tight.

"Does that please you?"

"Yes, yes! I want you in both places—yes, push your finger deeper. Fill me. I—"

She screamed and ripped her nails down his back. Around his cock, her cunny pulsed and squeezed.

His brain exploded into flames. Every muscle went rigid and he pinned her to the floor as his body bucked and writhed with his orgasm. Wave after wave tore through him. His muscles liquefied, his head seemed to shatter.

His cock swelled to three times its size before finally, mercifully, shooting his come deep inside her.

Her fingernails scraped into his ass, sending a last whoosh of seed through him, until he was certain every possible ounce had drained. But she began lifting to him again. Almost unconscious with pleasure, Marcus shuddered as her tight walls pulled along his sensitive shaft.

"No, no, angel, I can't." He rolled off her, collapsed at her side, his arm flung over her warm, damp belly.

Venetia felt wonderful, sated, heavenly, splendidly alive—goodness, what had she done to him?

She rolled up onto her hip and gazed down at Marcus. He flopped over onto his back and grinned at her. Slick with perspiration, his dark hair hung over his eyes, which still looked dreamy and dazed. Against the woven green-gray pattern of the rug, his golden-bronze body was beautifully displayed.

His nipples were taut, his chest hair soaked and matted down. A small cut marred the perfect sweep of his jaw—a nick from the straight razor he'd used on his face in the morning, the one that had cut her corset.

Excitement rushed through her, setting her nerves tingling. Making love to him had been as magnificent as she'd dreamed, and now, he was stretched out alongside her, hers to explore. But she felt too uncertain to touch him.

He traced the length of her arm with his fingertips, coasting to her neck. His turquoise eyes glowed. She felt treasured.

"You want more, don't you? I can see it in your eyes." He gave a playful groan.

Shyly, she met his heavy-lidded eyes. "My virginity is gone. There's no reason we can't enjoy sex all night."

His low, masculine laugh rumbled. "You plan to kill me, don't you?"

She frowned. His cock slumped against his thigh, still long, but spent. "You mean . . . you can't?"

"I can, sweeting. If you let me have a little rest." He ran his fingers along her breasts, down to her nipples. Goosebumps trailed in their wake. "But you must be tender."

"No. I'm hardly sore at all." She toyed with his cock, velvety soft and surprisingly heavy. To her delight, a drop of rich, white fluid rolled out of the tip. But he yelped and eased her hand away.

"Verrry sensitive," he warned, huskily. Flicking back his untamed hair, he cast a heated gaze over her, lingering at her eyes, then her quim. "Are you certain you aren't sore?"

Venetia's enthusiasm, her raw lusty need astonished Marcus. He'd thought she would want to cuddle and go to sleep. But Venetia slid down his body and coiled her fingers around his soft cock. She stuck out her tongue and licked it lavishly from hilt to tip.

God, she was a natural. Adorable.

Then she took his floppy member entirely into her hot, sweet mouth. Arousal shot through him. She teased him mercilessly with tongue and teeth. Blood rushed down to his cock, leaving him light headed.

His cock began to swell, pushing against the sharp edges of her teeth.

He drew her back, whispered. "I want to harden completely inside your cunny, Vee." He urged her to stand, and as she did, he planted a kiss between her thighs. His semen clung to his lips afterward. Licking them, he tasted her ripe juice and his sour, tangy seed.

His body was aflame, but he forced himself to ask once more. "Are you certain?"

"Yes."

"Then hold on to the edge of the bed and bend over."

To ask her to assume that position was unforgivably sinful. But he couldn't resist having a view of her drenched cunny from behind. A tempting, precious diamond. From behind, he eased his finger into her sheath, into liquid fire, and stirred. The sight of her round, smooth bottom had his cock standing proud once more.

She circled her ass in the most tempting way, slowly spread her legs wider in an invitation Marcus couldn't refuse.

Venetia gasped as his staff filled her wet quim and she had to grip the sheets to keep from being pushed forward. This was so wickedly wonderful. To present her up-tilted bottom to him, to be taken from behind. She felt a little twinge as his cock nosed inside and she hesitated.

Should she do this?

Oh, but she couldn't resist. And the pain was gone. Arching her back, she pushed her bottom toward him.

Hands on her hips, he held her and began to thrust. In that slow, sensuous way she now knew so well. Turning her head, she saw his face. Alluring agony turned his features into harsh planes, his mouth into a tense gash. His entire being seemed to be concentrating on fucking her.

She loved it—loved to lift her bum to feel him smack hard

against it. Her thighs shivered with the contact as his thrusts quickened. Her breasts bounced.

She angled forward, forcing her bottom back, taking him so deep she felt the push against her womb. She bent low, so her breasts grazed the silk sheets of the bed.

God, yes.

And he, the wonderful devil, began to thrust harder. So hard he lifted her to the very tips of her toes each time he drove deep.

Over and over. Faster and faster.

"Yes, be fierce!" she begged. "Be wild—I love this!" She felt the tug at her anus—felt her bottom slacken, open for him. His finger slid in. Once again he teased her derriere and her nub, while plunging in her quim—

Pleasure exploded inside her, raced through her, shattering between her thighs. Lush waves rolled over her. Her body sang to it, soared with it. She fell to the bed and he collapsed with her, buried deep. Lost in her own ecstasy, she dimly realized he was coming too. Groaning her name, jerking with his powerful release.

"God, God, it's never been like this," he vowed as he slumped against her back.

Did he truly mean it? How could she, a novice, give him pleasure that he'd never known before?

Heat. Venetia was curled up against something hot. She opened her eyes. The rumpled bed stretched before her—heat and the tickle of soft hair and satin skin was against her back. Marcus' arm stretched over her. She rolled beneath it, to lie on her back. His eyes were open, thoughtful. Without words, with only a soft smile, she hooked her arms around his neck. He was hers—she knew it as she drew him down on top of her.

Was she dreaming? No—it was more wonderful than a dream.

He kissed her lavishly, then moved down her body and pleasured her quim with his mouth. Her thighs were sticky with his semen. He could taste his come and hers inside her . . . she was drenched, sore, but she felt desire mount. He suckled her until she came. The orgasm rippled over her and she fell back in rapture. The second left her gasping. The third left her delirious with sensual delight, unable to speak, her throat raspy from her cries.

She knew he was rigid. "Let me please you." she whispered.

But he wouldn't. He cradled her in his arm and reached down to wrap his large hand around his shaft. She didn't understand. Why did he not want her?

Uncertainty must have shown in her eyes.

"You need to be treated gently." He began pleasuring his organ in his tight fist. Venetia watched his thrusts, studying the rhythm, the pattern, the way he slid his palm over the head on every third stroke. Then, nervous, she reached down and fondled him, too. She squeezed the head. He moaned and came in a sudden rush of white seed onto her fingers and his. Together they'd pleasured him, and together they tumbled into sleep once more . . .

Freshly baked bread. The rich scent of chocolate. The scents swept into her dreams and Venetia blinked open her eyes. Her arms stretched wide across the bed. She was alone.

"I didn't want to wake you."

Marcus' soft, sensual voice brought her entirely awake. Sitting up, she saw him at her escritoire, a single candle casting warm light on his haggard face. His long legs stretched out on either side of the dainty seat. He was fully dressed. She saw her own handwriting slanting across the paper he held. Her list of suspects.

He pointed to the tray pulled up at her bedside. Enormous. Covered by silver dishes. Marcus walked over to it. "Apparently the cook sent up a magnificent feast to buoy your strength."

Before her eyes, he seemed to throw off his tension, as though doing it to comfort her. Venetia sat up and hugged her knees. Strength! She had been shot at. She felt strangely calm about it now—as though it had not truly happened to her. Was it because she spent a night lost in erotic pleasures? Had making love given her the warm courage she now felt in her soul?

Marcus poured a cup of chocolate and handed it to her. "How are you feeling, sweeting?"

Before she could drink, he cradled her cheek.

"I'm fine." How inadequate that sounded. She struggled to understand. "I feel in a muddle. I was shot at. I made love. All in one day."

His lips sparked fire on her cheek. Even his simplest touch gave her strength. "Have you been awake long?" she asked.

"A few hours." He filled a plate with food and placed it on the bed at her side, then straightened, scrubbing his hand over his jaw. "I admit I left you alone for a while. I did lock you in. Found Swansborough downstairs. Tackled Chartrand. No one knows where anyone was yesterday during that madness." Anger flashed in his eyes, as he paced along the end of the bed, and spoke tersely in time to his strides. "No one knows who fired the shot. No one has an alibi for the time. It has stopped raining now, and I expect repair on the bridges will start. It won't be long before the magistrate arrives. A day. Two at the most."

She watched his long strides. She'd read of caged animals, exotic tigers that prowled along the bars, intent on becoming wild again. Venetia shivered. It was as though he'd said bluntly 'we only have to survive another day'. She gulped down the entire cup of chocolate. It scalded on the way down.

"None of the gypsies were seriously hurt, just badly frightened. They pulled up camp—but they can't have traveled far. They must be hiding on the estate."

She remembered children hiding in their mother's skirts. "Would Lord Chartrand attack again?"

"He drank himself into a stupor last night and is too bedeviled to cause trouble this morning." Marcus reached out for the empty cup, placed it on the tray.

"A sign of guilt?" She nibbled at her toast. "But why shoot me? No one could know that I had the book in my pelisse pocket."

"Whoever wants that book knows that both you and I have read it."

She swallowed slowly. "I learned more about Lord Brude's secrets. He has a stronger motive than plagiarism. He admitted he had an affair with his sister-in-law and fathered her child." So many secrets. Secrets worth killing for. "You think someone wants us . . . dead . . . to keep his secrets safe?"

Marcus was seated at her side, giving her more chocolate. His hands soothingly rubbed her shoulders. "Thank you, sweeting, for respecting my secrets. And I vow I will keep you safe. Someone tried to kill you." He spoke calmly but she felt the resolute power behind the words. "I intend to catch him and I intend to see him pay."

"But would any of these powerful men be made to pay?"

"I will ensure it." His voice was low, deadly. "I'll kill the blackguard who shot at you."

She knew in a heartbeat what he meant. He would see justice at pistol point.

He rose from the bed. "I am going to have to leave you again, Vee. Promise me you will stay here with the door locked."

She pushed down the blankets. Her plate slid off her lap. "Where are you going?"

He held up the lock pick. "I plan to search our suspects' rooms. You are staying here."

"I'm not! I am coming with you."

Venetia's hands trembled as she untied the ribbon that bound a stack of Lady Yardley's letters. She opened the first, straining to listen for sound outside in the hallway. Marcus moved in complete silence. How he could slide out a drawer without a squeak or open a door without a groan, she couldn't imagine.

Her gaze slid down to the signature. A first name only. Lancelot. It couldn't be the man's true name. Then she saw the crest on the page. Swansborough. She read the letter.

. . . I have learned that L. Harcourt is attending Chartrand's. I will deal with her for you . . .

She felt the soft whisper of warm breath on her neck and almost leapt out of her skin. She turned and glared at Marcus. "You mustn't startle me. I almost screamed." She waved the letter. "Lord Swansborough came her to assist Lady Yardley."

He inclined his head. "I am not surprised. Lady Yardley cared for his younger sister when his parents were killed—carriage accident. He has always been close to her."

"So he, too, has a motive." She slumped.

Marcus groaned. "We've searched the rooms and learned nothing except we have one more suspect."

"He has an alibi for Lydia's death but he might have tried to injure me to get the book." And, in their search, she'd discovered many of the fetishes of the guests. Wembly's collection of spanking paddles. Lady Yardley's painful-looking nipple clamps. Montberry's collection of lady's drawers. Lord Brude's habit of snipping pubic hairs from his lovers—a practice detailed in his journal. Night had fallen and she felt dejected. Confused.

"We'd best return to our rooms, love," Marcus said. The guests were at dinner—they'd used the time to search, but she knew they would return at any time.

She retied the letters, fussed with the bow, and slid the letters back in the secretary's drawer. She reached Marcus as he opened the door a crack. "Ssh," he whispered, "Chartrand and his wife are in the hallway."

Venetia slipped around in front of Marcus and tucked in between his chest and the door.

Chartrand's voice floated to them, cold and hard. "No matter what Aspers asks, tell him nothing about the past. What I did, I did for you."

"You didn't." Tears streaked Lady Chartrand's cheeks. "You said you wanted me, you didn't really. You have always loved her. Catherine was your first love. You never forgot her."

"I strangled her. I watched her die. I promise you that I never loved her—" The rest came softly and Venetia strained hard but couldn't hear.

Lady Chartrand struggled to control sobs. "What of Lydia?"

The low thrum of Chartrand's voice. "I arranged a near miss with a carriage in Hyde Park. A footpad armed with a knife . . . intended to scare . . . but she didn't scare . . ."

"You wrapped your hands around her throat in front of Polk—in front of a servant—would you have killed her in the gallery?"

"Hold your tongue, woman. I will not let you destroy me." Chartrand snatched hold of her sleeve.

Lady Chartrand wrenched from his grasp and ran down the hallway. Venetia recoiled at the look of raw fury in Chartrand's gray eyes, but he stormed off in the opposite direction.

Chartrand had arranged the accidents that Juliette had hinted at. He had admitted to attempting to strangle Lydia. "He must be the one," Venetia whispered.

"We can't be certain," Marcus countered, grasping her hand. "But it is safe for us to go."

"But I've just realized the way to catch the murderer," she whispered as they stole out into the hallway. "A brilliant, simple plan."

CHAPTER NINETEEN

"No," Marcus growled. "Absolutely not."

"But luring out the murderer is the best plan," Venetia protested. "He wants the book, we can use it to trap him. I would announce that I would be on the terrace alone, and then, when he strikes, you would catch him." Nude but for her stockings, she was perched on the edge of his bed. She crossed her arms beneath her breasts.

"No. I'm not using you as bait, Vee. Absolutely not." He slid her stocking down.

"It is the only way—" Why could he not see that?

"I am not risking your life, love." He drew off her last stocking and let it flutter to the floor. "Nor am I letting you out of this bedroom tonight."

He strolled to the bedside drawer, opened it. She knew what was there. A riding crop, ropes, and shackles. "Marcus—"

He dangled several lengths of black velvet rope before her eyes. She caught her breath. "Tonight," he said, "I plan to sweep you into an odyssey of erotic pleasures."

She giggled at that, as nerves and excitement tumbled in her belly.

Holding the ropes, he slipped his arm around her waist, and drew her into a bone-melting kiss. She broke away and tentatively touched the velvet restraints. "What do you plan to do?"

Eyes teasing, he wound one rope around her arm, the velvet a soft caress against her skin.

"Tonight you will be my slave."

She wished to be independent, how could the thought of being bound excite her so? "What if I say no?"

"I know you want to explore this, love. Trust me." He brushed a soft kiss on her mouth. "For this to be a delight, you must trust me."

Venetia understood. *Which Belizique picture fascinates you most?* She remembered Marcus' question. How excited he had been. She'd been so uncertain. She fantasized about ropes and submission yet had never truly thought she would let a man do such things. But slipping her hand into Marcus', she whispered, "I can trust."

"Close your eyes."

She did, but let her lashes drift up just a bit, just to peek.

"Trust," he murmured, and so she closed her eyes tight. She tensed as the velvet ropes touched her wrists. But he didn't bind her, he trailed the ends along her arm, up to her shoulder.

Velvet brushed her back. Even with eyes closed, she knew he was standing in front of her, mere inches away. The ropes skimmed high, brushing the curve of her spine. Then pressed lightly against the back of her neck.

She felt as though all the air had squeezed from her chest.

"Follow me," he urged, his voice as dark and sensual as the velvet. He tugged, the velvet pushed against her nape, and she moved as he bid. Trusting him.

"Stop here." Hands encircled her waist, lifting. As her bottom brushed smooth silk, she knew she was on the bed. She let him ease her back.

"Delightful," he murmured. "Open your eyes."

"Must I do everything you command?" But she did open her eyes, wanting to see him.

"Silence." He grinned, wickedly. "You may only speak when I allow it. You may, however, cry out your pleasure."

Every inch the arrogant peer.

"Stretch your arms above your head."

She complied, brushing them against the silk counterpane. Watching him, watching the fire that blazed within his eyes. A flame that was more than just a reflection of candlelight.

"Put your wrists together."

The bed dipped and creaked as he sat at her side. At the first loop of velvet around her wrists, she stiffened. Embarrassed, a little afraid, ashamed at her excitement. Surely decent women did not like such games.

But she did.

The velvet wound tighter.

"Try to free yourself," he instructed.

Valiantly, she did, but couldn't move her hands an inch. Then he tied another rope to the loops that imprisoned her and secured that one to the head of the bed. She fought, trying to move her arms, but all she could do was thrash them from side to side. And only a few inches.

But watching him watch her struggle . . . that set her quim blazing . . . his cock would bob upward each time she arched and tugged. His juices oozed out and dripped down his length.

"Now," he mused, tapping his chin. The ropes danced as he did. "To tie your legs apart . . . or together?"

"Together?"

He flashed a smile. "Together it is, then." He pressed his fingers to her lips. "Remember, slave, silence."

She might be the slave but she saw he couldn't draw his gaze away from her.

"First, ankles." He slid her legs together. Before she could even try to pull them apart, he'd wound a rope there. Her ankles rubbed, she shifted her feet to find comfort. He paused, let her do so, then pulled the ropes tight. Knotted them.

His hair shadowed his face as he worked on her knees. Excitement rippled through her. She was soaked between her thighs, soaked and burning. Hotter than she'd ever been.

He trussed her thighs, binding them tight. Even the squeeze of them drove her mad. She was panting greedily. But he couldn't enter her this way . . . what would he do?

With his large, strong hands, he arranged her and she stayed relaxed and obedient, following his direction. Ending up on her knees, with her head against the bed, her arms stretched in front of her and roped in place. Her bare bottom stuck out at him.

"A rope between your legs to saw against your clit . . ." he mused, and slid one in, drawing it back and forth, literally sawing the fabric against her. Each stroke sparked a jolt of desire.

But her satisfaction was not his goal, she soon realized. At first she sighed in relief as he teased her with his fingers from behind. As he opened her nether lips, then caressed her clit. She must look . . . submissive with her bum in the air, her breasts crushed against her knees. She tried to rock against his fingers, but as she neared climax, he withdrew them.

"Patience, my lovely slave."

Something large and blunt pressed against her nether lips. He was going to take her in this position. Oh yes. Yes, she wanted it. She pushed back against him, trying to draw his rigid cock inside. But he had other ideas. First he rasped the length of his cock against her clit, thrusting between her tightly squeezed thighs. Oh so good! She savored it, then struggled to reposition, to ensure that he slid in.

He pulled away. "Not yet, my sweet."

The mattress rose beneath her, and she turned her head to watch him leave. Panting. She was so close . . . she tried squeezing her thighs together, wriggling that way, desperate to come.

He returned with the gleaming brass box of toys. Let the lid drop back. But she couldn't see what he took out. She strained to look—the embroidered silk rasped her cheek.

"Curious?" He dangled it before her by its chain. The two golden balls reflected the candlelight, spinning before her.

To her surprise, he popped one in his mouth, toyed with it on his tongue. She was melting with lust. To be led was exhilarating.

When he moved behind her, she could no longer see. Her sense of touch, her hearing, was all she could rely upon. Hands caressed her derriere. She heard his harsh breathing, hers, and the licking of flames in the fireplace.

Something warm pressed against her bottom. His finger, massaging oil into her. Arching back, she relaxed for him. Pop. In went the ball, and her muscles closed tight around it. The links of the chain teased her entrance. Moaning, she waited for the next. Felt a light tug that had her quim throbbing. But he pushed the next ball there, into her cunny. And flicked the chain. The links teased the bridge between quim and ass, his playful tugs had the balls moving inside her.

"Squeeze tight on them," he commanded.

She fluttered her muscles around them, bringing herself to the brink—

He bent and laved the length of the chain with his tongue, stroking that most sensitive place. He ran his tongue around the rim of her anus, tangling with the chain, wetting her . . . reached around and touched her clit, just a touch—

Her orgasm slammed through her. Legs and arms bound she could only rock and buck with it. She wrenched her head to the side, to cry out, to gulp in breaths.

Heavens! She rode it forever, squeezing, pulsing, a slave to sin.

But the orgasm faded, sense flooded in. She suddenly felt exposed. Embarrassed. As though he knew, he instantly began to untie the knot that dug into the side of her thigh.

The bonds around her thighs went slack. He stroked her flesh, which stung and burned a bit, but the discomfort had been exciting itself. His touch was so tender. As he released each rope, he gently rubbed and kissed her skin.

Her gaze met his as he rubbed her wrist. Her fingers hurt as sensation replaced the tingling. Shame evaporated as

Venetia saw his enormous cock. "Could I . . . could I try to tie you up?"

Marcus's brows shot up. He hadn't expected that question. But Venetia was crawling around on the bed, derriere wiggling, as she gathered up the ropes. He almost always played the dominant. Being bound, being completely under a woman's power made him nervous.

Yet what would Venetia do? She had no ulterior motive. All she wanted was pleasure and play.

"Yes," he groaned. "You may." And he stretched out on the bed, arms and legs splayed.

He expected her to attack from the floor—to tie him up from the side of the bed. His heart thudded as she straddled his waist, the ropes held tight in her hand. Damn, he loved this position—her cunny stretched wide, its heat and wetness pressed against his skin, her full, bounteous breasts hovering over him.

She bent, stretched to reach his right wrist and her breasts dangled over his face. Lifting, he kissed the nipple. She squirmed on him, and he mercilessly suckled her as she tried to wrap the rope around his wrist.

"There." He felt pressure, she fashioned a knot, but it was loose. Still, he wanted to indulge in the game, pretend he was her captive.

"You have the most . . . seductive wrists," she confided as she tied his other arm. "I am incorrigible—even the sight of your bare wrists arouses me."

Her confession aroused him. His cock was as rigid as the bedposts and standing nigh as tall.

The wench crawled over him to bind the end of her rope to the headboard. He cocked his head to watch. Then she turned on his waist, waggled her bum in his face, attended to his ankles.

"Apart for you," she murmured as she secured the first rope.

"Now that I am your prisoner what do you plan to do?"

"You must not speak. Now you are the slave."

He chuckled, but the truth of her words struck him. No woman had ever tempted him so.

The wicked wench left the bed. He almost begged her to return but held his tongue. On his back, he had a perfect view.

Her red hair shimmered down her back as she fetched the vial from the table. Charmingly intent on her work, she drizzled oil into her palm, then withdrew the two gold balls from the dish of washing water and dropped them into her hand. She rubbed them within, then unfurled her fingers to show how they glistened.

He swallowed. Hard. The rope bit into his ankles and wrists in the most erotic way, but what truly enticed was her expression of power, excitement, wanton desire.

Gold glinted as she circled her nipples with the balls—the chain reached the span between them. She trailed the balls down the curve of her belly, dipping them in her shadowed navel. Dangling them by the chain, she swung them in front of her cunny. His throat was tight. His cock lifted off his belly.

"I want to do something forbidden."

Intrigued, he watched as she knelt onto the bed between his spread legs.

Then he knew. His ass clenched, his cock jolted. A squirt of fluid hit his belly—his cock's abundant lubrication. Her delicate hand held the balls against his bottom, eased them between his tight cheeks. All the while she watched his face. Licked her lips.

"May I?"

"God, yes." He fought to relax as she pushed the ball. Sweat beaded on his forehead. Pleasure uncoiled through him as she pressed the smooth ball against his anus, as his entrance parted. Groaning, he felt the first one pop inside. Then the second. Lord, the feeling of it . . . the pleasure . . .

"Climb on top of me," he begged hoarsely.

She looked tempted. Shook her head.

"Tempt me, Vixen. Drive me wild. Pose for me." Adopting graces was a skill taught to young ladies. To watch a nude woman adopt lovely, angelic poses had him leaking on his belly.

He'd planned to drive her wild with seduction—she'd turned the tables on him. She used two ivory wands in her poses. She playfully spanked her quim with one, then bent and presented her derriere, stroking a wand between her cheeks. She teased her bottom with one wand, her quim with the other.

He was panting. Sweating. His anus pulsed around the balls, heightening his need.

Wearing a saucy smile, she climbed onto the bed. Touched the wand that was wet with her cunny juices to his nipples. He moaned and arched against the ropes.

Her hazel eyes glowed like glass lanterns. She stroked the wand along his cock and the sight of the white length parrying with his cock made him both hot and uncertain. The combination set his heart pumping harder. Her finger twined around the chain, teasing the bridge between his balls and his ass. She pulled. One ball popped out. His anus clenched and pleasure shot through his brain. The second popped out. He gritted his teeth to keep from exploding. She stroked a wand between his arse cheeks, and he groaned in sheer sexual agony.

"I *know* what I wish to do!" she cried.

Leaving him in sexual torment, she disappeared through the connecting door to her room. Lying spread-eagled on the bed, unable to see, Marcus wrenched against the ropes. He gained slack, but try as he might, he couldn't lever up enough. Something scraped along the floor. Her trunk.

She returned with a paintbrush in her hand.

"What are—?"

"Silence," she commanded. Then she giggled. Ah, a true

dominatrix she would never be, but she was a delight at playing games. She sashayed to his side, climbed onto the bed.

She touched the brush to his hard nipples. "Tell me, which of my pictures is your favorite?"

"There are many." He moaned as she stroked the brush across his chest to draw rings around his other nipple. Straining, he saw she had no paint on the brush.

"Tell me them all."

"*The Page Turner*, for I like to imagine the next scene—when that innocent young woman finds herself penetrated by two aroused gentlemen. By another man and me."

He heard her breath hitch. She stroked the brush up the center of his chest, along the line of his throat. "And I love *The Luncheon*, where an orgy has broken out at a proper outdoor luncheon. I can picture us like that, you lying on the table, me feasting on your juicy quim."

The bristles touched his lips. Traced them. "Now, when I look at my work, I think of us . . . like that. Do you?"

"Yes," he hissed. "When I look at all of your pictures, I think of you with me."

She retreated, drawing the brush down to his navel, dipping in, then trailing down . . . down.

Closing his eyes, he savored the sensation as she brushed his ballocks. The pressure as the sable tip flattened had him jerking against his bonds. She drew the brush up and down the shaft of his cock until he moaned in pure hunger. A true sensual artist, she painted the sensitive head, swirled around the ridge, stroked the taut line of flesh at the back. She hit a spot that sent explosive pleasure rocketing through his skull. He howled, thrashing back against the ropes.

"Marcus . . ."

He felt her weight settle across his thighs. Yes. Pleasure and agony roared through him as she bent back his cock, preparing to mount. He kept his eyes shut and focused on the tight grip of her hand on the shaft, her heavy breathing, the brush of crisp hairs against the bulging head. His heart galloped with anticipation. Waiting to slide into her tight, sopping wet cunny—

A thunderous bang had his eyes open. A dark shape streaked in through the connecting door. Venetia screamed and fell onto the bed, but the assailant grabbed her, and dragged her to the floor. Marcus drove his arms forward, thrust his legs to the side, trying to break the velvet ropes. They held tight.

Dressed entirely in black, masked, the man hauled Vee to her feet. Her eyes were wide, face stark white. Wrenching her head back, the blackguard pressed a blade to her throat. A weak croak spilled from her lips. In a husky voice, he snarled, "Where's that bloody book? Give it to me, else she gets her throat slit."

Marcus ripped at the knots she'd tied. Damn, she'd played the game too well, she'd made him a true prisoner.

"Stop! Another move, milord, and I cut her throat." Hand fisted in Vee's hair, the man pulled her head back, forcing her neck to arch against the blade. Her whimper of pain ripped through Marcus' soul.

Boiling with hatred, fury, rage at his position, he could only obey. Stay motionless.

"Ye're looking less impressive now, milord," the intruder sneered. He nodded toward the toys on the bed. "Do ye stuff all those into this tart?"

Marcus reacted from the gut at the words, arching forward. The villain pressed the knife tighter to Vee's throat, making her gasp.

"I want the book, milord. Now."

Hell, who was behind the mask? The accent was rough but the voice was disguised and muffled. It could belong to any man in the house. Clad in black, standing in shadow and shielded by Vee, the bastard appeared muscular, tall—a build that could belong to any of their suspects.

"The book is in her trunk," Marcus said. "Untie me and I'll get it for you. Let her go."

"It's locked—" Vee stopped, trying to pull back from the blade. "I . . . I can't speak."

Damn. Only Vee would protest. Only Vee would point out to a killer the idiocy of his actions.

"You can stay right where ye are, milord," The man mocked and he pushed Vee forward, forced her to walk toward her room. "Now, let's get that book, sweetie, and then I'll be off."

It gave Marcus time. Twisting his head, he tugged his right wrist hard against the bonds. She'd left slack at least. Enough to get his teeth on the knot. To rip, tear, pull, gnaw. His first tug tightened it, but not by much. Shifting, he found another spot to rip. The knot loosened.

From Vee's room, came the sound of something dragging across the wood floor. Her trunk. Then her voice rose, filled with fear. "I've hidden the trunk key. Let me get it."

A thudding sound followed. As though the villain was kicking the trunk while Venetia got the key.

The knot slackened, then opened. His wrist ached, his hand prickled and he flexed it quickly. He tore the next knot open. Ripped the ropes of his feet and slid off the bed, taking care to make no sound. Venetia, bless her, slammed the wardrobe doors open and made a loud attempt to find her key, swishing dresses, banging the doors.

Noise that made the killer nervous. "Keep it quiet," he barked.

Pressed tight to the wall, Marcus peered around the doorframe. The villain's back faced him—he didn't expect a bound man to cause him trouble. Venetia had just dropped a gown to the floor, shaking in terror.

Did he have time to grab his thin sword from his walking stick?

"Ye're stalling." The arm lifted, the blade glinted.

Marcus launched forward. He tackled the villain and slammed his right fist into the man's face from behind. The knife arm slashed back. He jerked to the side—too late. Cold metal slid into his flesh. Tore upward. Jerked free. Instinct and pain sent him backing off, the villain took the advantage to turn and slice up with the blade.

Expecting it, Marcus sprung back and the bloodstained tip slashed air. But he drove forward with his right fist, snapping the villain's head back as his fist smashed into his jaw. He pushed his advantage, following with a left uppercut. His knuckles split on contact and came away red—smeared with blood from the killer's nose. The villain's hand went up in instinctive protection. Marcus drove his right fist into the bastard's gut. He sagged back.

Marcus moved fluidly, the training from Gentleman Jackson's ring guided him. He landed a volley of blows but the knife blade slashed wildly at him, forcing him back.

Venetia screamed. From the corner of his eye, Marcus saw her charge forward. A poker high above her head. Just a fractional hesitation. But the blackguard spun.

Venetia swung the poker down. It smashed into the floor and splintered wood where the killer's feet had been. With a cry, she dropped the poker. Marcus lunged to grab it, but the assailant chose to flee rather than fight. As Marcus sprang after him, poker raised, the man jumped up onto the windowsill. The open window—the way he'd gotten in. It was a two-story fall.

Crashing and cursing met Marcus as he leaned out of the window. Bushes below had broken the fall and provided enough shadow to swallow up a man dressed in black. Moonlight slanted over the lawns but trees made wells of shadow. Marcus spotted movement several yards from the house, but the killer vanished again into blackness.

Blast. No point launching nude out of the window to take up the chase.

"Marcus! You're bleeding!"

CHAPTER TWENTY

God, she had the hands of an angel. Leaning back on his bed, on top of folded sheets, Marcus groaned softly while Venetia cleaned his wound. The wet cloth felt strangely cold as it slid over his opened flesh, but it dulled some of the pain.

"Does that hurt?" she whispered.

"A little," he admitted.

"I'm sure it hurts more than that." Lashes soft as velvet screened her eyes. "Thank you," she whispered. "For rescuing me."

Against his will, laughter came. He remembered her wild swing with the poker, her angry, coarse curse of "Shite!" Pain lanced his side, but it was worth it. The laugh cleared his head.

He struggled to sit up. Her small, splayed hand tried to push him back. "What are you doing? It needs to be dressed. And laudanum—"

"No opiates." Hell, he needed a clear head. He looked down at his wound. A glancing blow at his hipbone and the cut wasn't deep. It hurt like the blazes. Had the blade struck higher, not hit the bone, it would have gutted him—

He eased her pale hand away, swung his legs off the bed.

"You can't get up!"

"Sweetheart, I have to. He's given himself away. I gave his

face a good pounding and he's going to show it. A split lip, bruises. All I need to do is round up the men on the estate and we've got our killer."

"Now? Your wound needs bandaging."

He met her frightened gaze. "I'm going to catch him. Tonight. It's all over."

She pressed a gauze pad to the slice along his hip, firmly, but gently enough not to cause pain. She moved his hand to it. "Hold that in place."

Clamping the pad as she asked, he yanked the bell pull to summon Rutledge. Who could he trust to guard Venetia while he searched? The women? Servants? Some brawny footmen whose innocence he could readily judge—he would know they were innocent if they didn't bear the evidence of the fight.

Marcus sank back to the bed. Blood loss left his legs shaky, but he fought the tremble in his muscles. Venetia firmly kept her hand on his shoulder—to keep him her captive—while she gathered up bandages and pins. Deftly, she wound the fabric.

The brush of her fingers over his skin was magic—not just sensual magic. Something different. Something he only vaguely remembered. Comfort. "You're very good at this."

Her gentle voice soothed. "Good works in the village. To keep us above reproach. Mother insisted that we must battle gossip about her absentee husband by throwing ourselves into charity work." She pinned the snug wrap of bandages swiftly and neatly, the pressure easing pain.

He'd never seen this side of her, this gentle nurturing side. What a wonderful wife and mother she would make.

"Marcus, I—" Her face was stark white. Her eyes were deep green in the light, watery, like jade stones in a flowing brook. "I want to go with you."

"No. Absolutely not. You'll be safe here—I'll post a guard." He brushed a quick kiss to her trembling lips, then slid to his feet to yank on his clothes.

So softly he knew the words were meant only for her, she whispered, "I can't bear the thought of losing you."

Marcus rested his hip on the edge of Chartrand's desk, holding the pistol he'd acquired from his host's collection at his side. Loaded and primed, it was a reassuring weight against his palm.

A footman stood by the row of windows and Rutledge stood by the door. For once, the butler looked shocked and appalled.

"What in blazes is going on?" Wembly stormed into the drawing room, running his fingers through his tangled hair. "Trent, what do you think you're about?"

Candlelight fell on Wembly's face, revealing it clearly. Wembly's face was unmarked. Not a bruise. Not a split lip. No sign of a beating.

Within ten minutes, Brude, Montberry, and Swansborough had barreled into the room, enraged at being hauled away from their sexual pleasures. They were debauched men— they'd continued to seek entertainment even though the orgy had halted.

Each man wore his innocence plainly on his face.

Time ticked by. Chartrand did not appear.

Montberry drew himself up. "Trent, what is the meaning of dragging us from our beds?"

"An assailant with a knife dragged me from mine. I thought I'd return the favor to the man responsible." He watched his peers, saw no sign of guilt. But they were gentlemen all, accustomed to masking emotion. He gave out succinct details of the assault.

"And whoever attacked you will bear the bruises," Swansborough concluded from the brandy decanter where he sloshed a glass full.

Marcus called out to Rutledge. "Where is Lord Chartrand?"

The butler stepped forward. "Not in his bedroom, my lord. I sent Roberts in search of him."

And Roberts had not returned with Chartrand. The man who had reputedly murdered his wife was not showing his face.

"We search for him," Marcus said grimly.

With the sentry on guard—Williams and Davis, two footmen with unmarred faces and barrel chests—Venetia couldn't leave the room. She paced the floor in front of her fireplace. She was terrified for Marcus, and worse, she was left out of the action and adventure. It drove her mad.

She'd thanked him for rescuing her—he had saved her life and she was being churlish to actually resent him for it.

Resting her hands on the mantel and bowing her head, she knew she didn't truly resent him. She was frightened. Not over murderers but of the stark truth staring her in the face. She'd come to London to rescue herself, determined to do it. And she hadn't—the magnificent, powerful Earl of Trent had had his hands full rescuing her.

He'd rescued her from her career. Rescued her from ruination—or, rather, tried. Rescued her from landing in a cauldron of trouble by seeking adventure at an orgy. And he'd most definitely rescued her from death.

She'd wanted to believe a woman could rescue herself. She'd had to believe it—she couldn't go blithely on pretending to hope that Rodesson would protect his family. And what had she done? She'd failed.

Which man had attacked them? She'd been close enough to smell his sweat and she still did not know. He hadn't smelled or sounded like a gentleman, but that might have been a disguise.

Which of them? Chartrand? Brude? Wembly? Montberry? Swansborough? It was so hard to picture any of those arrogant gentlemen as the rough villain who had held a knife to her throat. It certainly hadn't been a woman. He'd been strong. She'd felt his hard chest pressing against her back. And he'd been aroused—she'd felt that too.

Her stomach was churning and she rested her head on the carved mantel.

She lifted her head so quick her neck cracked. Her pictures. Would it help to look at them? She'd sketched every gentleman here. Perhaps studying them might stir recognition. Might give her a clue.

Unlocking her trunk, she pulled out her paint box. She'd jammed it hurriedly in before. As the lid opened and brushes and bottles tumbled out, she realized she'd forgotten to lock it. With a sweep of her arm she herded up the fallen equipment and dumped it back it. Locked the box with care, pulled out her sketchbook. Paused. Lydia's journal was beneath it. They'd read it over and over and found no real clue. Each guest had a motive. Tentatively, she touched it. Marcus' secrets were no longer there. Had Lady Ravenwood been the victim of incest? Had he been protecting his sister's secrets?

Why did he believe his mother's words that he was unworthy of love? Any man more worthy of love, she couldn't imagine!

The red leather-bound book lay there. Outwardly innocent, but it was the most sinful thing she'd ever seen. Venetia dropped her paint box back in the trunk on top of the book and pushed the trunk under the bed.

That book had driven someone to the most unthinkable crimes.

Marcus crouched, ignoring Chartrand's sightless gray eyes to study the ugly slash across his throat. The white of his windpipe showed amidst red, oozing flesh. Christ Jesus.

The dust of hay twinkled in the lamplight. Hooves clopped on stone as horses paced and tossed. Fierce snorts came from frightened animals, who smelled blood and death. A roan stallion threw his flank against the stall gate and sent the boards straining on the chain. The head groom caught his tether and began settling the beast.

The other two grooms—boys with thin chests and unruly hair—crowded around him and Chartrand's body.

"Coo," breathed one.

"Blimey," added the other.

Straightening, Marcus sent Rutledge to alert the other searchers.

Chartrand's body had been shoved into an empty stall, head landing against a bale. Blood had rushed from the slice at his throat, making a river of red along the floor.

The largest groom, a big man with gray threading his brown hair, came striding over and doffed his cap. "Can we move 'im, milord? The horses are spooked."

Marcus nodded. No clues to the killer, other than boot prints smearing the long trail of blood, but those vanished at the stable door. If the knife blow had come from the front, the killer would be sprayed with Chartrand's blood.

Who? Who was left? The women. Lady Yardley. Lady Chartrand. The various courtesans. He couldn't believe a woman had done this. She wouldn't have the strength to fight off Chartrand. Or to have fought with him in his bed-chamber. And he was certain the bone structure he had de-stroyed with his fist belonged to a man.

"Were it the gypsies, milord?" asked the tallest lad, the one with spiky red hair.

"No," the head groom said, "They packed up and left. Scared off."

Who did that leave? Servants. Had one of the servants been paid? He'd have to get Rutledge to round up every man on the blasted estate. He asked the head groom, "Did any of your lads get in a fight tonight?"

The groom crossed his arms over his massive chest. "Naw, not one o' mine."

"Aye," chimed in the redheaded lad, "But I saw a footman in the carriage house. Fetching something for a gent, he said. 'Ad a busted lip and the start of a shiner on one eye. Said he'd pinched the arse of the wrong wench."

"There's a curricle missing, milord," the youngest groom

added breathlessly. "And Mr. Wembly's grays are gone too."

"Which bloody footman was it?" Marcus barked.

On her bed, legs tucked beneath her, Venetia opened her sketchbook. Which one? Which one?

The first sketch—her naughtiest. John and Cole entwined after sex. Two limp cocks resting side by side, John's head bowed on Cole's chest. She turned to the next.

A portrait of Lydia. She lifted the page, intending to toss it over, then paused. Lydia had been very beautiful. Cupid's bow lips—Venetia was proud of the way she'd caught the shape. The only odd feature was Lydia's nose, straight but wide, with a rounded bump on the end. Large, round eyes. She had sketched in charcoal, so the eyes were rendered in black, with circles of white to show the reflection of light, the life, in them. Lydia's eyes had been the color of the night sky just before dawn—midnight blue, rich with violet.

And the next. Lord Chartrand tapping Trixie's curvy bottom with a riding crop while her hand had just smacked Mr. Wembly's hard and nude derriere. Unfinished, capturing only their forms. Venetia nibbled her thumbnail. Could her attacker have been Lord Chartrand? Had he been that big and broad?

It had been such a blur. She'd been so shocked—

Or could it have been Wembly who was slight but tall, and blond? Could he have disguised his mocking, jaded drawl as a ruffian's coarse voice?

She stared at her unfinished portrait of Montberry, captured as he watched a scandalous display—Lady Chartrand and Rosalyn positioned head to quim and lavishly licking. The war hero stood as tall as Marcus. Venetia was certain— almost—that the masked man had been shorter, but not by much.

She glanced at the clock on the mantel. A quarter of three.

Was Marcus downstairs? Had he found all the men? Why hadn't she heard anything yet?

She turned the page.

Another unfinished sketch. Lord Brude, dark, brooding, and gorgeous. With long fingered hands, and an unusually long tongue. Not the sort of thing to help identify a masked and gloved assailant when he stood at your back.

Or Lord Swansborough?

Her pictures weren't helping at all and she was at the last one. Lady Yardley caught in a passionate moment with the raven-haired footman, Polk. A few strokes captured the poignant emotion shining in her ladyship's eyes, the cocky triumph in his—

Why hadn't she seen it before?

The footman's face . . . Lydia Harcourt and Polk the footman had the same features. His were broader, coarser, more masculine, but they were the same. The same chin. The same nose. And the eyes—she was relying on memory—but the color of the eyes was the same.

It could not be a coincidence. Lydia and the footman were related. Quite closely, she guessed. Brother and sister? Her mind whirled. Polk had brought brandy to her room the day Lydia was killed. He was upset, agitated. Of course he would be, if his sister had been murdered!

Had Lydia come here seeking his help or protection?

It seemed a strange coincidence that her brother would be Chartrand's footman—

The man who had attacked them had dark eyes, so dark they could have been black, like Lord Swansborough's eyes. But given the faint light, the mask shadowing his face, they might have been midnight blue.

They could also have been brown.

Why would Polk strangle his own sister? His soon-to-be wealthy sister?

She must find Marcus and tell him. Tucking the sketchbook beneath her arm, she raced for the door. She turned the key in the lock. Blast. Her guards.

Well, their job was to guard her, they could just as easily do it while taking her to find Marcus. She pulled the door open. Two bodies sprawled in the hallway by her door. She saw crumpled crimson livery. Gleaming boots with toes pointing up.

She shrank back. Her arms wrapped around her sketch-book. As she stared down at the men, skirts came into view. Black skirts.

"I want me mistress' book. Now."

Venetia's horrified gaze slid upward. A pistol was leveled at her chest. She stared into the cold, merciless eyes of Lydia's maid Juliette. The grim faced woman who had shed tears over her employer's death.

Juliette's hand shook. Venetia's heart skipped a beat, realizing that Juliette was scared. Perhaps as much as she was. And that frightened her the most. Juliette could shoot her by accident.

"Yes," Venetia hastened to promise, "Yes, I can give that to you." She glanced down. "Are . . . are they dead?"

"Easy enough to coax the louts to toss back some laudanum laced spirits." Juliette sneered, stepped over one footman, pausing only to spit on his chest. "Laughed at my flirtations but were happy enough to drink the port I brought." She crossed the threshold, pistol held out. Instinctively, Venetia retreated. Had it been Juliette all along? But Juliette hadn't the strength to push over the urn or to strangle two powerful men.

Could she knock away the pistol? Did she dare? In her moment of hesitation, Juliette clasped both hands around it. "Move!" she screeched.

A gambler like her father Venetia would never be. "It's in my trunk," she admitted. "Under the bed."

"Get it out and be quick about it." Juliette closed her door. The lock clicked with finality.

Venetia turned, moving mechanically toward the bed, the trunk. Fear seemed freeze her. Could she get the fireplace poker? She'd have a hole blasted through her back before she could use it.

She dropped to her knees, lifted the fabric that skirted the bed.

"Drag out the trunk and open it."

Venetia dropped to her knees and pulled the trunk from beneath the bed. Her knee bumped something hard and cool. She glanced down.

The small glass bottle of turps lay on the carpet. It must have fallen out of her trunk before as she'd pulled out her sketchbook. Shielding it with her body, she closed her hand around it. Expecting Juliette to catch her, expecting to get shot.

"Drag that out farther. Where I can see it."

She obeyed. The bottle of turps weighed heavy in her pocket. Juliette looked in. Checking for weapons, Venetia guessed.

"The book. And be quick—if ye take too long, I swear to *le bon dieu*, I'll shoot."

Venetia rose, holding out the leather-bound book. "There."

And now she was of no use to Juliette. She bit her lip. There would be no reason for Juliette not to shoot her.

But Juliette pointed toward the door and the pistol drooped a bit as the maid's right hand trembled against the weight. "You're going to come in very handy, lovey. A ticket to buy me and Tom's freedom."

Venetia swallowed hard. A foolish, dangerous question fell from her lips. "Did you shoot at me yesterday?"

She flinched at Juliette's chuckle. "I wanted yer out of the way. Nosing in and asking questions. You and 'is lordship. Besides, ye wouldn't be so pretty dead, would ye? My aim's better at close range, I promise ye. Now move."

* * *

Venetia. Her name sang through Marcus' mind. If Tom Polk, the black-haired footman, intended to escape, would he do it without Lydia Harcourt's book?

Marcus sprinted up the lawns toward the house, through fingers of moonlight and pools of shadow. He'd sent the rest of the men in search of Polk. He had to know Venetia was safe. Questions raced, as fast as his footfall.

How did a footman know about the book? Had he bedded Lydia and she'd confided her grand scheme? Lydia would never do that. Confusion reigned. Was the footman in someone else's employ?

He couldn't remember Tom Polk's appearance, though the servant apparently had dark hair.

The fountain loomed ahead, a stone circle surrounded by trimmed roses. A cherub stood in the center, a ghost in the silver-blue light. He felt the thud of stone through his boot soles as he reached the flagstone path. The house lay ahead. Light gleamed in the windows. He knew which light was Venetia's and he looked up toward it as he ran.

He gripped one pistol in his hand. Deep in his pocket, the second gun he'd grabbed from Chartrand's cabinet swung against his legs.

Ahead lay the oldest wing of the house, the gardens, and the clean black edge of the woods. Beyond was the muddy road. He'd carried Venetia on that path, when the rifle ball had exploded just above her head—

A gray-white ghost shimmered against the trees, near the path that led to the gypsies' camp. Statues on the edge of the wood? Distorted by distance and wind, the whinnying of horses came to his ears.

Lungs burning, Marcus slowed, taking a few strides to think. Were the horses lashed to a tree waiting for Polk's return? Or was Polk at the reins, preparing to flee?

What if Polk had the book?

What if he'd harmed Vee?

That couldn't happen. It could not happen. Strange how the brain flung out words in a moment of fear. Min's words. *And you know that if you lost it, your heart might never mend.*

Which path to take? Up, to the house, to find Vee, to know she was safe? Down, to the horses and carriage, on the chance he could capture Polk before he escaped?

His feet turned toward the house.

CHAPTER TWENTY-ONE

"I didn't touch yer tart, milord," Tom Polk protested, his hands raised above his head.

Marcus rested his gloved finger on the pistol's trigger, its barrel aimed directly at Polk's heart. He fought panic—panic that roared in his brain and gripped his heart. *Vee wasn't in her room. Vee was gone. Vee . . .*

He had to keep his head, it was the only way to save her. The gentlemen were scattered around—anyone could have Vee. The quickest link was the blackguard standing before him. Black clouds had swallowed up the moon, and in the dark, he could barely see the man. "Then who are you working for?"

"Yer won't shoot me, milord. You'll never find your little tart if you do, will ye?" A sudden cocky grin lit up Tom's face. Shadow hid the bruises, but the bastard's words were thick, muffled, as though spoken through swollen lips.

Marcus couldn't judge if Polk knew where Vee was or if he was bluffing. But he had to gamble to keep the upper hand. "And if you won't talk, Polk," he bluffed in return, "You're no use to me, and I'd enjoy watching you bleed out."

Polk's lips split in a wider grin. His teeth showed in the dark. "Here's your little bit of muslin, now, milord."

Shocked to his soul, Marcus swung around. Who—?

He saw nothing but movement, then moonlight fell again,

bathing two black shapes stealing down the last rise. One was slightly in front, taking careful steps. A shaft of light glinted along a silver pistol barrel held by the second figure. The one in front pushed back her hood, exposing fiery hair and her pale oval face. Venetia.

"You don't move unless I tell you. Keep walking." A woman's voice. Rough, sharp and vicious.

Venetia stopped a few feet from them, her lovely face showing horror, frustration, and embarrassment all at once. The wind caught the unknown woman's hood and threw it back. Lydia Harcourt's hatchet-faced maid, Juliette. Her phony French accent was forgotten. The woman took a step forward and pushed the pistol against Vee's heart. She sneered. "Give Tom your pistol, milord."

"You have only one shot," Marcus said, forcing arrogant ice into his voice.

"Enough to kill her," the maid snapped.

For a frozen moment, Marcus held onto the pistol. Any move, no matter how fast, and he might sacrifice Vee. No, he couldn't risk it. He tossed the pistol in front of him and it thudded into the shadows. "It's yours for the taking."

"Pick it up, Tom," the maid ordered.

He had a moment's advantage, while Polk bent into the shadows, but Juliette's narrow eyes fixed on him. Her finger slid back and forth across the trigger. His throat dried. The bloody thing could fire by accident.

Marcus saw the shock in Vee's eyes, the hollowness of despair. He smiled at her, a soft, gentle uptilt of his lips. Promising hope. She smiled back, faith shining in the shadowed hazel-green of her eyes.

"Let her go," he commanded the maid. "You have me."

"Having her gives us both of you," Juliette threw back and victory radiated from her small, black eyes, her sallow face.

Polk jumped to his feet. The footman held the pistol loosely in his hand, cockily pointing it at Marcus' heart, as though goading an attempt to grab it. "Turn around and run, milord." Polk laughed, mocking, triumphant. "You toffs are cowards at heart."

Marcus felt the weight of the second pistol against his hip. Resting in his pocket. To draw it out now would be a mistake, but he wanted nothing more than to send the ball into Polk's open mouth. Time. He needed time. And he knew men like Polk. Men who liked to grind a bootheel into a dying man's heart. Polk would want to talk.

"You can shoot me if you like, but I'm not leaving while you hold her." He turned to Juliette. "At least draw the pistol back. Allow her to breathe."

The woman looked like a toad. She grinned. "But this way just a flick of my finger—just one jerk—and she's dead. And that is keeping you where you are, not moving a muscle, isn't it, milord?"

Juliette was growing more calm, more confident, while Polk was beginning to twitch. Marcus put his attention there, drilling the man with an autocratic glare. "You've been a cunning man, Polk," he allowed to buoy up the bastard's ego. "But what was it all for? Why did you kill Lydia Harcourt?"

"I'm not admitting to that, milord." Polk sneered. "I wanted her book, true enough—"

"You're Lydia's brother—" Vee cried and then Juliette yanked on her hair, forcing her head back. Exposing her delicate throat. The cloak-draped arm shoved the pistol harder into Vee's ribs.

"Shut it, bitch," Juliette snarled.

"I painted sketches—Lydia and Polk have the same features—" Vee stopped as Juliette's hand struck her cheek.

Marcus wanted to break Juliette's hand off her wrist.

"Half brother." Polk grinned, waving with the pistol. "So I thought I'd get her book and get what I deserved. I asked Lyd for some blunt to get me out of England. She owed me, the bitch. I smashed our da's skull with a shovel to save 'er life. Almost killed 'im. She'd bitten his privy parts when he forced them in 'er mouth. But after what I did for 'er, she decides not to give me the money."

"Tom! What in blazes are ye doing, ye damned fool." Shut yer yap!" The maid's screech silenced Polk, who glowered at her.

"Shut it yerself, ye shrivelled hag," he returned. "Ye're the stupid cow who couldn't even find her bloody book. I won't be dangling from a rope at Newgate, I promise ye. No offense, guv, but you lot 'ave your 'eads up your arses."

Marcus gave a cynical shrug. "If it is money you want, you stand in the perfect position to get it now, don't you? You have me. Release the woman and you can name your price."

"I'm thinking I can have both," Polk said. "What would you pay to save your bloody hide, milord?" Polk paced back and forth, jabbing in his direction with the pistol as though hoping to make him flinch. "You bloody toffs. I got sharped at cards by a bloody viscount who dealt from the bottom o' the deck. And the bloody cheating toff sent a thug to knife me when I couldn't pay up—"

"Tom, would ye shut your mouth—"

"You shut yours, woman," Polk barked. "Chartrand squealed like a stuck sow when I sliced his windpipe. He saw my knife and promised me a king's ransom to spare him. As ye can see, that weren't enough."

Marcus gritted his teeth against Polk's laughter but the footman leered at Vee. "As for your lightskirt, milord, I think I'll keep 'er with me for a while. I'd like to get a squeeze of 'er pretty tits."

"You touch her and I'll—"

"What'll you do, Trent? I've got the weapon. I'm glad she didn't get flattened by the urn. A waste of a nice, slick cunny, that would've been. I saw her pretty arse when she had ye tied to the bed. What a luscious tart, she is. I'll definitely stretch her wide before slitting her throat—"

"Enough, Tom!" Juliette cried. "God almighty, stop thinking with your prick!"

Venetia shuddered in horror at Tom Polk's threat. Her heartbeat throbbed in her throat. Helplessly, she watched Marcus. Coiled and ready to spring, he didn't dare move. Fury and tension rolled off him in powerful waves. Moonlight reflected on his eyes, blending vivid blue-green with silver moonbeams.

"But he's enjoying himself, Juliette, enjoying himself by tormenting me." Marcus' deep, calm voice was mesmerizing in the dark. "He wants my lovely Vixen, and who can blame him?"

Venetia bit back a cry as Juliette prodded her ribs with the pistol.

"This tart?" Juliette snapped. "You could buy a dozen of the likes of her for a guinea. Now, my lord, I have a good idea what Mrs. Harcourt's book is worth. Shall we say fifty thousand pounds? For your life?"

Venetia prayed neither Polk or Juliette would notice her hand was buried in the pocket of her skirt. Juliette had been oblivious while they'd crossed the grass in the dark. Her fingers fumbled with the turps bottle that rested deep in her pocket. With one hand it was almost impossible to work out the stopper.

No, not impossible. I will succeed!

"For hers," Marcus said.

Venetia almost lost her grip on the stopper. He would pay fifty thousand for her! It was an unthinkable amount of money.

"You're stalling," Juliette snapped. "We need to get moving, Tom. Get 'er up in the bloody coach."

In her head, Venetia screamed in frustration. She needed time. Just a bit more. Would she die? Would she lose Marcus forever? Blast, don't think of disaster! Think of escape. Her fingers felt numb on the cork stopper.

The blasted thing would wiggle but it wouldn't move up!

"You'll never make it to the end of the road," Marcus said, "There are armed men waiting."

"And we've got her," Tom crowed. "They won't touch us."

"Let her go." Authority resonated in Marcus' deep voice. "Use me instead. I can be your way out. There's no need to hurt her. No one would shoot you if you have a pistol at an earl's head."

Venetia's heart stuttered. Again, Marcus had offered his life in place of hers. It was so noble, so wonderfully brave . . . but no, no, she just needed time.

She shook her head at Marcus. Rolled her eyes down toward her skirts. How to signal without giving herself away? Her gaze met his and she tried to will her thoughts to him. *Marcus, please, I have a plan.*

"No, milord. I'm not about to let her go."

Rage flashed across Marcus' face. *No, Marcus, patience.* His turquoise eyes met hers and she saw deep pain, fury, and guilt. *Understand me, please. Just be ready. I've a plan. Be ready.*

Had Marcus' brow lifted? It couldn't be, he couldn't possibly hear her thoughts. She didn't dare wink! But she believed he saw, he understood.

"We should take them both," Juliette snapped at Polk.

He caressed the barrel of the pistol. "Don't need 'em both," Polk argued, "He's what we want. Though I'd like a go at her."

The stopper moved up a hair's breadth. Venetia's heart swelled with hope. She desperately smothered her little gasp of exhilaration. Rocking her fingers back and forth, she forced it out a little more.

And then, as the narrow end of the stopper slid up, it moved easily—

Venetia's heart beat in a steady, loud rhythm. She counted to it. One . . . she eased the turps bottle up. Turpentine splashed on her hand, cool, wet, stinging. She prayed she wouldn't blind Juliette. Two . . . she drew the bottle from her pocket.

Three.

Arcing her arm, she threw the bottle's contents into Juliette's face and grabbed for the pistol. She pushed down the maid's rigid arm as the woman shrieked.

The pistol went off, the roar deafening, the smell choking, and the shock forced her back. She released Juliette.

A second explosion filled her head. She jerked around. Marcus!

Marcus stood, straight, resolute, bathed in moonlight. His arm outstretched, a silver-barreled gun held in his hand. Polk's face was like a waxwork's, and he toppled like one, arcing forward, his face slamming hard into the ground.

"Vee!" Marcus lunged forward.

She saw a flash as Juliette slashed up with a knife from her skirts. Venetia screamed but Marcus reacted before the cry left her throat. He grabbed Juliette's wrist, and twisted it back until the knife tumbled from her hand. It fell, silver blade pointing down, and the earth swallowed it up.

Marcus wrenched Juliette's arms behind her back and held her there, pinned. "Vee, love, are you all right?"

She nodded, the acrid taste of gunpowder burning her throat, and hurried forward, stumbling on her cloak. She dropped to the ground and yanked the knife from the damp soil. The pistol had fallen from Tom's hand. It lay beside him. The ground must be soaked with his blood.

She heard Marcus threaten Juliette with the gallows. Juliette screamed curses, then fell silent.

"Vee—" Her name spoken in Marcus' soft aching voice caught her attention. "What are you doing?"

Hand shaking, Venetia clasped the pistol. She realized what she was doing. Tidying up. But she couldn't just leave weapons lying about. And Marcus needed a pistol to hold on Juliette.

He was trussing Juliette's arms with cord. Binding them tight. Juliette hung her head and tears streaked her cheeks. "Tom . . . Tom . . . Tom . . ."

Venetia handed the weapon to Marcus, warily watching Juliette, who swayed in the wind. Finally, Juliette's knees seemed to give out and she dropped to the ground, sobbing as though her heart was breaking.

Venetia felt Marcus' gloved fingers slide over hers, easing the pistol from her spring-tight grasp. His turquoise eyes shone into hers. Admiration—she saw admiration there.

"Vee, what in blazes did you throw at her?"

"Turpentine. I—I brought my paints, you see."

Now, at the end, there could be no more secrets. Venetia touched her cheek as she entered the library, her hand on Marcus' arm. Beneath her bonnet, her face was bare.

Lord Aspers, the portly, white-haired magistrate, was alone in the room. Early morning sunlight flooded in behind him. Venetia felt tears well, in relief and sorrow at the irony of a beautiful day.

Lord Aspers conducted the interview with tact and care. Venetia paused only when he asked for her real name.

Marcus laid his hand over hers. "You must give it."

Trusting in Marcus, she replied, "Venetia Hamilton." And she continued with the rest of her story smoothly, until she had to explain her sketches. "Portraits," she lied, face tingling with warmth, "And it was in those that I saw the resemblance between Lydia Harcourt and Tom Polk."

Aspers leaned back. "It appears that you were both forced to act in self defense. I see no reason for Miss Hamilton's identity to be revealed, or any need for her testimony. As for Lydia Harcourt's book and manuscript—we have Polk's confession as made to you, Trent. We know he murdered Lydia Harcourt and Lord Chartrand."

"So no reason for anyone's secrets to be revealed," Marcus said.

"No need at all," Aspers echoed. He picked up the red, leather-bound journal, the manuscript tied with the scarlet ribbon, and strode over to the fireplace. Hand on the mantel, Aspers fed both to the flames. "Though Lord Brude has spoken of assisting in the financial situation of the family of his late secretary. The man was a very talented poet, I believe."

"We're free to return to London, then?" Marcus asked.

"Indeed, Trent."

At the doorway, Venetia stopped. Aspers was standing at the desk by the windows, jotting a note on a sheath of paper. She reached out and caught Marcus' hand. "But all the others are leaving. They will be loading into their carriages. They will see me unmasked. Once they do, I won't be able to paint portraits in London."

"No," Marcus said, "You won't."

Last night, he had said nothing about her painting. She had even shown him her sketches. He'd looked at every one, reserving comment.

She'd stood watching, hands clasped behind her back. Waiting. At the end, he'd frowned. "You didn't draw any pictures of me."

Not what she'd expected. "I thought you wished me to stop doing that," she'd answered.

Quietly he'd said, "Let me tell you once again, I am in awe of your brilliance. Saving us with a bottle of turpentine was absolute genius." He'd brushed a kiss against her temple.

"You saved us, Marcus. If you hadn't moved so quickly—"

He'd kissed her mouth then, and put her tongue to more delicious use than speaking, and then carried her to bed as the black-pearl sky welcomed dawn.

But now, she knew the pictures were standing between them. She didn't understand how he felt about her painting. Was he angry?

Again Marcus said nothing. He drew something from his pocket, let it spill from his hand in front of her. Fine, gauzy veiling. Smiling, he tied it around her bonnet. "Not masked, but still a mystery."

But she could see through the veil—how much did it disguise?

He tucked her hand in the crook of his arm and led her to the front doors of Abbersley. The foyer was deserted except for Rutledge, who stood by the open doors, looking correct and austere.

"Is Lady Chartrand improving?" Venetia impulsively asked the butler as they passed. Poor Lady Chartrand had broken down completely in the drawing room and admitted Chartrand had killed his first wife. She'd sobbed pitiably into her hands, and wailed, "He killed her. I had nothing to do with it. He promised he'd done it for me but he hadn't. She was going to run away to Italy with another man. He couldn't let anyone else have her. His first wife, his first and always love—"

Laudanum had quieted her and let her sleep. Lady Yardley had kept a vigil by her bedside, soothing her. Venetia felt relief knowing that Lady Yardley's son would be safe from lies and scandal. Her heart ached for Lady Chartrand, who had apparently adored her husband. Another doomed love.

"I believe she is, madam." Rutledge bowed.

Taking a deep breath, Venetia walked down the steps on Marcus' arm. Her wide-brimmed straw bonnet and veil obscured her face, but she soon realized that no one was looking at her. On the circular drive a flurry of footmen and grooms prepared carriages. The guests hurried out and swept toward their vehicles, relief stark in their faces. Apparently Lord Aspers had informed all that the books were destroyed. The Duke of Montberry looked stoic and impassive as he boarded his magnificent carriage. Lord Brude looked wilder, more brooding than ever. Mr. Wembly was disheveled, his cravat askew.

Lord Swansborough paused to kiss her hand. "*Au revoir*, my dear Vixen," he murmured.

Panic, cold and numbing, raced through her. How much could he see? Swansborough smiled warmly. "I can only see a hint of your loveliness behind the veil, my dear. But even if I could see you, I would never reveal your identity. I owe you a debt of gratitude."

He winked! Then he swung up into his tall curricle, took the reins and set his four coal-black horses trotting.

A footman held the door of Marcus' gleaming black coach—the two drugged by Juliette were still recovering. The sight of the impassive face, the crimson and silver livery, made her shiver involuntarily.

Marcus drew her back. For a few moments, they were out of earshot of servants, of guests. "Are you all right, my love?" he asked gently.

My love.

She nodded. She kept one hand on her bonnet as the spring breeze tugged at it. Marcus twined his fingers with hers. "Let us go back to London. Home, together. And on the way, there is something of great import we must discuss."

CHAPTER TWENTY-TWO

"What do you plan to do with your sketches, love? Your orgy sketches that don't include me." As the carriage lurched forward, Marcus untied the big bow at Venetia's throat and tossed her bonnet away.

He wanted to take her thoughts away from the fear she'd faced. Wanted to throw off his own memories—the roar of the pistol, the explosion as the ball ripped into Polk's body, the mind-numbing fear of losing Vee that still rose up to haunt him—

He knew of only one way to do it.

Her brilliant, emerald-flecked eyes shone at him.

"I have no idea," she admitted softly. "The truth is, I enjoy drawing erotica. I love to create the stories, I love to make the pictures sensual and beautiful and arousing. I've been trapped for my entire life, denying who I am, trying to be a virtuous woman. Now I want to be free."

"And how exactly do you wish to be free?" A frown creased his forehead at the uncertainty and relief on her face. "What is it you need, Vee?"

"I just needed to be honest." She turned and laid her hands on his thigh, and the intimacy of her touch made Marcus' heart pang. "You will never let me paint your nephew's portrait now," she said. "Never help me start a London career.

I'd always thought that rakes could not be reformed but I am the one who cannot. I never knew who I was—proper lady or bohemian artist. Now I know. You have shown me."

He cradled her chin. "Who are you, then, sweetheart? I believe you are an entrancing blend of both."

Her lips widened into an engaging smile. "That is what I feel, in my heart. I am a little of both—"

"The best of both," he broke in, speaking from his heart.

She flushed, the sight bewitching. He couldn't help but laugh softly as she tipped up her chin. "Thank you," she said.

"Painting is a part of your soul." He untied the ties of her cloak and pushed it from her shoulders. "Your talent is so richly a part of yourself. And I want you to be free."

"But how can I? It's impossible."

He undid the front buttons of her gown. No shift. Two perfect ivory breasts tipped with erect rose-pink nipples popped into view. He kissed the swell of her breasts, aware of the quick jump of her chest.

"I think we should travel around London in a closed carriage with you naked beneath a cloak. My secret treasure," he said. He took her left nipple between his lips, between his teeth, and raked along the velvety soft length. Her moan electrified him.

He lifted her white skirts, revealing sensible stockings, pale ivory drawers. Hooking his fingers in the waistband, he slid her drawers down her legs, whisked them away. He ran his hands up to stroke sensitive inner thighs and springy nether curls, to caress her hot quim.

Her hands busily worked at the buttons of his trousers. She freed his cock, and pleasure and need washed through him. He ripped his waistcoat and shirt open.

"Sit astride me," he urged. He jammed his fist behind his cock to hold it upright, steadied her as she poised over him, pussy wet and ready. Her skin was hot satin beneath his touch. With a breathy moan, she sank down. Her cunny engulfed him to the hilt, her full bottom pressed against his groin.

Up and down, she rode.

"Slowly," he murmured, "Draw it out. Torture me, love."

And she did, her eyes closed, her head tipped back in ecstasy. She drew up until only his tip was held snug, then slid down, her muscles straining to control, to move agonizingly slowly. Heat rushed over his shaft, exciting him beyond belief.

"You grew inside me—bigger, thicker."

Marcus laughed at her amazement. It had never been like this—this intimate—with anyone but Vee. "Now, do whatever you want to me," he invited.

He expected frantic bouncing, but she clutched his shoulders and ground her quim into his groin, without lifting. She rubbed hard and urgently, sawing herself against him, squealing with pleasure.

If she wanted it hard and rough and deep, he was more than happy to oblige. Launching his hips up, driving his cock deep, he lifted her into the air.

Her hands closed on his chest, fingers gouging. Her hair tossed around her as she rode him, untamed, beyond control. This was his wanton artist—an utterly exciting and entrancing woman riding him to ecstasy. She pinched his nipples hard. Her face was a mask of hungry need. Her teeth sank into her lip.

She was wild. Passionate.

His.

"Oh God!" Her nails tore into him. Her body bucked on top of him, then she fell forward, her hair flying through the air to slap his face. He felt the rush of her juices around his cock. Wildly pulsing, her pussy gripped him tight. Ignited him.

Shoving up, he drove his entire cock hard into her, crying

out as the first spurt released. The rest rushed out like a torrent.

Blackness took him and he heard hoarse, guttural cries. Then melodic feminine sighs. Then his harsh breathing, her desperate pants, the clatter of the carriage wheels.

Something satin-smooth pressed against his chest, pushing out air. Her hands. She lifted her head. "You yelled so loudly."

He moved her arms away, sucked in air. "You almost killed me, sweet."

"I did?" She wore a look of astonishment, one that quickly became a glow of pride. The naughty wench rocked her hips.

He grabbed her hips. "No—no, love. I'm too sensitive."

But she kept moving, taking him to a level of pleasurable agony he'd never known. Any other woman he would have unseated in an instant, but he let Vee play. And she brought him to an explosive brink of desire and pain. His brain throbbed with the sensation as his cock hardened again.

She couldn't understand how intense it was but he forced himself not to stop her, enthralled. Moving her hips in a sensuous circle, she toyed with him, her eyes alight with power. Her tight, fire-hot walls caressed his swollen shaft, pulling him to and fro. She pinched his nipples again, and pleasure arced between those aching nubs and his thick cock.

He didn't care if it killed him.

"Fuck me, Venetia," he begged, "Fuck me hard again. Slam your cunny on me. Rip your nails into me. Give it to me."

The lush slapping sound of her sopping wet quim taking his rigid cock filled the carriage, filled his head, filled his soul. She raked her nails along his chest, his shoulders. She ran the sharp tips up his neck and he began fucking her like a wild man. He clamped his hands on her breasts once more, and rammed himself into her. Chanted her name like a man possessed.

She answered by screaming out his name. By meeting his

brutal thrusts with a pounding rhythm that threatened to bang his brains out of his head. He had to make her come, had to make her explode. Desperate, half-mad with pleasure, he slid his hand down between their joined bodies.

As out of control as he, she rode hard, filled with him. She rubbed her clit against his bent fingers.

His cock felt in danger of exploding, of being torn to shreds by his next climax, but he didn't care. He needed to drive deep, to fuck hard.

"I want to make you come," he rasped. "I want you to come so hard, you explode on me."

She screamed, rocked on him. "It's so intense. So good, so good, so good!" She cried his name then, over and over with each thrust. He watched, mouth dry, throat burning, body dripping sweat, as she rode him. Desperate, he clung to control. He would make her come before giving in. He was on the brink, a slave to his rising orgasm, to his need to come, but damn, he would please her first.

Victory was his the instant she arched back and screamed. One glance at her bobbing breasts, at her agonized face took him over the edge.

Like cannon-fire, his orgasm shot through him. He joined her in wild pleasure, ravaged by his release, weakened by it. He blinked his eyes open, still seeing colored spots. Awed by her power.

Mutual release. Perfect bliss. Hell, he loved it.

She slumped on him, as exhausted as he. Laughing, he stroked her back. Her dress was hot and damp. "How do you survive multiple orgasms, my love?"

Her giggle washed over him, soft and sweet. "Sometimes I barely do," she admitted.

Venetia sensed a change in Marcus, a tension in his body. He raked a hand through his damp, disheveled hair. The smile he usually wore after climax—one that was delighted, awed, and smug in a most masculine way—disappeared. His eyes didn't have that lazy post-bliss heaviness. His expression became serious.

Her dazed delight slipped away. She straightened on his lap. What was wrong?

Intense, solemn, his gaze held hers. "We will marry, Vee."

She blinked. "M—marry?" Startled. Confused. "Marry. But—no. No, of course not."

"No? Of course not?" He blinked, too, as if he didn't understand her words. "We will. I took your virginity, sweeting. Offering marriage is what a gentleman does."

She understood. His father had not behaved as a gentleman—he caused a girl to take her life. He had done something incestuous.

"I can't—no, I won't force you into a duty marriage, Marcus. The idea is preposterous. You are an earl. Earls do not marry illegitimate artists."

He brushed back his tumbled black hair. "It isn't preposterous. I insist on marriage. I will not ignore my responsibility—"

She slid off his lap, landing on the seat beside with a thump. Fingers shaking, she tried to close her buttons. "I am not your responsibility. I don't need you to rescue me! And I refuse to enter a marriage to prove a point of honor."

But even as she protested, she knew the truth. She wanted to marry him. That was the madness of it. To sleep every night with him? Wake up every morning? Have his child . . .

He couldn't be thinking beyond his honor. Her, a countess? Impossible. If he presented her to the ton as his bride, the matrons would feed on her like gulls on carrion. In Maidenswode, she'd seen how petty, vindictive, and vicious fine ladies could be. If they discovered she was the daughter of an erotic painter—

He cupped her chin. "We are going to marry."

She pushed his hand away. She would not force a trapped man into his *punishment* for making love to her and, for all his libertine ways, Marcus was more trapped than she had ever been.

She would not compound one tragic mistake with another. She didn't need marriage. She could go back to the country where no one would ever know she had given her virginity—and her heart—to the magnificent Earl of Trent at an orgy.

"Vee, what if there is a child already?" he asked.

That reminder stopped her cold. In the heat of wanting him in her bed, she'd forgotten that consequence of making love. But what was better for a child—a duty marriage or a mother determined to raise her child alone?

Venetia stared helplessly into Marcus' handsome face, which seemed harder, more resolute. His emotions were masked to her. She had to choose, from their example, which upbringing had been the happiest. She couldn't.

"I think we could have a happy marriage," he said. "We're both lovers and friends."

But no mention of love. Love! Love would make no difference to who they were. But she wanted to hear the word on his lips. She wanted that, like a fool. She waited, unable to breathe. Waited for those words.

"We haven't known each other long but I believe we could rub along. We could be happier than my parents, I'm certain."

But he didn't speak of love.

Venetia shook her head. "I don't believe in duty and propriety, Marcus. I would rather be independent than trapped. Society would laugh at me—at us. And worse, it would taint your family. Marrying me would hurt your sister and your nephew."

He recoiled at that. "My choice should have no bearing on Min."

"But it does and well you know it. Marcus, your duty must be to your family."

"Obstacles," he snapped. "An earl can overcome obstacles to get what he wants."

It startled. "You want me so much?" But even an earl

could not so easily stop scandal. She sensed he knew that. He had come to an orgy to try to save his family from scandal. She realized he had feared all along that he might fail.

"Do you want me?" he asked.

Want. Not love. She had been afraid of love. Her rakish father had broken her mother's heart because her mother had loved hopelessly. But now Venetia feared she couldn't exist without the intimate partnership, perfect friendship, and passion she'd found with Marcus. She could say yes . . . but that would ruin his life.

"You've saved me, Vee."

"With the turps—"

"With you. With everything about you. Your courage. Your heart. Your sensuality. Your bravery in a society that binds itself in ludicrous rules. I want you to save me from hellish, lonely unhappiness. I spent a lifetime looking for dissipation to make me forget what I didn't have. I could never forget you, Vee. Be with me. Be mine."

His family—the family who meant so much to him—they'd be appalled by his choice. Humiliated. But she wanted him. She loved him.

She tried to push back the memories of her mother. The loneliness of her mother's life as she waited for those few clandestine visits with Rodesson. The tears afterward, when she left London, left the man she hopelessly loved.

"I—would you want me to be your mistress?" Venetia tried not to think of what it would be like when Marcus married, for he deserved to marry for love.

Mistress. Marcus stared at Vee. He couldn't believe that was what she wanted. Her eyes looked so uncertain. Did she fear his refusal or did she despise having to offer herself as a mere mistress?

He knew only one thing. The need to protect Vee had become the hunger to possess. To have her as his for all time.

She'd said 'no' to his offer of marriage and his damn heart had ached like it would never mend.

Mistress. If she became his mistress, he could buy her a house, fine gowns, a magnificent carriage, everything she desired. He could sleep with her at night, wake with her in the morning.

He wanted her. More than anything. More than he had ever wanted his father's approval. Even more than he had needed his mother's affection.

"That would ruin you in the eyes of society. And destroy your sisters' chances at happy, rewarding marriages." His heart felt as heavy and black as a chunk of lead.

Vee slumped back in her seat and turned her face to the window. They'd crested a hill, and the sun-kissed green of the English countryside stretched out beneath them. "Then—" Her voice shook. "Then it's impossible."

She lay on something firm and warm. Wriggling as she wakened, Venetia discovered a hard ridge pressing against her derriere. Her head jostled on the velvet seat. She shook herself awake to discover she was laid across Marcus, her bottom bouncing on his lap. Her cloak lay over her and his hand was on her hip to steady her.

She tried to push herself up. He caught her hand and helped her. Street flares lit the outskirts of Mayfair, balls of indistinct light in the nighttime fog.

"Would you like to see your father first, before going home?"

Sleepiness dropped away instantly. Her father! He'd had no word from her, so had no idea that Lydia Harcourt was dead and her secrets were ashes. But Venetia couldn't speak through the tightness of her throat. She could only nod her head.

Impossible. Marcus wanted her, she wanted him, but it was all impossible.

Her father's street, the fringe of the fashionable world, was crammed with carriages whisking hopeful upstarts to lavish balls. She pulled on her bonnet, dropped down the makeshift veil. "Thank you." How inadequate that was. But what else could she do? Cry? Reveal the love she knew she shouldn't have for him? To what end? "I can hire a hackney to take me home."

The carriage stopped, she heard the thump of the groom's boots on the street, and she stood, ready to go.

Marcus got up, too, bent in the low carriage. "You are not hiring a bloody hackney. I am coming in with you."

Before she knew what she'd done, she pushed at him to make him sit. But he stood, unmoved, her hands pressed into his chest. "Do you intend to shout at him?" she gasped. "Over my career?"

"I think he needs to understand exactly what you endured to save the family he should be responsible for."

As Marcus helped her down from the carriage, he brusquely waved aside her every plea. Even her tears didn't move him. He wrapped his arm around her waist and firmly directed her to the house. She thought of what the physician had said. *He is on the mend, and if he takes care, should recover fully.*

Would Marcus' anger cause her father to have another attack? If Marcus hurt her father, could she nurse him, fix him, make everything well again?

Directed by the butler to her father's bedchamber, where he was still resting, Venetia stopped on the threshold. Shocked. A woman sat on a stool by the bed. She wore a deep blue dress. White curls were piled atop her head. The woman held Rodesson's hand. Venetia felt foolish anger rise—because Rodesson had a woman with him—until that woman turned.

"Mother?"

Olivia Hamilton's hazel eyes widened. "Venetia? Where have you been? Charles told me he had no idea where you were."

Venetia felt Marcus' hands slide over her shoulders. He propelled her into the room, then stepped around her. "Mrs.

Hamilton." He bowed as her mother, open-mouthed, rose from the stool. He flicked a glance to her father—an autocratic glance. "Rodesson."

Her father, propped up by pillows, had color in his cheeks, and his eyes glowed with energy and life.

Venetia summoned her courage. "Mother, may I make the Earl of Trent known to you."

At Olivia's stunned expression, Venetia feared her mother might have an attack of the heart.

"What is this about, Venetia? What are you doing with Trent?" her father barked.

Venetia drank in her father's unusual costume. His nightshirt had ruffles and he had a bright kerchief tied around his neck, like a gypsy. "Please don't trouble yourself, Father—"

"Pray take a seat, madam," Marcus broke in, addressing her mother. "I believe it is time that both of you knew exactly what Venetia has done to protect you."

"There's no need—" Venetia cried, but her parents spoke as one.

Her mother gasped. "Protect us? Venetia—I don't understand."

"Ah, lass, what have you done now?" Pain and guilt lined her father's face.

Venetia opened her mouth to protest—she'd been rescuing them, after all—when Marcus insisted, "They need to know."

Suddenly Venetia decided she did want them to know. She was tired of secrets. Tired of taking care. She dropped onto a chair by her father's fireplace. "Oh go ahead! Tell them!"

In his deep, magnetic voice, Marcus painted her to be a heroine—a woman who had gone to an orgy and risked scandal, a woman who had hunted down a murderer, a woman who had saved herself from certain death. By the end of his tale, she felt rather proud of herself.

Until her mother shrieked, "An orgy!"

Trust her mother to worry of that, not of murder and violence.

"Indeed. An orgy." Marcus inclined his head. Limned by firelight, he exuded power, strength, nobility.

Her mother turned a furious face to her father, who turned furious eyes to Marcus. "You blackguard, I should call you out—"

"Father!" Venetia cried.

Apparently unperturbed, Marcus continued, "I went to protect her. I did not. There is one other thing you both need to know."

Venetia leapt from her chair. She threw panic-stricken glances at her guilty-looking father and shocked mother. "They don't, Marcus. Truly they do not."

"I believe I can guess."

She flinched at her mother's look—horrified, disappointed.

"I know exactly what happened," Olivia swept on. "And so you ruined her. And there is no recourse at all, is there?"

Her mother's aching gaze fell on her. "Were you foolish enough to fall in love with him?"

And then Olivia dropped her face into her hands. "You have ruined yourself. It's because of your painting. I tried to stop it. I thought if I didn't let you paint, I could change your nature. But you are exactly as your father is. A man can be that way—dashing, seductive, wild, and he pays no price but enjoyment. A woman cannot. I should have done anything to stop you coming to London and disgracing yourself by painting—"

"I like her nature." Marcus interrupted. "And her painting."

Face strained, her mother looked up at him. "It's scandalous. Shocking. A good woman should not think of—"

"Sex?" Marcus asked. "Of all the ways lovers can enjoy pleasure? Why not? Her beautiful pictures entrance every man who looks at them."

Venetia felt her heart sing as Marcus smiled at her. "Why shouldn't a woman create erotic art and teach the world what women want from their lovers?" he asked.

"And not very long ago, women were burned at the stake, my lord," Olivia countered. "I wanted Venetia to be happy. I want her to live a conventional life."

"Were you unhappy?" Venetia approached her mother slowly. Uncertain. Her mother had cried. But she had also laughed and smiled. Had the laughter been false?

"You do not think it is wrong for her to paint?" her mother asked. "When because of it, my lord, you ruined her."

"I asked her to marry me," Marcus said. "She refused."

"Because I ensured that she doesn't belong in those circles any more." Her mother jabbed her finger against her own chest. "Because she is illegitimate. Which is my fault. Because she is Rodesson's daughter, which is also my fault."

Impulsively Venetia ran to her mother's side. "It isn't your fault." She glanced at her father. His illness had changed him. He looked older, sober, yet still handsome.

"You're correct, lass," Rodesson said. "The fault was mine—"

"Do you blame the earl for taking your innocence?"

Venetia flinched at Olivia's direct question. "No," she said, "I made the choice."

Her mother touched her cheek, her eyes wistful. "If I had been dutiful and had married as my father wished, I would have married a gouty old man. I would not have had you, Venetia, or your sisters. I would not have smiled upon you after you were born and felt the grip of your fingers on mine. I would not have seen you and Maryanne and Grace embark on your journeys to womanhood. I was impetuous and romantic but I was never unhappy that I had you girls. I was never unhappy that I had the man I loved, even for only a little while. But I am unhappy that I ruined your—"

"Blast it, woman, I am the one to blame." Rodesson threw off the sheets, and leapt out of bed. "I made a mistake, Olivia. I thought you would be unhappy with me. I've spent a lifetime trying to forget how unhappy I've been without you. Those snatched visits only reminded me of how deeply I cared, of what a fool I'd been. I want to make things right now, right by you and by my daughters."

Venetia stared down at her father's outstretched hand.

"Tell her the truth, Livvie," Rodesson urged. "She needs to know that you admire her talent, her courage. I've never known a woman as strong as my dear Venetia."

She'd always thought her mother was ashamed of her.

Her mother hugged her. Tightly. "Venetia, I love you dearly. I am so sorry I tried to steal away the very thing that makes you who you are."

Wrapped in her mother's arms, breathing in warm lavender, Venetia understood. Her mother had only tried to change her because her mother felt guilt. Her mother had suffered for so many years for following her heart. Olivia hadn't deserved that.

Venetia hugged her mother back, giving herself to the comfort of the embrace. She looked to Marcus. Deep happiness shone from his eyes. Happiness for her.

She felt her father clasp her hand. "I wanted to believe I was a wild and passionate artist," he said. "I feared that being conventional would stifle me. I was a young fool. A library of books doesn't warm a heart or fill a soul. Only love can do that. You, Trent, are a fool if you don't love my Venetia."

Venetia's heart almost stopped.

"I like to think," Marcus drawled, "That I am not a fool."

Marcus did not directly say that he loved her. But for one delicious month, they met in secret and Venetia learned of the true delights London offered. They drove to Richmond by moonlight to tour the park, and she rode Marcus beneath the night sky. He hired a boat on the Thames and they lay naked beneath a blanket, drinking champagne and watching the stars glide past. He gave her a lesson in riding in Hyde Park at dawn, proving that a woman could sit astride her lover's cock on a stallion. At Vauxhall, they reached simultaneous orgasm as the fireworks exploded above them.

She had no time to paint—she lived every fantasy in Marcus' arms. With wicked words, he placed other men and women in their bed—in fantasy only—but it added spice to delicious sex.

She attended every event masked and disguised, even wearing a blond wig. They encountered Viscount Swansborough on one sizzling night at Vauxhall, with a masked red-haired woman on his arm. Venetia had been astonished—in hair color and build, the woman was exactly like her. And Marcus and the viscount had exchanged a secret grin.

She knew, without a doubt, she was madly in love. But, without a doubt, she knew she could not have Marcus. They couldn't keep their secret forever.

And on a warm, starry, lovely May night, he sent a note with the most shocking request . . .

"He's adorable," Venetia whispered. She'd cradled many babies in Maidenswode, as Olivia had helped their tired mothers. She marveled at David, just as she'd marveled at each one she'd held. His head was so soft and delicate and impossibly small. And it had the strangest shape, not round at all, but a bit . . . squashed.

Lady Ravenwood beamed, her blue-green eyes alight. Venetia was so touched that she was allowed to hold her ladyship's special treasure. That Lady Ravenwood would trust her, invite her into her home, and be so welcoming and warm.

Holding David's cuddly weight, Venetia glanced at Marcus, who sprawled in a chair across the room, laughing with his brother-in-law, the handsome Viscount Ravenwood. Her heart soared at even the most stolen look, but she saw Marcus' expression become grim as he looked toward his mother, who sat, unmoving and silent, by the fire. Marcus had introduced her to Lady Trent. The countess' large, watery turquoise eyes had moved over her and then Marcus, looking blank, as though she could not even see them.

"I see a little of Marcus in him," Lady Ravenwood confided.

Venetia gazed intently at baby David, searching for a resemblance. He possessed large, round blue eyes and tiny dark lashes. The sweetest cupid's bow mouth blew bubbles at her.

"Marcus loves you very much, you know."

Venetia glanced up, startled. She still could not believe that Marcus had openly told his sister and brother-in-law that they were lovers. What lady received a mistress? A remarkable one, Venetia realized, looking into Lady Ravenwood's beautiful face.

Her ladyship smiled. "Marcus loves you very dearly. He told me about all your adventures. The risks you took. I must thank you, Miss Hamilton."

"I don't understand."

"You were protecting me, you see. Marcus did not want to tell me at first, but I guessed when he spoke of the blackmail. I could see it in his eyes. The most damning secret Lydia Harcourt had over my father was what he did to me."

"I—I'm sorry." The secret was what Venetia guessed, but she didn't know what to say.

"You must understand that Marcus has never forgiven himself for not protecting me. It almost destroyed me. I felt as though I had allowed it to happen because I obeyed my father. I felt as though I had betrayed my mother. I didn't feel I deserved anything, certainly not happiness in marriage and family." Lady Ravenwood met her eyes with a solemn gaze. "Only Stephen knows of this. But I am telling you because you must understand how this devastated Marcus. He tried to confront Father once, when he was a schoolboy. He even struck Father and our father almost whipped him to death."

Venetia's heart trembled. She stroked along the baby's blanket-clad tummy. "But what could he have done?"

"Nothing. Marcus ensured that I married and found happiness. He gave me a miracle but he still blames himself. He feels responsible for everyone. I want him to find happiness too, Miss Hamilton."

"So do I." Her view of the baby became blurry.

"I think he could find it with you. I think you would make a most admirable countess."

Venetia bit her lip. From his chair, Marcus turned and smiled at her. He couldn't have heard, but her heart tumbled in her chest. "I—I am not of his world. I can't—"

"Such things do not matter to him. He wants to follow his heart."

It hurt Venetia to protest. "But there would be scandal, my lady—"

"Min, you must call me Min."

"Of course, your—" Venetia broke off, shared a giggle with Min. "And I am Venetia."

David's face tensed, his fine dark brows drew down. He made fists and little choking sounds came out. Venetia knew to lift him to her shoulder, but the wail came out before she could. With a smile, Min took him.

Min held David to her shoulder, rubbing his back. "Scandal is not the end of the world. I have faced the threat of scandal for most of my life. And with Marcus' help, I survived it. We can weather scandal, Venetia."

"But the Countess would be devastated if he married me, wouldn't she? And his mother's opinion matters to him. What she told him when he was young, it hurt him deeply—" Venetia stopped. Should she have been so blunt?

"She told him he was like our father." A soft, knowing smile touched Min's mouth. "Marcus told me a great deal about you, Venetia. I think you fear you will hurt Marcus the way Rodesson hurt your mother. You aren't like your father, Miss Hamilton, any more than Marcus is like his."

"No, he isn't anything like his father," Venetia agreed.

"See? You have your father's talent, but in matters of the heart, you are much wiser." Min's smile widened. "For one thing, it hasn't taken you twenty-four years to realize how wonderful Marcus is. You understand what is truly important in life."

Venetia didn't know what to say, but baby David broke the quiet instead. The tiny creature gave an enormous belch and a flow of white curdy milk launched out. It splattered over the blanket Min wore on her shoulder. Instead of being horrified, Min patted him. "What a good boy!"

Marcus and Viscount Ravenwood shared a laugh. Venetia blinked back tears. Yes, she wanted Marcus to be happy. But would she be making him happy if she married him and brought scandal into his life?

Leather creaked as Marcus rose from his chair. He and the viscount strolled toward her and Min, but Min darted over to meet the men halfway.

"I wish her to hold David," Min implored. "You talked me out of trying before, Marcus. Please . . . I would like this so very much."

Venetia caught her breath. A quiver of fear leapt to her heart. And then, to her surprise, Marcus walked to her side, and she realized he wished to ask her opinion, even on such an intimate family matter.

He stood close enough for his breath to tease her ear, and her heart thudded as he confided, "Mother doesn't even remember Min and me most times. I fear that she might panic while holding David, and hurt him. I thought I'd convinced Min not to try this, but today, she's stubborn as ever."

But Venetia glanced at Min and saw the raw hope there. "We could watch your mother carefully. Surely it could help her to hold him."

The viscount joined them. Ravenwood placed his arm around his wife's waist. Worry touched his eyes, but he nodded to Min. "I'll stand by, in case—"

"No." Min shook her head. "I think it must be Marcus and me." She gave her husband a kiss on the cheek, then left him to walk to her mother's side.

Marcus strode over as Min bent, offering David. In a soft, compelling voice, she asked her mother, "Would you like to hold him?"

Venetia saw emotion flicker in the countess's eyes. Warmth? Understanding? A smile moved the pursed, wrinkled lips. Thin, gloved hands reached out. Min eased David into the frail arms and stayed close.

The dowager gazed down at David as though she had no idea what he was. But then she began to coo. And rock her arms. Venetia saw Marcus smile and she felt a watery burning in her eyes again. He was down on one knee, at the ready. Watching the worry in his eyes made her heart ache. He was so concerned for his baby nephew. His eyes sparkled and she guessed he was touched to his soul by his mother's welcoming reaction.

He was a magnificent man—one capable of the deepest and strongest love. And she loved him hopelessly.

CHAPTER TWENTY-THREE

"Why Covent Garden?" As Marcus escorted her into the private box on the second tier, Venetia stared down upon a scene even she couldn't have imagined.

"I promised you a night at the theatre." Marcus gave a seductive grin. Masked by a strip of black leather, he looked sensual and dangerous. He'd worn a hooded cloak, as had she, and now that they were ensconced in the velvet and gilt box, he slid it off and tossed it aside.

"The masquerade is notoriously sinful," he explained as he helped her take off her cloak. "Do you remember when we traveled to the orgy, and you told me about your painting? The one in which an auburn-haired woman pleasures an earl in full view of the theatre? That is a most enticing fantasy."

A shiver of anticipation raced down to her toes, setting her quim on fire in its path. But her heart ached too. A week had passed since she had met Min, since Min had urged her to accept Marcus' proposal.

He brushed a kiss against her neck. "I am glad you decided to come out with me tonight, Vee." He walked around to her side and took her hand, leading her to the front of the box.

"I'm sorry to have refused you so long—I needed time to think."

Marcus' turquoise eyes glittered in the glow of the wall sconces. "I guessed you wouldn't be able to resist this. Here, with the drapes at the sides, we can do whatever we wish, while watching the fun below."

Venetia rested her hands on the gleaming rail and looked down. Below, the scene was wilder than Chartrand's orgy. Most patrons were masked. The gentlemen wore traditional evening dress but the women wore the most revealing costumes. Fanciful concoctions of feathers, silk, and wings. Many women were completely bare-breasted and dozens of men suckled wantonly at their nipples.

"It becomes more lewd later."

More lewd? There was a couple standing, with the woman's legs around the man's hips and he was lifting her up and down, working faster and faster, obviously making love to her.

"It wasn't this that tempted me to come," she said. "I wanted to be with you again. I didn't care where."

"Vee—" Marcus dropped into the seat behind her, then grasped her hips and drew her down, so she was seated on his lap, facing out. Her bottom pressed around the hard ridge of his cock. She was wet, utterly aroused by the wickedness.

"Can the people below see us?"

"If they look up. But they won't know who we are."

Raucous laughter, ribald shouts, female squeals rose to them, and the melody of a waltz swirled up to them.

"Do you wish to live out the fantasy of my painting?" She twisted on his lap and laid her hands on his shoulders. He moved her to him, until his breath teased her lips. Venetia saw vulnerability in his eyes, in the firm set of his mouth.

"I have to talk to you about something first," Marcus said. "Minerva told you about the past, didn't she?"

Even as he asked Vee the question, Marcus wasn't certain he was ready to make the confession he knew he needed to make. But he could no longer avoid speaking about it.

Vee nodded. "I don't know why she confided in me."

God, she was beautiful. The most beautiful woman he'd ever known.

"Min appreciates your discretion, your strong sense of honor," he told her. "And she knows how much you mean to me."

"She told me you convinced her that she deserved to find happiness in marriage and family," Vee said softly. "You are such a wonderful man."

Music and laughter swirled from below, now dim and distorted as though muffled by fog. The world around them was golden with candlelight, but their booth was intimate. A place for confessions.

"No, hell, I'm not. I only confronted my father once over what he was doing and then I succumbed to cowardice. I hit him, he whipped me, and I returned to school, cowed and beaten."

She touched his cheek. "You couldn't have done anything."

"I could have stopped it."

He met her gaze, could almost believe he saw faith in her eyes. Faith, belief in him, love.

"You have no reason to feel guilty," she whispered, "Don't you understand that it hurt you too?"

"There's something else you need to know. I need to tell you."

"You want to share your secrets with me?"

"I killed my father." He spat it out, direct, cold, without pretty words to dilute the crime. But her warmth fought the cold that always wrapped around his heart when he remembered.

Her brows drew together. "Because of your sister?"

She wasn't condemning him. Hell, she was trying to understand.

"Yes, for Minerva. But what provoked it was a girl's death—Lady Susannah Lawrence."

"Yes," Vee nodded. "I remember."

"I told you I confronted him, but not what happened after, when he sobered up. He was leaving—to head down to the nearest inn to get foxed again and tup the local barmaid. Something snapped in me. I chased after him, carrying the blade from my walking stick. I don't know what I planned to do with it. I was half-drunk myself."

"What happened?" Her voice was soft, calm. She cupped his jaw with her warm palm. A balm to his aching conscience.

"He laughed at me. Mounted his horse and moved to ride off. I grabbed the reins, startled the beast. He fell off its back, cracking his head on the ground. But I was driven by fury. I pinned him there with the blade, shouting threats at him, telling him how much I hated him. An instant later he clutched his heart with one hand, raised the other to me, and cried out in pain."

"An attack of the heart?" Her eyes were dark and grave.

He glanced away, toward the gilded stage and the unfettered sexual play in the pit. "It didn't kill him. But the second one in the night did."

Anguished, he rested his head in the crook of her neck, nuzzled her warm skin. "I caused them. My mother blamed me for it."

She drew him away to meet his eyes. Her eyes shone. Bright. Beautiful. Like a glimpse of dawn after a long storm. "No. Your father caused them. Perhaps it was his guilt. But it was not your fault. What happened to your sister, to your father, was not your fault. You only tried to make things right. Your mother was wrong—you weren't responsible for his death. I think she has put herself in a prison of unhappiness because she couldn't give love." Venetia slid her arms around his neck. "I love you—not despite your pain, because of your pain. I have never met any man so deep of character, so honorable, so worthy of love."

He touched his lips to hers—not a kiss, but a jolt of warm pleasure. "I love you, Venetia. My heart and soul belong to you. I cannot imagine living without you. I want you, now and forever."

"Of course you know I love you, too."

"Of course." Marcus chuckled softly. "I am the most fortunate man alive to hear those words." He pressed his lips to hers again.

Venetia gave herself to Marcus' passionate kiss, but when he stopped to stare lovingly in her eyes, she gave him a saucy smile. She slid from his lap to land on the carpeted floor on her knees. Wearing a brazen smile, she undid his trousers. He watched as though transfixed, eyes bright, his breaths fast and hard.

His spicy scent enveloped her as she worked his cock free from his clothes. Far below them swirled a maelstrom of raucous laughter, ribald shouts, female squeals.

Wild excitement coursed through her and she flashed him a brazen look before opening her mouth wide, gobbling him as deep as she dared.

Earthy taste . . . velvety texture . . . his tense hands on her shoulders telling her how much he liked it. She sucked him deep, let him out, swirled her tongue, trying every maneuver she could think of. She twirled the hair on his abdomen, lightly bounced his swollen ballocks.

"God, sweeting . . ." Gripping her arms, he lifted her to her feet. He lifted the skirt of her gown and he dropped to his knees. Mouth wide, he took her. His hot breath flowed over her already scorching quim, his tongue licked wetly over her slick flesh. To be licked and eaten in front of the crowd . . .

Scandalous. Enthralling.

Venetia closed her eyes, swaying like a slender tree as he pleasured her. Suddenly she found herself lifted off her feet. Her bared bottom slid across fabric. Opening her eyes, she saw he'd placed her back on the seat. His hand was clenched around his cock—it looked huge. Thick and ready and all for her.

She parted her legs wide, hooking her thighs over the arms of the chair, wanting him.

Desire glazed his eyes at the sight of her. She caught her breath.

Braced on one arm, he lowered. His cock touched her lips, she reached down, held them open. Their moans chorused as he sank inside. He filled her so much, so tightly, so perfectly. Another waltz rushed over them as he thrust slow and deep and beautifully inside her. Pleasure flowed with each stroke, each push against her womb. All she could think of was his thrusts, the building delight, more and more—

She exploded in pleasure, pulsing deep in her quim, in her heart, in her soul. He came, too, shouting loudly. She heard the gasps from below, the sudden silence, then cheers and applause welled up. Braced on his arms over her, Marcus kissed her lips. They shared a laugh over the clapping and catcalls, then he left her.

Sated and dazed, Venetia turned slowly as Marcus went to his tailcoat.

Now she knew the answer to the question she'd posed while painting the theatre picture—what would her jaded lord do with his hands when his auburn-haired love knelt between his legs?

He would whisk her into his seat, make love to her until her heart and soul took flight, and give her earth-shattering pleasure.

Marcus took a box out from his tailcoat's pocket. A small, velvet-covered box.

Nude, he dropped to his knee at her side, and flipped open the lid of the box. Venetia blinked. Candlelight glinted off the facets of a heart-shaped emerald. Enormous. Surrounded by winking diamonds.

"Not quite as lovely as your eyes," he said. "I told you I can't live without you. I can't imagine my future without you. Not as mistress—but as lover, soulmate, and wife."

"But—"

"Min wished us well, sweeting. She wants us both to be happy. As for your sisters—your marriage to me would bring them into society, guarantee them vast dowries, and give them the chance to find happiness and love."

She trembled as Marcus lifted her left hand. He held the ring to the tip of her finger. "Will you marry me?"

A marriage proposal from a naked earl? She couldn't help but giggle. The beautiful ring blurred into vivid green stars as tears of joy welled in her eyes. "Of course."

His laugh—and the catch in his throat—rippled over her. She felt the coolness of the band slide down her skin.

Marcus kissed her fingers. "But, I understand if you don't wish to face society right away. I thought a private ceremony at St. George's. Then Italy."

She held the ring before her eyes, turning it to and fro. "Italy?"

"A sun-soaked villa in the country that inspired your lovely name."

"But we would leave our families, you mean?" She met his eyes—beautiful and exotic and rich with happiness beneath his long, thick lashes.

His fingertip traced her lower lip, sending a tingle of desire through her sated body. "Not forever. A trip to spend time alone together. For you to paint and for us to indulge our senses and enjoy every pleasure we desire."

"I would like that," she said.

Their lips touched for a leisurely kiss, but she broke it to murmur, "You spoke of painting? I know I can't paint erotica. And I understand about my career—"

His lips parted in one of those wicked grins that melted her heart and set her entire body on fire. "Why can't you paint erotica?" he asked. "Or have your career? Perhaps a collection of works by a mysterious lady?"

Shocked, she cried, "We can't! Think of the scandal if the truth came out!"

"But we will be safe and happy in Italy." His turquoise eyes sparkled at her. "And when we are home, the choice is yours. I support you in whatever way you wish to follow your heart. But before we leave, would you paint my nephew's portrait first?"

"Of course," Venetia said, around the lump in her throat.

"And then I plan to keep you busy sketching pictures of our children."

She laughed at that. "I love you," she whispered, unable to think of anything more poignant, important, or brilliant to say. Yet those words ignited a light in his eyes that stole her breath away. "Your eyes. I wonder if they are the same color as the Mediterranean?"

He laughed, too. "I've no idea, my love."

"Well, now I have a lifetime to try to capture that color."

Marcus' elegant fingers cupped her chin. As his lips lowered to hers once more, he promised, "I have more sinful plans for our future."

Acknowledgments

Sincere thanks go to my critique group for all their support and words of wisdom. Also, many thanks to my agent Jessica Faust, and my editor Hilary Sares, for their wonderful enthusiasm for my work.

Here's a hot sneak peek at Noelle Mack's RED VELVET,
available now from Aphrodisia . . .

Home. Bath. Bed. The three little words that meant the most to Dee at the moment. She'd dragged the suitcase through the lobby, looking around for the doorman in case there were packages that had been delivered while she was in China, but he was nowhere to be seen.

The elevator door closed silently and she counted the floors going up in her head, almost staggering down the hall to her apartment when the doors opened. Exhausted, Dee unlocked the door and got her suitcase over the threshold without bothering to turn on the lights. She shucked her clothes and tossed them on the floor, then headed into the bathroom, stark naked and shivering a little.

Her thighs and butt were sore from endless hours of sitting on a plane, but she was home. Bath next. Then bed. Tomorrow was another day and if she was lucky, she'd sleep right through it.

Dee crouched by the tub, turning on the faucet full blast, and tossed in an extravagant handful of pricey bath crystals, a gift from a fabric supplier, so she could afford to waste them. The jar was already half empty.

The gift basket had also held a scented candle at least a foot high, lovingly created by a hive of very busy, very talented designer bees just for her, if she wanted to believe the label. She could almost see them patting it smooth with their little black paws. If bees had paws. Whatever. She had been saving the candle for a moment like this.

Dee took the basket down from the cabinet shelf and unwrapped the delicate, crinkly paper around the beeswax pillar, ready for a little atmospheric soaking. She twiddled the wick upright, then remembered where she kept the matches. She padded back to the living room, scrabbled in the box over the fireplace, lit the candle and carried it back.

The tub was nearly brimming and Dee set the candle down on its wide ledge. She shut off the faucet and let some of the hot water go down the drain so it wouldn't overflow when she got in.

Her bathroom was her refuge—a beautifully appointed space, like the rest of the apartment. Something she couldn't possibly afford as a start-up designer, but it had been her graduation gift from Uncle Is, who owned the building. And to whom she would be in hock for the rest of her life, Dee thought unhappily.

She reached into a deep cabinet for a stack of fluffy folded towels to place next to the huge tub. A bowlegged table held spritzy little bottles of beauty products and two-week-old copies of rag trade publications. Her mailbox was probably crammed with new issues.

She stepped in, then kneeled, letting the water cover her thighs and her butt, feeling its penetrating heat soothe her nerves and melt away the stress of travel. Dee sat back, arranging a terrycloth-covered inflatable pillow behind her neck.

Then, echoing faintly through the porcelain, she heard footsteps in the apartment downstairs coming into the bathroom right below hers. As expensive as the building was, a lot of the construction costs had gone into luxury surfaces for the interiors, and it wasn't all that soundproof. She waited for the clonk of a toilet seat flipping up. She didn't hear it.

The new inhabitant of 16B would have to flip up the seat because he was a guy. Unless he was a hardcore bachelor who never put it down. She didn't know too much about him besides his name, Tom Driscoll, noting it on the row of mailboxes after he'd moved in three weeks ago.

Dee had seen the delivery van on her way out to buy a weekend's worth of fashion magazines and newspapers and thought he was one of the movers at first. Tom Driscoll's arms were massive, chest ditto. Legs, long and muscular. Dark hair, dark eyelashes. Blue eyes. Worn jeans with an eye-catching front bulge, topped by a frayed T-shirt with a few paint spots.

Never mind the moving day clothes, she'd thought. He had to be making a lot of money to buy a place in this building. She'd scoped him, knowing he was watching the movers manhandle a ten-foot black leather sofa down the truck ramp and not her. Dee had slunk away the second he'd turned toward the door with keys in hand and a big grin on his face.

Not that he would figure out that her apartment was on top of his unless she introduced herself and told him. Too bad. He was definitely the kind of guy she wanted to be on top of. Not that she had the time for a romance.

Maybe someday, she'd thought on her way back, swinging the plastic bag of magazines and munching on a Swiss chocolate bar. He'd been directing the unloading of still more black leather furniture. He had to be single and he had to be straight.

Bachelor pad black leather was the first thing a live-in girl-friend kicked to the curb, and gay guys didn't think it was cool. Not even retro cool.

Dee sank lower into the water, settling into a state of blissful relaxation. She reached out with a dripping foot and turned on the hot water faucet with her toes, thinking about her China trip and the problems of the new bra prototype. Scratch that, she told herself. Think about Tom Driscoll. Think about sex.

She let the hot water trickle, in the habit of topping off the tub until the bath was exactly the temperature she liked. Then she heard the click of a medicine cabinet door being opened in the bathroom below. Maybe he was shaving for a late-night date. Dee could imagine what he would look like bare-chested, a towel tied just above his groin, sorta covering that interesting bulge.

She wouldn't mind investigating it, playing with his cock and balls while he slapped shaving cream on his face and told her to quit it, giving her a Santaesque smile in the middle of all that white foam before he picked up his razor.

Nothing nicer than kissing the baby-soft, freshly shaved face of a just showered, totally naked man.

Dee slid a hand between her legs. If he were on all fours over her right now—she mentally moved the action to her own personal cloud nine, her antique fourposter—with his mouth on her pussy, licking and nipping her labia and thrusting his tongue deep inside, she'd be in heaven.

Just the thought of looking up at a set of heavy balls and a thick, erect cock, her head resting between two strong thighs while he satisfied her first, aroused her to fever pitch.

Her fingertips touched her clit, brushing over the sensitive tip. Over and over. She would tease his scrotum with her own tongue, licking all around, warmly, lasciviously, feeling it tighten and his cock get thicker, wanting him to get totally hot while he serviced her but not be able to come . . .

Dee opened her eyes, looking dreamily at the ceiling—and realized that the water in the tub was almost over her shoulders. She sat up, screwed the faucet handle the other way, and got out gingerly, being careful not to slosh.

She listened for more signs of life from the apartment below but heard nothing. *Thanks anyway, Tom. Nice to have met you. Maybe you can join me in the bath sometime.* She smiled as she wrapped a towel around herself and used another to dry her legs and arms. The first towel fell off when she wrapped yet another around her wet hair and she left that one on the floor, rubbing her feet in it to dry them.

Dee, soothed by her hot soak and stimulated by her fantasizing, decided to take it a little farther. Her skin was dry from the long hours on the plane. Her legs and ass could use some lotion. And her breasts too. Best for last. She could get close to climax with some just-right fondling and nipple attention, especially if she watched herself do it in the bathroom's tall freestanding mirror.

Then she could finish off with a vibrator in her bedroom and fall asleep. Not a bad way to end a generally disastrous day. She put a folded towel on the ledge of the bathtub and sat on it, reaching for the lightly scented lotion, pouring a warm stream over one stretched-out leg and catching the excess in her palm, rubbing it into her skin in long strokes.

She did the same with the other leg, then stood, rubbing her oiled hands over her ass cheeks, savoring the sensual pleasure of handling herself just the way she wanted to be handled.

The steam had cleared enough for her to see her blurred reflection in the freestanding mirror at one end of the bathroom. Dee wrapped a fresh towel around her lotioned-up hips and ass, sliding it back and forth, enjoying its nubby texture on her skin. She danced a little, a basic bellydance wriggle from a half-remembered class, making her heavy, firm breasts bounce. Dropping the towel, she took both her nipples in her fingertips and tugged at them. They got longer instantly and she bent forward, bare ass out and legs apart, like she was about to push her breasts into the face of a seated man.

Suck them, Tom. Big, gorgeous tits with long nipples. I know you want to. Just looking at them makes you hard.

She grabbed the bottle of lotion, shot a stream into her palm and rubbed it over both breasts, circling the nipples, then pinching them gently. Dee closed her eyes, wanting to imagine her new downstairs neighbor more than she wanted to see herself. Her breasts would more than fill his big hands. She hadn't been nicknamed Double Dee in high school for nothing.

The rest of her was shapely too, with hips that curved into athletic legs and a comparatively narrow waist. But it was the tits that had made the boys stare; and the men, for that matter.

Some days she'd hated it. Some days she hadn't minded. Depended on who was doing the staring.

Now, if Tom Driscoll were looking at her tits, hungry for them, going crazy from watching her caress herself, she wouldn't mind that at all. Dee cupped her breasts from underneath and squeezed them together, admiring the deep vee they made.

Want to put your cock there, Tom? Nice and tight and well-oiled. It's intense if you're into it. Or you can get on your knees and tease my clit while I play with my nipples. Get down. Tongue tip only. Flick it. Yeah . . . like that.

The condensation on the mirror had nearly cleared. She studied herself, imagining Tom Driscoll again, kneeling in front of her to eat her pussy. Her fingers were a more than adequate substitute for a masculine tongue, but she didn't want to come without at least the fantasy of a man doing her. Going solo was fine, but sex with a hot guy was better.

She bent forward a little, her big breasts swaying, her other hand coming up to brush over the nipples. Dee began to move her hips as she masturbated, putting her whole body into it.

She began to moan under her breath, saying Tom's name in a breathy whisper just to have a man's name to say, until she heard the bathroom door open.

Dee's eyes opened wide. There was a man in the mirror with her, just in back of her, barefoot and bare-chested, wearing only jeans. Tom Driscoll.

He grinned. "Looks like I got here just in time."

Dark. Thrilling. Highly erotic. Don't miss BLOOD RED by Sharon Page. Coming from Aphrodisia in January 2007 . . .

The Village of Maidensby, Yorkshire, 1818

Can you imagine both our mouths on you, love?
Althea sighed as the seductive male voice whispered behind her. His warm breath danced over the nape of her neck, stirring loose strands of her hair.

A moan spilled from her lips as his big hands closed over her shoulders, slipping beneath the straps of her chemise. One pair of hands—a gentleman's hands, long fingered, elegant. Hot, slightly rough, and all too real.

How could a dream stir her senses so?

Her dream lover massaged her shoulders and the controlled power in his touch vibrated through her. His fingers stroked the top of her spine. A bolt of desire raced down and exploded between her legs, drawing out a gasping sob from her very soul. A desperate sound. A plea.

For mercy? Or for more?

With a low chuckle, he held her as her legs melted beneath her.

Against her ear, his husky voice promised sin.

Can you imagine my hands and his worshipping you?

No. She shook her head, and that, too, felt real. No, she could not begin to imagine it. It was too scandalous. Too forbidden.

How could she, a virgin, be dreaming this?

Then perhaps it is not a dream, Althea. Perhaps it is a premonition.

No, she argued. It is a dream. Only a dream.

His head bent to her neck. His silky hair brushed her tingling skin. She shuddered at the gentle scrape of pointed teeth. But she could not pull away, even as he drew the straps from her shoulders. He'd unfastened the tapes and the neckline gaped at her breasts, exposing them. He tugged it down further and she grabbed at his hands to rescue her modesty.

No, sweet. Let us enjoy.

Her mouth dry, she stared down at her pale curves tipped with puckered nipples, small and pink. Two large male hands framed her bosom, holding the lacy neckline.

She'd never truly looked at her own breasts, not with the interest, the fascination, of these men. She'd never caressed them, never.

For the first time, the second man spoke. *Beautiful.*

Her gaze riveted on him. He lounged on a massive bed, shirt open to reveal sculpted muscles, swirls of golden curls and dusky pink nipples. Skintight buff breeches encased his powerful legs. His long fingers skimmed over his crotch, stroking the thick curving ridge that lifted the fabric. Her body ached in response. Her heart hammered, lodged in her throat.

His long golden hair fell across his eyes, shadowing his beautiful face. Only moonlight lit the room, glittering as it fell across his dark eyes. In the bluish light, his hair glimmered like moonbeams, but she knew, the way dreamers did, what his coloring must be.

Aren't they? Satin brushed her back as the man behind her moved closer. The buttons of his waistcoat pressed into his spine. She felt engulfed by him, small, delicate.

But not afraid.

She tried to twist around to see the man behind, but she couldn't. He seemed formed of light and shadow. Only his hands were rendered in detail. The backs traced with veins, the knuckles large, the fingers astonishingly strong yet graceful. Mesmerized, Althea watched his fingers release her fragile chemise, which dropped to her waist.

She swallowed a cry as those sensual hands cupped her naked bosom. Her tight, swollen breasts fit into his big palms like ripe apples. He lifted them, displaying them to the other man.

Pinch her nipples, suggested the man on the bed and he flicked open the first button securing his breeches.

Thumbs tapped her hard nipples, shocking her with jolts of pleasure and agony. He strummed them, and she arched back, thrusting her breasts forward. He wasn't so gentle anymore. He squeezed tight, plucked, pinched, and tugged at her nipples. But she loved every coarse, rough caress. He knew far better than she what she wanted. What her breasts enjoyed.

The man on the bed shifted to his knees. His lean muscular abdomen rippled. Waggling his brows with teasing amusement, he drew down his open breeches to the middle of his thighs, revealing his small clothes. His intimate parts, etched in relief by shadow and silvery light, pulsed as he moved.

She caught her breath. Strangely, in this room, with these two men, in this startling, wonderful dream, she couldn't speak. Perhaps she wasn't allowed to—because she should be protesting her innocence. She should be fleeing for safety.

The man on the bed possessed large, beautiful hands too. Hands tugging down his linens, struggling to release his . . .

His cock, love.

The man behind her arched his hips forward and she felt the ridge, hard as a poker in his trousers, jab against her bottom. His hips swayed, bumping his staff across her derriere.

It must be a dream. It had to be a dream.

The golden-haired man dropped his linens, freeing his cock. She understood the term "rampant rod," which she'd heard whispered by maids. This thing seemed to have a mind of its own. It wobbled, swayed, and grew longer before her astonished eyes. A nest of hair surrounded it, a cap crowned it, and it glistened as though wet. Moonlight played along its length, revealing a spine along the back that led a dangling sack that must be his ballocks. The maids called them jewels, as though they were incredibly precious.

She couldn't draw her gaze from it as he slid from the bed. As he pulled off his boots, kicked off his clothes. He swaggered toward her, his cock standing proud, straight and tall, amidst the thicket of golden curls. She could tell he was proud of it, too, and his hand settled around it in a possessive gesture.

Her legs trembled as he gave one long stroke to the base and back up to the tip. Behind her, her other lover arched hard against her, trapping her thin chemise between the cheeks of her bottom as he pushed his clothed cock against her.

It had been delicious to be caressed by one man but to have two touch her at once was a sensation unsurpassed. Someone tore her chemise away. Ripped it from her and tossed the tattered garment aside. Four hands moved over her skin, hot as candle flames, smooth and sensuous like a silken robe. They didn't touch her between her thighs but coasted flat palms over her dark red pubic curls.

Althea shuddered, caught in a horrifying cusp between fear and unbearable arousal. Their hands were pale, stark against the peach tinted skin of her tummy and breasts.

As though they'd said, one, two, three, go, they both bent and took her nipples into their mouths. Her cry rang out into the room. Both nipples in hot male mouths at once. Both nipples lightly scraped by pointy fangs.

As they began sucking in earnest, they took on their own unique rhythms, the contrasts more stunning than having them work in unison had been. Golden hair spilled over her neck and face from both sides. Two hard male members bumped her hips, one nude, the other clothed.

Hands parted her thighs and she whimpered in relief. Their tongues licked her nipples. Their fingers slid between her nether lips. She was slick, scandalously wet and hot. From their groans, she knew the men liked the feel of her wetness on their fingers. Liked the musky perfume floating up from between her legs.

Something built inside her. She sobbed with it and began to rock against their hands. Seeking more. Needing more.

Yes. Yes. Their voices joined, a chorus urging her on. Their mouths moved over her, pleasuring her nipples, her neck, capturing her mouth. With her lids almost covering her eyes, she couldn't see who kissed her where. She gave herself to them, floating between them.

A finger touched the entrance to her bottom and she gasped. Fingers stroked the top of her sex and she screamed. She ground herself hard against their big hands. Harder. Harder.

Make yourself come, sweetheart.

God, yes, come for us, love.

She drove relentlessly, gasping, moaning. *Yes, yes, yes.* She cried the word over and over. A frenzy gripped her, possessed her. She snapped inside. Pleasure swamped her like a wave and her body bucked over their fingers. They held her tight, praised her, groaned with her.

Oh. Oh, yes.

Her eyes shut tight, plunging her into a velvety darkness as the throbbing faded into a light-headed joy.

Faintly she heard a wicked voice murmur against her ear. *"You have never been bitten, have you, angel?"*

Weak, Althea shook her head. But for their arms around her, she would dissolve into a puddle on the floor. She was powerless. Powerless.

Can you imagine the erotic pleasure of having both of us bite you?